RECKONING
THE GATES LEGACY,
BOOK 4

Books by Lorenz Font

The Gates Legacy Series

Hunted - Book 1

Tormented - Book 2

Ascension - Book 3

Reckoning - Book 4

Redemption - Book 5 – Coming soon

Indivisible Line

Feather Light

Pieces of Broken Time

The Prodian Journey Series

Rise of Alpha

Reckoning

The Gates Legacy, Book 4

By
Lorenz Font

Trenda "Tbird" Lundin
Without a doubt, ours is a unique friendship, booger butt.
I'm grateful for the momma-bear love as well as your
friendship, support, and devotion to my work
and well-being.
With love and gratitude.

Glossary

Incomis Sippanus—A disease that can be transmitted from vampire to vampire or vampire to human through feeding or sexual intercourse. Symptoms are similar to leprosy or AIDS, including painful lesions and clouded white irises. Consumption of human blood alleviates visible symptoms but also speeds the disease's progression. Harrow Gates is the first known carrier of the disease.

Vampire Council—Governing authority of the vampire world, consisting of ten purebred vampires called Elders.

Harem—Goran's mistresses, beautiful redheaded vampires who are trained in combat.

Dangeran—Metal with the strength and weight of titanium that has been infused with diamond bits, used in the construction of most vampire weapons. Vampires cut by Dangeran will disintegrate unless the wounded area is cut from their bodies.

Arnis—Three-foot-long wooden sticks used as a sparring weapon.

Kalimetal—Metal version of Arnis. Three-foot-long sticks infused with Dangeran. Animal pelt is woven to the handle to provide a safe grip.

Blanch Room—A large secured area inside the Vampire headquarters that houses humans before and during transition.

Mentha—A plant extract believed to have a calming, numbing effect on vampires.

Great Vampire Revolution—Uprising by a group of revolutionary vampires seeking freedom from Goran's rule in the 1960s.

Pure-Blooded Vampires—Elite class of vampires on the verge of extinction, they are able to reproduce and can read minds. Each possesses a unique gift, and they must feed from pureblooded vampires of the opposite sex to survive.

Tack Enterprises—A company owned and operated by Pritchard Tack that manufactures guns for the military and private companies. Profits are used to support a large group of fighters, researchers, and medical personnel who are working on finding a cure for the disease *Incomis Sippanus*.

Vampire Rebellion—A small resistance by vampires in upstate New York. Reason for the uprising is unknown.

"Please don't hurt him," the woman pleaded.

Cyrus stepped out of the darkened patch he'd been hiding in and broke into a sprint. The air was stifling, and even at midnight the summer heat was on full blast. He moved quickly, passing parked cars and rundown establishments, while his boots slammed against the pavement with dull thuds. From the corner of his eye, he saw Gentry streak across the street in pursuit of their newest project.

The male vampire they were chasing was fast, considering his ailment. His determination to elude them made Cyrus wonder what in the hell the guy was worried about. In the six months since the cure had been introduced, a flood of diseased vampires had lined up on their doorstep. Well, "doorstep" wasn't an accurate term. They had an address where the infected could sign up to receive treatment. After attending a few counseling sessions, they were deemed ready for the gift of Malin's blood. The half-vampire, half-human child of the Vampire Council's new leader, Rohnert, had no idea how precious he was to the race. From the time he was two months old, he had been contributing small amounts of blood, which was used to cure those infected with *Incomis Sippanus*.

Tack Enterprises certainly had come a long way. What had begun with one man's search to cure his infected daughter was now an organization dedicated to protecting and treating diseased vampires who had, until recently, been hunted down and reviled. No matter how slow the production of the antidote, the positive results spoke for themselves. Harrow Gates, the unwitting source of the contagion, had taken over Tack Enterprises upon the death of its founder. He led the Tack team in its efforts to respond to the countless requests for help from the vampires who suffered from his legacy.

"He's going to jump." Gentry's warning broke into Cyrus' ruminations, and he refocused.

Their target male had reached the harbor. He stopped, looked over his shoulder with a laugh, and plunged into the water.

That was where Cyrus drew the line. He wasn't going swimming. Skidding to a halt by the edge of the waterfront, he traced the man's trajectory.

There was no sense in wasting precious time and resources on someone who didn't want their help. It was time to move on.

"Have fun swimming," Cyrus muttered under his breath.

"Where to now?" Gentry asked from behind him.

Gentry had been an excellent addition to their group. A soldier loyal to Rohnert and the Council, he had served as the royal babe's bodyguard since the child's human mother had been killed. When he found some downtime away from his prime responsibility, he was another point of contact for those who sought the cure. Cyrus was glad to have his help on patrols.

"Back to the facility."

They returned to the deserted street and found the woman waiting for them. Her face fell when she realized her runaway son was not with them.

Cyrus offered an apologetic smile. "If he doesn't want our help, we can't force him. I'm sorry."

"He doesn't know what's good for him," she said, her voice breaking.

"That is why we prefer that they come to us on their own."

"Will you give him another chance?"

How touching. If all mothers were like this female, then there might be some hope left after all. At least Rohnert's reign had put a stop to the shunning and slaughtering of the infected ones that had been carried out under Goran's rule.

"Of course. Gentry here will take care of him." Cyrus turned to leave.

The woman caught his arm, and when their eyes locked, she offered a feeble smile. "Thank you. You're heaven sent."

Cyrus didn't bother telling her that he and heaven were poles apart. The truth was he was living on borrowed time. His sworn vendetta against Zane, the man who had robbed him of his humanity, cast a shadow over whatever was left of his soul. Once Tack Enterprise's new venture was up and running, he planned to heed the dictates of his heart and follow a different path. He wanted revenge.

It was easier said than done, of course. There were a million things that needed his attention before he could pursue Zane.

The moment they reached the underground facility, Rayce paged him with a summons to come to the control room. Then his phone beeped with a message from Harrow to meet him in the I-room. Yeah, he was everyone's go-to guy.

"Go ahead. I'll catch up with you later." He slapped Gentry on the shoulder and made a beeline for the control room.

Goran's grandson, Zane, had breached the security of the Tack Enterprises' original underground facility, and the damage had been substantial. They'd had to abandon the facility and set up shop in a refurbished warehouse. However, since then the place had been retrofitted and given an extensive makeover, and they had been able to return after Goran's defeat. The Vampire Council had begun to move in a positive direction under Rohnert's guidance, but Cyrus' blood still boiled whenever he thought of Zane, the asshole who had changed him. His *daddy*, as Tor never failed to remind him.

"You need me?" Cyrus asked when he entered the control room.

Rayce spared him a quick glance before returning his attention to the bank of ten monitors. His mop of brown hair was sticking out in all directions, which made Cyrus wonder if the man had trouble sleeping—or just grooming. If it was the former, that would make two of them.

The tech guy punched the keyboard, and several monitors flickered then zoomed. "Look at this," Rayce said.

Cyrus directed his attention to one, and his heart skipped. Isidora was inside the shooting range, firing a Sig. Her form was perfect. Her stance was wide enough to withstand the recoil, and her focus was intent on the target.

She had been a diligent student—always on time, never missing a session—but she preferred one-on-one instruction, which still baffled him. Not that he was complaining.

"Um . . . what made you think I needed to see this?" he asked, eyeing the younger man with annoyance.

Rayce gave him a sheepish grin. "Well, she's your student. I thought you might be interested in keeping tabs on her progress."

And there you are, folks. The teasing has already started. Cyrus regulated his breathing before flashing his fangs at the human. "Stop hanging out with Tor. He's turning you to the dark side."

Cyrus took one last look at the monitor before exiting the room. Rayce's laughter followed him as he made his way to the I-room. Blast the damn human. He was lucky his control room was such a godsend.

Harrow and Tor had complained about the lack of privacy before, but Cyrus had thought it was silly. After all, it was for their protection. However, now that he was under the microscope, he realized he wasn't crazy about the cameras pointing in every direction. Their fallen leader, Pritchard Tack, had been too involved in his people's affairs.

Cyrus opened the door of the I-room and found Harrow watching the same segment. "You guys are not funny," he said, marching straight to the libation station. He picked his favorite bottle and poured.

Harrow turned and snickered. "You're like a brother to me, and you know I only want what's best for you, right?"

"Cut the crap, Gates. What do you want from me?"

Harrow turned somber, which made Cyrus roll his eyes. *Here we go.*

"I want you to be happy . . ."

"Oh, please. Not that speech again. Can we just skip the sentimental bullshit so you can tell me what you want to do with the Naples account?"

That should shut the boss up. Slap Harrow with business decisions to take the focus away from Cyrus. It always worked.

Harrow gave him a knowing look—no doubt the man had caught on to his evasion tactic. "You have a meeting with the CEO tonight?"

Cyrus nodded and put the glass to his lips, downing the first of many drinks of the evening. At the rate he was going, he might as well buy stock in Caol Ila. He'd been drinking the single-malt whiskey like it was water.

"I'm meeting him at his home. I told him I have an early flight, and that was the only open time in my schedule." That was bullshit, of course, and Harrow knew it. Cyrus had reserved his daytime hours for scouring the city for traces of Zane, who had vanished without a trace.

Harrow gave him a dubious glare but said nothing. Cyrus waited while he pulled a sheet of paper from a folder, signed it, and handed it to Cyrus.

"That should seal the deal. Tell Jack that his order is guaranteed to ship in four weeks."

Cyrus scanned the contract, and after a thorough check, got to his feet. "I'll pass it on." He turned to the door.

"Hey, man, are you sure you're all right?" Harrow asked, removing his sunglasses to look him in the eye.

Despite the cure, the damage to Harrow's sight had been too extensive to reverse. Looking into his whitish eyes was a bit creepy, but these constant questions were getting old.

"I'm great. Couldn't be better."

Cyrus left him shaking his head and marched straight to his bedroom. Any more questions about his state of mind and he was going to scream. He slammed the door and collapsed on the sofa. If everyone kept treating him like a live grenade, he really would explode. He glanced at the digital clock on the wall and gritted his teeth. His appointment with the guy from Naples was in an hour. If he wanted to make it on time, he'd better get in the shower quick.

Isidora worked the mouse and slid her target closer. On inspection, it was riddled with bullets, which were concentrated around the chest area. This made her smile. She moved the target back then reloaded.

This had been her nightly ritual since she began training with Cyrus eight months ago. Once her teacher left for the night, she would engage in nonstop practice, further developing the skills she wouldn't have imagined she possessed in her wildest dreams. Under Cyrus' tutelage, she had tried several different weapons, and the guns seemed to be the ones that worked best for her. She and Cyrus also spent countless hours sparring, which had produced dismal results, in her opinion. Though he continued to encourage her, she wished he would give up on ever teaching her hand-to-hand combat.

She had been cooped up inside ever since she arrived—first in the warehouse, and then in the underground facility. It wasn't much different from the conditions she'd left behind, except that instead of being hidden away in a mansion, she was thirty feet underground, in the company of both humans and vampires.

However, this time it was no one's doing but her own. She hadn't expressed a desire to leave the facility. This was because the first and the last time she had ventured outside her sanctuary, her world had been turned upside down. Her beloved Finn had been killed trying to defend her, and the little hope she had of a normal life had blown away with his ashes.

When her family's mansion had been under attack, everyone she loved perished to save her. It was a sacrifice she was beginning to understand. Her father had been tight-lipped every time she asked why she was sequestered. He had been trying to protect her from the ugliness of the outside world. Her family had been keeping her existence hidden from the man who would wish to possess her to further his ambitions. When she'd found herself alone in a strange place, surrounded by people she didn't know, it had been a rude awakening.

She missed her parents so much. Sometimes, all she could do to keep herself together was to believe that the higher being had something good planned for her. Maureen, her best friend, had given her life for her, along with Finn. Isidora just hoped she could make a difference and their deaths wouldn't be in vain.

Pushing aside her gloomy thoughts, she focused on the target once more. Isidora cleared her mind of all the clutter, zooming in on the limbless, headless torso and firing. The sound exhilarated her, and the force of the recoil pulled at her strengthening muscles. She was getting better.

The door suddenly opened, and Jordan, Harrow's mate, walked into the room. Her red hair was pulled into a severe ponytail, but her eyes were much kinder than they'd been the first time they met. After Goran's defeat, Jordan's personality had undergone a drastic change. The female had been one of Goran's many creations, and her life's purpose had been to eradicate the vampire. Since her mission had been accomplished, the facility inhabitants reaped the benefits of her new positive outlook.

"Issy, you've already proven yourself with the guns. I think you're ready for the Kalimetal," Jordan said. Her eyes had the familiar twinkle they held whenever she suggested the idea.

Isidora put down the gun and removed her protective goggles and ear plugs. "I'm not as graceful as you want me to be. We both know it." She smoothed her long floral skirt and headed to Cyrus' desk. Without him around, she took comfort in spending her quiet hours using his desk to read.

"Well, let's see. Recalling my first time, I wasn't exactly well coordinated. Ask Rohnert—he'll tell you how many times he wound up smacking my hands with the Arnis," she said, referring to the nonlethal weapons used for Kalimetal training. Jordan shed her jacket to reveal a well-formed upper body that hadn't lost its feminine curves. "And you have to lose the skirt. I believe in freedom of movement, but dresses and skirts would be a liability during a fight."

Issy nodded. "I'm open to suggestions."

Allison, the coheir of the Tack fortune and Pritchard's daughter, had asked her several times what she needed. Too timid to impose on her benefactors, Issy had asked for the type of clothes she had been used to wearing at home.

"If you're serious about this, I'm going to get you the proper clothes, although I think it'll be better if you choose what you prefer." Jordan sat on the chair, grabbed a pen and paper, and scribbled down something. "Here— it's the link to a site that carries every style you can think of. We have an account with them, so all you have to worry about is finding what you want."

When Issy glanced at the paper, she grimaced. She hadn't been taught how to use the computer, let alone go shopping on the Internet. Her father hadn't believed in modern technology, preferring to raise his daughter according to the old traditions.

"Hey, what's with the long face?" Jordan was too perceptive.

Isidora shook her head. "Nothing."

Jordan studied her for a moment and then sighed. "Tell me if I'm overstepping my boundaries here. I'm going to make a wild guess and say that you're not quite sure how to use a computer."

Issy looked down, feeling suddenly small. For Christ's sake, they were in the twenty-first century, but she'd been left behind after being isolated from the outside world all her life. She slowly nodded. There was no use hiding it. When she looked up again, Jordan was watching her with those kind, amber eyes.

"You have nothing to worry about. I'm going to teach you everything you need to know."

Grateful, Isidora could only smile.

Rohnert collapsed on the chaise after concluding his fourth official Council meeting. He had retreated to his personal chamber in the hopes of getting a short reprieve from the never-ending demands of his position. Being the head of the illustrious group was just as tough as he'd imagined it would be.

The Vampire Council was going through rapid and extensive changes. This growth pleased him, but his energy was at an all-time low. Even so, repeated pleas for him to take a break had fallen on deaf ears.

As long as he stayed busy, he couldn't think, so he filled his time with his child, the Council, and training. He didn't want to remember why he was taking care of a growing son single-handedly—didn't want to think of the massive hole in his heart that his mate left behind when she died. Teaching and training gave him the chance to impart his knowledge of martial arts, but they also gave him an outlet for his pent-up rage. He was hurting more than he let on.

Parenthood had its rewarding and frustrating moments. Both Jordan and Allison had been a great help to him. When the two female vampires offered their babysitting services, Rohnert had taken them up on their offer, knowing his little boy would be in good hands. They would give their lives for Malin and protect him as if he were their own.

A loud knock sounded at his chamber door. There was no need to look to know who was waiting outside. His visitor's thoughts were clear, even at a distance. Such a loud inner voice could only belong to someone with an equally big mouth.

"Come in, Tor," he called out and leaned against the chair to wait.

Tor opened the door with his usual flourish, chuckling. "You're a piece of work, you know that?"

No matter how long they'd been friends, Tor still couldn't come to terms with Rohnert's mind-reading skills. He gave a hearty laugh.

It went without saying how grateful he was for Tor and Cyrus' help with the new soldiers' training. Tor had been a mean machine, working the troops to the ground under the watchful eye of Wendell, who had been appointed tactician and weapons expert after Bretania's disappearance. Cyrus also had been pitching in whenever his schedule permitted.

Tor sat on the ornate chair opposite Rohnert and glanced around. "You know, I still can't believe that you're actually here. This place is creepy. All those wood carvings, heavy curtains, and artsy-fartsy paintings don't suit your style."

"What is my style, if you would be so kind as to enlighten me?" Rohnert lifted his legs and rested them on the table.

"Well, first of all, that robe makes you look fat," Tor said and then laughed.

Rohnert shook his head. Some people would never change. "And what kind of clothes should I be wearing?"

Tor pretended to think. "Jeans, black shirt, and your Kalimetal."

The vampire might have been an ass, but he was also an integral part of the group when things got rough, so Rohnert was willing to tolerate his endless witticisms.

"And what about the decor?" he asked, looking forward to a good laugh.

"It's grandpa-ish. Makes you look old."

"What should we do about it?"

"Um, I have the newest issues of *SI* and *Playboy*. The centerfolds could breathe life into this lonely place." The moment he said the words, Tor drew back. "Man, I'm sorry. Foot-in-mouth disease is next in line for a cure."

Rohnert faked a laugh. Indeed, he was lonely, and he feared he'd never find a reason to *really* smile again. It might have been six months since his mate's murder, but not a minute went by without Shelly making an appearance in his mind.

Every memory he had of her only strengthened the conviction that he'd never get over her. Time didn't heal some wounds. He couldn't stop the longing in his gut, erase the memories from his mind, or fill the void in his heart.

He'd learned the art of faking it just to appease those around him. It was easy to pretend that he was all right instead of answering questions about his mental well-being. In truth, he was sick of it—sick of his whole goddamned life without Shelly.

"It's okay, my man," he finally said.

Tor watched him with those concerned purplish-red eyes, staring long enough to make Rohnert uncomfortable.

"Rohn, you'll have to talk about it at some point, you know."

Talk? Talking would make it more real, and he still couldn't wrap his mind around the idea that Shelly was gone. His very soul refused to accept the finality of it.

"Well?"

Rohnert eyeballed his friend. "Well what?" He wasn't about to pour his heart out.

"Well, if you don't want to talk, maybe we can go out and paint the town red." Tor smiled, exposing the sharp point of his fangs.

He knew this was Tor's futile attempt to lighten his load, but Rohnert wasn't ready to open up. Hell, he wanted to be left alone and deal with his miserable life.

"Excuse me, but I have some important Council matters to attend to," Rohnert said by way of dismissal. He didn't look Tor in the eye, afraid the vampire would see right through him.

He did, but thankfully didn't prod further. "I'll be in the training room if you need me."

After Tor had left, Rohnert bolted to his feet to walk off the anxiety. He didn't want to go there—not to the place where darkness, sadness, and isolation shackled him. His muscles were coiled tight while he paced the room like a caged lion.

Bretania stirred from a short, nightmare-ridden sleep. Her lids fluttered open, and the piercing glow of the light, no matter how insignificant, stung her eyes. For some time now, darkness had been her constant companion. It didn't take a genius to discern the problem. She had been hoping the great Shaman could aid her, but alas, Lukan had failed to respond to her summons. With difficulty, Bretania pushed her body out of bed, feeling her energy seep away with the slightest movement. She braced her hand on the nightstand.

"Greta." Her voice came out strangled.

Her loyal housekeeper answered her call but then stopped dead in her tracks. Judging from Greta's expression, the sight before her was gruesome. The scent of the lesions was far from Bretania's preferred Chanel No. 5, and the thoughts swirling in her servant's mind confirmed what she already knew. She was a card-carrying member of the diseased.

Despite Greta's qualms, she rushed forward to steady her mistress. Fire raged down Bretania's throat when her faithful servant's scent strengthened as she moved closer. The hunger didn't listen to reason nor adhere to proprieties or scruples. If she denied its call, she would go mad.

"Madame, you must not exert yourself." Greta hefted her onto the bed.

Blocking out the guilt and pushing pride aside, Bretania eyed her servant's jugular hungrily. This was her life now, and there was no denying what she had become. With the element of surprise on her side, she was able to grab Greta by the shoulders and pin her against the mattress. Bretania mustered enough energy to overpower her victim, despite the woman's resistance.

"Shh, this is going to be fast," she whispered in a voice that sounded foreign to her ears.

In quick movements ignited by the hunger she had denied for months, she punctured the skin, probing deeper until she caught the sweet taste of blood.

Her salvation.

Bretania sucked at the vein with greedy pulls, taking what she needed to build her strength. Then she did the unthinkable. She utilized her talent for manipulating weak minds to insert thoughts into Greta's cerebrum. The one person who had been aware that she possessed this gift had taken his knowledge to the grave.

Goran, damn the man. He'd sent her and a group of vampires on a suicide mission that had spelled trouble from the get-go. Their little rebellion had been no match for the Elders' army of disciplined fighters. Had she not used her gift to escape, she would have perished in the battle.

Inside Greta's mind, she planted vicious images, ruthless ideas, and added a fondness for butchery into the mix. Spreading the disease was first and foremost on Greta's mind, and it would be her mission from now on. Life had handed Bretania lemons, so she would squeeze everything to a pulp and leave a trail of bitterness and carnage in her wake.

With one last look, she got up from the bed, marveling at her renewed strength. The night was far from over. While her servant went through the writhing pain of the transition, she had better things to do. There were questions that required answers.

Energy coursed through Bretania's veins. Gone were the dreary nights spent cooped up in her apartment. This was her time to shine and deliver a blow to the belly of the beast. She would take down those who had thwarted and denied the legacy of her beloved. Hatred burned inside her while she wrapped her body in a black-hooded robe. She holstered her weapons around her waist and took one last glance in the mirror, pleased to have the chance to regroup and build her army.

Bretania smiled at the mirror, studying her disease-ravaged features. Her once onyx eyes held a tint of whitish discoloration, and her formerly smooth, silky skin had taken a light pallor, with painful lesions running across her limbs, torso, and face. Her pale, full lips still held a drop of blood from the feeding, and she greedily licked it off, savoring the taste.

She would go to whatever lengths were necessary. After all, she was married to the ruling blood line, and by the grace of that union, she would take what was rightfully hers. The tip of her sword would ensure this path, and damn anyone who dared stand between her and her goal.

When she stepped outside, the city's inclement weather greeted her. The rain and annoying humidity of summer were enough to dampen her spirits, but she persisted. She wanted to get the ball rolling. The prospect of revenge sent tingles down her spine as she turned toward the most densely populated area of the city.

Cyrus took his time under the icy spray—the shower was the one place where he could think, away from the close scrutiny of his friends. With two vampires equipped with mind reading skills, he had learned to control his musings around them. Picturing a gunfight, a movie scene he enjoyed, or even a calming seascape did the trick. He had grown used to Rohnert, but having Isidora around still made him edgy.

After getting out of the shower and drying off, he dressed, gelled his hair, and secured a few weapons underneath his custom-made blazer. When he inspected himself in the mirror, his reflection made him laugh out loud. Like a wolf in sheep's skin, his outward appearance would fool everyone. The severe crew cut he preferred made his brown hair look like angry spikes, thin and rigid. His square-shaped face was taut and hard, his lips were drawn into a straight line, and the furrows that creased his forehead had deepened. Other than the beige blazer and the dark shirt concealing his muscled and tattoo-covered arms, he looked like the bounty hunter he had been before Pritchard rehabbed him.

Leave it to Allison to soften his hard edges by supplying the duds she wanted him to wear. If he hadn't had a soft spot for Pritchard's daughter, he would have canned the outfit. However, that might scare business clients away. Cyrus looked older than his actual thirty-seven years, and he felt it in his weary bones. He took one last look at himself in the mirror and took off for the garage.

He was paying close attention to the contract in his hand and not where he was headed when he almost bumped into Isidora, of all people.

"Hi," she said, looking shy after their near collision.

Cyrus felt stupid when she observed him. He wished he had on the sort of clothes he was more comfortable wearing. He felt his face grow warm under her gaze.

"Hey, how's it going?" He tried to keep his voice even, hiding that she made him uneasy.

"I didn't see you in the training room today." She kept looking at him and wringing her hands.

Good to know he wasn't the only nervous one. *Damn it.* Cyrus had prided himself on coming to grips on everything in his life, but this young woman was making him feel like a teenager with his first hard-on. Sure enough, his pants were growing tight even now.

He grunted. "I was busy."

Cyrus looked at the wall behind Issy, not wanting to get lost in the abyss of her sable eyes. Sometimes, he sensed that she wanted more than fighting instructions from him, but he knew he was just imagining things.

A clipped answer was the best he could do. At the moment, he felt too raw and vulnerable. The last thing he wanted to do was make an ass of himself in front of the beautiful vampire. She might be advanced in years, but she maintained a youthful appearance, making Cyrus look much older than her. Sure, once turned, his aging had slowed down, but still the thought of their outward differences made him cringe. He should be ashamed of himself for wanting her, but curiously, he wasn't. She continued to watch him, and he bet his life she was trying to read his mind.

"Listen, I'm in a hurry. I might catch you tomorrow if my schedule permits." He turned and walked away.

He heard her speak just before he cleared the door to the garage. "I'm looking forward to it."

When he turned to take one last look, he caught the little smile on her face. Cyrus gripped the folder tight and let out a long exhalation while he surveyed the available vehicles in the showroom. He strode over to the brand-new, yellow Dodge Challenger and whistled. He was taking this baby for a ride tonight. His need for speed would be satisfied by the four hundred horses under its hood. He jumped in, pressed the start button, and revved the gas. Dust followed in his wake the instant he cleared the underground tunnel.

Peace and quiet had their rewarding moments, Cyrus thought as he drove away from the underground facility that had been his home for the past four years. The solitude gave him a chance to contemplate the path his life had taken. He'd seen the groundbreaking rise of Tack Enterprises under Pritchard's leadership. Before his demise, the fallen leader had entrusted his life and that of his daughter, Allison, to Cyrus' care. Pritchard had given him a home, forged a new path to his wayward career, and made him family.

It was too bad his loyal friend, Lambert, wasn't around to witness the fruits of their hard labor, but he had been killed protecting what he revered most—life. It was a sacrifice he'd made to preserve another, bringing an abrupt end to the beloved peer and decent human being.

Cyrus sighed and pushed the sobering memories aside to focus on his meeting.

Before his abduction, he had been conducting most of Tack Enterprises' business alongside Allison. Since Pritchard had promoted him to liaison and business advisor just before Harrow took the helm, most existing connections preferred to continue dealing with Cyrus. If there was one thing Pritchard had worked hard for, it was this company. He had built it from the ground up. Tack Enterprises had become a successful guns supplier for military units around the world, and their contacts were as vast as the oceans that separated them.

The new Naples account would be huge. Even though it was a private company, the size of the order was an opportunity they couldn't pass up. It was an account he'd been working on before Zane kidnapped him, so he was surprised that his clients hadn't given up and taken their business elsewhere. Grateful for their patience, Cyrus made a point of dealing with the CEO of the company on a more personal level, managing communications himself that could have been handled by another employee.

While the employees and allies of Tack Enterprises had been caught in the fight of their lives, production had slowed. Since Rohnert had secured the highest seat in the Vampire Council, they were able to focus once more on business. Harrow had more time to run the underground operation, including supporting various organizations and managing the donors for their blood supply. The business front was handled by Allison, which took some of the weight off Harrow's shoulders during Cyrus' absence. Now that he was back in the flesh, it was business as usual. He just wasn't human anymore.

Arriving at the swanky neighborhood that boasted the Pierre penthouses, he emerged from the car, tossing the keys to the waiting doorman. He smoothed his jacket and strode into the building. He knew where to go, having received an e-mail from the secretary with directions.

Inside the elevator, Cyrus glanced at himself again. He curled back his lips to check out his hardware—nothing but prominent canines there. The ding-ding of the elevator sounded, and he emerged with confidence.

A rather creepy-looking butler answered the door and led Cyrus to a seating area, where he was told to sit and wait. When Cyrus watched the man walk away, he noticed the bulge underneath his dark jacket. The guy was packing some serious weapons. Cyrus contemplated this while he glanced around his lavish surroundings. Museum grade artwork adorned the walls, decorative lead crystals as thick as his skull were perched on the fireplace mantle, and thick draperies framed the floor-to-ceiling windows that hugged the entire room. The setup reminded him of Pritchard Tack's residence.

Footsteps sounded, prompting him to straighten and focus on the hallway. During his several phone conversations with the client, Cyrus had drawn a mental picture in his head of a short, balding, pompous millionaire. The gentleman who appeared was a far cry from what Cyrus had imagined.

Tall and fit, Jack Drago's dark, calculating eyes met his. "Cyrus, we finally meet." He extended his hand.

Cyrus rose to his feet and accepted the outstretched hand. Their handshake was firm and filled with confidence, and they watched each other like opponents sizing up their competition before a fight. "It's a pleasure to meet you, Mr. Drago."

Drago gestured for Cyrus to take a seat and then dived straight in to business. "Do you have the contract?" He took the seat opposite Cyrus and produced a gleaming Montblanc pen from the pocket of his crisp, tailored shirt.

"I do." Cyrus spread the contents of the folder on the coffee table and fiddled for the signature page. "I appreciate your taking the time to meet with me. My flight is in two hours, and I didn't want you to wait any longer."

Drago gave a hearty laugh and took the papers from him. "I work well during the witching hour."

He took his time to inspect the contract in its entirety. Cyrus glanced around, sensing something that he couldn't quite put his finger on. They were alone in the room, but it felt like they were being watched.

The scratching of the pen sounded when the CEO affixed his signature to the document. "How long before I receive the first shipment?"

"Mr. Gates is guaranteeing delivery in four weeks."

"Very good. My assistant is wiring the funds as we speak. Is there anything else we need?"

Cyrus gathered the paperwork and stashed it back in the folder. "I believe that is everything."

Jack Drago nodded and stood. "If you'll excuse me, there are still some personal matters I must attend to. Norris will show you to the door."

"Thanks for doing business with us." Cyrus offered his hand, but the man waved him off as the butler appeared in the doorway.

"I'll call on you again if the need arises. I appreciate the house call." With that, Drago left the room.

He was rather odd. Cyrus couldn't quite put his finger on what was off about Drago, but he had been suspicious of everyone since his transition. Nowadays, he eyed every situation with skepticism that bordered on paranoia.

"This way, please." Norris preceded him to the door. Even the butler was acting weird. "Have a pleasant evening."

The door closed behind Cyrus, and he got the distinct feeling that the man wanted him out fast. Well, that made two of them. If it hadn't been such a big account, he would have assigned one of their yuppie employees to do the legwork and spared himself the trouble.

Once back inside the muscle car he'd borrowed from the Tack garage, Cyrus decided to experiment with its power. At this ungodly hour, the streets were almost deserted. A test drive wouldn't hurt. He slammed his loafer on the gas pedal and the machine responded with a mighty roar. As he changed gears, the car soared along the quiet street, the engine responding like a powerful animal with every shift.

Exhilarated, he went several blocks before slowing down to a cruising speed. He had nothing scheduled for the remainder of the night. Cyrus wanted a little time away from the underground facility so he didn't have to guard his every thought or have his movements be subjected to constant monitoring.

When Cyrus turned on to the main thoroughfare, he heard a stifled scream. He zeroed in on the sound until it led him to a narrow alley. Once he'd killed the engine, he left the car on the street and checked his holster for weapons.

In the darkened alley, he found two men cornering a woman, and he walked in the direction of the conflict. None of them noticed his arrival.

"Please let me go," the woman begged, but one of the men grabbed her by the arm and twisted it behind her.

"Women shouldn't walk around looking sexy if they don't want men to pay attention."

"I'm begging you. Please stop." Her voice held fear and panic.

Cyrus placed one hand inside his jacket, ready to draw his weapon at a second's notice. "The lady asked you to let her go."

Both jackasses looked in his direction like deer in headlights.

The man who held the woman found his tongue first. "Why don't you mind your own business? Go find yourself another whore."

His companion brandished a knife.

Cyrus narrowed his eyes, tracking every subtle movement. He eyeballed the woman, who continued to beg for her freedom.

If this got down and dirty, she might wind up being a casualty.

"Didn't your mother teach you to respect women?" Cyrus inched closer.

"Shut the fuck up if you want to live." The knife wielding dumbass moved toward him.

There was a faint zipping sound, and Cyrus knew the other man was going to try to take the woman. He sprang into action. Instead of using his weapons, he kicked the knife from the man's grasp. Several quick movements followed as he hit the man in the face and kicked him in the stomach until he was on the ground, clutching his belly.

Cyrus turned his attention toward the other human, realizing too late that the guy had a gun on him. Before he could palm a weapon of his own, the trigger-happy fuck fired.

Drago retreated to his bedroom after Cyrus left. With the promised delivery, he was one step closer to his goal. The thought made him smile. The countless hours it had taken to set his plan in motion, along with the thousands of dollars spent to secure the weapons, were worth it.

His motivation for building a multimillion-dollar business empire had been revenge. The prestige that came along with his amassed wealth paled in comparison to the prospect of getting even with Cantor, the man who had broken his mother, Catalina's, heart.

Before becoming Rohnert and Goran's venerated father, Cantor had wooed Drago's mother, impregnated her, then cast her aside and mated instead with a higher-ranking female. Ridiculed after this rejection, Catalina had run and hidden as far away as she could. She was taken in by another coven and gave birth to Drago, but then she fell into the hands of an abusive vampire.

After the male took his mother as a mate, Drago spent years becoming familiar with hardship. At an early age, he was forced to kill and collect bounties. When his sadistic stepfather killed Catalina, Drago had discovered that he wasn't averse to murder and revenge. He became addicted to the sound of a dying breath. It was a melodious whisper that sent chills down his spine and brought a smile to his lips.

Fueled by hatred and greed, Drago devised his master plan. He scraped together every penny he could and built a following based on extortion, bribery, and false promises. Money cast a blinding spell, and he used it to his advantage.

Upon Cantor's death at the hands of his younger son, Goran, just Rohnert stood between Drago and the highest seat as the new leader of the Vampire Council. It was not a challenge as far as Drago was concerned. He planned to park his own ass on that throne one day soon. It was about time the Vampire Council experienced a new type of leadership. With Drago, they would build effective relationships with other covens under one rule. His.

The human world presented an easy path to his grand entrance. He made his first million with the help of unsuspecting humans who wanted a piece of the pie Drago offered. Manipulating stocks was easier than he would have expected. Insider trading became his forte, and he was able to elude the watchful eyes of the SEC. His focus had turned to Tack Enterprises, the biggest manufacturer of the guns he coveted. It was a privately owned company, and he needed their product to reach his ultimate goal.

Their representative had guaranteed shipment within a month. This marked the beginning of his plan to take over the Vampire Council. With a powerful army behind him, all he would need was one other piece to complete his life's purpose—his half-brother's death. Drago would achieve the complete eradication of Cantor's line from the whore who had usurped Catalina's rightful place.

A tingle ran down his spine at the prospect. He was ready to stake his claim, and the anticipation was like a shot of adrenalin to his heart. He could almost taste his victory, but he would be patient awhile longer. It would be worth the wait.

"Damn it." Cyrus looked down at the entry wound in his stomach. Thank God it hadn't been a Dangeran bullet, which would have blown him to smithereens. He almost bared his fangs at the pain but stopped himself before anyone could spy his fangs.

"I can't believe you ruined my jacket." Moving faster than human eyes could follow, he unloaded one of his daggers. He flung it toward the triggerman, clipping him on the leg.

The human staggered and fell to the ground, releasing the frightened woman in the process. She began screaming, and, afraid this would attract unwanted attention, Cyrus moved even faster, disarming the man and securing the weapon.

"Let's get you out of here now." He took her shaking hand and led her out of the alley.

"You've been shot. Maybe we should go to the hospital." Hysteria rose in her voice while her clammy hands tugged on his arm. "You could've been killed."

Cyrus knew that blood had started seeping out from the wound, soaking his shirt. He'd been stabbed before, but this was far more painful.

"Don't worry about me. Are you going to be okay?" He glanced over his shoulder at the two men, who were still down on the ground.

"Yeah, but . . ."

"Miss, you better leave now before those bastards get their second wind."

The woman hesitated before she wrapped her arms around him. "Thank you. Please, you have to get to a hospital." Her smile was shaky, but he saw genuine concern in her eyes.

"I'll get myself there. Now go."

She hesitated before fleeing. Cyrus watched her flag a taxi down. He debated whether to finish off the assailants, but he wasn't ready for an early checkout, so he staggered back to his car. Once he'd started the engine, he activated the voice control directory. "Dial underground facility."

Dangeran bullet or not, the injury hurt like a bitch. He had maybe fifteen minutes to get himself back in the compound if he didn't want to bleed to death. Hopefully, he wouldn't pass out until he was safe inside.

The phone rang, and Rayce answered. "Cyrus, what's up?"

"I've been shot. ETA fifteen minutes. Let Rick know." Cyrus hung up before Rayce could start asking questions. He drove fast, hoping he wouldn't attract attention from any cops along the way. It would be difficult to explain his situation.

The traffic didn't help. Cyrus muttered profanities each time he hit another red light. He glanced at the dashboard clock. Ten minutes had elapsed, and he still had twenty blocks to cover. His strength was waning, his legs were numbing fast, and the scent of his blood was doing a number on him, making him want to throw up.

Impatient, he pounded his fist on the steering wheel. "Move it people."

By the time Cyrus was in the general vicinity of their underground hideout, his eyesight was blurred and his clothes were soaked in blood.

The gate was opened and Cyrus barely cleared the side of the steel door. Upon making it to the subterranean parking, he slammed on the brakes just before his vision dimmed and he slipped into oblivion.

Isidora had been waiting with Rick in the parking structure after getting the frantic message from Rayce. She watched the car zigzag its way to a vacant spot, almost swiping the Humvee's rear bumper. Cyrus' head slammed against the steering wheel when the car sputtered and then hit the wall.

"Oh, my god." She gasped and sprinted over with Rick, while Harrow and Jordan trailed from behind. They reached the car within seconds, and she yanked the door open. She drew back at the sight of Cyrus passed out in the front seat, covered in blood.

When Rick tapped her on the shoulder, Isidora whipped her head around in anger. "What?" Her voice almost sounded like a growl.

The doctor gestured to his nonexistent voice box. *You have to focus. I need you to tell Harrow to help me get Cyrus out of the car.*

It took a moment to remember that she was the doctor's only means of communication with the others. "Harrow, Rick needs help with Cyrus."

"On it!" Harrow positioned himself and pulled Cyrus from the car. "What the hell happened to you, bud?" he asked. Their leader moved fast, lifting Cyrus while Jordan put the car in park. They all ran back inside the building and raced to the clinic, which was already humming with activity.

Cheryl had Rick's preferred classical background music playing when Harrow laid the unconscious vampire on the operating table.

"Rick, you will do whatever it takes to save this guy," Harrow said and parked himself in a corner of the room.

The doctor nodded and hustled over to the sink to wash his hands.

Isidora felt a sob building up deep in her throat, and tears threatened to escape when Rick communicated his first instructions for Cheryl. "Start the IV. I need six units of blood, stat." Her voice sounded hoarse, and Jordan walked over to her.

"Are you okay?" The other woman peered at her.

Isidora gave a tentative nod. This was not the first time she'd seen a gunshot victim. Ever since she'd started interpreting for Dr. Rick Whitaker, she had experienced her fair share of life and death situations, but this patient was different. It was Cyrus, her teacher . . . and friend.

Cheryl's movements were efficient as she followed the doctor's orders. The nurse showed great presence of mind while she prepared the bag of blood and IV and then found Cyrus' vein. Isidora waited for Rick's instructions, glancing at Cyrus every few seconds. Numbness crept up her body at seeing him in such state, his immaculate beige jacket stained red.

She locked eyes with the doctor when his mental instructions reached her. "Rick is ready to operate. He wants you guys to wait outside."

Rick's thoughts were calm, but her interpretation of his orders came out abrupt and panicky. Harrow's pasty eyes lingered on Cyrus before he led Jordan out of the room. The doctor had already begun cutting through the material of Cyrus' shirt.

Sorry, dude, but you'll just have to buy a new one. Rick's joke made Isidora want to punch him in the face.

Feeling helpless, all she could do was to hold Cyrus' hand. She kept squeezing, hoping he would respond, but he was dead to the world. At least he wouldn't feel the pain. As Rick inspected the entrance and exit wound, she knew he was buying time for the anesthesia to take effect.

They both glanced at the clock then looked at each other.

"Rick, please help him. Do it now." Her plea sounded desperate, even to her own ears.

It was the longest night of her life. She waited, listening to Rick's inner ramblings while he explored Cyrus' abdomen. It was a big comfort to know that Cyrus was in good hands.

The monitor beeped, and Rick's quick mental orders put Isidora on alert. "Rick needs three units of blood." Cheryl moved fast to get a bag from the clinic's stash and hook it up next to Cyrus' IV.

It took several hours before Rick looked up, but the procedure had been successful. For Issy, being privy to the doctor's unspoken thoughts had made the long wait bearable. Today, she was thankful for her gift.

The bullet had hit a small artery, but Rick didn't foresee any permanent damage. The immediate cause for concern was the massive blood loss, which Rick was monitoring. Otherwise, the prognosis was good and the injury was not life threatening.

All we can do is wait. Rick took off the bloodied gloves and tossed them in the biohazard bin. While he and Cheryl took turns washing their hands, Isidora studied Cyrus' features. In his unconscious state, his face appeared softer. The harsh lines around his mouth were absent, making him look more vulnerable than usual.

"I'm going to get a cup of coffee. Would you like some, Dr. Whitaker? Issy?" Cheryl asked.

"Rick could use one, no cream, one sugar. None for me, thank you." Isidora's response was automatic.

The nurse was a tortured soul. As much as Cheryl tried not to think of her personal affairs, Issy had overheard her errant thoughts about a man named Zane. It made her wonder about the male Cheryl was pining for, but her strict upbringing prevented her from asking. It was bad enough that she knew the poor woman's business.

Are you all right? Rick touched her shoulder.

Pivoting to face the doctor, she saw the worry in his face. "Yes, I am. Why do you ask?" She smoothed an errant hair away from her face.

You look like you need a friend. Do you want to talk about it? Rick's earnest expression made her want to cry, but she shook her head.

"Go drink your coffee. If you don't mind, I'll stay here."

Sure. You know where to find me. Rick nodded and exited the clinic without a sound.

Isidora moved to the chair in the corner of the room. It didn't matter if Cyrus woke up three hours from now or the next day. All she cared about that he wasn't alone.

Zane looked up when the door opened. Hill walked in, and his demeanor gave the answer before he spoke it.

"Nothing boss. The place is quiet as a cemetery."

Hill and his sidekick, David, had been back on Zane's payroll since he learned of Goran's death. Although he didn't trust them completely, they were Zane's connection to the outside world. His injury still made it difficult to get around, and he required assistance with his external transactions.

He studied the human for a moment. There was no reason for Hill to lie about this particular assignment. As luck would have it, Zane had inherited a gold mine from Melissa, his grandmother. A lawyer had contacted him some months ago about her will. It turned out Grandma had left him a sizeable fortune.

The revelation was a welcome one. Zane made sure his resources would last for a long, long time by being conservative in his financial matters. Gone were the clothes, cars, and tech toys. After he sold his Manhattan penthouse, he invested the proceeds of the sale in stocks.

"Get David to go every other day to check," he said, waving his hand in dismissal.

"You got it." Hill watched him for a moment before taking his leave. If the human had questions about the abrupt changes in Zane's behavior, he kept his hole shut. And that was how Zane preferred it.

Zane returned his attention to the computer monitor and the Internet search he'd been performing. Locating Cheryl was like looking for a needle in a haystack. The warehouse where he'd found her before had become a ghost town. There had been no recent activity in the area. Perhaps they'd moved back to the underground facility.

He wanted to see the female nurse again, to do right by her.

And why is that? asked the nagging voice of a conscience he never imagined he had.

Aside from his desire to comfort the woman, he drew a blank when he tried to explain it to himself. Maybe it was time to let the absurd idea of locating her go. She knew the number where he could be reached. It was best to leave her alone and go on with his empty existence. Zane closed the browser and gave up on the idea.

It was funny how solitude could mess with a person's head. After all his troubles, he had come to realize that he was alone. His grandfather's sick machinations had cost him both his grandmother and his father, Demetrius. Even Goran himself had perished in the end.

Being alone had never bothered Zane before. Growing up, he had been a self-centered, self-serving bastard. He was content to live in the lap of luxury, bedding different human females each night and hobnobbing with the city's elite. Somehow, after his brief captivity, his perspective changed. For the better? He didn't know anymore.

Zane crossed the hallway of his inherited penthouse and entered the exercise room. Thanks to the enumerable properties Melissa had bequeathed to him, he was set for life. Despite his newfound resolve to live a meager existence, he didn't have the heart to sell this particular property. It was his last link to his family and the only tie he had left to the people who'd loved him.

Using a cane to keep his balance, he hopped on the treadmill. He hoped the machine would help expend some of this nervous energy.

The equipment whirred to life. Zane held on to the handlebar and eased into a walking pace to begin his workout. He tried to clear his mind and concentrate on the task at hand. His left leg began to throb—a reminder of what the Dangeran metal had done to him.

Even after a thorough check, several granules remained lodged in his skin. They had most likely embedded themselves in his muscles. Harrow sure knew how to disable his enemies. Although Cheryl and Celia, his faithful housekeeper, had managed to remove most of the metal Harrow drilled into his body, it was impossible to find it all without going to a hospital and demanding help from a doctor. The small particles wouldn't kill him, but he'd never be the same.

Rohnert and Tor left the Council headquarters upon hearing the news about Cyrus. They plowed through the city streets to get back to the underground facility, where they found Harrow and the rest huddled inside the I-room.

"Can someone tell us what the hell happened?" Tor asked the moment they walked in.

Harrow, Jordan, Allison, and Gentry looked up. Dr. Rick Whitaker was also present. Rohnert soaked in their emotions, seizing their unspoken thoughts to gather any information he could get.

"We have no idea. Rayce reported that Cyrus called to say he was shot and to get Rick ready." Harrow waved them to some chairs.

Rohnert perched at one end of the table. "No one can extract any information from him?" he asked, looking around for Isidora.

"He passed out seconds after he made it back. He hasn't woken yet," Harrow said.

"A regular bullet?" Rohnert turned to Rick.

The doctor nodded, and a one-sided conversation began. He listened while Rick explained Cyrus' injuries at length. It was both a gift and a curse to have the doctor there with them, since he'd lost Shelly in the attack that led them to landing the mute doctor's services. The man's presence reminded Rohnert that his mate was never, ever coming back.

"Rick is certain that Cyrus is going to be fine. The regular bullet suggests that Cyrus was shot by a human. However, Cyrus has not been feeding enough. It took more than six units of blood to stabilize him."

Tor pounded his prosthetic hand on the table. "What the hell is up with this starvation bullshit? Didn't anyone get the memo that we need to feed to live?" His question may have been general, but his glare was focused on Rohnert.

Rohnert couldn't help feeling defensive. "Everyone has their own issues."

The remark seemed to further incense Tor.

"Regardless of issues, everyone needs to feed, hydrate, whatever. There is no way around it."

It was clear that he was targeting Rohnert. How the vampire knew he hadn't fed was anyone's guess. The last time had been six months ago, when Shelly was still . . .

Christ, he wasn't going to go there again. Even if Isidora was able and willing, it felt wrong to take someone's vein. It felt like he was cheating on his wife.

"If you're thinking what I think you're thinking, stop it, brother." Tor was looking at him. "You're not betraying Shelly's memory by taking what you need to survive."

Crossing his arms, Rohnert glared at the big-mouthed vampire. "Since when did we start talking about me?" The hint of challenge was clear in his tone.

"Since you ascended to that throne of yours. You're the leader of our race. It's my duty to remind you that you're a fuckin' ass for neglecting yourself."

Harrow, always the peacemaker, jumped in. "Boys, boys, let's not get into this right now. What I want to know when Cyrus wakes up is what he was doing getting involved in human affairs."

Tor snorted, turning his attention to Harrow. "You're not the only Boy Scout in the group, you know." This brought some laughter to the tense group.

"Well, all we can do now is speculate. If there's nothing pressing to discuss, I'm going to swing by to check on Cyrus before I see my son." Rohnert got up and left the room. He hated being the focus of Tor's nagging.

He covered the long hallway to the clinic in no time. Isidora looked up when he walked in, releasing Cyrus' hand as if she'd been caught doing something improper.

Rohnert took stock of her thoughts. The woman felt strongly about his friend, which was fine and dandy. "How is he doing?" He parked on the chair on the other side of the bed and faced the female vampire.

The stress of the situation was reflected in her young face, and Rohnert had the urge to reach out and comfort her, but he kept his hands in his pockets.

"It's been six hours since Rick operated on him. I'm getting worried."

Rohnert nodded in understanding. Cyrus had been in this situation before. He got lucky this time. Good thing that his stout vampire constitution would make healing faster than it would have been for a human.

"He should wake up soon. Don't worry." He took one look at Cyrus and knew Rick was right about his feeding habits. The vampire's face was ashen.

His head whipped when he caught an errant thought from Isidora. "Jesus, Issy. You haven't fed since you got here, have you?"

How could he have forgotten? After Shelly passed away, his whole world had fallen apart. He hadn't thought about his responsibility toward the pure-bred female who had been orphaned after her parents were killed in a raid. While the others could live off the blood of fellow vampires, humans, or even animals, pure-blooded vampires like him and Isidora required the blood of another pureblood, male or female. But he'd be damned if he would ask Wendell or even Icarus if he could suck on their veins.

"You had a lot on your mind. I've been fine until today. The smell of blood was too strong." She threw a quick glance at Cyrus' face, but he was still dead to the world.

"I suggest you wait no longer."

Isidora hesitated. This made Rohnert edgy. It had been a while since someone had taken his vein. Since Shelly had been human, there was no need to provide this service to his mate.

"Let's do it now." He stood up before his nerves got the best of him. "We'll come back here right away once we're done."

Isidora followed Rohnert to the hallway, where the great leader of their race hesitated and stopped to face her.

"I, ah, can we do this in your bedroom?" Rohnert sounded distracted, but that was understandable. It wouldn't feel right to do this inside the bedroom he had shared with his wife, no matter how clinical the process was.

"Of course. This way, please." Isidora led the way to the elevator. They traveled three floors down in utter silence. They both were privy to each other's thoughts, so words weren't necessary.

Isidora's heart was pounding hard by the time they covered the long corridor to her room. She turned on all available lights to make Rohnert feel comfortable before gesturing to the couch. This was pure necessity, she kept reminding herself. No feelings or emotions attached. Rohnert sat down on the couch and closed his eyes. From then on, he blocked her off, barring her from his private thoughts. Isidora did the same to him.

She was unsure how to go about the process. Before tonight, she had drunk from one person, Finn. Their usual encounters had been very physical and involved torrid foreplay. After he was killed on their first day in the city, she had been drinking the blood of an unknown human donor from a glass. What she and Rohnert were doing was new to her.

Through her indecision, her feet brought her closer to her blood donor. *This is dispassionate. Don't make anything out of it,* she mentally scolded herself. One look at the straining veins on his neck, and a feeling of claustrophobia began to close in on her. It had been too long since she had gotten an ounce of pure blood inside her.

"Issy, don't punish either of us for this. You need to feed. That's all you need to tell yourself. The longer you hesitate . . ." Rohnert's voice sounded broken and resigned.

Her heart did a major flip, and she realized that she was making a big production out of it. "It's been a long time . . ."

"I know." He let out a long sigh.

"I don't know how to do it anymore."

Rohnert opened his eyes, and there she found comfort and compassion. He patted the cushion next to him.

"Come here."

She followed his command and sat next to him, leaving ample space between them. Rohnert closed his eyes again, and his face relaxed.

With the hunger gnawing deep in her belly, Isidora knew that waiting longer would be dangerous for them both. She placed one hand on the base of his neck to tilt his head. His skin was warm, inviting even.

Disregarding the dread coursing through her like wildfire, she took his vein. The moment her fangs punctured his skin, he drew his head back, giving her more space. The first pull was like a bolt of lightning that spread from her head down to her toes. She drank in greedy gulps, marveling at the power his blood gave her. It was sweet and warm, and she tugged hard until Rohnert groaned. His hand moved to the small of her back, pressing her closer. Their bodies touched, and his warmth was like a promise of safety and protection.

She was close enough to feel the vibration of his body in response. Her temperature spiked at the eroticism of feeding. This was supposed to be unemotional and clinical, but it was difficult to overcome the urges of a soul long denied.

Rohnert was pushing her away before she realized what was happening. He was on his feet in a flash, jiggling his arms and shaking his head as though he was trying to rid himself of the sensations.

"Wait," she said when he darted to the door.

The great leader stopped in his tracks and turned to face at her. If guilt had a face, she was looking at it. Rohnert's usual serene features were drawn tight, his forehead was creased, and his lips had thinned into a straight line.

"I haven't sealed your wound." There was blood oozing from the puncture site.

Rohnert wiped the blood off with his palm and shook his head. "It's all right. I have to go and check on Malin."

"Thank you," she managed to say before the door closed behind him.

Replete, Isidora sat back on the couch. She could feel the effect of their blood mixing together and the strength that came with the feeding, and she slid down the soft cushion, her eyelids growing heavy.

As she fell into a relaxing slumber, her mind dipped into her memory of the man she used to feed from. Finn had been gone for seven months, and his absence still cut deep. Her thoughts of the man she'd once loved carried her into the turmoil of a dream-filled sleep. Theirs had been a young love stunted by the cruelty of life and the machinations of one evil man.

Then in the haze, she saw Rohnert's glory, his sacrifices and loss. He waded in the murky waters of confusion, torn between his responsibility to his people and the desire to step away. This was the cross he had to bear, and she'd be damned if she let him carry the weight on his shoulders alone.

Cyrus' face came into the light. The proud and broken vampire she had come to know.

How could she help him? Was it possible to tear down the wall between them? Would he let her penetrate the solid armor he had built around himself?

Cyrus' mind slammed into high gear the moment he emerged from the mist that separated sleep from reality. When he stirred into consciousness, the first thing that came to mind was the memory of a conversation he'd overheard, despite being out for the count.

A female's voice that might have been Issy had been talking to a male. The deep, low voice belonged to Rohnert. What was his role in all of this? Cyrus tried opening his eyes, but the damn things were like a ton of bricks. Even his body refused to cooperate when he commanded it to move. His hearing seemed fine, though.

He recalled listening to the heart-to-heart, but his brain short-circuited on him, refusing to accept the significance of Rohnert's offer to Issy. Cyrus' mind refused to process the idea of her feeding from Rohnert.

It might have taken hours or even days before awareness seeped back. At last, he surfaced. His lids fluttered open and he breathed deep.

The first thing Cyrus saw was the white ceiling, and then he registered the sound of familiar beeping. His arms were heavy, and the rest of his body ached. Then his memories of that ill-fated night returned. He had been in a dark alley, talking some sense into two human males. There also was a woman. Then the deafening sound of gunfire, followed by pain. It was the same pain he'd felt two years ago. He was in the hospital, in bed, safely back in the underground facility.

Jesus. At the rate he was going, he would need nine lives like a cat. For now, he would bask in being alive. Zane wasn't safe from him yet. His thirst to hunt the bastard down was stronger than ever.

He tried to lift an arm, but his hand was holding something. He dug deeper, willing himself to feel, to get the full sense of what was weighing him down. Soft and warm—a hand. Cyrus inclined his head to get a better view. Red hair. His heart somersaulted, and his eyes stung. No, this was too unreal.

Cyrus was a realist. A relationship between him and Issy would be too good to be true.

He concentrated on the simple act of removing his hand from her grasp. Even though his head was screaming at him, he wanted her touch more than anything.

Cyrus was a typical male, for crying out loud. Of course he wanted to keep holding this woman. More than that—he wanted her in his arms, to possess her, and make love to her. Damn. The bullet had messed with his head, not just his body. It had been ages since he'd been with a woman. He had managed to stay away, but this angel next to him was doing a number on him. He felt his shaft growing hard at her touch. Indeed, it had been too long, and his body reacted to the sexual hunger just like any man's would.

"Damn it," he muttered under his breath. Cyrus swallowed the lump in his throat and tamped down the urge to run his fingers through her hair. He longed to feel her body against his and make love to her until she shouted his name.

But after his traumatic experience, he was likely to fuck things up. Hell, he wasn't even sure she'd want him after she realized what Zane had done to him. He wasn't even sure he'd want her to find out.

Cyrus put a lid on his arousal. Men didn't yield to the weakness, to self-pity. They didn't hold on to false beliefs of happy-ever-after. Just look at how Rohnert's fairy tale had ended—in a nightmare. Cyrus' luck was bound to be even worse.

Isidora jumped to her feet. "Cyrus, I'm glad you're awake," she said, pushing a wisp of hair away from her face. She seemed genuinely happy.

"How long have I been out?" He couldn't meet her eyes and hoped to high heaven she wouldn't notice the wood he sported underneath the flimsy sheet that covered him.

Instead of answering him, she reached across the bed. Her arm accidentally rubbed against his bare chest when she retrieved the call button. Cyrus shrunk away. "Rick, he's awake," she said into the instrument.

It took less than a minute before the door burst open and Rick breezed into the room. The doctor's mouth moved, but unintelligible sounds came out. He shot a glare at Isidora, who seemed stunned into inaction. She was staring at Cyrus, her eyes glistening.

More incoherent sounds came out of Rick's mouth before Isidora snapped back. She looked at the doctor, her face turning beet red. "I'm sorry. Oh, Rick wants to know how you feel."

Cyrus hated this silent conversation around him. He felt like an outsider crashing a party, knowing he wasn't welcomed. "I feel like a superstar." His voice sounded gruff, and his throat felt like sandpaper.

Rick chuckled without making a sound. He took the chart by Cyrus' bedside and scribbled something on the paper.

"Are you in pain?" Issy translated the doctor's question.

"Does the burning in my stomach count?"

The doctor nodded. "I will give you a pain medicine to help with that."

"While you're at it, throw some sleeping pills my way, will you?"

Isidora stared at Cyrus while she relayed the doctor's answer. "Sure thing, after I check your wound."

"Hey, doc, I don't mind the silence. Is it possible to have you and me alone here while you do it?" he said, unable to look at Isidora.

Cyrus didn't want to hurt her feelings, but being in the same room with her made it impossible to think or even breathe. Isidora left without a word. Of course he felt wretched, but he needed space to gather his bearings.

While Rick snapped on a pair of gloves, Cyrus kept his eyes shut, hoping the doctor wouldn't see his hard-on. A wisp of air swished when Rick lifted his hospital johnny. Cyrus groaned, knowing that Rick had seen the bulge underneath his hospital gown. He couldn't bear to see the doctor's reaction, so he kept his eyes closed. There was a slight pressure around his abdominal area while the doctor removed the bandage. The inspection didn't take long. Before he knew it, new dressings were in place.

He felt a tap on his shoulder. Rick held up a piece of paper, and Cyrus scanned the scribble and then laughed. "You want me indoors for three weeks? You gotta be kidding me."

Rick shook his head then turned to write, then showed him again.

"Just try to tie me to the bed, and I'll send you back to the hospital you came from."

That wiped the smile off the doctor's face, which made Cyrus want to take back his words. He might be hurting, but he had no right to intimidate the man who had saved his life. He felt like an ass. "Hey, Rick, that was a joke, okay?"

Green eyes met his before Rick nodded. He scribbled fast and then showed Cyrus the paper.

"You're still going to keep me for three weeks? And you call that fair?" More scribbling. "You mean it?"

Damn, this doctor wasn't any different from Shelly. The door burst open, and Cyrus swore under his breath. It seemed like the entire facility was out in the hallway, judging by the noise.

Cyrus struggled to sit up. It wasn't cool if everyone saw him flat on his ass. The alarm sounded, prompting Rick to push him down against the mattress.

Rohnert came in first with a warning from the doctor. "He's going to put you to sleep right now if you don't behave yourself."

"At least let me sit up." He glared at Rohnert while he pushed the button to move the bed into an acceptable position.

Soon enough, he was surrounded by vampires and humans alike. Cyrus pasted a smile on his face. Sitting up placed some pressure on his stomach muscles, but to hell with pain. The tough-guy act was difficult to let go. At least, everyone was on eye level.

"I think it's time to change your SOP." Tor slapped him on the shoulder.

"What do you mean?" Cyrus drew back.

"Your constant injuries are beginning to bore me." Tor shook his head in mock disgust, and then grinned.

"You're just jealous because you're down two to one," Cyrus quipped.

"Stop it. This is not a joke." Allison gave Tor a good-natured slap on the arm.

Tor grabbed Allison's arm and drew her close. "Mm. Such a public display of affection is not a good thing, woman."

Allison laughed while Jordan rolled her eyes.

Then Jordan turned to Cyrus. "You have to take better care of yourself." She looked like she wanted to cry.

Cyrus took Jordan's hand that was resting on the side of his bed and kissed it. "I'm touched by your concern, but stop the sentimental shit. Don't make me get up from this bed and kick your ass. You know I'll do it, right?"

Jordan's eyes flashed. "You're too much, you know that?"

"Oh, I know. Gotta keep my reputation intact." This made everyone laugh.

Harrow grew pensive, and Cyrus knew that the vampire had something in mind. With Harrow, you had to wait until he was ready, and it was always a slow simmer.

Rohnert situated himself in a corner of the room, seeming content to watch the rest. Cyrus was certain that the vampire was reading each of their minds, so he kept his head clear, not willing to share his deepest and darkest secrets. Over time, he had learned to protect himself from the vampire's unusual gift.

There came the throat clearing as Harrow shifted his weight. *And here we go.*

"Okay, gang. We have a few new leads, which I have discussed with Rohnert at length."

"Leads?" Tor was all ears.

Harrow nodded, and his eyebrows dipped lower, disappearing behind his sunglasses. "While we're hard at work providing the cure, intel says that we have a generous source that is spreading the disease around."

A collective groan spread through the small room. Cyrus couldn't believe his ears. Wasn't that just dandy? Pritchard and Harrow had moved mountains to find a cure, and now someone was intentionally spreading it? That was wrong on so many levels.

"Care to elaborate?" asked Barth, a human fighter who'd survived the fierce battle at Catskill Mountain.

"The details are sketchy, but several vampires who sought our aid said they were recently infected. They were held at gunpoint—by a TE-18, nonetheless."

A *TE-18*? "What the fuck . . ." Cyrus couldn't believe what he'd just heard.

They were the sole distributor of that particular weapon. It was a product they had introduced a year ago and had made available to just a few select clients. This newest creation was a lighter and much shorter variant of its predecessor, the TE-15. It had more accurate aim with its improved sniper-scope, and since it was magazine fed, the weapon was hell in one small package. If it landed in the wrong hands, World War III could be on its way.

"How did those infected escape?" Tor asked.

"They had no choice but to submit. They knew there was a group that could help cure them, so it was better to suffer for a bit than end up dead." Harrow ran his palm through his blond hair in frustration.

"What do you propose we do?" Gentry stepped closer to the foot of the bed.

Rohnert replied this time. "We're going to utilize a combined team to do patrols. Since we're not one hundred percent sure of the validity of the news, we're not going on the offensive yet. We'll gather more facts, and then we'll reconvene and figure our next step."

"Sounds like a plan," Tor said, cracking the knuckles of his right hand.

"I'm going to establish a team from our side to help Rohnert's Council guards. I need a group of maybe fifteen for this particular endeavor." Harrow turned to Tor. "Mind taking the reins on this one?"

"Sign me up, will ya?" Cyrus said in a quiet voice.

All heads turned to him. "I hope you're joking." Harrow shook his head.

Rohnert waved his hand. "Rick says it's time for our friend to take a long nap."

Before Cyrus could process what that meant, the doctor had pushed a needle into his IV line. The goddamn bastard was putting him to sleep. "Dr. Whitaker, haven't you heard payback's a bitch?" Cyrus said just as the first wave of feel-good coursed through his veins.

"What the hell are you doing?" Cyrus hated the panic in his voice.

"I'm going to see how long a fucking grown man can keep his mouth shut." Without saying more, Zane ripped Cyrus' boxers off him.

"Get away from me!" He tried to twist his head around, but Zane's foot was jammed against his neck, preventing him. Sweat trickled down his temples to the floor. Then his legs were spread apart, wider and wider, until he could feel his skin tearing. He bit down on his lips to keep from crying.

"Having fun yet?"

"Fuck you," Cyrus said through gritted teeth.

Then with one mighty thrust, something was rammed in his ass—sick and painful. His mouth opened, and he cried out.

"Don't you just love the sweet sensation of torture? Are you ready to tell me what I want to know?"

"Go . . . to . . . hell . . ." he managed to say between waves of unthinkable pain.

"You first," Zane whispered in his ear. "Do you have any idea what I have jammed up your ass?"

"I'm sure you'll tell me."

Waking up on the tail end of his scream, Cyrus writhed from the pain of his fresh stomach wound. He looked around in the darkness and recognized the dark blue walls, the framed movie poster, and the bright light from the neon beer sign. He was back in his room, thank God. Drenched in sweat and clutching his abdomen, he struggled to get up then headed to his walk-in closet. Removing the shirt was a pain, so he decided not to put on a clean one.

A knock sounded on the door. Damn, he should have requested a room somewhere near the garage where no one would hear his nightly screams. Time and again, he'd told Tor not to bother, but the vampire didn't understand the concept of . . .

"Open the fuckin' door, or I'll break it down," Tor said through the thick wood that separated them.

Same shit, different day.

As usual, Cyrus yanked open the door and glared. "I told you not to bother. I'm fine, solid in the head. I'm not going to explode anytime, and I'm taking the pain medication."

Tor grinned. "Damn, I love your people skills. You bring tears to my eyes." He shoved past Cyrus, carrying a bottle of his favorite, Patron Silver, along with two shot glasses.

Cyrus closed the door behind Tor and hobbled to the couch. "Are you deaf or something? How many times have I told you not to bother checking on me?"

Tor placed the bottle and glasses on the coffee table and flipped him the bird with his prosthetic middle finger. "When my girl is out on babysitting duty, sleep is hard to come by. Then if you scream like a bitch, what do you expect from me? Just go quietly into that good night?"

Cyrus glared. "Shut up and pour."

"The boogeyman got to you again?" Tor uncorked the bottle and filled the shot glasses to the brim.

"I was dreaming of J Law."

"Hmm . . . I see you have a soft spot for younger women." Tor handed him a glass.

Talk about setting himself up. Cyrus raised his glass in Tor's direction before the bastard could say something that might lead to bloodshed. "*Kampai*, brother." They both drank and then slammed their glasses down on the table.

Tor was watching him. "Cy, Issy is over fifty years old, so you're technically younger than her. Maybe if we use hair dye, you could look like a prize stallion again."

Cyrus glared daggers at him. "Drop it, Burns, or I'll fuckin' shave your head in your sleep."

His friend had the audacity to laugh while running his fingers through his thick dreads. "This is my crowning glory. Females swoon over this." Then Tor's expression sobered. "You and I have been together through a lot of shit, and you know I have your back, right?"

Cyrus rolled his eyes and nodded. Tor, though afflicted with foot-in-mouth disease, was as tight and loyal as you could get. Just like a fucking dog that wouldn't go away. The idea made Cyrus laugh. "Don't bore me, Tor. What are you trying to tell me?"

Tor got up and paced the room then poured another round of shots. This was going to be a long night. After handing Cyrus a glass yet again, he sighed. "The nightmare is not going away, and we both know it. If it would help to talk about—"

"Save it. Not interested. I'm fine." Cyrus downed the shot. "Why don't we watch a movie?" Tor was a sucker for action movies or anything that featured blood and gore.

There was no answer. Cyrus felt a little bit of remorse, but he shook it off right away. The vampire should know by now that he wasn't going to sing. There was no way he was going to talk about what had been done to him. The humiliation and pain weren't worth rehashing.

Cyrus strode to the entertainment console that housed his precious movie collection. He chose an all-time favorite action flick, with gun-slinging and smack-talking that would entertain them without requiring any more conversation. He slid the disc in the player and pressed the play button.

"What are we watching?" Tor poured another shot.

"I'm your huckleberry," Cyrus said, quoting a line from the movie.

Tor hooted and whistled. For the next hour and a half, they watched *Tombstone*, often reciting the familiar lines. It gave Cyrus a reprieve from questions he didn't want to answer.

The bottle was empty by the time the movie ended. Cyrus shooed Tor out of his bedroom before he could begin his inquiries and platitudes again.

He needed peace and quiet. Regardless of what others might think, he was fine—fine with the knowledge that the day of reckoning was coming soon. Doc Holliday was right. Hypocrisy would only go so far.

Bretania inhaled deep before releasing a long, contented sigh. Two weeks into her full acceptance of her new lifestyle, she felt like a million dollars. She had given in to the call of her new nature, and the blood had eased the pain stemming from the disease. What was the point in crying about the past? All she had to do was seize the moment and live for the future. It wasn't so bad from her point of view. Perched high on one of the tallest buildings in the city, the possibilities were endless. She marveled at the grand vista around her and spread her arms.

All it had taken was a little ingenuity on her part, and the plan had been set in motion. Build an army, give them the best training, and she was well on her way to claiming what was hers.

"Ready?"

Bretania glanced at her second in command.

Reid's red eyes flashed as he cracked his knuckles in anticipation. The man was as smart as they came—lean, trim, and with the right amount of wickedness in his heart. All she had to do was groom his innate skills and feed his ego with false promises, and she had a mean machine at her disposal. It didn't hurt that the bastard was able and willing to feed her heart's desire and find her unsuspecting, gullible vampires and humans.

Upon learning of her mate Goran's death, her perspective had changed. It wasn't easy at first, because anger had consumed her. She had been angry about his betrayal. He had withheld vital information about his disease and had sent her away. Now, it made sense to her. Goran had sent her away so she would be spared death at the hands of their true enemies.

Keyed up and ready to go, Reid rose to his full six-foot-one height and looked at his men. The army Bretania had brought together was filled with stout fighters, riled up and prepared to carry out her bidding.

Her strategy was unprecedented, so she was testing the waters. She tugged on the strap of her weapons before raising her hand to give the signal.

"Stay alive," was all she said before free-falling over one thousand feet to the ground. She heard the group follow suit, and soon they were gunning down dingy alleys and long, dark stretch of streets to the famed Rockefeller Center. Beneath the structure lay the headquarters of their powerful race, unknown to humans and civilian vampires alike.

During Goran's rule, the first order of business after someone left the Council walls for good had been the removal of their access to the mysterious door for re-entry. For all she knew, her entry access had been revoked, but she had to try. There was business to conduct, scores to settle, and people for whom she was responsible.

They reached the general vicinity, and Bretania smiled. The filmy entrance was still there, waiting and beckoning her. She listened for any possible danger lurking in the darkness before gesturing for everyone to follow her. Her plan was already in place. She had given each fighter the layout and his particular mission, along with an order to kill anyone who got in their way.

The entrance led them to a staircase in the furthermost wing of the headquarters, close to the Blanch room. Surprisingly, the area that once reeked of blood and despair was immaculate and sterile. It didn't carry the scent of death that she had associated with it.

They advanced in quick and silent movements. All she sensed from the headquarters' inhabitants was their contentment and the general feeling of safety. That was about to change.

"Remember, I want them all," she reminded her team. As the ten able-bodied males scattered in every direction, she ran toward her former chamber. The hallway was quiet, but it wasn't a surprise when she encountered some resistance.

There was no hesitation on her part when she gunned down two former comrades. Nearby cries and gunshots sounded, and she knew the mission was underway. They had to move fast.

She turned the corner in the direction of her chamber and found two soldiers closing in on her, while more footsteps sounded behind them. "Madam, are you back for good?" one guard asked, smiling at her.

Ah, just what she'd expected. Unsuspecting fools would be easy to subdue or annihilate. Bretania smiled and watched as the guards relaxed. This was her cue to unleash hell. With economized movement, she unstrapped her automatic rifle, fired a round, and felled the five or so guards in her path. When they disintegrated before her eyes, she felt no remorse. The only emotion taking over was the intense desire to get even. Nothing more.

Bretania entered her former chamber and raked her eyes over her belongings. Everything remained untouched. In fact, she couldn't gather any scent that indicated anyone had entered her quarters at all.

Rohnert was a sentimental fool, and that was the vampire's weakness. Well and good. Bretania worked fast, taking some treasures and the most important thing in her collection, the necklace Goran had given her during their mating ritual.

She closed her eyes for a brief moment, trying to sense the activities within the Council walls. Their timing had been good. Most Elders were away, and the guards were fulfilling their duties elsewhere, thinning the defenses inside. After gathering the thoughts of her group, she was ready to go.

Bretania took one last lingering look at the place she had called home for at least a century and fled to the hallway strewn with the ashes of fallen soldiers. Too bad Rohnert was too much of coward to come out of his hiding place. Rushing footsteps of backup soldiers drew closer, drowning out the cries of the children they'd come to collect.

"We're ready, your highness." Reid was holding Nathaniel in a chokehold, half dragging the young vampire toward the exit. The rest of her army was holding on to three others, and pure terror shone in the children's eyes.

"What happened to the other two children?"

Reid shook his head, and she knew what it meant. They were out of time. Their window of opportunity had been utilized, but it was time to go.

She did a quick mental headcount. Not shabby. They'd lost five men in the raid. Bretania gestured for everyone to head to the exit, took one last look at her old stomping grounds, and then jumped through the portal. That might well be the last time she would set foot inside the Council walls until the moment she returned to stake her claim to her rightful place.

The trouble with Issy's ability to hear everyone's innermost thoughts was the intimate knowledge of the burdens each of them carried. As much as she wanted to block the voices around her, it was next to impossible. Cyrus' internal ramblings and nightmares were the toughest to ignore because she was drawn to him. Even though he had made it clear that he wanted to put distance between them, she couldn't stay away.

Tonight, he had another nightmare. It was the most telling of all by far. Hearing his inner turmoil brought her newfound respect for the way the man managed to hold himself together.

Maybe if she could learn all the fighting tactics and excel in every weapon, Harrow might allow her to go on rotation. The thought of going out there still scared her, but the desire to avenge Cyrus was even stronger. She began to wonder if Jordan or maybe Allison would show her some of their tricks. Cheryl had told her one day that Allison used to be a quiet and unassuming lady. In Issy's mind, Allison still projected that persona, except she had more confidence.

Could Isidora be that way, too?

There was so much to learn. The lingo, the body language, the subtle nuances of interacting with others, and even the pop culture were enough to give her a headache. Everything was happening too fast for her. One day, she'd been busy plotting a way out, and in a blink of an eye, she was all alone in a strange city, surrounded by a curious mix of characters. This was the life she had missed out on, and it was about time she tried to catch up.

She was leading a new life now with a new set of friends and family. Even if her heart was still mending from the loss of her loved ones, it was time for her to move on and get with the program.

Hugging the pillow to her chest, she closed her eyes and tried to block Cyrus from her mind. She could do this. Isidora would win him over because she believed they could help each other. Even if they didn't fall in love, she'd have someone to share the lonely nights. With these thoughts, her body began to relax, and she smiled to herself.

Two weeks into his unscheduled break, Cyrus swore he'd go mad. It felt like he was wasting away. He was unproductive and fast becoming a basket case. His inability to participate in training and patrols was driving him to the brink of insanity.

He longed for action and wanted the feeling of being needed. The longer he stayed within the four walls of his bedroom, the closer to the edge it pushed him.

Rick had checked on his post-op wound and changed the dressing in Cyrus' bedroom, because he refused to go in the clinic and see Isidora. He doubted if he would be able to keep his hands to himself if she ever decided to touch him again. Of course, he gave no indication this was his reason, and the doctor was game enough to do the house call. This required no talking on their part, which was all right with him. If Rick had something to say, Cyrus didn't give the human a chance to say it, often shooing him away even before he reached for a piece of paper to write on.

He'd been reduced to sitting in front of the television, scanning the cable channels for movies. When that didn't work, he tried light workouts, which led to intense pain that prompted him to stop.

Today was no different from the past days. He sat on the couch, wishing for something that would take his mind off the shitty things that he had no business thinking about. He managed to avoid seeing Isidora, but she had kept his brain occupied with thoughts of her.

What could she be doing now? How was she after the feeding? Damn it! He didn't want to go there, didn't want to imagine her taking the vein of another, especially a male. What the hell could he do about it anyway? He wasn't royalty. His vampire blood was second rate, nothing that would nourish her and make her thrive.

All he had was a heap of emotional baggage that was heavy enough to sink a ship. Besides, she was better off with the likes of Rohnert, or maybe Rick. Someone who would cherish her and take care of her in ways he couldn't. Sex was all Cyrus could offer, and even that left a bad taste in his mouth.

Cyrus groaned, putting an end to his idiotic self-deprecation. His lethargy was making him act like an ass, and a jealous ass at that. It wasn't his style. He'd never been in a long-lasting relationship, or any relationship that held significance. He wasn't a monk, by any means. Being unattached suited him just fine. In his line of work, he was better off being single—no one to worry about and vice versa. He had loved two women in his life. They were Mrs. Tyler, or "Mom" as he called her, and Linda, his foster sister. Both were out of his life now. His foster mother had been taken by cancer, and Linda had been taken back into the system.

Cyrus, on the other hand, had taken off. He'd worked odd jobs, getting in and out of trouble until he met Lambert. They had shared the bond of living in the foster care system—going in and out of households that never felt like home.

Having similar backgrounds enabled their friendship to grow. They never asked for details of the past, and they watched each other's backs. The pair had been working as bounty hunters until they met Pritchard Tack, and their lives took a turn. For the better? Who knew, but at least he'd found a small measure of peace and belonged to a family, however dysfunctional it might be.

Man, he was a bundle of shit these days. All this inaction was making him think about things that he wanted buried deep. He had shed his last tears for his mom and had continued to curb the desire all these years to visit Linda for her own safety. No one was going to chip away at his resolve now. Not even the beguiling young vampire with haunting eyes.

A knock sounded from the door.

"Fuck it," he muttered. Tor should get a life or find someone else to annoy. He'd had enough of the vampire crowding his space. Cyrus wobbled over to the door and yanked it open. "Now what? Can't you see that I have . . ."

He swallowed the rest of his words. Isidora stood outside, her face flushed and her eyes miserable.

"Issy, what's wrong?"

She shifted her weight from one foot to the other, a nervous habit he had noticed from the beginning. "Can I come in?" she asked, sounding tentative.

There went his resolve to keep the girl at arm's length. Cyrus opened the door wider and stepped aside to let her pass. "Is something the matter?"

When she brushed past him, he had to suck in a breath to keep her scent from wreaking havoc within him.

Isidora looked around, hesitated, and glanced over her shoulder at him. He gestured toward the sofa and watched her with keen interest while she sat down. Her proximity was already causing his mind to go into overdrive and his body to heat up. This prompted him to sit at the end of the couch, keeping a safe distance between them. Then he took a pillow to cover the unwanted bulging inside his pants.

"Issy, what is going on?" he asked again.

"I'm troubled."

Her eyes were beseeching him to say something. *Say what?* "If this is about my dream last night, don't worry about it. I had a hyperactive imagination as a child."

She looked dubious. "I didn't mean to listen, but you do it so often."

Maybe sleeping wasn't an option anymore. Cyrus watched her with growing unease. He could control his mind's rambling during his waking hours, but the dreams—the nightmares were beyond his control.

"Look, I'm sorry if that is an inconvenience for you. I'll try not to—"

Isidora cut him off. "You're not listening to me. I don't care if you scream every night, but what you have in there is troubling you." She pointed to his chest. "I want to help."

Okay, so the woman had a temper on her. Hmm . . . something he hadn't pegged earlier. "There is no help needed here. My problem, my concern." He shrugged.

"I don't want to overstep my boundaries. I just want to help you." She jutted out her chin and met his gaze straight on.

Cyrus gave a mirthless laugh. "What can you possibly do for me?"

Her gaze didn't waver. "I can hold you while you sleep." It was spoken without hesitation.

He stared at her, unable to process the idea. Yeah, sure. That would put him on the laughing stock list for sure. "No, thanks. I'm fine."

"Why are you so stubborn? Why are you refusing my help?" Isidora asked, seeming hurt by his refusal.

Cyrus broke eye contact and got up. He needed to shake off her effect on him. "My dear naïve little girl, you're not thinking straight. People talk. Sleeping in my bed would not be a good addition for your chaste résumé."

He searched his mind for an explanation of what he was feeling. Sure, he was physically hungry since he'd managed to neglect feeding on a regular basis. Her easy relationship with Rick made his chest hurt, and he often worried about her. The latter was nothing he hadn't felt before for the other women in the facility. He cared about them. Nothing more.

She lapsed into silence. Just when he thought that she had accepted his refusal, she spoke again. "I thought you were different when we first met. You seemed caring, easy to talk to, and approachable. Now, I don't know anymore."

Cyrus hardened his heart. The woman was going to unravel him with her heartfelt words. "Issy, please, I'm all right. What I want you to do is go back to your room—"

The squealing of the alarm cut his entreaty short, and they looked at each other. Cyrus saw confusion in Isidora's eyes.

He stumbled while making his way into his closet, but firm hands caught and steadied him.

"Thanks." He grabbed his Glock and a handful of daggers. His wound throbbed at the suddenness of his movements. "Go back to your room and lock the door. Don't come out until you hear from me."

Isidora shook her head. "I'm going with you. You can hardly walk. Besides, I'm quite capable of handling myself." She raised her long skirt up to her thighs and pulled out a gun from a holster.

Damn. He twitched at the sight of her creamy skin. Any higher, and he would have grabbed her and had done with it. He shook his head at the mental image. It wasn't the right time. "Issy, don't be stubborn. I can manage. How can I protect you if you won't listen to me?"

Instead of responding to his plea, she looped her arm around his waist. "I'm ready to go." The determination on her face made him want to crush his lips to hers—and then make her understand the stupidity of her actions.

Instead, off they went into the hallway, with Isidora supporting his weight. She was steady and calm.

Then a voice blared from the speakers. Harrow's. "All hands are needed in the I-room now. I repeat, we need everyone in the I-room now."

Humans and vampires were clamoring for the elevator by the time they got there. "Let's take the stairs." Isidora steered him into the narrow stairwell.

Man, this was the most embarrassing moment of his life. Still, he couldn't ignore the heat her body sparked in his. This was a bad idea on so many levels, yet he wasn't sure he had the strength to push her away. Not with her soft body rubbing against his skin.

Issy looked up at him then, and he was sure as hell she'd heard what he was thinking. In an effort to save them both from embarrassment, Cyrus tried to pull away, but she just pressed her body closer.

Cyrus grunted with every step. Rick had been right. Even three weeks was stretching it. His scheduled liberation was one week away, and he was nowhere near ready. He was covered in sweat by the time they made it out of the stairwell. Tension blanketed them the moment they entered the I-room.

Almost every single resident of the underground facility was gathered inside. Even little Malin was there, tucked inside Allison's arms. Cyrus did a fast sweep and noticed quite a number of people missing.

Marcus, a vampire, got up and offered his seat to Isidora. She thanked the soldier, but then she pressed Cyrus into the vacated spot. "Take it. You shouldn't be up on your feet."

He was about to argue when Harrow began speaking.

"There has been an attack at the Vampire Council headquarters. Rohnert, Tor, Gentry, and a handful of our men are en route to check for damage and casualties."

"Who are the perpetrators?" asked Robin, one of Alonzo's recruits who was known to be a hothead.

"Preliminary reports are saying it's one of the Elders they thought was dead." Harrow removed his sunglasses and rubbed his eyes.

Cyrus looked at the fighters, and he could sense their frustration. An attack on one was an attack on them all.

"I don't believe this. I would have thought VC was a fortress," another vampire said.

"Rohnert shouldn't take this sitting down," one of the human fighters said. "This is an outrage."

There was a loud murmur of speculations and expressions of anger that roared around the room until Harrow pounded his fist on the table. "Believe me, Rohnert will do everything in his power to find whoever is responsible."

"What are we going to do about it?" Firman asked.

Harrow looked at each of the fighters in attendance. "Since Rohnert is a valued member of our team, we are looking at this as an attack to us, too. I'll be conferring with Cyrus and Firman about our position and how we can help. But this also might have been meant as a distraction."

"What do you mean by distraction?" Marcus asked.

Allison took over the explanation, which made sense. She'd been in the thick of it all. "About a year ago, our group experienced simultaneous attacks on our business and home fronts. We lost many men in our upstate home, but when we sent fighters to that location, another call came from our office building requesting backup."

"With those incidents in mind, I want everyone on full alert. If you must sleep with your weapon next to you, do so." Harrow stood up and rested his palms on the table before launching into a full-scale briefing about facility protocols and the location of the secret exit. While their leader went on, Cyrus' mind slipped into high gear, running different scenarios in his head.

This couldn't be happening again. What would it take to fortify their facility enough? Rayce had been glued to the monitor with Angus as his backup. They had secured the gates, even added an electric shock fence surrounding the mile-wide area. For Christ's sake, they wouldn't be able to come back from another strike like the ones they'd gone through before.

He felt a pair of hands on his shoulders, kneading the knotted muscles and urging him to relax. Cyrus couldn't resist the pressure or the softness of the touch.

"That is why we need to learn how to fight and watch each other's backs," Isidora whispered in his ear. The warmth of her breath against his skin made him acutely aware of her closeness.

Cyrus took a sharp intake of breath. Jesus. The woman would be the death of him. He looked over his shoulder at her and saw the hint of a smile on her beautiful lips. That also meant she knew what he was thinking. Damn it. An attractive girl and mind reading were a bad combination. Definitely bad for him, anyway.

Out of the corner of his eye, he saw a quiet figure watching them, unmoving. He raised his head and met Rick's gaze head-on. The human didn't falter. Instead, he released a long sigh.

Cyrus returned his focus to Harrow when the vampire began to wind down the emergency meeting.

"Do you want me to stay here with you?" Issy murmured into his ear.

He shook his head. "I'll be fine. Thanks." The room emptied out until just he, Harrow, and Firman were left.

"What do you suggest we do?" Harrow turned to him.

Cyrus took his time responding, taking into consideration their numbers, the balance of experienced and new fighters, and the possibility of another attack. "As much as I would love to send our best men over there to help out, I'm afraid we can't do that while we're in the process of rebuilding. What I can do is step up the training of new recruits. Once we get a new batch to full capacity, then we can send some to help. I don't want to be blindsided."

Harrow pondered his recommendations while Firman stroked his chin, deep in thought. After a few moments, Firman offered his suggestion. "On some of our patrols, we've heard discontent throughout the community over this group that is spreading the disease. Most vampires have expressed a desire to fight back. I didn't think anything of it before since we're in rebuilding mode, but now I think it's a good idea to gather as many willing souls as we can."

Cyrus studied Firman. The vampire had been an invaluable addition to their team and had shown his worth as a leader during the attack on the office building. He might have appeared young, but his calm behavior and sound judgment were traits they needed. Although Cyrus hadn't had the chance to work with Firman in the field, Harrow seemed to have taken a liking to the fighter.

"I think Firman has a good point. We should explore that option. And since Rick hasn't cleared me to engage in strenuous activities, I think it's also a good idea to let Firman run the training for the time being. I will help out with the schedule and tracking of fighters."

Harrow ran his palm over his face then sighed. "Okay. I think you're right." He turned to the fighter. "Firman, if you need help with training, ask Isidora to help you out with the guns. I've seen her with those weapons, and I think we hit the jackpot with her."

Cyrus wanted to protest, but Harrow shook his head. "We both know you've taught her well. She needs this, too."

"Fine, but she's never to go on rotation." Cyrus would make sure of it. Issy's place was in the safety of the facility—right where he could watch her. He tried not to envision her lovely face and waved off Harrow and Firman's questioning gaze.

Rohnert's lips parted away from his teeth when he took in the carnage in front of him. The air grew thin, and it felt as though he would suffocate with anger. His grip tightened on his Kalimetal, and he wished he could strike out and give in to the mounting rage within. So much death. Just when he thought things were looking up, this had to happen.

"I'm going to check from room to room." Tor's features darkened, and he left before Rohnert could respond.

Gentry bristled. "Sire, what should I do with the remains?"

Rohnert wanted to ask, *what remains?* but caught himself. "Take whatever ashes you can collect, and we'll put them in a jar as offering."

The centuries-old tradition had been long forgotten, but he owed it to the people who gave their lives to be given proper burial rites. There was no telling who had perished or survived until he got an accurate head count.

"Right away, sire." Gentry was gone in a flash, leaving Rohnert alone in a state of anguish and confusion.

He looked around the room then closed his eyes, trying to gather the scent of those who had wreaked havoc on their peaceful haven. A small part of him wanted to thank the higher power that had protected his son from the intruders, but that was so wrong. He was supposed to keep everyone single person safe, not just those he loved.

Rohnert began to dart from one chamber to another investigating. It seemed the Elders had survived. Wendell's private quarters were undisturbed. So were Serena and Icarus' quarters. He hastened his movements until he had covered the inner wing and made his way to the area belonging to the children.

In this part, he caught a scent . . . something familiar. Then a slight movement from behind made him aware of a presence. He brandished his weapon, ready to pounce.

"My lord, it is I," Icarus said, his palms up.

"Who were the perpetrators?"

Icarus pointed his chin up, his eyes fluttering shut. Rohnert watched as the Elder's copper hair twitched, his body growing taut. Then his eyes flashed open.

"Bretania." The elder breathed. "She was here."

There was no way Rohnert could have recognized the scent since he'd been gone for such a long time. Bretania had been his replacement as the tactician and weapons expert, and she'd worked her way into Goran's favor.

"Are there any survivors?"

"Most soldiers are out, which was good timing. I found some servants and a few soldiers scattered around. According to reports, we were able to take down a few of the attackers."

"Have you called the others?"

"Yes, sire. Serena, Regrita, and Wendell are rounding up the survivors as we speak."

Rohnert shook his head, unable to wrap his mind around the killing of innocent people. Then Icarus' errant thoughts struck him.

"They took the children? Which ones?"

Icarus nodded. "Wendell is trying to find out now."

"What would she want from . . ." he stopped himself as the crystal clear implications dawned on him. Of course Bretania wanted the children— Goran's children. With their mothers killed in the carnage upstate, she was all they had. Although Rohnert had tried hard to draw the kids out of their shells, their innate defenses had been up from day one, especially the oldest boy, Nathaniel.

"What I don't understand is why she just didn't ask for them. Why did she feel the need to kill?" Icarus had caught on to his line of thinking.

"That's what I'm going to find out soon." Rohnert made a promise to himself in silence. Another vow he was piling on top of many others.

Avenge Shelly and Alonzo's death by killing Goran—check. Spread the cure—check. Lead their race back up from the ground—struggling to get that done. Find closure about the disappearance of Shelly's body— impossible. And now this. Sure. Yeah, he was up to the task.

They had covered the entire children's floor, but aside from occasional piles of ashes, there were no other traces of anyone else. Their hasty sweep produced nothing more.

Loud footsteps sounded from the hallway, and Wendell came into view, followed by his trusted men.

"Rohnert, the headcount of missing soldiers is about fifty." Wendell's despair was palpable.

What do people say in situation like this? I'm sorry—let's move on and rebuild? A lump formed in Rohnert's throat, making it impossible to utter a word. More deaths. Would this ever stop?

"The children?"

"Nathaniel, Marian, Rhiannon, and Esmeralda are nowhere to be found. Sawyer and Liv are with Regrita right now."

Rohnert remembered each of the kids. Nathaniel became the oldest of the brood after Demetrius was killed. The teenage was firecracker, often speaking his mind without being prompted. He had inherited his father's temper. His sister, Marian, was more into fashion and her appearance, like most human teenagers were. Unlike her, Rhiannon was most often seen reading, and she had a healthy appetite for blood. The toddler, Esmeralda, was a sweet thing, too young to realize what was going on around her.

Then there were the two children who remained. Sawyer was the exact opposite of Nathaniel. Quiet and content to be alone, it was rare to see the boy interacting with others. Liv was a younger version of Rhiannon and had been caught on several occasions taking more blood than was allotted to her.

Unable to find appropriate words of consolation, he tackled a safer topic. "Inform the rest of the Elders that there will be an emergency meeting. I have important business to attend to, but I'll be back in no time."

Wendell inclined his head, his eyes shifting to the ground. "What about the children, sire?"

Rohnert blinked. Now that their headquarters had been compromised, there was no guessing if Bretania would come back for the ones left behind. "We will discuss that matter during the meeting."

He left the room to find Tor waiting for him, a grim expression on his face. They exited the Council walls in silence, though Rohnert knew the exact feelings of his friend. They had seen so many casualties during their time patrolling the streets and protecting their friends. This was no different.

As soon as they reached the underground facility, he went to Allison and Tor's room to pick up his son. Malin was still fast asleep when Rohnert laid him in his crib. Then, the shrill ringing of the phone sounded.

"Rohnert, what did you find out?" Harrow's voice sounded strained over the phone.

"Nothing much. I just came back to call on Lukan. What's up?"

A long sigh came through the phone line. "Got a call from Leo. Gail is acting up saying she wants to come home."

Parenthood was something foreign to all of them. Rohnert could just imagine what was in store for him and his son. Then the picture of the two children left within the Council walls jarred his vision.

"I'm sorry." What else could he say? He was no more experienced with parenting than Harrow, who had cared for the human girl for almost two years. Gail was a sweetheart, orphaned when her mother was taken by Goran and turned into one of the members of his Harem.

Harrow made a clucking noise. "I'm going to leave tonight with Jordan. There's no telling how long it'll take us. I'm going to leave Cyrus in charge, with Tor as his backup. I swear Cy is going to go postal soon without something to do."

Rohnert knew Cyrus well. The vampire was rock steady, but he had his fair share of secrets. Though he often kept his thoughts private, Rohnert had caught glimpses of the demons the man was fighting. Privacy was something Cyrus needed, and Rohnert was not going to crowd him by asking too many questions.

"I have a favor to ask. You can say no, and I'll understand."

Harrow chuckled. "The great Rohnert is asking for a favor. I gotta hear this."

Rohnert ignored the jibe. "Most casualties in the palace are soldiers. It was Bretania."

There was silence for a few seconds before Harrow spoke. "I'm still waiting for the favor."

"Bretania took most of the children, but left two behind. There's a possibility she might come back for them." Again, the silence loomed, so he continued. "I'm wondering if I could bring them here for an indefinite period while I'm assessing the safety of Council headquarters."

Harrow remained silent, and Rohnert understood the leader's concerns. He waited.

After a few moments, Harrow cleared his throat. "You know how I feel about their father, but I'm not one to punish children for their father's mistakes. They are welcome here. Just make sure they behave. We have humans living with us."

Rohnert sighed. "Thank you. I'll make sure they are monitored every moment of the day."

"Call if you need anything else."

"Sure will."

After they hung up, Rohnert took a moment to check on Malin. He hovered over the crib and watched his son. In deep sleep, the baby's mouth was moving in a sucking motion. Rohnert's chest tightened at the thought of Shelly, and he reminisced about the time she'd first breastfed their son. It had taken Malin some time to get into the rhythm of sucking, which had made Shelly cry in frustration. When mother completed the bond with her son at last, it had been a touching scene. They were a family.

Rohnert took a step back and gathered himself. There was no point in rehashing the tender moments for they brought him more pain. He strode to the closet and pulled out the wooden chest.

He brought the chest to the middle of the room and lifted the heavy lid. In it were the ceremonial purple robe, the gingko beads, and the candles needed to perform the summons. Shedding his leathers, he donned the robe before shoving the chest aside. He lit the candles, gripped on the beads and closed his eyes. Though his heart continued to be troubled and the last thing he needed was to be in the company of the shaman, this had to be done.

Rohnert began chanting the ancient words to call upon their race's priestess. It was not an easy task, considering his ill-feelings toward the woman and her master. As far as Rohnert was concerned, Lukan and Gastarius, their diviner, could go to hell. They had known Shelly's death was imminent, and yet they did nothing to prevent it from happening. Instead, they had stood on the sidelines and allowed the prophecy to pass— to fulfill the sacred divination. Bullshit.

The trademark wisp of air was followed by smoke that festered inside the room, and then Lukan appeared. Her features seemed subdued. The usual smile was missing from her once calm face. She wore a hesitant expression when she lowered her hand for his acknowledgment.

"You called upon me." Lukan's voice quavered.

Rohnert pulled her hand to his lips for the briefest moment and then stood up. He was determined to forgo the rude remark about to leave his lips. "Yes. The Council has been compromised. Many of my men were killed. You must surround the area with your blinding spell, or whatever it is that you do." He watched her lovely face cringe at his request. "While you're at it, put a spell around this facility, too. I want my son safe at all times."

The last part was not a request.

Lukan closed her eyes and pressed her lips together. Rohnert resorted to reading the great shaman's mind. It was considered rude to invade the higher being's thoughts, but he was past worrying about decorum. If they wanted him to run the show, then they'd better cater to his wishes.

The woman was debating between several potions to use. While her mind was devoid of any other thoughts, Rohnert could perceive static, and this told him the Shaman was blocking him from further probing her mind.

She began chanting words he hadn't heard before—melodious, enchanting, and somewhat disconcerting at the same time. A cloud of gray smoke danced around her as she waved her hand in a symmetrical pattern and continued to chant.

Rohnert remained transfixed until the session ended and the room again was bathed in darkness except the faint glow coming from the candles. Lukan took a deep breath and then met his gaze.

"I will go to the Council house and perform the same ritual." Her voice was unusually hoarse.

"Thanks," he said and turned away.

"You are most welcome." Lukan's mind suddenly opened, allowing him to see more than he wanted. Shelly's death, Goran's demise, and her remorse. "Rohnert, I want—"

"Save it, Lukan. The die has been cast. There's nothing left to say."

No apologies, no excuses, and certainly no offer of sympathy.

Without a word, Lukan disappeared, leaving a trail of melancholy that gripped his heart and weakened his knees.

Cyrus reached the clinic level after getting a message from Rick that he wasn't going to make the scheduled house call. He approached with cautious steps and noticed the clinic was busy. There were muffled voices streaming into the hallway, so he slowed his stride once he got closer. The door was ajar, and through the little opening, he saw Tor standing next to Allison.

He was about to turn and leave when Tor glanced over his shoulder. "Hey, what's up with you, brother?"

"I'm good. What's going on here?" He tried to get a peek past Tor's big body, which was blocking his view.

"Issy had a little accident—"

That was all he needed to hear. Cyrus pushed Tor aside and burst into the clinic. "What's wrong with Issy?"

Several heads whipped in his direction, including Issy's. She was sitting on the examination table, face pale and scrunched in pain. He did a quick visual inspection and found the small laceration on her right arm. Rick raised his hand and gestured for her to interpret.

"No sudden movements. It makes it tough to concentrate, and I want this stitching to look nice and neat."

Cyrus stopped dead in his tracks and hissed. His common sense told him she was fine, but his nerves were already skyrocketing and ready to explode if he didn't get an answer. "What happened to her?"

Allison stepped closer to him and laid a calming hand on his arm. "She was practicing using the dagger with me when she slashed her arm by accident," she whispered.

"Did you remove the Dangeran? Are you sure it's all gone?" He directed the question to Rick, his tone a bit more forceful than he'd intended.

Issy's eyes were pleading when she translated Rick's answer. "Get him the hell out of my clinic."

Tor moved quick and hustled him out of the room, and Allison trailed behind them. "You heard the guy. He's trying to concentrate."

"I was asking a question, and no one will give me a straight answer." Cyrus felt his body shaking with rage.

"Cyrus, I told you what happened. What else do you want?" Allison was right up in his grill. The little girl he used to give piggyback rides was standing in front of him, her eyes flashing with aggression.

"He wants to make sure she's okay. Cyrus is crushing on our Issy." Tor chuckled, leaning against the white wall.

Cyrus flashed up to the guy and grabbed the collar of his jacket. "I'm not in the fucking mood, so stop pestering me." He gritted his teeth, trying his best not to rip out the vampire's throat.

Tor held his hands up, prosthesis and all, but he bared his fangs as well. "I'm not pestering you. Check yourself out. You look like someone stomped over your rose garden. Lighten up, will you? I was there watching the whole time. Rick removed every single piece of the Dangeran metal, so chill."

Although Tor was showing equal hostility, he didn't bother prying Cyrus' grip off him. Allison managed to wedge herself between them. "Hey, hey. There's no need to get all wound up. You know how Tor is. It's his lifelong goal to annoy us."

Cyrus relaxed his hold, in spite of his jacked-up nerves. "Is she going to be okay?" He released Tor and moved away, feeling the burn of his injured abdomen. The three-week-old gunshot wound should've been healed by now. Thanks to his less than regular feeding habits, the process was taking longer than anticipated.

Allison smiled and kissed her mate. She whispered something in Tor's ear before the vampire disappeared back into the clinic. "You saw her. She's fine. Maybe a bit shaken, but she's okay."

He sagged on the cold tile floor and rubbed his face. "I got a bit carried away. I'm sorry."

Allison was the lone soul who would dare attempt to get close to him. She wrapped her arm around his shoulders. "Don't worry about it. I know how you are with all the women. I saw how you were when Mom and I . . ." She let the words trail.

Perhaps the memories were too fresh, even after all these years. He'd always been overprotective of the women in his care. That was the prime reason Pritchard trusted him with his family, until Allison's mother killed herself.

Cyrus looked up and saw Allison's eyes gleaming with unshed tears. "You know you're special to me. With Issy, I feel like she needed someone to watch over her. I remember the horror in her eyes when they killed her friend, and she had never set foot outside of her home. Everything is so new to her."

Maybe it was the waning adrenaline that made him prattle like a child. He shook his head and laughed. Allison sighed before joining in. They sat there for a few minutes, staring at the stark white walls in silence. It was another thirty minutes before the door opened and Rick stepped out of the clinic. He strode straight to where Cyrus and Allison were sitting and propped himself against the wall next to them.

The doctor released a long sigh and closed his eyes. Without his voice box, there was no telling what he wanted to say. The three of them sat in total silence until Isidora emerged, followed by Tor.

"I want to talk to you, Cyrus," Issy said, hovering before them.

Cyrus let his gaze run from the tips of her boots, up her skirt-covered legs, to her face. He glanced at the bandaged arm before he nodded.

"Thanks, Ally," he murmured then kissed her on the forehead. Next he offered a handshake to Rick. "I'm sorry for barging into your clinic like that."

Rick rolled his eyes and shook his hand.

Cyrus pulled himself up with difficulty, realizing he should be in bed. He caught Tor looking at him and sucked in the pain. Under normal circumstances, Tor would already be flapping his gums, but he merely watched Cyrus.

"Hey, we're tight, right?" he asked, landing a slap on Tor's back.

Tor raised his head and smirked. "Strung tight, dude."

He had no idea if he was stalling, but when he met Isidora's eyes, he found nothing but determination on her face. "Where do you want to talk?" He matched her much smaller strides.

"Where can we have a little privacy?" Her voice quivered.

That would be in the bedroom. But dear lord, he wasn't even considering the option. "The training room." By this time, most of the fighters were either getting ready to head out for their patrol duties or retreating for a much-needed siesta.

There was no response, so they walked the rest of the hallway in tense silence. Even if he'd wanted to make small talk, one thing kept popping in his head. He still felt an immense urge to protect her—to keep Issy from any harm.

As he had hoped, the training area was deserted. He closed the door behind him and followed her to his desk. On top of the table were books that didn't belong to him.

Isidora seemed to have caught on. She removed the books and threw them on the floor. "Please sit down."

Cyrus walked around the table and took a seat. "Issy, first of all, I want to apologize for my behavior. It wasn't my most shining moment."

Isidora studied him, her lips quirked while her eyebrows furrowed. Not for the first time, he wished he'd gotten the same mind reading gift the pure-blooded vampires possessed. It would be a nice not to have to guess what was on her mind for a change.

"Would you tell me what got you all jumpy back there?" She leaned forward, resting her arms on the table. Cyrus was tempted to lie, but one direct hit with her intense gaze made it impossible.

"I have this overwhelming need to look after you," he mumbled. It wasn't easy to express himself these days. Well, that was a lie. It had never been easy to talk to anyone except Lambert, who had been like a brother to him.

A myriad of expressions crossed her face—surprise, sadness, elation, and disbelief. She took her time in responding. When she did, it didn't have anything to do with his previous statement. "You need to feed. I gathered your thoughts when you were in the hallway." Isidora placed her hand on top of his.

Her skin was warm, sinfully warm, and Cyrus couldn't handle the emotions that came with her touch. He drew his hand away. "It must be tough having to live with the bullshit you hear every day."

From her hunched shoulders and the way she ran her palm along the smooth surface of the table, he could tell she had something on her mind, and it wasn't along the lines of yeah, I love the mind reading crap.

"I want to you to take my vein."

Isidora's statement was given with conviction, which made him curse. "You can't be serious."

"I'm dead serious."

"Why would you do that?" It was difficult to erase the erotic images from his mind, especially when she was sitting across from him in all her glory—beautiful, caring, young, and oh-so-inviting.

"Because I want to feel needed, wanted." Her voice was low, as if the revelation had sapped all her energy.

"What a naïve thing to say. Besides, you've been servicing Rohnert. I think you're already doing a great service to the race doing that alone."

"Are you naturally callous or just plain scared?"

Cyrus watched her with defiance oozing from his pores. How could she call him out like that? Did he look scared? He'd never had a reason to be around females who elicited unwanted emotions before, and he wouldn't start now.

The shutters began their ascent, marking nightfall and the start of a new day for them. If Cyrus had a choice, he'd be out patrolling or fighting. He'd be anywhere but here with a woman who evoked a wanting and longing he dared not give in to.

"I don't know what you're talking about." He pushed his chair away from the table and stood up. It was easier to think when he was moving. He paced back and forth, to the window, to the end of the room, creating as much space between them as possible.

The darn woman had no concept of personal space. She flashed right in front of him—close enough for him to get a whiff of her provoking scent and the heat radiating off her body.

"Oh yes, you do. You deny yourself what you want and need."

Isidora was too close for comfort. He reached out and pushed her away, just to get some breathing space. Man, he was screwed. "I know what I need, and I'm sure it's not your vein." He turned away, but not before he caught the look of hurt that crossed her face.

Feeling like an ass for pushing her away, he reached out and touched her cheek. "My sweet girl, you're too potent for your own good. Go now before I lose whatever shred of self-control I have."

"You're too stubborn, Cyrus. I'm throwing myself at you, and you don't have the sense to take what you need."

"Would you do this for anyone who needed help? Offer yourself?" That didn't come out right.

There was no doubt Cyrus had crossed the line, but it was too late to take it back. He closed off his mind from her. All the same, if he had a woman, although the thought alone was laughable, there was no way he would he share her with anyone.

Isidora stared at him with eyes brimming with tears. Cyrus hardened his heart. He wasn't going to falter or give in. Although he might want her, he was much too tainted for her. She needed someone who could take care of her. A royal bloodsucker like Rohnert could do it for her.

As the first of the tears fell on her flushed cheeks, Cyrus sucked in a hard breath. It was better for her to think he was an asshole rather than let him do something they both might regret.

Bretania studied each of the children while they sprinted back to her hideout. Their faces gave away their emotions—exhilaration, confusion, and fear.

Nathaniel's dark eyes returned her gaze. The teenager, who sported the body of a man, was Goran's son with Marchesa, one of the female bitches from the Harem. He was young, but his keen stare and rigid muscles didn't belong to a boy. He had his father's features—the proud nose, thin lips, and remarkable brow/cheekbones/jaw that had made him ruthless as well as enchanting. The one thing that reminded Bretania of Nathaniel's mother was the color of his hair. Red—annoying and reminiscent of her dead mate's perversion.

"What are your plans?" Nathaniel asked.

She smirked. This was new. The boy, who hadn't seen much in his short life, was already questioning her about her goals. She cursed Goran for his strong genes. Just the same, this boy could be a good ally, gopher, pawn, or whatever need be.

Too bad they hadn't been able to snatch all the children in one sweep. The odds of her getting them all together were slim to none. She was certain that Rohnert would have Lukan change the spells surrounding the

VC headquarters. What a pity. It would've been a big, fun party to have all Goran's progeny in one place. Oh well. She'd gotten the most useful of them. The oldest of the brood would be a precious addition to her growing army.

Marian looked up at Bretania, waiting for her to answer.

"I'm building an army. I intend to show them that your father's legacy lives on. He may be dead, but we will get back control."

Marian's eyes twinkled—deep, dark, sinister pools of secrets waiting to be set free. Bretania smiled. Even though she had her work cut out for her, these little darlings would be a great asset to her in the long run.

Reid held the littlest one, Esmeralda, who had fallen asleep on his back, while the other girl, Rhiannon, was trying to keep up with everyone's strides. Once they reached the front of the high-rise building, the children hooted with approval.

"Is this where we're going to live now, Bretania?" Rhiannon asked, tugging at her hand.

Bretania sat on her heels until she was at the child's eye level. Rhiannon was around eight or nine years old. She had her mother, Yara's, upturned nose, creamy complexion, and full lips. Tall for her age, she had Goran's black hair and calculating eyes.

"Yes, Rhia. You will be sharing a room with Marian and Esmeralda." Bretania patted the little girl on the head in assurance. "I will get someone to come in for homeschooling."

Rhiannon wrinkled her nose. "Do we have to?"

"Yes, we do. Stop asking too many questions," Nathaniel responded.

They rushed to the back entrance that led to the stairs. Climbing the tall structure was a piece of cake. Besides, this would keep them off the humans' radar until Bretania could move everyone to her family home on the outskirts of the city.

The moment she opened the door, the children's eyes grew large as saucers. Growing up within the impressive walls of the Council had its down side. They were far too inexperienced with the outside world. Instead of the lavish surroundings they had been accustomed to, the condominium's furnishings were simple. It had a much bigger space to roam around. After all, less was more. With six bedrooms, they would be a little cramped, but the five men they lost would free up two rooms.

Greta, her housekeeper, appeared at the hallway, and her red eyes watched the children with amusement. "I have the rooms ready as you ordered."

Bretania smiled. "Kids, this is Greta. If you need anything, let her know." Then she turned to the oldest child. "Nathan, you get the room at the end of the hall. You'll be alone for now, but if we collect more men, you'll be sharing with them."

The boy-man nodded, no questions asked, and that was how Bretania liked it. She took Esmeralda from Reid, as the toddler was showing signs of strain. She cradled the little one in her arms before shuffling the other two girls into their bedroom.

"Remember, you don't go out unless I know and you have company. You don't talk to anyone, especially humans."

Bretania placed the little girl on the bed and then removed her shoes. One look at Rhiannon and Marian and she could see the stress of the journey on their faces. "When was the last time you fed?" she asked the oldest girl.

"Two weeks ago." Marian shrugged, busy twirling her windswept hair.

No wonder Esmeralda appeared somewhat lethargic. "Marian, watch your sisters while I'm out. I'll be back in a few minutes." Bretania was out the door before the teenager could respond.

This was going to be bit messy, but they needed a quick fix. Bretania exited from the 10th floor window and scaled her way down into the darkness. This way, she could get a feel of the people around her by listening to their inner blather. The back alley provided a direct entrance for homeowners who preferred to park their own cars, and it was also a gathering spot for the bottom dwellers of the human society. This was where she would get the children's dinner. Spotting a lone soul leaning against a wall and smoking a cigarette, Bretania proceeded in the man's direction.

Taking great pains to act like a junkie, she staggered and shook her body with small convulsions. "I . . . I need a hit, anything you can give me."

The man crushed the cigarette with the sole of his shoe and then leaned forward, just in time to catch her from falling. "Hey there, you precious thing. What do you need?" His lazy drawl told Bretania that he was high, which suited her just fine, and the reek of alcohol from his breath meant he would be an easy target.

"Coke, freebase, crystals, anything you have."

"Hmm . . . aren't you one hardcore girl," the man said, skimming his mouth along the nape of her neck.

Disgusted, Bretania endured the little kisses raining on her skin. She held on to his shoulders, appearing as helpless as she could. The human's smile made her want to vomit, but she waited with patience she hadn't possessed before tonight.

"Do you have something for me?"

"Of course. Big Daddy has something for you, all right." The fool smiled wider, showing a set of crooked teeth.

Once she knew the man was distracted, Bretania gripped his shoulders and head-butted him hard enough to turn his lights out. His grip slackened, and he slumped to the ground. Plunging a dagger into the stupid human would've been easier, but she hated blood on her furniture and floor. This was the best option she had, considering her choices were kind of limited at the moment.

Easy as pie, she grabbed the man by the ankles and swung him over her shoulder. It would be a bit tough to get him through the window, so she opted for the stairs. She was lucky that the stairwell was free of humans when they made it back to her place.

Bretania kicked open the door and delivered her catch to her wards. She dropped the man on the floor without care and summoned the girls. "Go feed, but leave some for Esmeralda. I don't want any mess. Keep your clothes clean."

Marian's fangs elongated while Rhiannon's eyes went wide at the prospect of an unscheduled but welcome meal.

Bretania proceeded to the bed and roused the little one. Poor thing, she had been through a lot. First, she'd lost her mother, Milla, one of Goran's pets who had been sent to the massacre by their father, and then Goran was gone himself.

The man roused just in time for Marian to sink her fangs into his jugular. A scream bounced off the walls, but Marian quieted him down by covering his mouth with her palm. The younger sister took the left wrist right away and began her greedy pulls. Thrashing and trying to push the children away, the drug dealer wasn't strong enough to ward off the children.

Esmeralda's eyes fluttered open, and dull, crimson irises stared back at Bretania, disoriented. Bretania picked her up and brought her down to where the feast had already started. Feeding instincts for vampires were like breathing. The scent of blood and their hunger was all they needed, and this alone would point them to the right direction. The little girl's internal GPS fired, her nostrils flared, and her eyes widened. Her little fingers took hold of the struggling man's wrist and struck to get her fair share.

Bretania smiled in satisfaction when the stranger's eyes fixed on her. "Thanks. I know, I know. That was great acting on my part. If you want to live, nod your head, and I will extend mercy to you."

The terror-besieged man nodded at once.

"Good, I have just the task for you." Bretania left the girl's room and crossed the hallway to her own bedroom. She had another project that needed her attention.

Zane had just stepped out of the exercise room when he found a message waiting on his cell phone. He checked the unfamiliar number before listening to the recording.

Your name was given to me by someone very important in your life. I want a meeting with you as soon as it can be arranged. Call me at this number so we can talk.

He listened to the recording again, trying to get a clue as to the identity of the female voice. There were no telltale noises in the background to give away the location. Zane limped over to his laptop and tried to put a trace on the number.

Nothing came up. He could attempt to dig deeper, but he didn't feel threatened enough to warrant going the extra mile.

The important people in his life were dead. Demetrius had been killed by Harrow. His grandmother, Melissa, had been sent to an early grave by his grandfather, along with all the members of his harem. There was no one else he could think of.

The message intrigued him enough to give the caller a moment of his time. Not that he was busy these days.

He redialed the number and waited. It took three rings before it was answered.

"You're ready to meet with me?"

"Who is this?"

"That's not important right now. Tell me if you want to hear what I have to say." The voice held an authority that made Zane more curious.

"Sure."

"Meet me at Vintage in an hour. I'll be waiting by the corner booth, close to the back exit. Come alone. If I so much as suspect that you brought company, I will abort the meeting by killing you."

Whoa, firing threats already? "How will you know it's me?"

"Believe me, I will know." The woman hung up before Zane could respond.

Sunrise was in three hours, so there was a lot of time to do some damage. Zane walked into the shower, still running the odd conversation through his head. First of all, no one had his phone number except Cheryl and grandpapa. The latter had already bitten the dust, so this left the human female.

Zane shook the idea from his head. Cheryl had disappeared without a trace. That possibility was out. After his shower, he changed into jeans and a white cotton shirt. Then he packed his holster with daggers and his faithful Smith and Wesson, donning a leather jacket to hide his ammo.

The woman might have talked him out of bringing backup, but she couldn't stop him from arming up. If this got down and dirty, there was no way he'd be caught unprepared and unable to defend himself.

"Where are you headed, boss?" Hill got up as soon as he spotted Zane.

"Stay alert and wait for my call," was all he said before walking out the door.

"Boss, I'm going to patch through a call from General Krever," Rayce said over the intercom, interrupting Harrow's phone conversation with a client.

"Put him through."

Harrow concluded his conversation just in time for the incoming call. He picked up, wondering what news the general had for him.

"Leo, how are you?"

"Harrow, I have a little concern I want to talk to you about."

Leo wouldn't even bother calling him unless it was about his little girl. Harrow and Jordan had just come back from checking in on Gail the day before. "I'm listening," he said, leaning on the desk.

"It's Gail . . ." Leo hesitated.

He just about jumped out of his chair. "What's wrong with my baby?"

"She's fine. Nothing's wrong with her physically."

Harrow let out a sigh of relief. "Then what is it?"

It was Leo's turn to heave a long breath. "She's not herself today. She's quiet and distant. So I sat her down this evening, but it took some time to draw her out."

His little girl, distant? Gail was a chatterbox. The girl never stopped talking or asking questions. "Tell me what she said."

"She misses you and Jordan, and she wants to come home."

"Again? But we just saw her yesterday."

"I know."

In his mind, Harrow knew that keeping the girl close would be selfish on their part. They'd decided to have her stay with Leo so she could have a shot at the normal life they could never offer her. It was painful to be apart from their adopted daughter, but under the circumstances, this was the best thing he and Jordan could do for her.

"What are you thinking?"

General Leo Krever had always provided a steady voice of reason and guide for them. Pritchard's friend and Allison's godfather, the man was family to them all. He had been their contact with the outside world and a protector from the challenges the humans posed for them.

"I think you and Jordan should come back and talk to her again. Maybe spend a few nights here and see what you can do to ease her mind." Leo sighed once more.

"I think that is a good idea. I will let Jordan know, and we'll hit the road by sundown tomorrow."

"Tell me what?" Jordan asked from the doorway. He hadn't even noticed that she'd walked in.

"Leo's on the line—"

Jordan was next to him in a blink of an eye. "It's Gail, isn't it? How is our baby?" There was a tinge of fear in her voice. She gripped his arm, and her eyes were flashing brighter than usual.

"Leo, I better hang up. We'll see you tomorrow. And thank you for calling me right away."

Harrow pressed the end button and stood up. "Hey, she's fine." He explained the details of Gail's behavior and the general's suggestion for them to visit again and spend a longer time with her.

Jordan sagged in his arms, and he absorbed her weight. "I thought something happened to her." Her voice quivered.

"Growing pains is what it is," he said into her hair while stroking her back.

"It's too soon. She's not even eight years old."

"She's seven going on twenty." Harrow chuckled.

Jordan joined in his laughter. They held each other for a while. With the demands of the business, facility affairs, and the new recruiting group, there was less and less time for them to be together.

Maybe it would be good to get away. "Why don't we take her on a short trip? We could maybe take Angus with us so she won't be cooped up in the hotel all day."

Jordan looked up at him with a smile. "I think that is a brilliant idea, Mr. Gates."

Harrow inclined his head, pleased at the prospect of spending time with his girls. "Then I must see Cyrus and Tor about running operations while we're away."

She slapped him on the butt. "Go!"

He brushed a light kiss on her lips, but Jordan pulled him closer for a more intimate exchange. Their kiss deepened as his body started to react. If they didn't stop right this moment, who knew how long it would take them to pry their hands off each other.

Jordan must've been thinking along the same lines, because she pulled way. "We can continue this *discussion* when you get back."

She licked her lips, and Harrow felt himself come alive. "I will be back soon so we can continue to *talk*." He waggled his eyebrows and left before he could change his mind.

Flicking open his phone, he punched in a three-way call to Cyrus and Tor. "I need you guys in the I-room, stat."

It didn't take a long time before the two men arrived. Tor didn't seem happy. His dreadlocks were in disarray. Harrow must have interrupted something important.

"This better be a matter of life and death, Gates." Tor grunted as he sat down.

Cyrus, on the other hand, was the picture of boredom. Harrow watched him lower his body into a chair.

"Is everything okay?" Cyrus asked after finding a comfortable position.

"I'm leaving tomorrow at sundown with Jordan to see Gail."

"Is she all right?" Concern was written all over Tor's face.

Cyrus sat up straighter. "What's wrong with Gail?"

Harrow launched into an abbreviated explanation, and Cyrus and Tor agreed with his decision to leave right away.

"This brings me to why I called you both here. Since Rohnert has his hands full with Council business, I need you both to run all operations in my absence. Cy, monitor the production line and the delivery to Jack Drago and the usual stuff here in the facility."

"Sure. Got no problem with that." Cyrus saluted.

"Tor, monitor the influx of our diseased friends, and you're still on patrol."

"Yup. Don't worry about anything. We'll keep you posted. Kiss our little rebel for me," he said.

Cyrus seemed to be weighing something in his mind, which prompted Harrow to probe. "Cy, are you okay?"

"I'm fine. Tight, really tight." Same answer every single time.

Cyrus had been a tough character as a human, but as a vampire, he was like a pet piranha. *Domesticate at your own risk.*

"FYI, Rohnert will be bringing two of Goran's children from VC headquarters to stay here for the time being." Cyrus and Tor made a face. "Rohnert assured me that he would have someone watching over them twenty-four-seven, so no worries there."

"In the spirit of unity and camaraderie, what in the hell was Rohnert thinking?" Tor asked.

"We do what we can to help," Harrow answered. Deep down, trepidation reigned in his heart, but the need to give assistance where it was needed won against any other reservations he had.

"It's your call. One wrong move from either of those kids, and I will personally hand them their punishment," Cyrus said and then left the room.

Cyrus paced inside his bedroom, disgusted by the idea of the impending arrival of their unwanted guests. He was all for helping the down-and-out, but this went beyond their scope of responsibility. It might backfire and blow up in their faces.

Oh, well. What was new?

Christ, he was being a hypocrite. Had he forgotten where he came from? His past? After all, he'd grown up in the system after being given up for adoption as an infant. It wasn't a cakewalk by any means. Often, he felt he had no right to be happy.

How many foster homes had he been removed from because of static? Being unwanted sure left a nasty stain on him. Most of his foster parents had just been concerned with the government stipend that came with him.

He'd sworn back then that he would make it on his own, but at a tender age, he found trouble and was brought to yet another a foster home. Mrs. Turley was the last option for him, but she had been different. She cared for him and the girl she'd adopted. Linda had been abandoned by her birth mother after she was born with congenital paraplegia. She was a happy girl, despite her physical woes. It seemed like he'd finally found a home and a family he could call his own. However, his happiness had been short-lived. His mom died of cancer, and Linda was placed in another family's care. The only two women he'd ever loved had been taken from him.

The sudden urge to hear his sister's voice burned inside him. It wouldn't hurt to check on Linda. He lifted the phone and selected the undetectable line, dialing the number he knew by heart. He waited for someone to come on the line.

"Hello?"

"Is Linda Wilson available?" He tried to modulate his voice in an attempt to conceal his identity.

"This is she. Who's this?"

Cyrus gripped the phone, unable to say anything. He held his breath. Maybe it had been a bad idea to call her. She was doing much better, and he wouldn't want to reenter her life the way he was now.

"Hello? Are you still there?" Linda asked again. Her sing-song voice hadn't changed.

Without saying anything, he pressed the end button. Jesus . . . he was screwed. Cyrus had stopped caring for people altogether for fear of losing them. Life hadn't been easy after he'd lost his mom and Linda. Trouble had followed him everywhere he went, and he had given up hope. He took shady jobs to stay afloat. That all changed when he met Pritchard. Maybe it had been his reputation in the underground world that prompted the billionaire to put him on the payroll. Cyrus would never know.

Pritchard had treated him with kindness and respect, something he hadn't expected from the successful businessman. Soon after, he'd hired Lambert to join his team. Imagine, a lowlife running the show. Who else but Pritchard Tack would've taken a chance on a character like him?

Lambert had been his best friend, the one person he'd trusted with his life story, and he was taken from him, too. So were Pritchard and Shelly. How many more had to die before he stopped caring? Damn this shit. Cyrus was sick and tired of worrying. He had a reputation to uphold. What had happened to the man who used to ooze confidence? He couldn't afford to go soft now. There were people counting on him to be strong.

Cyrus stopped by the mini-refrigerator and yanked it open. In it were bags of donated human blood for his consumption, the one type of feeding he'd known since his transition. Shelly had given him his first meal, and it was as satisfying as eating cardboard. It filled him up, but the taste could be better. Gone were the T-bones and ribs. This was all about nourishment and staying upright.

Then he thought about Isidora and her offer—sweet, tempting, and stupid. The woman had no idea what her proposal had done to him. Just thinking about her made him hard, which was wrong. Besides, what would he know about taking a vein? He was a goddamn virgin in that respect.

From what he had gathered from all these years living with vampires, feeding was an exhilarating and erotic experience. He was all for exhilaration. But erotic? That was an alien emotion. After all, he was so messed in the head that he would just end up ruining the moment. If he were being honest with himself, any form of physical intimacy would unhinge him—and not in a good way. The possibility of him sucking her dry while pounding into her was too likely a scenario. Not a good way to treat a woman.

Cyrus shoved the mental image away and settled on the couch with the bag of type O. He tried to relax and clear his mind by watching television. Soap operas were prevalent in this time slot, but romance made him twitch. He hadn't known love in its purest form—not that he had anything against it. There were some things that were not meant for him.

You're an idiot, Crackenbush, and you know it, his inner voice taunted him.

He stared at the bag lying in his lap. There were so many things he had to get used to with being a new vampire. The incredible strength and energy were something to celebrate, and so were the speed and power. What didn't help was that his feeding was messed up and his sole purpose in life now was to kill Zane.

Cyrus had no business thinking of the beautiful Isidora. No business allowing her to creep inside his head and his heart. He wasn't going to allow anyone to derail his plans. Besides, he wasn't built for anything loving, even if all he could think of was seizing her mouth with his.

"Humph." He was better off living outside his head if he wanted to survive to exact his revenge. A raging hard-on wasn't going to help.

Then a soft knock sounded. There was no rest for the wicked.

Cyrus threw the bag of blood on the nightstand and heaved his body off the couch to answer the door. It seemed like life had other plans for him. He found Isidora standing outside, her eyes beseeching.

Cyrus opened the door, his face ravaged with a sadness Isidora couldn't fathom.

"I came to change your mind," she said before she chickened out.

She was determined to do this, but Cyrus' reaction to her arrival had her second guessing her decision. He continued to stare at her, unmoving until she touched his arm. Then he jerked back to life.

"Why?"

Her gaze dropped to his hands, which were gripping the door as if he wanted to crush it. Had she been such a nuisance? Was it so hard for him to accept what she was offering him?

"I know you haven't fed . . ." Her words trailed off. Something about Cyrus made it difficult for her to get her point across. She tried again. "You can insult me all you want, but it's not going to change the fact that you need to feed. If you don't give your body what it needs, you're not going to be worth a damn to anyone."

Cyrus sighed and stepped aside, creating enough room for her to pass. She took the opening as a welcoming gesture. At least he was allowing her into his room. Now, she just needed to not screw this up.

He gestured toward the couch. With her head held high, she walked past him and took a seat. The sound of the door closing caused her breathing to falter. *Oh God, am I really doing this?*

Issy wanted to say something conversational, something that might spark a common interest, but she drew a blank. Her sheltered past didn't give her much material to talk about. She'd heard from Cheryl that most of the male inhabitants in the facility were into action movies, Cyrus among them. Isidora wished she could throw out a movie title they could watch, but nothing came to mind. And Cyrus was acting all predatory, covering the length of the room in a few strides.

He stopped by the little built-in bar, took out a bottle, and started pouring. She stared at his powerful body. It moved like a magnificent stallion, ready to bolt. She knew she had to say something before he kicked her out.

"Cyrus, I don't mean to sound like I'm prying. Believe me, I want to give you the privacy you deserve, but I can't tune you out. Everything you think about makes me ache to help you." She cringed at the way she'd expressed it.

He pivoted and the expression on his face told her that she had gone too far. "What makes you think I want your help?"

That stung, but she wasn't going to let him push her away. Isidora stood up and took a few steps toward him. "I listen to you night after night, even during the daytime. We've both lost people we loved, and I know we could help each other forget."

Another blunder, but she wouldn't apologize for it. She had spent nights crying herself to sleep, trying to block out her hurt and his, too. It didn't have to be out of love. This was just two people who needed each other to get past the hurdles fate had thrown at them.

Cyrus' crimson eyes snapped, and his hand curled into a fist. Isidora waited, expecting him to throw her out. She couldn't blame him if he cursed her. Instead, he just stood there, watching her with calculating eyes that made her want to crawl under the nearest rock.

After a few tense moments, he relaxed and chugged the contents of his glass, then poured another one. He downed the amber liquid and set the glass down on the bar. "What are you proposing here? You want to warm my bed and service me?" The sardonic tone made her want to claw at the wall he was building up between them.

"I want to be a friend, someone who can help you forget your woes. And I hope you could do the same for me."

He laughed, a mirthless sound that poked at her heart. "You're so naïve, my little girl. You have no idea who I am and what I can do to you. Regardless of what you think you know about me, you haven't heard even half of it."

By this time, he'd closed the distance between them, and they were standing face to face.

Isidora didn't step back, even though his proximity threatened her. This was what she wanted. Why else would she come knocking on his door? She needed him as much as he needed her, even if he wouldn't admit it.

Yes, she might be naïve, but in her mind's eye, they were perfect for each other. Two creatures lost, gasping for air, and looking for a safe refuge from harsh reality.

"I might have crossed the line by coming here, but you can't turn me away. You need me as much as I need you."

"Why do keep saying *need*?"

"Because it's true."

Until that point, Cyrus hadn't sounded hostile, but when he lifted his hand, she shrank back in fear.

"I won't hurt you, if that's what you're thinking."

As she stared into his eyes, she knew he was telling the truth. Cyrus had been gentle with all the females in the facility. She had seen his tender side when he interacted with Allison, and even Jordan and Cheryl. He rearranged the assignments of every female fighter until he was satisfied that they were away from major conflicts. Yes, she believed that he wouldn't hurt her.

It was when he brushed his hand down her cheek that she felt his tenderness firsthand. It was a slow caress she hadn't expected from a man with so much strength in him. Isidora leaned into his touch.

"I know you won't." She closed her eyes. If this was as far as he'd allow himself to go, it was enough for her.

"Issy, you have no idea what your offer is doing to me." Cyrus' breathing grew ragged.

"What am I doing to you?" She opened her eyes just in time to see the hunger etched in his face, his fangs elongating until they were punching his lower lip.

"You make me want to rip off your clothes. Stop teasing a hungry dog with a big bone."

In this quiet moment, Cyrus was all she wanted. The air grew electric, and the magnetism between them was undeniable, so strong she could touch it. Her gaze slid down to the massive tenting in his pants and couldn't deny her own hunger.

"You're going to kiss me."

"Damn right I will." He closed the small gap and crushed his mouth against hers, his kiss hard and filled with urgency.

Issy rode the tide, tasting, stroking, and feeling the jolt of life from his lips. She pressed her body closer, but he ended the kiss abruptly. *Way too soon.*

"You better run, little girl." He turned away.

"I'm not going to run. Take what is freely given to you." She touched his shoulder, caressing the taut muscle.

What in the hell was he supposed to do? The warmth of her hand burned through the layers of Cyrus' clothing. God, he was such an asshole. He was breaking the promise he made to himself to keep her at arm's length. To keep his distance—because everyone he'd ever loved had been taken from him.

Cyrus was losing ground. His body was overheating, reacting to her closeness. Yet, looking into her dark eyes, he found warmth and longing that mirrored his.

"You're reading my mind." It wasn't a question. "How does it work for you?" This was a last ditch effort to keep his hands off her.

Issy's eyes flickered, telling him that she knew he was distracting himself from the attraction between them. It surprised him when she answered.

"It's weird most of the time. For instance, I hear Barth thinking out loud when he pleasures himself." She coughed and reddened at the confession.

Cyrus had to laugh at the sight of Issy's discomfort. "That must be tough for you."

She nodded and continued caressing his shoulder. Her touch unnerved Cyrus, but in all honesty, he didn't want her to stop.

"I hear conversations, which are easier to ignore. The more intimate details and private thoughts are harder to block out. It never bothered me before because where I came from, it was different. I was among people I was familiar with. Here, it's overwhelming. I've heard stuff I never thought possible."

"Do you hear me a lot?"

Issy lowered her eyes when she nodded. "I know enough."

"Am I making you uncomfortable, my dear Issy?"

She nodded, but then as if she'd had a change of heart, she shook her head.

Cyrus shivered from her touch and looked at her mouth, wishing he could taste her again. "What do you think we'll gain from this?"

Isidora licked her lips, and he almost came undone. He felt his body quake under the immense pressure he could no longer deny.

"Comfort."

"How can you be so sure?" He drew her closer, and the first order of business was to run his fingers through her glorious hair. Each strand felt like silken thread, magical and fever inducing.

"We both want the same thing. Please stop thinking, Cyrus."

"I have no idea what to do. I haven't done this before."

Issy smiled and tilted her head, offering the vast expanse of her neck. "Find the vein, the biggest one you can see. Sink your fangs into me. Close your eyes and let your instincts guide you."

Cyrus swayed under the intense weight of what he was about to do. He stared at her skin and focused on the vein—thick and throbbing, seducing him to taste. This was the offer of a lifetime. Was he going to take a bite?

Damn him, because he was. His knees had weakened under the weight of her invitation. Cyrus began compartmentalizing his emotions, shutting down reason, and giving in to his need. He cradled her face and kissed those luscious lips before he skimmed downward. When he found her vein, he opened his mouth and took the plunge.

When his fangs punctured her skin, he closed his eyes as she had suggested. Her body arched, molding into his until her breasts were pressed against his chest. The first taste was just what the guys had described to him. It was like a fine wine or a single-malt whiskey aged to perfection. He tugged harder and let his hands roam across her back, rubbing, feeling, and touching her body.

He could get used to this. Blood, as he was finding out, was better taken from the source and not in the bag he'd come to know. Issy began rubbing her thigh against his while she moaned, and the sensation left him reeling. *Was he ready to take all of her?*

Then his high was interrupted by his doubt. He wasn't ready to go all the way. He shouldn't.

Cyrus began to pull back, but Issy refused to let him go, linking her hands behind his neck. "Don't stop."

God, he didn't want to stop. This was a slice of heaven he'd never thought possible. So he tugged some more, letting the thick liquid slink into him like fuel. Her blood was jumpstarting his sputtering system, and he felt rejuvenated, alive, and unbelievably hard.

Afraid to lose his last ounce of self-control, he unlatched his fangs but still held on to her.

Isidora swayed under his fingertips. "You haven't taken enough."

Cyrus took a step back to look at her face. Her eyes were wild, and it seemed like she was about to collapse. He wrapped his arms around her waist and cradled her to his chest then brought her over to his bed. This was the one place he never thought he'd have company. Now here he was, about to cross the line.

"You need to feed, too." He placed her on the mattress.

"I'm fine." Issy stayed still, and he could see vulnerability in her beautiful face.

"If you don't want to feed, would you mind spending the night with me?" The question was out of his mouth even before he could consider the possibilities.

He saw the desire in her eyes, but this didn't have to be all about sex. Even if it killed him, he wasn't going to degrade this woman by letting his filthy body touch hers that way. His cock was going to stay where it was, tucked inside his boxers, no matter how hard it got.

"I just want to hold you until you fall asleep. Comfort is what we need, remember?" Cyrus slung her words right back at her. He was an ass. After what Isidora had given him, here he was, making her feel like an unwanted piece of meat.

She smiled in understanding. "We'll comfort each other," she said and slipped under the covers.

Cyrus dragged in a hard breath before turning off the lamp and climbing into bed next to her. This was going to be a long night.

"It doesn't have to be," Isidora answered his unspoken thoughts. "Why don't you hold me? Then we can fall asleep together."

Issy turned her back on him as he moved closer. He wrapped one arm underneath her and let the other rest around her belly. Her scent was an aphrodisiac, making him want her even more.

Cyrus was okay with the little touches. *For how long?* He wasn't even going to consider that question anymore. For now, he would just bask in the sensation of having someone to share the night with.

He stared at the ceiling in the darkness long after Isidora had fallen asleep. This was for her own good.

"Thank you," he whispered against her hair just before his heavy lids gave out on him, taking him into the first restful sleep he'd ever had since his abduction.

Cyrus awoke with a start. The minute his eyes snapped open, he felt different. Everything about him radiated clarity. His mind, his body, and . . . whoa, he was even sporting a boner big enough to rival a baseball bat.

The source of these good feelings stirred in his arms. That explained his picture-perfect outlook.

They had spent the night locked in each other's embrace *for comfort*. Her words. He knew she was willing to give more, but he had put on the brakes. For one thing, he was unprepared. He believed in dressing for the party.

Also, given his long and muddy history, he wasn't ready to take on Issy as a permanent fixture in his life. She would leave, like all the others.

Although she had given him the best gift ever and he wanted her without a doubt, he wasn't willing to share. Rohnert depended on her for his nourishment, and that was a deal-breaker. Even so, his arms tightened around her as if unwilling to let her go.

Her chest heaved when her backside rubbed his erection. He was going to need an icebox to calm his body's response to her proximity.

"Hard at work already?" she asked and then turned to face him.

Cyrus could tell she knew what he'd been thinking. It was disconcerting to know that he was naked to her. Even with the mask he put on day in and day out, she would always see right through him.

Was he okay with that one unnerving detail?

"Will there ever be a day when you take a break from mind reading?" He studied her soft features. Everything about her spoke of femininity, proper breeding, and a life of luxury. Hello Rodeo Drive, welcome to Skid Row. The thought made him laugh.

Issy raised an eyebrow. "First of all, I've only heard of Beverly Hills from the show. Skid Row sounds more like my cup of tea."

"You're nuts."

"I'm nuts about you."

She cradled his face with her soft hands, and man, he tingled in every place imaginable. Why the sweet torture? Because he loved pain. He and pain were on first name basis.

"If you'd stop thinking about silly things, then I would leave you alone." She gave him a blinding smile.

"I'm trying here. It would be nice if you'd cut me some slack. Allow me to dwell on my misery. That is all I have."

Her expression sobered. "And leave you to exact revenge? How can you expect that of me?"

"I will do what a man must do. I'm entitled to vengeance. Until I get it, I won't be able to let go." The edge in his voice was the one part Cyrus regretted. "Look, I'm sorry. I'm not usually this uptight."

"Even if I understood your motives, I would still try to stop you. There's no need to apologize. We all have burdens that we carry." She smiled.

Cyrus contemplated her statement. They were two very similar creatures. "How about you? Don't you feel angry about the direction your life has taken?"

The smile faded, and she brushed her lips against his mouth. His breath hitched, and he was not sure what to make of it.

"There has not been a day I haven't thought of my parents, Maureen, or Finn. I miss them so much that it hurts to think of them. Like you, I want justice, but justice has been served, whether or not it conformed to my idea of fairness. Besides, there is nothing I can do. I'm in a strange place, at the mercy of others."

"Is Finn still on your mind?" Cyrus asked. He knew he shouldn't have, but a big part of him needed to know.

Issy hesitated while she searched his face. Then she nodded. "I still see the look in his eyes before he died. The vision still haunts me."

"Oh, baby, I'm sorry." He was an ass. All he had been focused on was his own pain. Not once had he asked her how she was dealing with her losses.

She gave him a brave smile. "It's okay. I try to shed the negativity when I can. There have been moments when I'm down, like last night. I wasn't just thinking of you."

"So you came to me for comfort?"

"Yes," she said, sounding breathless.

That breathless voice did a number on him. "Then by all means, come here and I'll give you comfort." He tried to project calm, but he knew he sounded like a bastard.

"Why do you fight it, Cyrus?"

"You're like fine crystal, woman. You have no business hanging out with cheap broken glass."

"Will you stop selling yourself short? Maybe you should take a good look at yourself in the mirror and see what I see."

"What do you see, Aladdin or King Kong?"

Isidora laughed and punched him on the arm playfully. "I see an honest man who is like the foundation for this place—someone who is willing to give his life for others. Also, it doesn't hurt that you have the kindest eyes and a killer body." She winked at him.

Cyrus couldn't believe his ears. The woman was zinging him with her charm, and he was getting hooked. "I believe the pretty lady is flirting with me." *Jesus, please don't let me fall in love with this woman.*

The smile she offered made him think of how she could easily manipulate him with her mind-reading talent. Working around the issue was going to be an uphill battle for him. As challenging as that sounded, it also felt good to know he wasn't doing it alone. Someone understood where he was coming from, and it was a liberating experience, as well as scary. He had gotten used to just looking through the display window all his life without ever having the ability to touch.

"We're about to change the way you look at the display window." She hit him again with her precious smile, and Cyrus swore under his breath. Then he held her close.

Zane drove the Porsche out of his affluent neighborhood to a rundown bar in a desolate part of the city. Armed with daggers, his faithful gun, and loads of ammo, he was prepared to kick ass if necessary. He guided his car toward the deserted street and parked across from the seedy establishment.

He got out and pulled his cane from the backseat. With its aid, he crossed the street and pressed the button to trigger the car's alarm. The activation sounded just before he entered the dingy bar.

The Vintage was a hole in the wall type of bar, filled with alcohol and drug-addled characters milling about in a euphoric daze. No one paid attention to him while he scanned the crowded room. From the outside, it had appeared empty. Zane knew whoever asked him to come had no intention of being compromised, and being around humans would negate the aggression stemming from any possible disagreement.

He let his gaze wander to the booth in a corner of the room. Since he was to see over the high wooden divider, he had to move closer. Eyeing the two exits signs, Zane began to form an exit strategy inside his head.

From six feet away, he got a clearer angle of the stranger he had spoken with over the phone. As expected, it was a female. Judging from the rigid set of her shoulders, she was ill-at-ease, which made this a level playing field. Then she turned around to look at him, as if she'd known he was standing there all along.

Zane closed the gap until he reached the table. "You wanted to see me."

She stood up and met his eyes. "Yes. Come and sit down." The invitation was casual, but her delivery told him that this woman was someone familiar with authority.

He took the seat opposite her, then propped his cane against the table. It didn't escape his notice that the woman's eyes followed his every move, lingering longer on the cane.

"Business hazard," he explained.

"Ah . . ." Her nebulous eyes turned calculating, and then she grinned.

Zane didn't like being under the microscope, and the sooner he was out of the limelight, the better for him. "You wanted to talk, so talk."

"Impatient man. It comes from your upbringing, I suppose." She smiled wide enough to expose her fangs. It was a smart move if she intended to instill fear from the get-go.

"Genes are a convenient excuse, so I'll use it." He leaned forward and let his arms rest on the table. It gave him a closer look at the female vampire in front of him. Her regal features told him which breed he was dealing with, and the medal hanging around her neck was a dead giveaway. The freckles dusting her cheeks were cute, but he wasn't into blonds. She was beautiful, in a wicked sort of way. But she wasn't . . .

"I see you're as smart as your father. I hope the similarities end there. He let his blind ambition lead him to an early grave." Her high voice was quite irritating.

"If you think I'm going to stay here and let you insult my father, then you're mistaken." Zane rose from his seat.

"Slow down, cowboy. I think you'll want to hear what I have to say." She eyed him. "Sit."

"Who are you, and why don't you just get down to business?" He flopped back down on the padded seat.

"The name's Bretania, and we are somewhat related."

What a surprise. Zane smirked. "And the reason for this meeting is?"

"Don't you want to know the family connection first?"

"Fine, enlighten me."

"I married Goran, your grandfather." She smiled and waited for his reaction.

"Damn," was all he said.

"I want to propose a business deal with you."

"I have money, courtesy of my grandmother."

"I offer my sympathy for your loss."

He nodded. "Are you taking over for Grandpapa now?"

A pained look crossed her face before she was able to school her expression. It wasn't lost on Zane. She'd gotten his full attention.

"Let's just say I'm not interested in ruling." Her voice quivered.

Zane could spot a lie from miles away, and this comment was screaming bullshit loud and clear. Then he remembered an important detail of this particular breed from a conversation with his father. He closed off his mind.

"Smart move," Bretania said when she caught on.

"Now, can we proceed?"

"I want you to join my army." She eyed his cane.

Zane rolled his eyes. "Yes, it could be a problem. I might slow you down."

"Care to tell me what happened?"

"Dangeran." He shrugged.

"Ah . . ." She let out a long exhalation while she openly let her gaze roam his body until he wanted to scream.

"I'm not into blonds."

Bretania's eyes flashed. "You're a cocky bastard."

"Knowing what you want is never a bad thing."

"Goran said you're effective in trailing and research."

Zane nodded, feeling his chest puff with pride. At least the cocksucker had realized his worth. "What are you offering me?"

"Find out the hideout of a certain group while I'm building my army."

"What do I get in return?" He began stroking his chin while maintaining the barrier to keep her from reading his thoughts.

"Power, money, prestige."

Holes. This conversation was filled with holes, but he wasn't done listening. "Tell me more." Zane smiled and leaned closer so that she could go over the details of how she would give him the three things he no longer cared about.

Rohnert stood up to address the Council Elders. "Thank you for coming at such short notice. This is an unfortunate day for us all."

The general emotions of the entire Council were sadness and gloom, but that was understandable. It wasn't every day that the place they felt safest was compromised.

"I'm sure you heard about the breach earlier. I can assure you that we are working to get to the bottom of it."

"Has it been confirmed that Bretania was responsible?" asked Clotilde, one of the newest members of the Council and the person in charge of functions and rituals.

"We have several eyewitnesses who have corroborated that report." Rohnert ran his palm along his head. "Is everyone in agreement with me that, if found, Bretania must be brought before a panel for sentencing?"

This had been an old practice before Goran rose to power. During his term, Goran had abolished the judging panel and had gone for a dictatorship instead. Although he pretended to listen to the Elders' suggestions, he had fallen into the habit of following his heart's desire. He judged each offender according to his whims, and if anyone had opposed his edicts, they were hunted down and eliminated. His unfair practices had come to light when Rohnert finally sat down to read the contents of the Black Book.

"Have new measures been taken to ensure our safety?" Regrita asked. As Wendell's assistant in the weapons and training department, Regrita took personal offense at the deaths of the guards she'd helped train.

Rohnert bowed his head. "I called upon Lukan to cast a spell around this place. It should guarantee our safety."

"Would it be prudent to move our families here?" Icarus stood up and paced.

Rohnert thought about the question. Was it advisable to house all Elders and their families in one place? "I'm not keen on putting all my eggs in one basket, if you know what I mean. But if you feel that your current residence is vulnerable, you're welcome to do what you think is best for you and your loved ones."

He began to lay out his suggestions for rebuilding their group. Fortification came first, since their structure had sustained some damage. Second, the loss of lives meant their numbers had suffered and would need to be replenished.

"I have a group of personal fighters who will increase our numbers when I move my family here to headquarters," Wendell said. Their tactician was all about safety, improvement, and preservation of their race, which was in line with Rohnert's personal principles.

"Your kindness is very much appreciated." Rohnert dipped in his head in respect.

Next, they discussed the rampant spread of the disease and the assailants who were working to counter the effects of the cure Tack Enterprises had in place.

"I suggest we start finding the source of outbreak." Icarus turned to Rohnert. "I can have half of my private soldiers work for the Council while Wendell rebuilds our army."

Rohnert thought about the offer. They had lost about fifty soldiers and were getting more in return. Maybe this was a turning point for them. With the extra manpower, the Council didn't have a reason not to deal with the growing contagion. He sat down and eyeballed each Elder and then nodded.

"I believe our friend Icarus has made a generous offer, and I'm inclined to accept. Let's make this endeavor our special project. I think it's in our best interests if we keep our plans on the down low. I have reasons for doing so, and I promise to share them with you as soon as I gather more proof."

Everyone expressed their support.

Serena cleared her throat, seeming uncomfortable. At their last encounter, she had offered her vein to him, and Rohnert had run away like a scared cat. He tried not to wince at the memory.

"Yes, Serena. Do you have something to share with us?"

She nodded. "We should start this program right away." There were murmurs of assent. "Although I don't deal with the outside world, my sources say that these intentional infections have become problematic. While we are working to eradicate the disease, a group is hindering our efforts."

"How so?" Rohnert stood up and started pacing. The constant movement helped with his thought process.

"A relative of one of my guards was in a public place and overheard a couple talking about an orgy happening." Serena wrung her hands in frustration. "This tells me that the spread is happening faster than we imagined."

Rohnert didn't have to visualize how gatherings of that nature would increase the spread of the illness. If such group did exist, then the Council was dealing with a bigger problem than just irresponsible individuals.

He sat down. "If we are to discover that this report is correct, we must be ready with a plan for how to counter the problem."

"If we encounter resistance, we must be ready to fight them," Wendell blurted. The usually calm vampire appeared surprised with his own suggestion.

"We're talking about large scale battle," Icarus said, not seeming comfortable with the concept.

Rohnert had to think fast. "What if we sit on this and meet again in two days? This is a big decision. I would appreciate a vote on the measures we plan to take so we can make the decree official. Also, in two days, we will have a ceremony to pay respect to all those we lost tonight."

Each of the Elders nodded in approval. Then Bardos raised his hand. During Goran's reign, August had been their finance wiz and had served the Council longer than anyone else. However, he had no children to take his place when Goran had him murdered. His younger brother Bardos was able and willing to serve.

"I think we should also start thinking about filling the vacated seats of our past members. I always believed that there is strength in numbers. It makes for a better decision if we have more opinions brought to the table." He grinned. "Just sayin'."

"We'll start that as soon as Icarus' group is situated here," Rohnert said. "Now, I have one last issue I want to bring to your attention. Two of Goran's children were left behind. Since we are rebuilding, I want to take them to my residence and keep them under the supervision of people I trust. Is this acceptable?" A ripple of consent sounded from everyone present. "If things don't work out, then we'll make other arrangements."

It didn't take Rohnert long to conclude Council business and ready himself to collect the children. Gentry waited outside the room, having been reinstated as Council guard after the attack on their headquarters.

Sawyer, a scrawny prepubescent boy with dark hair, looked up from his desk when Rohnert entered his bedroom. On the table, Rohnert found drawings, sketches of characters, and symbols. He concentrated on one character and gaped. If he wasn't mistaken, the man with shaved head and garbed in dark garment with two holsters crisscrossing his chest was him.

"You're good," he said, trying to break the ice.

"It helps with the boredom." Sawyer's eyes watched him, studying him with unconcealed interest.

"Is there anything you like to do besides drawing?" He got close enough to confirm that he was indeed the character on the picture.

"Bretania doesn't allow us to leave our rooms, so other than TV, there's nothing else to do."

"Is that me in the picture?"

The boy nodded and shifted his gaze down, as if he'd been caught with his hand in the cookie jar. "I hope it's okay. I caught a glimpse of you once, but my watcher said I shouldn't be caught doing this."

Though disconcerted, Rohnert nodded. "Did he say why?"

"No. He just said it was a long story." Sawyer stood up. Despite being just thirteen, he reached Rohnert's temple. What had they been feeding these children?

"I'm guessing your watcher didn't want Bretania to see it. I say you should do what makes you happy."

"Thank you," Sawyer said with a little smile.

"In light of what happened here earlier, I'd like to propose something to you."

His words seemed to have caught the boy off guard. Rohnert suspected no one had ever asked him about his preferences before. They were just hustled around, and no one cared how they felt or if they had any opinion.

"S—sure," the boy said.

Rohnert had always believed in full disclosure. "Bretania took your other siblings. You and Liv are the only ones left."

"Oh, yeah. My watcher killed the guy who came to get me before he died. I helped out."

"Then you must know that it would be in your best interest for you and your sister to come live with me."

Sawyer's eyes widened, and his smile grew bigger. "I would love to get out of this place."

"I would ask for a few things from you." Rohnert sat down on the chair across the desk, and the boy followed his movement with interest.

"Yes?"

"You don't go anywhere unless someone knows your whereabouts. It's crazy when we get worried about a missing person. Then there's feeding. I want you to respect our human friends. These are the two things I want you to do, nothing more.

It took several minutes for Sawyer to respond, but when he did, he was resolute. "I can do what you ask of me."

"Then we are going to leave now. If there are things you want to take with you, get them packed and ready within thirty minutes. Is this enough time for you?"

"I'll be here waiting."

Now, if Liv was as easy to convince, then they would be on their way in no time. Rohnert left the room feeling lighter, and he moved across the hallway to the little girl's bedroom. He knocked before he entered. In there, he found the five year old on the bed, propped on her elbows with a picture book.

"Who are you?" Her voice was curious and devoid of fear.

"I'm Rohnert—"

"Oh . . . you're the new leader, right?" Just like that, no fanfare or condemnation from the young mind.

"I'm also your uncle." What was the matter with him? Was that even necessary?

Liv's red eyes grew as wide as saucers. "Cool," she said. And just like that, her concentration was back on the book in front of her.

This gave Rohnert time to study the little girl for a moment. She was almost the same height and size as Gail, who was a few years older. Her strawberry blond hair was pulled into a ponytail. "I want you and Sawyer to come live with me. Is that okay?" he asked, trying to catch the girl's attention again.

"Okay. Is your house big like this? Is Creepy Bretania going to be there, too?"

Rohnert almost choked on the name the child had given her father's mate. "It's big enough for many people."

"Is she going to be there?" Her red eyes focused on him.

He tried to read the young mind, and the first thing he caught was unfavorable memories suppressed by fear.

"She won't be. Is that how you'd like it?"

"Groovy." Her attention was back on the book.

Groovy? What had these children been reading? Since Liv was still immersed in her book, Rohnert went to the closet and grabbed a duffel bag. He began the task of stashing anything he found inside and stuffed everything in the bag. If there were any items missing, he would have to beg Jordan or Allison to come to his aid. Besides, female stuff was as alien to him as sunlight.

Gastarius rose from his shallow slumber, feeling an excruciating pain deep in his gut. He adjusted his sight in the darkness, and his eyes flickered with sinister and disturbing visions.

For centuries, he had cared for and watched over the vampire race. There had been some hits and misses, but he had kept the people well, as far as his abilities allowed. Destinies couldn't be altered, and outcomes were off limits. Through it all, he had kept a constant vigil. There were moments wherein he'd longed to change people's fate, but the strict code he followed had guided him on his path.

Then it hit him. Lukan was smack in the middle of it all. She'd manipulated the events that led to Goran's madness, planting the diseased vampire to entice Goran and infect him.

That hadn't been enough for her. Next, Lukan had arranged the shooting of Rohnert's mate, which had led to Shelly's death. Gastarius' breath hitched when his mind's eye showed him an image of Lukan conniving with a ruthless creature and a long forgotten vampire sub-species. The heartbreaking visions of Lukan's treachery brought tears to his eyes.

Troubled, he pushed back the thin sheet that covered his frail body and rose to his feet. With measured steps, he walked to the window and stared out at the vast darkness. He was losing his touch. The gift that had aided him for centuries had begun to wane. There were no allowances to be made. It was clear that his time was up. If this was a sign that he must step down, then he must begin to prepare for the transition.

Struck by a blinding light that appeared out of nowhere, Gastarius fell to his knees. The die had been cast, and he could see the exact time and date of his demise. Gastarius closed his eyes and breathed deep. He'd expected this day to come, but he had never suspected that he would fall victim to one of his own.

After the vision disappeared, he struggled to his feet, eager to set the wheels in motion. It was about time he let Aemerria know she was ready.

Harrow glanced at Jordan. Her face was illuminated by the dashboard's orange glow, and he could tell how anxious she was to see their little girl. He squeezed her hand in a show of solidarity, and her expression softened. In the quiet time between them, Harrow allowed himself to go back to one of the most memorable moments in his life—the first time Gail had called him "Dad," during Pritchard's surprise party.

He had led Jordan to the dance floor while holding the little girl in his arms. Everything had been perfect—the music, the mood, and dancing with the two women who mattered most to him. It had been both odd and touching. Never in his life had he seen himself as a father with a family. If only the night hadn't been tainted afterward by the death of three integral members of their team.

Angus was being quiet in the back seat. The human was their youngest recruit. He had been Shelly's bodyguard before he was injured in the hospital rooftop conflict with Goran. The young man had proven himself trustworthy, and he would make a good companion for Gail during this little getaway they had planned for her. In the daylight hours, they needed someone who could watch their child in their stead. Angus was perfect for the job.

They reached the posh upper east side neighborhood and circled several blocks in search of parking. After stopping and engaging the car's alarm, the trio made their way toward the upscale town homes where Leo resided during the week. The area, which was a ghost town at night, boasted a collection of imposing buildings reminiscent of the Renaissance era.

"Are you okay?" Harrow asked. Jordan had been quiet during the drive, and he'd given her space to think.

"I'm fine. Just worrying about Gail." Jordan sighed. "Maybe we should take her home." She gave him a sideway glance. "The facility is under a spell now. There's no way anyone can infiltrate the barrier Lukan has in place."

"Let's see how Gail is, and then we'll decide what's best."

Jordan nodded. They reached the building, and a doorman let them in, nodding when he recognized them. The elevator carried them up to the eleventh floor, and when the car stopped, they could already hear Gail's excited voice.

"Mom! Dad!" she squealed the moment they emerged.

"Baby, how are you?" Jordan opened her arms, and the little bullet zoomed into her waiting embrace.

"I'm okay, but I missed you." There was the unmistakable tone she often used to tangle up their emotions.

Harrow grinned in spite of himself. "We've missed you, too." He sat back on his heels, and Gail moved to wrap her arms around his neck. He stood up and carried her into the living room, where Leo was waiting for them, folding the newspaper in his hand.

"I want to go home," Gail said, eyeing Angus.

Jordan took advantage of the opportunity to distract Gail. "Why don't you say hi to Angus? He's joining us for a little vacation."

Gail's face lit up. "Hi, Angus."

Angus saluted. "Hey there, missy."

Then she turned her attention to Jordan. "Where are we going?" She tried wiggling out of Harrow's arms before he was able to set her down on her feet. Once on solid ground, she began jumping up and down.

Harrow laughed. "It's a surprise. Now, settle down and let Mom help you pack while Leo and I talk."

"I'll be done in ten minutes, tops." Gail blasted out of the room like a tornado, ready to do some major damage.

Jordan gave Leo a quick hug then followed her.

"Harrow, how's the operation coming along?" Leo gestured for Harrow to sit down.

"It's fine, although it has been a crazy week. Hell, it hasn't stopped. Know what I mean?"

Leo chuckled then nodded. "You've inherited a big corporation and a lot of responsibility, my boy. It comes with the territory."

"I know, I know. It's never ending." Harrow stretched out his legs in front of him and sighed. "We're going to take Gail for a few days, take her for a little weekend getaway and assess the situation." He nodded to Angus.

"I think that's a good idea. Reaffirm your roles in her life and take it from there. I mean, she's always welcome here, but there's nothing that can replace the attention she gets from her parents."

Harrow couldn't agree more. "But she won't ever be normal where we are. She's surrounded by people like us—hardly an ideal atmosphere for a growing child."

"You'd be surprised. I've seen children grow up in the harshest environments and still make it. Don't underestimate your girl. She's resilient. I can vouch for that." Leo reached for his vape and took a long and contented drag.

Harrow smirked. He was aware that the general had been attempting to stop smoking. "I guess we'll decide what to do during this getaway. I'm glad you're kicking the habit."

Leo frowned. "It's about time. Ella has been nagging me nonstop. But I'm going to miss my cigars." The general launched into an in-depth explanation of the pros of using the E-cigarette, and Harrow and Angus listened with interest.

It wasn't long before Gail came barreling out of the hallway, followed by Jordan, Leo's wife Ella, and Heather, his granddaughter. While the women conferred, Gail hugged Heather, expressing her concern about breaking their playtime schedule.

"I'm ready," Gail announced at last. "I still want to know where we're going."

Harrow took the little suitcase and handed it to Angus before slinging Gail's backpack onto one shoulder. "You'll just have to wait and see." He shook Leo's hand. "Thank you for putting up with this little squirt."

"I'm not a squirt." Gail pouted.

This is going to be an interesting vacation, Harrow thought as he navigated the car out of the quiet neighborhood en route to JFK.

Cyrus stepped down from the treadmill after a thirty-minute run and felt like he could run some more. But with Rick hovering like a damn moth, he knew the doctor wouldn't hesitate to remove him from the exercise machine if he persisted.

The look of approval radiated on Rick's face as he scribbled his observations on a piece of paper. He flashed the note at Cyrus. *You're doing great. You can start with the weights next week. The wound is healing well.*

Cyrus felt like a winner. Feeding from Isidora had done wonders for his healing time.

"I'm feeling much better, thanks to your mad skills. Now you don't have to watch my workout. I'm sure you have better things to do."

Rick hunched over the paper and wrote fast. *Nice try man. I'm going because I'm sick of watching your ass.* He got up and pointed to his eyes and mouthed. *I'm watching you.*

"Yeah, yeah. Get out of here!" Cyrus landed a good natured slap on the doctor's shoulder. "Come back when you're ready for your training."

He went to his desk and checked the schedule. During his absence, Tor had stepped in for him, and so far there'd been no injuries or deaths on the patrols. Their group always welcomed the downtime. When their soldiers were able to focus on helping diseased vampires, his job as head of operations became much easier.

If it weren't for the daily demands of the business, he'd have been able to pursue his first and foremost personal goal—hunting down Zane. However, with the recent attack at the VC headquarters and the disease spreading again, he had to be patient. He wasn't giving up on his plan, though. The fire for vengeance continued to burn inside him.

A few more days and he'd be back on rotation. He was dying to get a taste of the outside world again. Being caged up for several weeks could bring a man to tears. The sound of the shutters drawing down signaled the end of the night. He glanced at his cell phone as the usual flurry of texts came in from every fighter returning to the safety of their facility. He began to breathe easier.

The door creaked open, and Isidora walked in. Cyrus watched her approach his desk. It was impossible not to pay attention to the sway of her hips, and he couldn't tear his eyes away from her while she drew closer. His gaze traveled downward. The graceful stride of her legs drew his eyes to her flowing skirt, and he longed to run his hands along the long legs it concealed.

Her cheeks reddened as a sheepish smile broke across her face. What was the point of hiding how he felt when he knew full well she'd read his mind anyway?

Cyrus' throat went dry, and he coughed to clear it. "Hey. What can I do for you?" He got up from his seat, wiping the sweat from his forehead.

Isidora walked right up to him and laced her arms around his waist. "I missed you," she said into his ear.

That was a surprise. "I've, ah . . . missed you, too." That sounded way too awkward.

His arms had nowhere to go but around her. Isidora was taking him into uncharted territory, but he couldn't deny the warmth that coursed through him at her touch.

She smiled in satisfaction and held onto him tighter. Just as he was about to pull away, the door opened, and Tor, of all the goddamn vampires in the facility, walked in.

"I . . ." He stopped in his tracks, and an idiotic grin broke across his face. "Am I interrupting?"

Cyrus pulled away, blinking like a deer in headlights. He ran his fingers through his short hair and coughed. "Um, no, we were, ah, just talking."

"Oh, okay. Well, I was going to check on the rotation for tomorrow, but since you're here, I guess you've got it covered, right?"

Just go, you bastard. The words were about to leave his lips when Isidora squeezed his hand and shook her head.

"Yeah, I got it." This was making him uncomfortable. Tor winked and chuckled his way out the door.

Cyrus closed his eyes and let out a sigh. "I'm sorry about that."

Issy closed the gap between them and rose up on her toes to kiss him on the mouth. Damn it. He was weak under such assault, and further denial would be criminal. Cyrus placed one hand on the nape of her neck and kissed back hard, probing and seeking entry into her soul.

The trouble with lip-locking was the inevitable hard-on that followed. It was natural. He knew that for a fact. Yet it annoyed the hell out of him since he knew he wasn't going to do anything about it.

"Don't fight it," she murmured against his mouth.

He broke away. Isidora was too close for comfort, and she was too damned sweet to learn about the torture he'd gone through.

"I want to feel you, Cyrus. Here"—she pointed to her lips—"and here." She placed her hands on the junction of her legs.

His eyes lingered on the sweet spot he hadn't experienced in a long time. "Impossible. Why me?"

"I don't know . . . I dig you." Issy passed her tongue over her lips.

Atta girl. She was sounding more comfortable in her own skin. Cyrus blinked then swallowed the big lump in his throat. "Issy, come here." She leaned into his embrace. "You have an idea what I've gone through, right?" Isidora nodded. "I'm not turning you away because I don't *dig* you. On the contrary, I'm about to explode here. But—"

She tilted her face up and placed her finger over his mouth, preventing him from saying any more. "No buts. Allow me to lead you to a place where we can have some measure of peace and happiness."

Jesus, her words were like bee stings, inflicting pain and numbness at the same time. Cyrus shuddered at the fearsome possibility that this woman was his ticket to hell. Was he willing to sell his soul to take one taste?

Issy's heart leapt in anticipation of his response. Between the two of them, the weight of their emotional baggage could sink the Titanic. Much of what Cyrus was going through was not a mystery to her anymore. Though there were times she could tell that he intentionally closed his mind to her probing, she knew deep in her bones she could trust him.

If she heeded his inner ramblings, she would run away. After all, he wasn't ready, and her healthy appetite for rough sex wasn't going to sit well with him, considering his horrifying experience. Isidora had heard bits and pieces from his nightly dreams. When she put it all together, she knew it would be best to take things slow. At the moment, she was working from instinct alone since his body language had been giving her mixed signals. He was fighting the attraction, and it was up to her to change his mind.

Cyrus kissed her nice and slow while his arms tightened around her waist. "I'm messed up in the head right now. I'm not sure if I won't go postal on you, Isidora."

Her name was spoken with gruffness, as though there were underlying sentiments behind his declaration—something he wouldn't dare say out loud or even allow himself to think. As much as she wanted to satisfy the raging need inside her, she realized Cyrus was fragile and begging to be handled with care.

"I understand. There's a lot going on inside your head that will only be resolved with time. Give me a chance one of these days to prove we could help each other. That's all I ask."

He reached for her hand and kissed it. The tips of his fingers were rough, but she could feel the humming of tenderness inside him. Time would be her ally. If and when the real Cyrus emerged, she wanted to be in the front seat to applaud him.

"You're precious, and I know it. Let me come to you once I have my issues sorted out. I'm afraid I'll hurt you when my past catches up with me." He bowed his head, and his voice dipped lower. "I will try to do right by you. In the meantime, allow me to get to the place I need to be."

Issy examined his face—the creased eyebrows, the hard lines across his forehead, and the bags underneath his eyes. The vulnerability and suffering beneath his tough exterior were at odds with his powerful persona. It made her ache for him. Isidora placed his hand on her chest. Man, she was falling for this guy—too fast and too soon.

"I'm not going anywhere. We have the luxury of time." That was a half-truth. Her body wanted him inside her now, but she would try to wait, for his sake.

"Feed from me, even if it's not enough. It would be an honor."

Even if her true makeup required her to feed from another pureblood, Cyrus would no doubt taste divine. With Rohnert in limbo after losing his mate, Issy wanted to spare him.

The scent of Cyrus' desire to please her was too much for her to handle, and she eyed the pulsating vein in his neck.

Issy shivered as her fangs elongated. She focused on the throbbing artery and took him.

She struck hard, and the muscles of his shoulders tightened. The first pull was sweet, like a thick gulp of sweet wine that coated her throat and crept through her system. Her neurons fired at full blast, and his keening cry echoed in her ears. The scent of sex hung thick in the air, but the taste of fulfillment battled against its mighty force. Cyrus had given a piece of himself to her, and that was enough.

"Thank you for letting me take a part of you," she said when she pulled back.

Cyrus cupped her face, his expression serene. "You have no idea how much it means to me."

In truth, he was helping her more than he knew. If he would just take a moment to listen to her pleas, he'd have a clearer understanding of her brokenness. Together, they could heal each other.

The intercom on Cyrus' desk buzzed with an announcement from Rayce requesting his appearance in the I-room. Stat. Cyrus snapped out of the heady trance he'd been caught in. Instead of feeling lightheaded or weak from the feeding, a surge of energy flitted through his veins. When he looked at Issy, he felt a sense of well-being.

"I have to go." His voice was guttural—an aftereffect of their surreal encounter.

A quick movement of her tongue across the puncture site sealed the opening. Then Isidora looked up at him. "See you later?" She wiped the remnants of blood off her mouth.

Cyrus grinned like a fool. Giving his vein to the woman he was crazy about was the most important thing he'd ever done. It was something he could get used to . . . except reality hit him. She would still require the blood of a purebred vampire. His blood, though freely given, wouldn't be enough to sustain her. This recollection clouded his high, but instead of giving in to the negative thought, he smiled and brushed a finger across her cheek. "I'll be happy to service you again," he whispered before he left.

Conflicted but satisfied, Cyrus almost skipped down the hallway on his way toward the meeting room. Man, he would give his left hand to be able to do that again and again. He pushed the door open to find Rohnert, Tor, Allison, Gentry, and Firman with two children. Everyone looked up and watched him approach the table without a word.

"What's going on?" he asked, wiping the grin off his face.

Tor chuckled but refused to look him in the eye. It was a matter of time before the vampire bombarded him with nonstop teasing. Cyrus wasn't looking forward to it.

Rohnert's intent focus alerted him that the vampire was digging into his brain in the hopes of plucking information from him.

"What?" he asked again, eyeing the kids.

Rohnert straightened and got up. "These two are Sawyer and Liv. They will be staying with us for the time being."

The little girl with strawberry blond hair smiled, showing her uneven teeth and prominent canines. The older boy was straight-up formal, dipping his head in acknowledgment.

"Kids, this is Allison, Cyrus, Tor, and Firman. You already met Gentry." Rohnert introduced them one by one. "If there's anything you need, you can come to us."

It wasn't every day they had young bloods in their midst. It felt weird to be in a room with children. Cyrus hadn't thought they'd be running a nursery, but as he'd come to expect, Allison's dormant maternal instincts kicked into gear. She rose and walked over to the little girl, her face filled with excitement.

"Sawyer, Liv, would you like to see your rooms?"

Liv bobbed her head with eagerness while Sawyer agreed in a quiet voice. Cyrus had reservations as far as the newcomers were concerned. Looking back into his past, he could sympathize with how they must be feeling. Cyrus decided to go out of his way to make the children feel welcome.

The children's departure left the room in silence, and Cyrus proceeded to the bar. "I'm taking drink orders," he said to alleviate the tension.

Tor was first in line. "Patron, double."

Gentry shook his head, and so did Firman. Rohnert thought for a second then asked for a double shot of scotch. Cyrus went to work right away while Rohnert continued to pace.

"What's on your mind, Rohn?" Cyrus slid the drinks onto the table one by one.

"I have a hunch who is spreading the disease." Rohnert took a drink, then tabled the glass.

"Who?" Tor asked.

"Bretania."

Crickets. There were a whole lot of crickets. Cyrus downed his drink in one gulp.

"What makes you say so, sire?" Gentry leaned forward.

"Lose the title. I'm getting sick of it." Rohnert glared at the faithful soldier who leaned back against his chair like a child slapped with a failing grade.

Rohnert wasn't in the mood. That much Cyrus could tell. His back was rigid, and his lips were set in a thin line. The leader's eyes were sunken with missed sleep, and his cheeks were hollowed out.

"Goran was infected before he died, so it's just simple logic." Rohnert slid his glass back to Cyrus for service.

He took their empty glasses and went back for refills. "If that is true, what's her reason for spreading the disease?"

"I put a ban on killing without due process, so it's easy for vampires to commit murder. If she's not caught, she can get away with her crimes without punishment."

Tor nodded. "What's your course of action?"

"The Council is going to reconvene, and we'll take a vote. I just wondered what your input would be." Rohnert sighed. "Too bad Harrow isn't here."

"I think we should get help to those in need. If an infected one is caught in the act of maliciously spreading the disease, I think we should be allowed to hand out a quick sentence," Cyrus said. Then he downed another glass. The alcohol made its way down his throat with a vengeance.

Rohnert stared at him, and Cyrus didn't so much as blink an eye. He meant what he said. Under no circumstances would he allow anyone to spread the violent disease they'd fought so hard to eradicate. The big kahuna nodded, seeming convinced with his argument. The rest of the room watched them, heads moving left to right like they were watching a ping-pong match.

"The fuck. How about letting us in on your silent convo?" Tor pounded his artificial fist on the table.

Cyrus bared his fangs. Aggression was fun, and he felt as though he'd swallowed a whole bag of it. "I won't take matters into my own hands unless I see malicious intent with my own eyes."

Rohnert walked over to where he stood and slapped him on the back. "As a member of the group who has been championing the cause for so long, I would grant a reprieve for such an act. I will make sure it's brought up in the meeting."

Rohnert's vote of confidence was a small measure of success for Tack Enterprises and for Cyrus. He felt good, like a goddamn Mr. Universe winner. This made him more eager than ever to join the rest in patrolling the streets.

Gastarius rarely left his chamber, so it came as a shock to Lukan when she found him waiting inside her little room.

"Your grace, what brings you here?" She flitted over to him and went down on her knees, head bowed low.

A heavy hand touched her head, and for a few seconds, a swirl of air encircled them. Lukan had the sinking feeling of what was to come, even though Gastarius had closed off his mind. She dared not look up to see the condemnation in his eyes.

The diviner drew in a sharp breath. "Rise to your feet and look at me."

Lukan stood up and slowly met his gaze. There was sadness in his eyes rather than the contempt she'd expected to see.

"What is it?" She tried to conceal her building anxiety.

"Child, how could you?" Gastarius stood up, and with feeble movements, paced back and forth. The sound of his staff hitting the wooden floor was the only sound.

She followed his movement. What could she tell him?

"Speak the truth." Gastarius glanced over his shoulder.

Lukan buried her face in her hands. "I-I don't know what to say."

"You were given the task to protect. I entrusted you with lives of countless people, and you betrayed me. Instead, you allied yourself with death and destruction." His grief was thick, and Lukan felt the walls closing in on her.

She kept her eyes on the ground, refusing the see the reproach in the old man's face. "I'm not worthy to be in your presence."

"Nor are you worthy of the faith I had in you." She heard the quiver in his voice. "This is my fault. I should have seen this coming. I'm losing my touch."

Lukan deserved his words and more. She had expected this to happen the minute the truth was exposed, but she hadn't expected the damning pain as his words knifed through her heart.

"I have loved you as my own. I've given you the greatest gift, to watch over our people."

That might be true, but she knew the old diviner had held some things back from her. She couldn't stop herself from answering this time. "I was always second best."

"Leave Aemerria out of this. You have disgraced yourself by allying with creatures focused on destroying our people. You altered the course of people's lives and played with destiny and fate. How could you allow greed and jealousy to cloud your judgment?" Gastarius stopped in front of her and pounded his staff hard against the ground. "You have been given amazing gifts, and yet you used them for your own selfish ends. I have no choice but to strip you of your title and banish you from the realm. You may no longer call yourself a shaman. I'm retracting every enhancement I've given you. Only your innate power will remain."

She reckoned her innate talents were still enough to help her. Gastarius knew that when he waved his hand. A burst of smoke engulfed her, and she fell into a miserable darkness. In that long moment, her body jerked and the lights dimmed until she couldn't see through the veil that clouded her eyes.

Lukan screamed from the prickling sensation that coursed through her body, and she cried from the emptiness that filled her heart. Shunned and terrified, she kept spiraling into the abyss until she was no more than an empty vessel.

"Are you sure Rick cleared you to go?" Tor narrowed his eyes.

Cyrus pulled out his cell phone and handed it to Tor. "Go ahead and call him if you want to check."

Rick hadn't given him official clearance, but he'd said that Cyrus should be good to go by the end of the week. Cyrus considered Thursday the end of the week since his nerves were shot. He needed to get out and breathe some fresh air.

Tor narrowed his eyes, but after a few moments, he slapped Cyrus on the shoulder. "It's all good. I'm just checking. You're too precious." Good thing Tor didn't call his bluff.

"Oh, fuck it, Burns. Please don't even try to annoy me tonight." Cyrus opened the outermost door of the facility. "Ready?" he asked.

"You never did tell me what's going on with you and Issy." Tor pointed his nose upward, a common practice whenever they went outside. It was their internal warning device for immediate danger around them.

Cyrus didn't answer and looked away.

"Nothing happened? Is it the age thing?" Tor glanced over his shoulder and grinned.

Cyrus nodded. If he gave an inch, Tor would just hassle him for more information. It was better to let the fool believe whatever he wanted.

There was no fooling his friend. "Sure. I know what I saw, but if you want to keep it a secret, be that way."

Tor was like a bullhorn with unlimited volume. Cyrus wasn't about to disclose what was going on with him and Isidora.

"Why don't you just shut your mouth and let me enjoy this night?" He broke into a jog, testing his legs. When they held up, he sprinted, leaving Tor to eat his dust.

"Dream on, Romeo." Tor caught up with him right away. They spent the rest of the run in silence, which Cyrus welcomed with open arms. From time to time, he glanced at Tor, checking the vampire's emotional grid. There was nothing but the same exhilaration written on his face. He was no doubt jonesing for an honest-to-goodness fight, too.

"Where to?" Tor asked when they reached the main artery into the city. Lights, tourists, and traffic greeted them.

"To the usual seat of the shunned and diseased." Cyrus took the lead and spotted a dive bar frequented by locals and tourists alike.

They bypassed the long line with just a nod to the doorman, who recognized them and stepped aside to let them in. The club was dark, and they elbowed their way through the crowd of bodies milling around.

"The usual?" Tor glanced at him once they reached the bar.

"Yep," Cyrus said and began his visual scanning. Hookers, drug dealers, businessmen with sorrows to drown, and curious tourists were the patrons on this particular night—nothing out of the ordinary. He turned around and focused on the collection of mid-range bottles on the bar's display.

He got to thinking. If Rohnert meant what he'd said about honoring Tack's goal, and Cyrus had no reason to doubt the vampire, then it was time they stepped up the mission. With Jones running the disease control operation, guarded by his toughest vampire recruits, he and the others should crank up their efforts to find the people spreading the infection.

The music shifted to a bouncy tune, and half the bar's patrons emptied onto the dance floor. Tor parked his rear on a barstool and beckoned him to take the one next to it.

His phone beeped, and a message was patched through. Cyrus pressed the button and listened. Funny, Jack Drago seemed to share Cyrus' night owl schedule. The request for a call back sounded urgent, and the account was big enough to get his personal attention. He dialed and waited for the ring. One, two, three, and . . .

"Hey, Mr. Drago. You called?" He cupped the receiver to muffle the noise around him. Amid the blasting music that drowned out most of Drago's voice, there were three things Cyrus heard loud and clear—fifty more crates, cash wired, and two weeks. This meant production would be cranking 24/7 to get the order done and delivered. Funds were no problem.

Their drinks came, although not as fast as he'd hoped. Cyrus threw back the drink before the bartender could move to the next bar patron and put the glass down. "Give me two more."

The guy behind the counter grinned and fulfilled his order right away.

"Aren't you all wired up tonight?" Tor scooted closer to be heard.

"We have a huge order and two weeks to get it done."

Tor whistled. "Well, you better get moving."

His drinks came, and he downed one after the other. When Cyrus got up, his ears picked up a convo at the end of the bar between two men, one gangster type and one dressed in an impeccable suit, complete with glasses.

"You want a little action tonight?" the gangster asked.

There was a short hesitation on the yuppie's part. "What kind of action?"

The gangster smiled, revealing the tips of his fangs. "I know what you are. Been watching you all night. You dig men."

Some feet shuffling came from the other man and some throat clearing. "And if I do, what are you going to do about it?"

Damn it. This would have been a good time to have Rohnert around. The vampire would have had the 411 on the gangster's plan right away. Waiting games weren't Cyrus' cup of tea. Itching to make a move, he dialed back his aggression and pounded a cool hundred on the counter. That should be enough to cover the six rounds, with generous tip to boot.

"We're headed out?" Tor sounded keyed up.

"Yeah. I have to get those orders filled."

"Mind if I stay?"

"I do. No one patrols by himself."

As capable as Tor was, they'd been down that path before. They always came with a partner or group. It was a bummer, since Cyrus would've welcomed the alone time.

Just as he pivoted to leave, he caught a sight of a familiar figure. So familiar his blood began to boil and his breath hitched. He palmed his Glock, ready to spring, but a powerful yank brought him back down.

"This place is crawling with humans. I don't think it's a good idea to go all Rambo right here," Tor said.

"Then he'll have an audience. It'll be an entertaining way to make an exit."

At that moment, Zane glanced their way and locked eyes with Cyrus. All Cyrus could think of was blasting the mother fucker. He stood up again, not heeding Tor's advice, and he aimed his gun at Zane. But as luck would have it, a hooker stood in front of him, blocking his shot.

Cyrus had no choice but to lower his weapon. "Hey, good looking. Want to have some fun tonight?" the woman slurred, and he could smell the alcohol on her breath.

"No." Cyrus sidestepped her and zeroed in on Zane's position. The guy was no longer there.

"Fuckin' shit," he muttered then pocketed his gun.

"Jesus, Cyrus. Would you just consider how Leo would be all over our asses with another vampire sighting?" Tor pulled his ass down onto the barstool.

True, the General had stuck his neck out for them many times—getting them out of sticky situations, diverting attention, and pulling strings to get their facilities done in record time. The least Cyrus could do was spare the man the headaches that would stem from the bloodbath he was picturing in his head.

Standing down was a tough order. He'd been waiting for this chance for a long time. Just one chance to kill Zane and get his revenge.

His phone vibrated, and Cyrus glanced at the display. "Barth, what's up?"

"Cy, we're headed back to the facility."

Cyrus glanced at his watch. It was only two in the morning. "Is everything all right?"

"It's too quiet. We've patrolled along the border of the city, gone to several clubs, and walked the streets, but there's nothing out of the ordinary. We even visited the warehouse to see if they needed our help. All is well."

An uneventful outing was always welcome. "Sounds good. I'll see you in a bit," Cyrus said then hung up. He glanced at Tor, seeing the man watching him. "Let's get back so I can fill Drago's order."

Tor took one last pull on his drink and set the glass down. "I'm ready, sweetheart."

Cyrus sneered as he made his way to the exit. Zane had been lucky tonight, but if Cyrus had anything to say about it, the bastard's luck would change soon.

Allison stepped back, surveying Issy's killer outfit, and giggled. She had a dreamy look on her face, and Issy could tell what she was thinking. Cyrus wouldn't be able to take his eyes off her.

"Jordan, what do you think?" Allison turned to the other vampire.

"Damn, Issy. You're going to give our Cyrus a heart attack." Jordan stood next to Allison and winked at her.

Issy stared at her reflection in the mirror. It did feel good to step away from the usual long skirts and loose blouses, but the skinny jeans and tank top with its low, round neckline was showing off too much skin. She couldn't help but frown, in spite of feeling good about her new clothes.

"I might catch pneumonia," she teased and then swirled around. The shiny boots had wedge heels, which gave her a little boost but still allowed her to move around without tripping.

"Oh, puh-leze! You're going to be fine." Allison dismissed her concerns. "Kidding aside, how do you feel?"

Jordan tapped her foot while waiting for Issy to answer.

Isidora glanced at herself again. "Well, I do look different. I have to get used to the tight pants, but I like it. Makes me feel like a new woman."

"That's good. I'm not going to let you catch pneumonia, so I got you this," Jordan said, handing her a shopping bag.

Her eyes widened. "For me?" She took the bag and glanced inside. Issy gushed before pulling out a leather jacket.

"Put it on." Jordan beamed.

Issy did as she was told. When she looked in the mirror, she liked the woman who stared back at her. The jacket gave her enough coverage but still hugged her bosom and her curves.

"Femme fatale," Allison quipped. "I doubt Cy will ever let you out of his sight."

"Uh, can we keep this to ourselves for now?" When both women stared at her like she had lost her mind, Issy explained, "I need time to get used to it. I don't want to feel uncomfortable around him."

It had taken her some time to get Cyrus used to the idea of being around her, and if she jumped at him with this seductress outfit, she might scare him off. Her intention was to reel him in and not drive him away.

"Sure, but don't wait too long. The skirt really has to go." Jordan snickered.

Allison clapped her hands with excitement. "I'm going to bribe Rayce to show us the footage when the time comes."

Issy squealed. "Don't you even dare!" She laughed and took another look at herself, and she liked what she saw.

"At the rate you kids are feeding, I'm going to need full-time help just to keep your cravings satisfied." Bretania smiled at the girls.

Marian, Rhiannon, and even little Esmeralda giggled at her. Their latest meal lay limp at their feet. In a matter of a week, the three girls had finished off two humans. Not bad, considering the hapless being would regenerate as another member of their army.

"I want more," Rhiannon said, her crimson eyes glowing.

Bretania laughed. Their appetites were insatiable, and their growth was rapid. Good thing blood donors were abundant.

"Jackson, we need another one," Bretania said, summoning the drug dealer she'd taken from the alley. Since he was a new vampire, he wasn't ready to fight, and this made him the babysitter-slash-meal planner for the children.

The vampire saluted and was out the door before Bretania could even voice her preference. Anyone with a pulse was good enough, but she was hoping for characters with a penchant for murder, types who were easily enticed with the offer of more deaths at their hands. Instead, the first two Jackson had brought with him were junkies—not that their tainted blood had any effect on the children.

On the surface, their arrangement was like your typical boarding house, with people walking in and out. It was a show put on for the young ones' sake, except for Nathaniel, who at the moment was busting his ass with the punching bag. The young man was driven, and the hatred in his heart was the very weapon she believed to be their key to salvation. With proper fighting instructions and weapons training, he was going to be an unstoppable force.

She had spent hours with Goran's son, training him and prepping him for what she had planned. Thirsty for knowledge, Nathaniel thrived under her, but their relationship remained strained. Often, she caught him concocting his own plans for revenge. He was young and inexperienced, and she feared that his impulsive nature would land him in trouble, so she harnessed his eagerness by working with him every moment she could spare.

Bretania hid her secrets from the three girls because they were too young to understand. Besides, she needed a dose of normalcy, a diversion from the thoughts running through her head. With their future home base almost ready for them, the growing lack of space would be solved. Sure, the girls asked a lot of questions, but her answers were as vague as mud. No one needed to know her heart's desires.

She heard a skirmish outside the room, and seconds later, Jackson walked in, dragging a rather large individual by the collar of his muscle shirt, and throwing him on the floor. Tattoos of every variation covered his biceps, spreading down to his wrists. Damn, the bastard came complete with his own set of sleeves.

"What the fuck is this, Sesame Street?" The man practically growled. "You promised some great stash."

"Jackson, I think you made a mistake." Bretania smiled and turned to the girls. "You'll have to wait while Jackson finds you another one. This guy's for me."

She pushed herself off the mattress and took over manhandling the poor human, whose eyes almost popped out of his skull at the sight of her elongating fangs. "What the hell are you?" he managed to ask.

"The better question is what am I going to do with you?" Bretania pulled him out of the room and crossed the hallway with powerful strides.

They reached her darkened bedroom, and she threw the man across the room and slammed the door shut.

The man rose to his feet, groaning and cupping his nose. "You broke my nose, bitch."

Nice! Bretania loved to fight, and this man was just what she needed. She kind of fancied a little foreplay at the moment, so she could fork and rearrange her meal before consumption.

"What are you going to do with me?"

Bretania flashed her fangs. "I want a piece of you," she answered.

What a turn on. The man's thoughts bulldozed into her. So this kinky piece of shit wanted a little slice and dice. Of course, she would oblige. What could be more satisfying than fucking the bastard while feeding from him? This was a sure-fire way to transmit her everlasting gift of pain and suffering.

"Then come and get me," the man said, thrusting his hips forward. She liked his way of thinking. She smiled and burst forward.

The man expected to lock lips with her, but she stopped just before their mouths touched. He reached out to snake his thick arms around her waist, pulling her closer. He felt good—solid. It didn't hurt that he wanted her, too. He was a bit cocky for her taste, but that would change once she worked on inserting ideas and principles in his head.

"Take what you want." He ground his body against hers.

"You don't have to ask twice." Her smile dripped like honey before she ripped the pants off his body, startling him. "You like that?"

"Rough is good." He reached out for her chin and planted a kiss on her mouth. Bretania couldn't help but smile.

She lifted the hem of her gown all the way up to her waist and then fisted his erection. In just a few strokes, the man was groaning with intense need.

"What's your name?" she asked. In one quick motion, she plugged his arousal between her legs.

"Mason." He pounded into her like a jackhammer.

"Mason . . . nice and solid. You'll like what I'm going to do to you next."

"Do it." His voice was growing ragged. It was the perfect time.

When the human male shuddered inside her, her lips twisted into a wicked grin and she bit into him with full force. She sucked harder until just an ounce of blood was left to get him to the transition stage.

"Congratulations. You're going to enjoy working for me." Her ominous laughter bounced around the four walls of her bedroom as she dropped Mason on her bed, petrified and writhing.

Cyrus got right to work the moment they set foot in the facility. After the past breaches, their operation had been confined to laptops and phone calls to ensure everyone's safety. Even the personal demonstrations performed by either him or Allison had been aborted. Since their clientele consisted of old and loyal accounts, their sales weren't affected. Aside from Drago's new business, their company existed to maintain their current list of clients.

Before the first attack, which had taken the lives of Pritchard, Rayce's predecessor Dante, and Jones' mentor Leroy, they operated from an adjoining building. Afterward, Harrow and Allison decided that demolishing the business structure would be best for everyone residing in the facility.

Cyrus nudged the mouse, and the computer buzzed to life. He scrolled through Drago's account and checked on the wired payment and the new order. Jesus, with fifty crates of their powerful guns, the man could start a mini war. Was it their responsibility to find out the intended use for those weapons? In the past, their contract hadn't contained a full-disclosure clause. Should they add one? Maybe a meeting with Harrow and their lawyers was warranted before he filled the order.

Harrow was due back any minute from his short vacation with his family. Cyrus logged off the system and decided he had time for a quick shower before Harrow's arrival. Stepping out of his office, he glanced down the long hallway and plodded along. At the end, he heard a door opening, and a figure emerged.

Sawyer, the young boy Rohnert had taken in, didn't see him as he walked with purpose up the stairwell to the next level. Wearing an oversized shirt and basketball shorts, the boy looked like a normal human kid. Sawyer's eyes were the only giveaway that he wasn't the usual preteen. The droop of the boy's shoulders stirred curiosity in Cyrus, so he decided to follow. He maintained his distance, until the boy disappeared into the training room.

Conflicted whether to check on Sawyer or leave, Cyrus stood outside and pressed his ears against the door to listen. He heard nothing except a whole lot of silence so he decided to check in.

In the center of the room with his face down on the blue mat and his legs tucked underneath him, Sawyer looked up to check on the new arrival. It didn't escape Cyrus' notice that his eyes were shimmering with tears. He opted not to approach the boy.

"Carry on. I'm just working on the schedule," he said in a gruff voice. Cyrus went behind the desk and sat down. From the corner of his eye, he could see Sawyer hesitating before he adjusted his body on the mat. He could hear a faint murmuring, but Cyrus couldn't make out the words and continued his pretense of being busy.

Cyrus leafed through the profile photos and bio data of their new recruits and the soldiers Wendell and Icarus had sent their way. He began the task of filing each paper in its proper folder in an attempt to feign disinterest.

The quiet suffering from the boy in the middle of the room was hard to ignore. Just when Cyrus thought he didn't have it in him to feel anymore, his instincts urged him to reach out. There had to be a reason behind Sawyer's tears, and he'd be damned if he wasn't going to do anything about it.

Minutes ticked by while Cyrus watched in silence, debating the best approach. Sawyer remained face down on the mat. It made Cyrus wonder about the child's mental well-being. Not many kids that age would spend time in quiet reflection. Just when he thought Sawyer had fallen asleep, the young vampire stood up and spread his legs. With his eyes closed, he lowered his hands to his abdomen and pushed, taking a series of long breaths.

Prompted by curiosity, Cyrus stopped pretending and leaned forward to watch Sawyer perform the slow and gentle movements. He wasn't a practitioner by any means, but as he watched Sawyer, he was mesmerized by the discipline and controlled movements flowing from his body, hands, and legs. As the boy continued with a series of low and high stances, Cyrus began to realize that it wasn't too late to learn this particular art. He recognized the martial art form from Rohnert's several attempts to introduce it in the past. The flow of Chi could do wonders for one's body and mind. Trying to make the least amount of noise, he got up and walked toward the mat.

Sawyer's eyes popped open during his approach, and he froze. Cyrus saw the fear in the scarlet orbs staring at him and raised his hands. "I don't mean to interrupt, but your movements are quite interesting."

The boy hesitated, eyes darting to the exit, as if deliberating whether to stay or bolt.

"Where did you learn Tai chi?" Cyrus asked, hoping to calm the panic that was coming off from the boy in thick waves.

"From the Internet." Sawyer's voice was a mere squeak.

Cyrus smiled, revealing his fangs. "What made you decide to take it on?" He had no idea what made him want to draw out the child, but here he was, making awkward small talk.

Sawyer glanced at the door again with apprehension. Just when Cyrus thought his question would be ignored, the child spoke. "I wanted to relax. According to the steps, it helps with the internal flow of energy within us. It keeps us attuned, not just with the nature but also with the life force within us." He clamped his mouth shut as though he had said more than he should.

"Hey, relax. Don't be afraid." Cyrus' tone came out more commanding than he'd intended. Well, blame it on his habit of talking to hard-assed adults in the facility.

"I . . . I didn't mean to disturb you. Rohnert said this is a good time to come here. He said most are out patrolling and that I can use—"

"You're fine. Don't worry about it. Rohnert is right. I wouldn't have been here if it weren't for some things I had to do."

By the look on Sawyer's face, Cyrus was doing a piss-poor job of putting him at ease. The boy still looked like he was ready to bolt, which was understandable. Being shuffled from one home to another could be a shock to a young soul. Cyrus should know. Been there, done that, and had the shirt to prove it.

"Why don't we make a deal?"

"Deal?" Sawyer's eyes were a pool of confusion.

"Yeah. Teach me Tai chi, and I'll give you some lessons in my street version of ass-kicking."

He reached out a hand for a handshake. Sawyer seemed to digest his offer while he studied Cyrus' face. Trust was a tough sell, especially for people who'd been on the receiving end of broken promises. It made Cyrus wonder what the boy had been through.

After a few seconds, Sawyer walked up and grasped his palm with a shy grip. "Deal," he said in a voice that held a healthy dose of doubt.

Drago sat on his balcony enjoying the evening peace when sounds of a scuffle came from nearby. He zeroed in on the stilted conversation forty-three floors down and listened. A vampire was hustling a human, who was a soon-to-be meal for his master's wards. Interesting.

He continued listening, blocking out everything except the one mental voice that had caught his interest. Scaling down the building, he stayed out of view and followed the ongoing argument. With the human outgunned and corralled, he was brought to the building, one floor below where Drago resided. Taking great care to stay unnoticed, he hid in the shadows, maintaining a good distance between them.

The event took an interesting turn when he heard a woman's voice, which led him to believe that he had found what he was looking for.

Bretania, the missing mate of Goran, had surfaced and was living in his building. How convenient for him. This was just too good to be true. Knowing the former member of the esteemed Council was a mind reader, he shut away his inner thoughts and continued listening. A grin spread across his face at this welcome development. Now that he'd found the missing link, his plan was off to a great start.

Once the house quieted down, Bretania slipped out her bedroom window and scaled the high rise onto the other side of the building. She ended on the balcony of the largest penthouse in the structure.

With her dark red nightgown blowing in the wind, she felt the chill rise up from her legs to her thighs and settle around her core, making her tingle. Filled with apprehension at the requested meeting, she stood outside the glass sliding door and waited.

The city's lights glowed in the dark, twinkling and tempting her to feast her eyes on the display instead of focusing on the impending encounter with the man she only knew as J. D. The door slid open, and gust of wind was sucked in, blowing the thick draperies. From where she stood, she couldn't see into the darkness inside. Without her weapons, she felt like a newborn child, naked and vulnerable.

As agreed, she had come alone and unarmed, and she regretted complying with the arrangement.

"You harbor so much doubt," a low but authoritative voice said from within. "Step in and let us get acquainted."

Hesitation prevented her from taking the first step right away. Bretania had always been confident, so this dithering was unusual for her.

"I'm a busy man." Impatience laced the man's tone, and it reminded Bretania of Goran. Important, impatient, and intimidating—not a promising start to a proposed partnership.

His words got Bretania moving, however. She reached out and parted the heavy fabric to let herself in. Darkness greeted her, and there was a malevolent air around her that was almost oppressive. A figure sat on the immaculate white sofa, garbed in a silk black robe. The glass partition slid closed, and the locks engaged. Although there were no other beings around them, Bretania could sense that her one hope for getting out of this in one piece was to abide by any terms the man would give her.

"I'm Bretania," she said unnecessarily.

The dark figure chuckled, a rumble deep enough to make her take one step back. "I think that has been established already."

Okay. Now what? Should I ask for his name?

"That's a good start," was a reply to her unspoken thought.

Disconcerted, she followed the man's suggestion. "Who are you?"

"I'm a guardian angel."

"My guardian angel?"

"You could say that," he said.

"Does my guardian angel have a name?"

"Call me Drago."

"Drago." She let the name roll on her tongue, liking the sound. "Why are you my guardian angel?" Bretania advanced into the room, not enough to see his face, but she got a whiff of his scent—heady, masculine, and definitely ready.

"I feel that I may be able to help you."

"What's in it for you?"

"Let's just say I want a piece of the pie."

"So we're speaking in terms of giving and taking?"

"You're astute. I like that in a female." The man stood up to his full height, towering over her five-foot-ten frame. He placed his hands in his pockets, and with a gait belonging to a person who knew his worth, moved in front of her.

Drago's eyes were dark, endless pools of wickedness she had only seen before in one man, Goran. His smile made the hair on the back of her neck rise. The man reeked of pure evil as he watched her with steady gaze.

"What do you want from me?" she asked once her system calmed down.

"Servitude. In return, you shall get what is coming your way."

"That is vague." With a sudden attack of boldness, Bretania reached out and took hold of his jaw, tilting it toward the little ray of light that streamed from the parted curtains.

He gave no resistance, though she felt the power surging through her fingertips when the man's jaw clenched. "Your audacity might land you in trouble."

"My meekness landed me in the heap of shit I'm in right now. Step into the light. I want to see all of you," she murmured.

To her surprise, Drago did as she requested. She started her look-see at his bare feet, lean and long. What did they say about men with big feet? Bretania couldn't hide her smile while she continued her visual exam, moving to his tapered waist that was covered by the silky robe, held together by a tie of the same material. His broad chest peeked out through the V of the garment and gave her a slight case of shivers. Strong and powerful men were her weakness, and she could already feel the desire coursing through her veins. When her gaze landed on his face, she saw cynicism in those shifty eyes, and the quirk of his mouth suggested she had opened a can of worms. He was a looker by every standard, but the evil underneath the thick veil of lashes churned her stomach.

"Like what you see?" He took her by the wrist and twisted it behind her as he spun her around. With his other hand, he pushed her hair away to expose the expanse of her neck. He sniffed her like a dog, and she closed her eyes, expecting him to take a bite. But he just hovered, skimming his mouth along her bare skin.

"I like . . ."

"It'll stay this way. I don't mix business with pleasure."

The rejection bit her like a vicious animal, and she flinched. Rage coursed through her until she shook beneath his touch.

"You're an ass—"

"As I was saying, you and I will have a great relationship. Consider this Christmas morning."

She was infuriated, and it became difficult to think. It took a few moments before she'd calmed herself down and regulated her breathing. Drago released her arm and turned to walk toward the glass door. Bretania followed his movements with her eyes while he stared out the window. She glanced at her surroundings and recognized the value of the display around her. It was obvious that money wasn't a problem for this creature.

"What are you proposing?"

"I lead, and you follow."

She laughed—one that echoed throughout the room. "I'm done following orders."

"A word of caution—I chose you, therefore, your fate has been decided."

He turned around, and Bretania witnessed his fangs lengthen to an unbelievable degree. His eyes flickered black, red, and white. Panicked, she took several steps backward, only to be met by a concrete wall of bodies—ones she hadn't noticed when she walked in.

The whole room was surrounded by tall, black-clad creatures. Their eyes glowed in their depthless sockets, and their mouths were filled with razor sharp teeth. When the room became bathed in light, Bretania felt she was waking up to a nightmare.

"Now, let's talk terms and expectations." Drago moved toward her, his strides predatory, and his expression held contempt. He was a perfect example of a man who would get what he wanted, no matter the price.

After her initial shock, Bretania squared her shoulders. "I don't enter into deals without my own set of expectations. If you need me to do something for you, then I want something in return."

Drago's eyes flickered before he nodded. "You drive a hard bargain, my dear."

Bretania laughed and then crossed her arms. "What did you have in mind?"

The moment Rayce alerted him to Harrow's arrival, Cyrus dialed his boss' number and waited. "Harrow, can we meet at the office in a few minutes?"

"Hello to you, too." Harrow chuckled. "What about?"

Cyrus felt a pang of guilt, but he couldn't wait. "This needs to be done in person."

"I'll come by your office. Give me five."

The line went dead, and Cyrus changed into his jeans and black cotton shirt in a hurry. His wound had healed well, thanks to Isidora's blood. The mere thought of her name evoked a sensation deep in the pit of his stomach. He had to work hard to keep from dwelling any longer on her if he wanted to be able to walk straight. Cyrus hurried to the office and fired the computer to life.

Within minutes, Harrow arrived, still garbed in his trench coat but minus the weapons. He took one look at Cyrus and nodded. They'd been together long enough that words sometimes weren't necessary to convey sentiment.

"Hit me." Harrow settled on the chair opposite his.

Cyrus turned the laptop around to show Harrow Drago's order request, plus the exorbitant amount that had been wired to their account. "We already supplied his first order, and the delivery was acknowledged sometime last week. I'm wary about this next order. Don't you think it's a bit too much for a private firm?"

Harrow pushed his sunglasses to the top of his head and tilted his head sideways to get a better look at the monitor. Cyrus had gotten used to the whitish color of Harrow's eyes. The deterioration process had stopped, and that was all either of them cared about.

Once Harrow had finished reading, he stroked his chin, deep in thought. "You think the guy is building a private army?"

"We're talking about automatics so powerful he could start a war."

"What are you thinking?" Harrow pushed his sunglasses back onto his face.

"I'm thinking of not filling the order and returning the money ASAP."

Harrow paused but then shook his head. For the most part, they were almost always on the same page as far as running the business, so this came as a surprise. "I think it's bad business, know what I mean?"

Cyrus understood, but his gut was telling him to can the idea. "What do you suggest?"

"Let's fill a third of the order and say we're having trouble with the production line. Return the amount corresponding to the unfilled portion of the order, and we'll call it a day."

It sounded logical, and for the sake of their business, a good call. Cyrus had no problem with it. "Sounds good. I'll get the ball rolling on this." He changed gears. "How's Gail?"

Harrow's expression softened, as it always did when Gail was the topic. "She's doing great. That vacation was what we needed. I guess we can't postpone the inevitable. Gail wants to come home. She doesn't care if she gets homeschooled or if her bedtime is different from ours. She wants to be here, and that is that."

Cyrus laughed. The little girl had her adoptive parents wrapped around her finger. "So when is princess coming back?"

"They're done with school. She wants another week with Heather so they can say proper goodbyes." Cyrus' eyebrows lifted, and Harrow grinned. "Her words, not mine. I swear she's a young woman masquerading as a child. Jordan will pick her up in a week."

They both laughed, knowing Gail too well. In truth, even Cyrus couldn't say no to her. No one could. One request from the exuberant child and everyone found themselves tripping over their feet to fulfill her wishes—whether it was for company to go swimming, an ice cream, or a buddy to watch her favorite cartoons. It was no surprise that Lambert had been smitten with her.

The thought of his dead friend brought home a bittersweet memory. Lambert had given his life to protect Gail. Cyrus didn't doubt that others would as well.

The loud alarm brought him out of his trip down the memory lane, and he followed when Harrow raced toward the door. Just as they made it to the hallway, Rayce's voice came over the speaker with an announcement.

"Two men down and en route. ETA three minutes."

Cyrus and Harrow looked at each other and sprinted to the clinic. Rick would no doubt have his hands full. With Cheryl as the only other medical staff member on their payroll, the doctor would need the extra hands.

Rick was already suiting up with Cheryl's help when they walked in. Sinatra was playing in the background. A few seconds later, Isidora came barging in. She held Cyrus' gaze for a second before taking her place next to Rick. As the silent conversation began, Cyrus watched Issy, studying her body language and guessing her frame of mind. She appeared solid, following Rick's guttural orders and relaying them to Cheryl with efficiency. Cyrus felt damn proud of her and how she had handled the changes in her life.

In a matter of minutes, the room started to fill up, and frenzy followed. Chase and Vince were brought in by several human fighters, both of them bleeding and pale.

"What happened?" Harrow asked amid Rick's orders being shouted through Isidora.

Matthew, another human fighter, walked toward them looking rather shaken. His face gleamed with sweat, and his clothes were soaked with his comrades' blood. "Scuffle broke out when three humans came at us outside the billiard hall, demanding we join them."

"Dangeran?" Cyrus asked.

Matthew shook his head. "Automatics. Damn, I had no idea what was coming until the bullets started raining on us."

"Rick said to get out if you can't give him a moment of peace," Isidora said. Her tone, no doubt, was as forceful as the thought behind it.

Cyrus stepped into the background, watching Rick move fast while Cheryl began working on the less severe case of the two. Accidents and shit happened. It was the name of the game. But for Pete's sake, a human or even a vampire had no chance against such powerful weapons. Multiple entry sites were exposed the moment Vince's garment was cut off.

It was a race against time. Cyrus tuned out the rest of the noise out and tugged on his collar, feeling caged in all of a sudden. This scent of human blood still did a number on his newly transformed self. He continued to track Isidora's movements with close attention while Harrow pulled the rest of the fighters out to the hallway to grill them for additional information.

In the midst of the tumult, one word drilled into his brain. "Clear!" Isidora shouted.

Cyrus left the room and stood in the hallway, far from Harrow and the crew. He'd heard those words one too many times. There was no getting used to it.

Isidora had a long day and couldn't wait to sleep off the effects of the evening. She came out of the bathroom after a long, hot shower that removed the aches and pains stemming from her long, excruciating night at the clinic. They had lost Chase, but Vince it was still with them. The question remained whether the human was going to survive his wounds for the critical first twenty-four hours.

Issy's plan for the night was simple. Read a book until she fell asleep. The adrenaline began to seep out of her, but her muscles remained coiled and her chest tight. She opened the book to the page she'd marked and started reading where she'd left off. Five minutes in, and she still couldn't get into the story, but her distraction was her fault, not the author's.

The memory of Chase's last breaths was seared into her brain. There was no getting used to the stench of death. The grim reaper had won yet again.

Then she heard a familiar sound—groaning and moaning. Most nights, she forced herself to stay away because Cyrus had made it clear he wanted to deal with his problems on his own. But tonight, she couldn't shut his thoughts away. It was times like these when her mind-reading talent was a curse. The pain he had been keeping to himself came out loudest during his sleep. Mixed with the vicious reminder of her parents, Maureen, and Finn's deaths, Issy felt she was about to crack. She knew where this dream would lead Cyrus. It took him into a dark place, and he would end up screaming and thrashing.

Jesus. How could he keep everything bottled inside?

Since sleep was out of the question, she gathered up her robe and slipped out of her bedroom just as the door to Tor and Allison's room opened. She saw the huge vampire walk out, his hair in disarray, heading for Cyrus' room.

Battling the urge to slip back unnoticed, she found Tor looking her way. In a few steps, he closed the space between them. His disturbed sleep was clear in his eyes after he'd clocked so many hours on the field. "Would you like to do the honors tonight?"

"I'll do it," she said without hesitation.

"Remember, Cyrus is gruff on the outside but soft on the inside." Tor turned toward his bedroom and saluted before closing the door.

Left alone to her own devices, Isidora wrestled with the idea of slinking back into her room, except she told Tor she'd take care of Cyrus. The moaning turned into an all-out scream, cementing her decision. She pounded on his door.

"Cyrus. Cyrus," she called. As much as she hated to draw attention to herself, there was no way around it. People were bound to check what was going on if he kept making so much noise.

Isidora continued to hammer on the door until Cyrus yanked it open. His eyes were bloodshot, and his mouth was set into a thin line. Then he recognized her.

"I'm here for comfort," she said.

He raked his fingers through his hair and opened the door wider to let her in. Without a word, he climbed back into bed and opened his arms for her.

In the darkness, she could see his acceptance, and she considered it a welcome change. Isidora settled in the space next to Cyrus. There were no words exchanged between them. He wrapped his arms around her, and she snuggled against his chest.

In the silence, she heard him sigh. "Thank you." Minutes later, he'd succumbed to sleep. This time, the nightmare didn't come, and he slid into a more peaceful slumber. Issy kept watch and paid close attention to his thoughts. She ignored her own exhaustion until she was certain that Cyrus was on his way to getting a good night's sleep.

Issy stepped out of Cyrus' room after several hours, knowing he wouldn't be surfacing any time soon. She thought it was best to keep his fragile ego intact, and they could do without the awkwardness. The man had enough torment in his life, and adding another strain to his pride should be avoided. Once in her room, she picked up the discarded book and resumed reading until her lids wouldn't stay open anymore.

Rohnert stood before the Council Elders and called the meeting to order. All six were in attendance. Judging by the determined look on their eyes, he could tell that each one had made their choice about the subject on the table.

"I'm sure it wasn't easy to come to a decision, but it's necessary to keep our Council effective. Clotilde, would you like to cite our first item of business?" He took the seat next to Icarus and let the female introduce the first of the three issues they were going to address that evening.

Clotilde stood up, gathering her robe around her. "Our first item is the motion to reopen a panel to handle the judgment of those in violation of the Council's rules. Those in favor of the motion, please raise your hands."

All six hands came up right away, and Rohnert breathed a sigh of relief. He took in the emotions of those around him. They were contented with the choice and comfortable that they'd made the right call.

"Bretania will have to stand before the panel once we find her," Wendell said.

With everyone in agreement, an official document was passed around for their signatures. Once the last name was signed, Rohnert stood up.

"I wish to address an issue that is important to me. I will move this to be a part of the Council's official business. As each one of you are aware, I have become part of a group of vampires and humans intent on eradicating the disease. Their goal is simple. Find the cure and offer help. Now that we have a cure at hand, they are hard at work, getting help to all afflicted parties. It saddens me that this current outbreak will put more obstacles in their path.

"I have been told by those closest to me that they wouldn't think twice about eliminating an immediate threat. I am concerned, since they would be subjected to the decree we've just passed. I'm formally asking you to grant permission to Tack Enterprises personnel to continue their quest without fear of repercussions."

The room went silent for so long that it reached an uncomfortable level. Rohnert paced until each member began asking questions.

"Are you certain of their integrity?" Clotilde raised the point everyone had in mind.

Rohnert nodded. "I will vouch for every single one of their members."

Bardos waved his hand. "How do we know that they are acting in the best interests of the race?"

"They were doing this long before the Council declared them enemies. These people are championing a cause, and they're prepared to die to make sure that the disease is eradicated."

"What are we going to do to ensure their safety?" Icarus asked.

"The group is well funded. They have their own security. All they ask from us is to grant them leniency so that they can achieve their goals."

"I have seen these soldiers on the battlefield. They are disciplined, focused, and admirable. I believe we should give them the chance to get things done. After all, we have bigger problems to worry about, like capturing Bretania and halting the spread of the disease," Serena said.

"We've fought alongside these people. They have integrity," Wendell agreed.

The room buzzed with voices as the Elders began conferring with one another.

"If any oppose this motion, please raise your hand," Clotilde said. No hands came up. "I move this motion be recorded and signed by all."

While another official document was passed around for signatures, Clotilde continued. "On the subject of Bretania, I'm opening a motion to pass a decree to capture her alive. If she resists arrest, then I move to introduce a 'shoot-to-kill' option."

This was a bold statement and in line with what Rohnert had in mind. He snuck a glance at the female, astounded by her courage in setting herself up on the firing line. Again, the room fell silent while each member digested the newest item on the table.

After a few minutes had passed, Clotilde opened the motion. "Those in agreement, please say aye." A thunderous response erupted, and the motion was rapidly passed. "Then last but not least, we have to fill the vacant seats in the Council. If you have anyone in mind, please state their names so we can set the wheels in motion." She turned to Rohnert and bowed. "If it would not offend, I would rather you handle this part of the discussion."

Rohnert dipped his head in acceptance. "We're going to do our due diligence and conduct the necessary investigations on the people whose names are mentioned tonight. Keep in mind that there are aristocrats we can call on, as well as civilians who have served the Council as best they could."

All eyes focused on him. This was an unprecedented step. No civilians had been called to take seats on the Council because they lacked a noble bloodline.

"All I ask is that you consider each nominee with an open mind. Let your instincts guide you, and I suggest no one discuss this with anyone until we have done our complete research into each person's background."

Wendell raised his hand. "I'm nominating the Desider, a cousin of our beloved Randolph."

"I would like Isidora, daughter of Iden, to be considered," Regrita said.

Bardos volunteered a name from another prominent bloodline. "How about Tiber?"

There were about ten names tossed around, including Harrow Gates. Serena pointed out that Harrow, though a civilian, had been a vital member of the group that helped them topple Goran's men. She also mentioned that Harrow had saved her life by endangering his own.

Once each name was written down for further discussion and consideration, the meeting was adjourned and each member left feeling elated.

Rohnert stayed behind to affix his signature on the documents and place them inside the steel safe for safekeeping. Since the Council was not set to reconvene for a week, he felt a little measure of peace knowing they were headed in the right direction.

He had a brief meeting with the soldiers, who was now headed by Gentry, and gave them their orders based on the Council's resolutions. Afterward, he shed his ceremonial robe and set out from the Council walls. Rohnert ran toward the underground facility, intent on getting back before Malin's bedtime.

His weakness was spending too much time worrying about Council business and less time with his son. He loved his child like no other, but there were moments when one glance at his baby reminded him too much of Shelly.

It was difficult to be constantly reminded that he was going to spend eternity alone, without the woman he loved, so he often tried to stay away. It wasn't fair by any means, and he felt like a fool for subjecting his son to his foolishness.

Rohnert was clearing the last busy thoroughfare when he caught sight of a woman seated inside one of the twenty-four cafés, and he did a double take.

The woman sported blond hair that reached her shoulders and a prominent nose. Rohnert screeched to a halt, not sure whether to chalk this up to hallucination or the need to feed again. His feet moved of their own volition and took him inside the crowded restaurant. What in the hell was he thinking? Shelly had been gone for months. What were the chances she would be alive and having a cup of coffee on a random street corner?

Zilch. Nada. Zero.

He ended up at the table, standing in front of the woman and her family. Yeah, she possessed all of Shelly's facial features, but she wasn't the woman who continued to haunt his dreams—the one he craved to see and hold once more.

"Sir, can I help you?" a waiter asked.

"No . . ." He stumbled to the exit. "Hell fuckin' no. No one can help me."

Rohnert continued at a dead run. He didn't stop until he was back at the facility and inside the comfort and isolation of his own room. Without stopping to think, he went straight to the bathroom and pulled out the dull dagger from the drawer. He made the first cut, savoring the pain as if it offered salvation before continuing the shallow slash. His brain began to slow down, and his arms numbed with every slice.

Each drop of blood provided comfort, anchoring him to reality. He was still alone, and Shelly remained dead. There was no changing his fucked-up destiny.

"Kids, I'm going out for the night. Do not give Greta and Jackson a hard time." The three girls giggled conspiratorially before Bretania closed the door. They were situated and comfortable in their new home, and there was enough room for everyone with more to spare. The split-level design gave her and the kids a bit more privacy away from the army she had built.

"Ready, mistress?" Reid was waiting for her in the foyer. He eyed her with appreciation.

"Where is Mason?"

"He's bringing the car to the driveway." Reid held the door for her as they walked out of her Tudor-style house. Since they were now located in Long Island, it would have been easy to run to her meeting, but since Drago had instructed her to dress in her finest threads, she had to travel by car.

Mason had turned out to be a good addition to her group. Aside from being her go-to fuck buddy, he was a reliable bodyguard who could help Reid. Though she could sense a brewing rivalry between the two, she was more than willing to bed each of them whenever she got the chance.

Reid opened the door to her Bentley and took shotgun as soon as she was seated inside.

"Where to?" Mason was watching her from the rearview mirror.

"Pierre penthouse," she said and gazed outside. The night was young and cool. Drago's invitation had surprised her. During their first few meetings, the man showed little interest in her. At the last one, he had been more attentive, showering her with praise and even surprising her by giving her a little tongue action.

His invitation to come see him tonight gave her hope that the man might be willing to go all the way with her. The prospect excited her.

After navigating the nighttime traffic, they reached their destination with a little time to spare. Both Reid and Mason got out of the car, and Mason tossed the key to the waiting doorman. "Leave the car in front," he said.

Once inside the elevator, she checked her reflection in the mirror. The yellow gown brought out the golden hues in her hair. It was a good thing that her regular feeding had slowed the progression of the disease and the discoloration of her eyes.

Reid and Mason knew what to do. Armed with every imaginable weapon underneath their coats, these two men were lethal. Even though she had forged an alliance with Drago, she still had to protect herself. You would never know what people might do those days.

The Nerocs were another thing. The vampires were much too shifty for her. Although she had a good read on their inner thoughts, it was safe to say that she wasn't planning on crossing any of them, especially the leader, Lord Marchec, whom she had caught staring at her.

The door to Drago's suite opened before she had the chance to knock. Norris, the butler, bowed to her. "Mr. Drago is waiting for you on the terrace," he said.

"Show me the way." She smiled.

She was led to a private elevator. After climbing several floors, the car opened onto a roofless veranda with strings of lights illuminating the entire space. With the city as a backdrop, it was too romantic.

Bretania turned around to her guards. "You can wait here."

Reid was more than willing to do her bidding, but Mason snorted his displeasure. Still, he backed away and faded into the background as she had instructed.

A uniformed server approached her. "Mr. Drago is sitting by the fire," he said.

Bretania looked around the open space and found Drago sitting on a lounger. When he spotted her, he got up, picking up two glasses and a yellow rose from the table.

"Bretania, you're a breath of fresh air." He kissed her on the cheek then handed her the rose and a glass of champagne.

"How did you know I would be wearing a yellow gown?" she asked then took a sip from the flute.

"I didn't. The doorman called up to me."

This made her smile. She stood back to appreciate the man before her. Dressed in an impeccable dark suit, proud, and achingly delectable, he looked like a prize stallion.

Drago grinned at her. "Do you like what you see?"

"You have no idea what I like."

"Oh, I think I do." He took her hand and led her to a comfortable-looking couch with mounds of pillows. "I know exactly what you and I would both enjoy."

The moment they sat, Drago took the glass and rose from her and laid them on the glass table. "I have to apologize for my rude behavior in the past. I want to make up for it." His eyes sparkled with mischief.

She was taken aback. "Drago, what are you thinking?"

Since they were shrewd enough to close their thoughts to each other, it was difficult to guess what the other was thinking. However, all of a sudden, Drago allowed her to read his mind. He wanted her, all of her, even envisioning the two of them together after they had taken power from Rohnert and the Council.

"Isn't that what you like?" he asked, his voice dipped low.

Bretania found herself licking her dry lips. The prospect excited her. She hadn't felt this way since Goran. With a snap of a finger, she summoned Reid and Mason.

"Please wait for me in the car." When they showed a hint of hesitation, she added, "Now." The two scrambled away so fast it was comical. She laughed then turned back to Drago. "Where were we?"

Drago sure didn't believe in wasting time. He pinned her against the sofa, devouring the expanse of her skin with his mouth until she was breathless and moaning. Without asking, he lifted the skirt of her silk gown, unzipped his pants, and in the blink of an eye was pounding into her.

"Goodness, don't you believe in foreplay?" she asked, riding the wave of lust.

"I don't believe in waiting, period, milady."

Bretania wound her fingers at the back of his neck and nipped at his lips. This was happening too fast, but she wasn't complaining. Drago was someone you didn't want to keep waiting.

Her body responded to his every move as he burrowed deeper into her. "Oh, Drago," she moaned. They were good together, too good.

"Bretania, explode for me," he whispered into her ear.

Her walls constricted and burst into a powerful climax. Bretania cried his name over and over in ecstasy, wishing the night would never end.

"Good girl. You're just as splendid as I always imagined you would be." Drago pulled out and zipped his pants before she could open her eyes. "You're exquisite, and you're mine."

Those words were music to her ears, and she reveled at her good fortune.

Turning down a big client involved finesse and some crafty maneuvering on his part. Cyrus felt it was best to conduct the business in person rather than firing off an impersonal e-mail. He tapped his fingers on the desk while waiting on his request for a meeting. After all, Jack Drago was a busy man.

Upon confirmation from Drago's secretary that the big boss had agreed to see him, Cyrus took his time dressing up. He took meticulous care to pick the right clothes, wanting to project a confident company even after announcing their inability to fill the entire order. His personal attention to the matter was an attempt to extend his deepest regret but not to the point of sucking up. It was imperative to maintain professionalism while trying to keep their business relationship intact.

He attempted to loop his tie, but the damn thing wouldn't cooperate. Either the knot was too fat or the narrow end appeared too short. After several tries, he gave up and left his room. Down the hallway, he pounded on Tor and Allison's door.

Tor answered, and an immediate grin broke out on his face. "What cha up to?" He glanced at the tie in Cyrus' hand.

"I need Allison." Cyrus walked in when Tor stepped aside.

"She's taken."

Cyrus laughed. "Don't I know it." He took note of Tor's bedraggled appearance and glanced at the bed. "Did I interrupt something?"

Tor scowled. "Payback's a bitch, right?"

"I won't be long. I just need help with this shit."

Tor made a huffing sound then gestured at the couch. "Do you want something to drink to take the edge off?"

He thought about it. "Hell, why not? Make mine a double, no ice."

Tor walked to the minibar and poured Cyrus' drink first and handed him the glass. "Meeting a special client?"

Cyrus chugged the drink before answering. "Yeah, Drago."

The door to the bathroom opened, and Allison came out with a big smile. "Need help with that, old man?" She breezed over to Cyrus and gave him a peck on the cheek.

He snorted and tipped her chin. "I don't know why I even bother listening to your fashion advice."

Allison went right to work, her eyes twinkling with mischief. "Because you're a smart man," she said. Her hands were fast, and no matter how Cyrus tried to remember the loops and knots, he could never replicate her work.

"The woman has spoken." Tor chuckled as pride shone in his eyes.

"I think you're ready to represent." She stood back and inspected her handiwork. "Not bad at all. Daddy would be so proud of you."

Not wanting to get caught in a moment of sentimentality, Cyrus handed Tor the empty glass and gave Allison an awkward hug. "Wish me luck."

Cyrus hurried along the hallway and took the elevator up to the top level. If he weren't wearing the suit and tie, he would have gone on foot. Too bad his outfit required a more civilized mode of transportation. He strode to his car and swung himself inside. When the classic car roared to life, he checked himself in the rearview mirror. Not bad—he'd cleaned up well.

The drive was uneventful due to the late hour, and he was thankful for the break from the city's usual snarling traffic. Parking remained a problem around the area, so there was a valet, who held the car door for him.

"No need to park too far. I'll be in and out." Cyrus handed over the keys and smoothed his jacket. While he walked to the elevator, he sensed a fair amount of static—a feeling born out of familiarity with being around vampires. He buttoned his jacket after checking his Glock. Yeah, he was paranoid as hell, but who could blame him? He'd been stabbed and shot, and neither experience was a picnic.

The butler answered the door with his usual gloom and doom routine, complete with calculating eyes and a sneer that made Cyrus want to punch him in the face. He held on to his composure while he was led to the same sitting room. While Mr. Belvedere took off to announce his arrival, Cyrus walked to the floor-to-ceiling windows and gazed outside. This time the lights inside were dimmed to a minimum, which did more justice to the scene before him.

No matter how long he'd been a resident of the Big Apple, Cyrus could never get used to the dazzling lights. Each time he looked somewhere, a building seemed to have sprouted out of nowhere, crowding the already tight space.

"I can't get used to it either. There's never a dull moment in this city," Drago said, stopping next to him.

Cyrus gave him a curious glance. He hadn't heard the man's approaching footsteps, which was rather odd. Humans had a knack for making unnecessary noise even when their lives depended on stealth.

"Mr. Drago." Cyrus extended his hand.

The man clasped his hand in a firm handshake and nodded to the couch. "This is a surprise visit. Did you receive the order?" Drago smiled.

For some reason, something about the gentleman was off tonight. It triggered Cyrus' defenses.

"That's why I'm here." He took the sofa, while Drago settled on a recliner. "I'm afraid we can't meet the full order. There's been some trouble in our production line."

Drago's smile disappeared, his lips twitching. "Is there any particular reason why you can't fulfill the order?"

Cyrus had the distinct feeling that his client was trying to read his thoughts. Then it dawned on him what was different about the man sitting in front of him. The CEO was flashing his fangs in a display of anger.

"Excuse me?" he asked, feeling rather blindsided.

How could he have been so dense all this time? Cyrus considered himself observant. How could he have missed this detail? Suddenly galvanized, his reaction was automatic. He closed all the windows to his private thoughts.

"Your reason for not getting my order filled in its entirety."

"Our production line is suffering from an unexpected delay, and I hate to tie up your funds. They were wired back into your account even before I got here." He stood up, feeling closed in.

Drago followed, not even attempting to hide his disdain. "This is unfortunate. I was planning on introducing you to more clients." He placed his hands inside his suit pockets.

Cyrus was prepared. If the fucker decided to pull a fast one, he wasn't going to just stand around and wait to be blasted. Prudence made him stand down while he watched the vampire pull a cigar from his pocket. Drago flicked his gold lighter and lit up. In a manner of seconds, the room was filled with a chocolaty aroma.

"I apologize for this inconvenience. Once we're back in full production, I will contact you."

Drago nodded through a thick cloud of smoke. "Very well. Keep this in mind. My business alone is enough to keep your company going, not to mention the referrals I can send your way. Remember, a solid business is something you don't fuck with. Don't even think for one minute that I won't take my money elsewhere."

Cyrus heard the threat, but he chose to ignore it. It wasn't the place or time to get all worked up. If his dear old friend Pritchard had taught him anything, it was never to burn your bridges. He reached out a hand, but the vampire ignored him, his attention focused on the rings the smoke was forming.

"I appreciate your business." Cyrus didn't wait for the butler to show him to the door. Once outside, he let out a sigh he hadn't realized he was holding. It had gotten tense in there. For a moment, he thought they were going to go at it.

He moved fast down into the stairwell and out of the building to the street, where his car waited for him. Once inside, he tugged his tie off and stepped on the accelerator, his powerful exhaust system sent a cloud of dust in his wake. He took out his cell phone and dialed the facility. Rayce answered in one ring.

"Get me Harrow." Cyrus turned onto the main drag.

Harrow came to the phone right away. "Cy, what's up?"

"Meet me at Sardi's. I have some interesting information for you."

"I'll be there in fifteen minutes. Hang tight." The line went dead.

Clenching the steering wheel, Cyrus navigated toward the more bustling part of the city. For as long as he'd been connected to Tack, they'd never failed to do due diligence. None of their inquiries had turned up that Drago was an aristocratic vampire multimillionaire.

It looked like Cyrus' loaded to-do list just got longer. He wasn't happy about it, but this latest discovery wasn't something he could sweep under the rug.

He concentrated on finding a parking spot. The tourist population was a pain in the ass at any time of the day, and it seemed like they were all gathered in the vicinity of the restaurant. Finding a place to park would take a while, unless he didn't mind doling out fifty dollars for one of those tourist parking traps.

After circling several blocks, he decided that parting with the money wasn't a bad idea if it meant saving his sanity. He honked his horn at a parking attendant, who ran to remove the cone to the crowded parking structure.

Cyrus handed the crisp hundred dollar bill and got out of the car while the man whistled at his baby. "Don't block my car." He left the attendant staring with open appreciation at his car. Well, what could he say? His '69 Shelby was a head turner.

Sardi's was an institution and his secret indulgence. Their jumbo crab cakes were to die for, and even if food didn't appeal to him anymore, he still wanted to keep up the tradition. He and Lambert had frequented this place back when they'd started working for Pritchard, and it didn't hurt that they were on first-name basis with the maître d'. The moment Lucio spotted him, the short balding man waved him in and magically produced a corner table.

"Luc, how are those creaky knees?" They shook hands.

The older man sighed and rolled his eyes. "Still upright, aren't I?"

Cyrus pretended to scrutinize his friend and then laughed. "That you are. You're looking good, old man."

A smile lit up Lucio's face. "I can't complain. So what'll be for you? The usual?"

Cyrus nodded. The restaurant served wines for the pre- and post-theater patrons. Somehow, Lucio would rustle up a bottle of scotch for him. He glanced at the front door when it opened and Harrow walked in.

Raising his hand, he waited until Harrow spotted him and headed his way. Cyrus watched his friend's approach. Harrow had indeed come a long way. No longer uncertain, he walked and talked like someone who knew his worth. The thing was, the male was worth fucking millions thanks to Pritchard's wealth, and it couldn't be denied that the vampire deserved the money he'd inherited. He was a hard worker without an off switch. The man would work himself to death if the situation called for it.

"What's going on?" Harrow slid out of his leather jacket, slung it over the chair, and sat down. "Are we celebrating something, or you just hate the idea of being alone?" He laughed as he sat down. "How many times must I tell you that I don't roll that way?"

Lucio returned with his drink and then took Harrow's order.

Cyrus watched Harrow take in the restaurant's main attraction, hundreds of caricatures of celebrities that lined the wall of fame. "I'm surprised you haven't been to this place before."

Harrow gave a shallow laugh. "In my heyday, I was a struggling actor. Places like this weren't affordable." He continued to glance around, paying particular attention to one ethnic beauty's cartoon portrait.

Cyrus got back to business. "I went to see Drago tonight. You'll be surprised to learn that the man walks on the dark side, too." He shook his head at the memory of the meeting.

Harrow leaned forward and rested his arms on the table. "What are you talking about?"

"The man is a vampire. How I could have missed it before still bugs me."

"What the hell?" Harrow's voice rose.

Cyrus looked around. It was a good thing the noise level in the restaurant drowned out Harrow's voice. "Keep it quiet. Yes, he's a vampire, and I have a bad feeling about him."

Harrow didn't any waste time before chugging his drink. Once done, he set the glass down and waved for another. "You got a backup plan?"

Cyrus had known that question was coming. Ever since Harrow had taken over the reins of both the business and their group of freedom fighters, he was all about backup plans.

He thought about it for a moment. There was no point in jumping the gun. It was too early to tell what Drago was up to. It would've been great if Cyrus had known all along about his client's nature. If he had Rohnert's ability to read minds, he wouldn't have been deceived.

"Not yet. Let's sit tight and wait. Since we're dealing with an influential character, I think it would be a good idea to keep our relationship open. I've got a gut feeling that there's more to Drago than we know."

"What do you mean?"

"I've had enough interaction with mind-reading vampires to recognize their tendencies, and I'd bet my life that he was trying to read mine while I was there."

"You mean we're talking about a purebred bloodsucker here?"

"Yep. I suggest we get Rohnert involved in this."

"On it." Harrow took his cell phone from his jeans pocket. In a matter of seconds, Rohnert had answered the call.

Cyrus tuned out their rest of the conversation when his attention was momentarily captured by a woman making her way in their direction. He watched with interest as other patrons glanced up, fascinated by the tall, desirable female, her eyes hidden behind large sunglasses, making her way to a booth not too far from his. A disturbing but familiar voice greeted her, piquing his interest. From his position, Cyrus could stare or listen. He opted to shift in his seat until he was facing the opposite direction, then he signaled at Harrow to keep his voice down.

Trying his best to appear nonchalant, Cyrus inhaled the air around him, and her scent confirmed her vampire nature. Without the benefit of a visual, he had to rely on his eavesdropping ability to follow the conversation. After the initial greetings, following the ongoing chat became difficult, despite his keen hearing. Their voices had toned down once they settled down to business.

Did they sense he was listening? To answer this question, Cyrus tilted his head in their direction and found the woman staring at him. Although he hadn't seen her before, he had the distinct feeling that their paths had been moving in the same direction.

Saying she was beautiful didn't cover it. She had an ethereal aura about her that seemed to mesmerize everyone around her. Her aristocratic vibe reminded him of Isidora, except Issy possessed an intrinsic kindness. The female glaring at him was downright vicious.

Cyrus had no problem with the stare down. In fact, he was beginning to enjoy being on equal footing with some of the snooty vampires in circulation. This particular one had more nerve than the rest of the females he'd come across. She never batted an eyelash underneath her dark lenses.

As far as he was concerned, the room and its occupants were nonexistent while he tried to stare her down. It wasn't until he heard the recognizable voice, the one embedded in his brain like a worn microchip, that he broke eye contact with her. It was a voice he'd be able to identify with his eyes closed. Zane. Rage jacked up his system like fuel, screaming for release.

By then, Harrow had finished his phone call and was seeking Cyrus' attention. "Hey, why don't we get out of here?"

Cyrus snarled and jumped out of his chair. "No. I have a score to settle."

Harrow's firm hand was quick to restrain him. "Buddy, this place is crawling with humans."

The hell it was. He hadn't survived degradation and humiliation to leave now without getting his hands around the bastard's neck.

Cyrus glanced around and found some patrons watching him with curiosity, so he forced himself to sink back into his chair.

"Fuck," he muttered.

Harrow leaned closer. "What's going on?"

Cyrus was in no mood to give Harrow the 4-1-1. "Nothing."

"Nothing works you up like—" Harrow no doubt realized what had gotten Cyrus all riled up when Zane and his female companion emerged from the booth and exited the restaurant.

"Let's go." Cyrus pulled out a wad of cash and threw it on the table. Palming his Glock underneath his coat, he walked out, ignoring Lucio's protest that he hadn't stayed long enough. Once outside, he glanced left to right and took a whiff of the air to guide him to Zane.

"Where did they go?" Harrow's looked around. There was no trace of Zane or the woman who'd been with him.

Cyrus cursed. Hell, he'd been so close.

"We can split up." Harrow was still checking their immediate surroundings.

It took a lot for Cyrus not to scream. He ground his teeth together. His heart raced at the lost opportunity, but he knew his time would come. He could feel it in his gut. The bastard would die, and the last thing he'd see was Cyrus' face staring down at him.

"No. We need to go back to headquarters." Killing Zane was his personal vendetta. He'd have to go at it alone.

From the expression on Harrow's face, it was obvious he wanted to pursue the asshole as much as Cyrus did. However, given his state of mind, heading back to the headquarters was the best idea.

"Fine, we'll do it your way."

They walked in the direction of the parking lot, neither interested in talking.

"Sorry, bud." Harrow patted him on the back before they went their separate ways.

"Yeah, me, too."

Isidora had been sitting in the control room with Rayce for the better part of the night in the hopes of catching Cyrus when he returned. She must've fallen asleep, because the next thing she knew, the tech guy was nudging her awake.

"Issy, Cyrus' back."

She lifted her face from the desk and focused on the monitor. He looked quite stunning in his suit, despite the scowl on his face.

"I have to go," she said and gave Rayce a hug, one that put a big smile on his face.

"You're welcome. Come back again if you need anything." She heard him chuckle before the door closed behind her.

With hasty steps, she raced down the corridor, lifting the hem of her long skirt to quicken her pace. Several fighters nodded in her direction as they passed, but none were bold enough to say a word to her. From their general thoughts, she came to understand the unspoken code between the males in the facility. She was their boss' woman, even if it hadn't been made official. This brought a smile to her face, even though some of the guys were wondering whether it was Cyrus or Rick she preferred. Either way, she was out of reach because she was a purebred vampire—a member of the upper echelon.

She knew where Cyrus was headed without asking for Rayce's help. The male spent most of his waking hours in the training room, checking on the schedule, spending time with Sawyer, conducting training, or killing time. She heard the muffled sound of the punching bag even before she entered the room.

The sight that greeted her when she opened the door took her breath away. Cyrus had shed his expensive jacket and shirt to reveal his muscular body, and it gave her the opportunity to devour him with her eyes. Isidora drank in his magnificent form, wishing she could trail her fingers along the ridged chest muscles. His attention remained on the punching bag, oblivious to her presence.

Cyrus was going at it with recklessness she hadn't seen before. His mind raged with anger, and he was intent on doing damage to the equipment. It was so beautiful to behold his glorious physique and the determination in his every movement.

Her palm gripped the door handle until her knuckles turned white. Cyrus was too potent, and as much as she tried to keep her distance, the invisible pull between them kept on reeling her in. A tingling sensation radiated through her legs, making her sweat. He had warned her on several occasions, but she wasn't listening. She had followed strict rules all her life, and it was about time to follow her instincts. How could being with Cyrus be wrong when it felt so right?

The question burned in her until she realized that he had stopped and was watching her. "What are you doing here, Issy?"

She didn't miss that his tone lacked welcome. He stood rigid, waiting for her answer.

"I wanted to share some good news with you," Issy said, feeling her face redden at being caught staring.

Cyrus drew in a sharp breath before he walked over to the desk. With marked weariness, he dropped onto the chair. "Tell me about it." There was still no hint of welcome in his voice, which made Isidora wonder if she'd made a mistake seeking him out.

Who else could she go to? The rest of the women were mated, and she'd hate to take precious time away from their men. Cheryl, the nurse, had more emotional baggage than Isidora could begin to fathom. Rick was too busy with the medical demands on his time. Cyrus was the only one left, and he was the person she most wanted to share everything with.

She followed him to the desk but didn't sit, blurting out her news before she lost her nerve. "Rohnert informed me that the Council has voted to have me sit in one of their meetings. It had something to do with filling vacant Council seats."

At the very least, Isidora had expected an acknowledgement, if not some form of encouragement. Instead, Cyrus pounded his fist on the desk while his face hardened into a formidable mask. It was out of character, and to be honest, frightening.

Issy blinked back the tears that threatened to spill. "I thought you'd be happy for me," she said, trying to control the quavering in her voice.

Cyrus huffed as his eyes raked her face with a hard stare. "I am."

She turned on her heel, wanting to get out of there fast. It had been a mistake to seek him out. Cyrus didn't care.

She almost made it to the door before Cyrus' arms circled her waist and pivoted her, pinning her against his rock-hard body.

"Let me go." The words came out pinched, and his proximity cross-circuited her brain.

The warmth of his breath caressed her cheek. "I can't. I won't. I'm sorry." His lips descended on hers.

Hard and harried, Cyrus' tongue probed, demanding a response. Isidora complied, returning his kisses with the fury he had stirred within her. She was angry and hurt, but she couldn't deny her excitement that he had pursued her this time. There might still be some hope for them both.

Zane released a long sigh the moment Bretania stepped out of his car. It wasn't easy to be in an enclosed space with a mind-reading vampire. It made him edgy to know she'd take whatever she could get from him. Chancing upon Cyrus and Harrow in the restaurant had fucked up his plans, but that may have been a good thing.

He loathed the prospect of reporting to Bretania, especially when her request was for the exact location of Tack's operation. Then there was Cyrus' unexpected appearance at the restaurant. Sardi's had been a close call. He hadn't expected Cyrus to be in the same establishment, let alone at the same time that he was meeting Bretania. She had been ready to start a fight back at the restaurant, even in the midst of all those humans. What had happened to the sacred decree to keep their existence on the down-low?

It was obvious the woman had thrown caution to the wind when she engaged in the stare-down with Cyrus. Her questions afterward had proven she had no idea that the people under her nose where the same group she had been tracking down without success.

Running away hadn't been a part of Zane's makeup before. He'd thrived on confrontations in the past, but his current disability made him tuck tail and run. So much had changed since his short captivity in the hands of

Harrow Gates. He had developed a pseudo-conscience, as well as a permanent limp, and a dreadful longing for a human female who wanted nothing to do with him.

Blame it on his DNA—his family tree was rooted in greed, carnage, and evil. His dead grandfather Goran, the king of all that was dark and malevolent, had stamped their future with doom. Demetrius, his father and the son of Goran and Melissa, had hated his existence because of his father. His mother's affection had done very little for Demetrius. Then Melissa, the headmistress of the Harem, had been sent to her death by his grandfather as part of his quest for supremacy. It was a good thing that Goran's rule had met its demise at the hands of Rohnert.

Nowadays, loneliness was his one constant companion, a permanent dark cloud hovering over him. Ever since he had been introduced to the concepts of kindness and compassion, his life had taken an abrupt plunge into confusion. These days, it was difficult to separate the need to avenge his father's death from the nagging desire to seek forgiveness from Cheryl, who had saved his life on more than one occasion.

He glanced at his rearview mirror and noticed a dark car trailing him. This was the problem with allying with people who didn't trust him, and vice versa. If Bretania had hopes of finding his hideout, she was in for a disappointment. Then again, he'd made many enemies. It could be one of the bastards he'd pissed off in the past instead.

Zane took a sharp left into one of the dark, deserted alleys, turned off his headlights, and waited. He kept the engine running and checked the rearview mirror once again. The car was at the mouth of the alley. Doors opened and several men stepped out with powerful toys. From what he could see, the guns they held were automatics.

Right. Zane was so not ready to die. He drew his gun and braced his hands on the steering wheel when the first gunfire erupted. The deafening sound of thud, thud, thud hit his bulletproof car—each projectile hitting the metal with a loud clang. He felt each vibration and flinched. These bastards were messing up his toy. It was his baby and had been a gift from his father. Their nonstop firing was sure to attract attention. Zane continued to bide his time.

When they stopped to reload, it gave Zane a short window in which to get out of his car. He jumped to the roof of the nearest establishment, expecting a barrage of firepower the moment he landed, but it seemed like the distant sound of sirens had spooked his attackers. Quick to return to their car, they fled the scene as if nothing had happened.

Zane seized this opportunity to hobble back to his car before the cops arrived. He fired the accelerator and drove away. A quick glance around told him that the interior had held up well, even if the exterior had sustained substantial damage. He blazed through connecting alleys, narrowly missing several bystanders. It was better than to risk getting in a tussle with the NYPD.

When Zane reached his townhouse, he activated the garage opener and pulled in. On inspection, the rear window, though ruined, hadn't shattered. Of course, it was half an inch thick. If those assholes had used armor piercing bullets, it would've been a different story. No doubt they'd used Dangeran ammunition, hoping to kill him, but they hadn't been expecting to find him in a bullet-proof car.

Damn it. Now he'd need another form of transportation until his car could be restored. Bretania had better watch her back from now on. If it was she who had ordered the hit, then it was a whole new ballgame.

Zane hurried back to his place and found Hill lounging on the couch. "Gather up some reliable men. I have an assignment for you."

There was no hesitation whatsoever from the human. "Right away. Anything else?"

"Yeah. Take out life insurance. You might need it." It wasn't a joke. Who knew what would happen in the coming days?

Cyrus realized he had gotten carried away. He was an emotional bundle of shit after sighting Zane and getting Issy's news was just icing on the cake. Even so, he didn't regret the kiss. He'd keep doing it over and over, except it wasn't fair to take out his frustrations on her. There was no doubt in his mind that sex with him wouldn't be pleasurable at the moment. His murderous mood might scare her away.

When he looked into her eyes, he found understanding there. With Issy's hands twined behind his neck and her delicious mouth providing warmth to his, everything felt right. She belonged with him. God, he swore her gaze would melt him into puddle. How could he resist her any longer?

His hands slackened their hold on her body, and he pulled away. "I'm so sorry. I shouldn't have kissed you."

Isidora was quick to answer. "I'm not sorry. Don't resist, Cyrus."

Mere attraction paled in comparison to his actual feelings for her. Maybe it was best to let her think this was all physical and nothing more. "You're talking about sex," he rasped. Without thinking it through, he grabbed her hand and pulled her to the door. "Let's get this over with."

Cyrus didn't wait for an answer but dragged Isidora down the hallway, to the elevator, and straight to his room. He didn't let her go until the door was locked behind them. She took a few steps away, wringing her hands.

"I don't want it unless you do."

He turned and gave her a hard stare. "Look at this." Cyrus pointed to the massive tenting in his pants. "Does it look like I don't want you?"

Issy looked down at the hard evidence. A small smile tugged at the corner of her lips. Their eyes met, and the blush that tinted her cheeks made him want to crush her with his body.

"I—I, you're right."

In two big strides, he seized her waist, holding her close. "You're not going to like how I make love to my women."

Her answer came in a throaty rush. "I'll take you any way I can get you."

Maybe he was just a change of pace for her—a blue-collar vampire, a novelty. "Why?"

"Because I'm falling—"

"No, you're not. You don't even know the first thing about a relationship. You've been cooped up, told what to do your entire life. You have no idea—"

"You're right. I've been sheltered all my life. Everything I do is examined under a microscope and subject to parental approval. I didn't have the freedom you enjoyed. Now that I'm on my own, allow me to make my own decisions, according to my feelings. Don't you dare tell me what to and how I should feel."

His body jerked, and his fangs elongated at her defiance. Something about the way Issy spoke made him see her in a different light. She might have been sheltered, but the woman in front of him was determined. Isidora knew what she wanted, and he was it. The thought made him harder.

"Damn it, Issy. I can't do it." *And I'm fuckin' lying through my teeth.*

"Yes, you can."

He raked his fingers through his hair in frustration. "I don't know if I can be gentle with you. You're beautiful, and you need proper loving—not a quickie, which is all I can give right now. Damn, Issy. Aren't you at least bit scared of what I might do to you?"

She shook her head, adding to his frustration.

"What if I fuck this up?"

"Slow or rough will work for me."

A lick of heat went through him. "Damn it. What do you want from me?"

"Nothing you're not willing to give."

That was it. He was going to crack. "This is all I can give you." Cyrus backed her up against the wall, his hand moving up her thighs. The delicious friction of his calloused palm over her silky skin sent shivers down his spine. Even with her clothes separating them, he could feel her ache for him, reacting to his light touch and the pressure of his palms on her bare skin. Her tiny waist was just as delicate as he'd imagined, and her skin was the color of alabaster, inviting and perfect.

He felt Issy shudder as he moved his hands up and down the curve of her body.

"This might not be what you're expecting," he whispered, losing ground.

"Stop talking. We're in this together." She moaned in his ear.

Pressed against the wall, Isidora lifted her legs, anchoring them around his waist—an invitation he could no longer refuse. Her chest heaved with her erratic breathing, and she arched her body to meet his touch. The smoldering desire in her eyes fueled his lust.

Cyrus lifted her skirt, intending to show her a good time, and Issy began fumbling with his zipper. He caught her wrists. "No, baby. This is all about you. Let me pleasure you for now."

Issy's eyes went wild. "But you need this, too," she said.

A flashback of ugly memories came to him, enough to dampen his mood. "Damn it, Issy. I can't."

"Cyrus, we can work on this together."

He shook his head. "All I want is to hold you and see the expression on your face when you come."

Sadness crept over her beautiful face. "Then take me to bed so I can touch you."

With Issy's legs still straddling his waist, Cyrus walked to his bed. "This skirt has to go," he said and pulled it down past her ankles.

Taking both her feet, Cyrus skimmed his mouth along each one, letting his tongue touch her soft skin in a sweet caress. When he trailed light kisses along her skin, he was rewarded Issy's toes curled, and her moans were like an electric current, waking him from a long slumber.

"Cyrus, you're killing me." Her voice was thick with emotion.

"I want to take my time."

All that was left was the lacy number that covered her. There was an immense feeling of possession that swelled within him when he pulled her body closer. He eyed the thin material while the delicious thought kept playing inside his head that she was his, and they were going to be together for the long haul. Idiotic, but he allowed himself to believe the lie.

Issy responded to him by opening her legs. Her body gyrated with pleasure when his teeth tugged on the material of her panties. Cyrus paused for a few seconds, letting his hands explore her flat stomach and the incredible curves of her body. Issy's moans lifted him, making his body hum at her reactions.

He seized the opportunity to lick the folds that were peeking through her thong.

She groaned. "Take it off, please."

Cyrus tore off her thong with his teeth with vicious impatience, then he grazed his mouth against her sweet skin, letting her enjoy the warmth of his breath and the firmness of his tongue. Issy rewarded him with shudders of pleasure. When the shredded piece of what used to be her thong was tossed on the floor, he unleashed his inner animal and began his assault.

He glided his tongue in, teasing, prodding, and licking. Issy responded by running her hands along her body while her thighs tightened around his head. At every chance he got, he stole glimpses at her as she worked her hands on her breasts.

There was no hiding it. Issy was wet for him. The thought made him growl, and she pulled on his hair.

Cyrus continued to dart his tongue in and out until he felt her tighten around him.

"That's it baby, wrap me up."

He picked up the pace, tonguing her wet walls. Her moans of satisfaction were fever-inducing, and he worked harder to please her. Cyrus shifted his position and placed a finger inside her, applying pressure until her groans graduated to an outright scream of ecstasy. He added another finger, and every thrust was rewarded by her sounds of pleasure as her fingers dug into the flesh of his shoulders, gripping harder when she neared her climax.

"I—I'm coming." Her body squirmed and shook as she exploded in a cry of pleasure.

"Come Issy, come."

Perspiration broke out on his forehead. He kept at it, enjoying the satisfaction of watching her ride her high.

They were both drenched in sweat by the time she surfaced from her euphoria. When she opened her eyes, he saw contentment there. It was the bliss he'd been dying to feel all along. With tenderness, Isidora kissed his face.

"Thank you," she whispered.

Cyrus smiled and let the happiness he'd found in her guide him. "My pleasure." He kissed her lips to seal the sweet deal.

Rohnert waited until the last of the Elders and their invited guests had settled before he addressed the congregation. It being a formal gathering, all the Council members had arrived in their finest robes. What was more important was that their behavior exuded peace and hope. The candidates had been instructed to keep this function under wraps, attend in their finest garments, and bring their significant others.

"As we gather here tonight, I wish to welcome our guests to this meeting, where we will welcome the new members of our Council."

Murmurs of disbelief rippled through the room. They came from the unsuspecting inductee themselves, who had been under the impression that they were merely visitors. After a rigorous background check had been conducted by Rohnert, Serena, and Icarus, the candidates for the coveted position were chosen based on their bloodlines, integrity, and contributions to the vampire race.

Rohnert dared not meet the questioning eyes of those he knew on a more personal level. He soaked in their emotional reactions and knew that while some felt undeserving, two in particular had not expected such an illustrious position.

He raised a hand to quiet everyone down. "We're ushering in an era of change. It's about time we let go of some old traditions and adapt to the ever-changing world around us. This induction will be different to those held in the past." He glanced at Harrow, who looked like he had been struck by an eighteen wheeler. "We've diversified our selection process by including a male who is not qualified by birth. He is nonetheless deserving of the position. This decision was based on his courage, dedication, and leadership. Let me start this induction process by introducing the first of our newest members.

"Ladies and gentlemen of the Council, I'm pleased to introduce a fine gentleman, whom I also happen to call friend, Harrow Gates." Rohnert smiled.

From where he was sandwiched between Jordan and another female, Harrow stood up with reluctance amid warm applause.

"Would you like to say a word?" Rohnert grinned, proud of his good friend.

"Damn. You blindsided me," Harrow said before bowing with grace.

Rohnert spoke above the din of laughter that followed that comical response. "Do you have anything more profound to say?"

Harrow removed his sunglasses, gave a sideway glance at a beaming Jordan, then took a deep breath. "This is an honor." He cleared his throat. "I promise to give everything in me to uphold the goals and interests of our race."

That short statement was met with loud applause as he acknowledged everyone with a wave.

Once people had settled down, Rohnert continued. "The next inductee is going to be the youngest member of our Council. If the basis of our decision was birthright alone, she would be a slam dunk. But this female had proven herself worthy because of her resilient nature in the face of adversity. She is of noble blood, raised in accordance with the dictates of our race, yet she is most comfortable aiding those in need and working alongside medical personnel to save lives every day. Let me present to you, Isidora, daughter of Iden and Chandra."

Issy rose to her feet. Rohnert watched her pale skin blush, but she kept her head held high. Cyrus sat next to her, which wasn't a surprise. What did shock Rohnert was the turmoil that was raging within Cyrus. The man was going through a multitude of emotions, bouncing from fear to pride, and then worry, doubt, and tension. Rohnert had known all along that these two had something going on, but Cyrus' appearance today cemented the fact in everyone's eyes.

He relegated his thoughts to the task at hand. "Isidora, do you have something you wish to say?"

Her sharp intake of break was followed by a loud exhalation. Then she smiled with a touch of melancholy. "I wish my parents were here to see this."

Her heartfelt declaration sobered the entire organization, especially those who had been familiar with her parents. Issy didn't offer anything else. She sat down and buried her face in Cyrus' chest. He, in turn, began whispering in her ear.

Rohnert went through the motions of introducing the next two inductees, Desider and Tiber, in a cloudy haze. His mind was glued on the weight of Isidora's words. They were both pining for the people they loved. How he wished Shelly was present, guiding him, loving him. Hot angry tears burned his eyes while he continued with the ceremony. It became unbearable as each minute ticked by and memories of Shelly still haunted him.

Sensing his internal battle, Icarus stood up and took over the bestowal of the Council medallion to each new member. Rohnert hung back and reined in his emotions until he could no longer control the grief, and he excused himself. He retreated to his chamber, ignoring Gentry's concerned inquiry.

Once alone in the confines of his room, he let go of the tears. Before he knew it, he heard a purposeful knock on the door. Rohnert caught the thoughts of Harrow, someone he didn't mind seeing him in this deplorable state.

"Come in." His voice croaked, and he buried his face in his hands in shame.

The approaching footsteps were light but determined. A warm hand patted his shoulder. "It got kinda intense there, huh?"

Rohnert nodded, thankful Harrow did not ask how he felt—because at the moment, he was feeling homicidal.

"I'm glad you're letting it out. This is all you can do right now."

Rohnert threw his head back and laughed. "I'm itching to kill, too."

Harrow took a step back. "Bro, I hope you're not serious."

Sure he was, but where could he direct his hatred? Goran was dead. Shelly would never come back. He angrily wiped away his tears with the sleeve of his robe. "I want to get out of here. I need to forget."

Harrow's eyes narrowed. "Well, since I'm now an official Council member, I think we have a good reason to celebrate. The guys are out in the hallway waiting."

A party was not his idea for ridding himself of his sorrows, but what the hell. Harrow and Isidora had every reason to celebrate, and he wasn't going to hold them back by moping around.

"Sure. Let me get out of this robe. I'll meet you outside."

Again, Harrow narrowed his eyes. Rohnert knew what the vampire was thinking. Damn Tor and his big mouth, divulging his purging practices to their leader. He laughed at this thought while he freed himself from the heavy robe and proceeded to the bathroom.

Rohnert was the highest ranking vampire in the Council, yet he was subject to Harrow's leadership in their little enclave at Tack Enterprises. He was fine with it. Whatever. There was no one he would rather have watching his back.

With a heavy heart, he pulled out the dull dagger from inside the drawer and clenched his right fist. Rohnert made a short clean slice on his inner forearm, drawing blood. He glanced at his reflection in the mirror when the first drop landed on the immaculate sink. Numbness crept in, and he took a deep breath.

"I'm so sorry, Shells," he whispered, not knowing what else to say.

"You've been real quiet." Issy spoke above the noise inside the bouncing club.

Cyrus tore his eyes away from the group of five vampires circling two human females on the far side of the room. Man, he was being an asshole. Instead of being happy for her, he'd been moping about the situation. He was ecstatic for her, but this promotion to one of the highest seats meant she would be away from him. Issy would be under someone else's protection, and that was a flat-out bummer.

"I'm just distracted." Sure. What a convenient excuse for brooding.

"I'm trying not to read your mind, but you have to help me here." Issy took his hand and squeezed.

He looked away, but he kept their hands twined. Her touch grounded him. The woman made him think of the things he wanted to do with her, but dark memories kept hovering over him.

"Cy, I know what you're thinking. We can work on it together."

The loud thumping of the bass added to the tension building inside him. He changed the subject. "Have you ever thought of getting a bodyguard?"

Issy's smile in response dazzled him. "I thought you'd never ask."

He might as well do the job, since letting Issy go out on her own would kill him. If Harrow and Rohnert agreed to it, he wouldn't mind stretching himself to the limit. Cyrus would rather take on the responsibility instead of assigning a newbie who had no idea what the role entailed. Yeah, what exactly did guarding an Elder involve?

Before he could voice his concerns, Issy was already waving to get Rohnert's attention. The vampire raised his eyes from the drink he'd been nursing. Cyrus knew the weight his friend was carrying and felt helpless because there was nothing he or anyone could do.

"You mentioned we could have a personal guard assigned to us. I want mine to be Cyrus."

Rohnert's response came swift and easy. "I think you've made a perfect choice, Issy."

"Thank you." Issy's voice sounded earnest.

Touched, Cyrus pulled her into an embrace. "If you ever disregard your safety under my watch, know that you will face my wrath," he whispered, just for her to hear.

Instead of acting annoyed, she offered a smile that dripped with promise. "Thanks for assuming the position."

He jerked up at the double entendre. "You're something else."

Issy blew into his ear. "There's no one else I'd rather have next to me twenty-four-seven."

The warmth of her breath made him shudder, and his circuits began firing. "You better not do that here in public." He turned to see Harrow and Jordan watching them with interest. "Why don't you two mind your own business and quit watching us?"

Harrow smirked. "And miss an unfolding love story? No, sir."

"Shut it, Gates." The duo laughed then began in a private conversation amongst themselves.

Cyrus grunted in irritation. He took a quick gulp of his scotch and looked across the room. The group of five vampires was missing. He shot a silent warning to Rohnert, who in turn looked at him.

"You're sure about this?" Rohnert was on his feet right away.

Harrow and Jordan glanced up, catching on. Cyrus nodded. They were outnumbered five to three, and there was no way he'd let Harrow and Rohnert deal with five vampires on their own.

"We can help," Issy offered.

He squeezed Issy's hand. "Baby—"

Thank God Rohnert took over, or it would have been hell trying to convince Issy to leave. "Jordan, take Issy home now. We're going out to check on something."

Jordan was fast on her feet. "Let's go," she said and grabbed Issy's hand.

The women left, despite Issy's nonstop protests. Cyrus got up and felt for his gun. It had been a long time since he'd had the thrill of stalking troublemakers. He went to the darkened patch that led to the restrooms. Farther down the hallway was the emergency exit. Harrow was right behind him, with Rohnert bringing up the rear. Tracking the sound around him, he pressed his ear to ladies room door and waited.

Nothing. He went to the men's room, but the place was empty, too.

"Ready for some fun?" Cyrus kicked open the exit door and wasn't in the least bit surprised when the alarm didn't sound.

"Preparation is the name of the game." Harrow came up alongside him, and they found the group in the alley, still haranguing the two females.

Judging by the wave of fear emanating from the cornered women, it didn't take a brainiac to know a decisive action had to be taken.

"Hey, assholes. What do you think you're doing?" Cyrus asked, his lips peeled away from his fangs.

Guns engaged in a matter of seconds while the shrieks and screams of the frightened women echoed in the stillness of the night. One glance at their weapons made Cyrus pause, but he had to act fast. He jumped up to avoid the first sling of bullets from the automatics, and Rohnert and Harrow deflected the incoming rounds with their Kalimetal.

Cyrus latched on to the wall like a cat, hanging on for dear life, and figured out his next move. He scaled the two-story wall, landed on the roof, and began firing on the men below without giving it a second thought. He had nine bullets in the chamber, and he knew better than to waste any of them.

Without mercy, he took out three in a snap while Rohnert and Harrow finished off the other two. The inevitable process of disintegration started, and the fireworks lit up the darkened alley.

"Happy fourth, assholes." Cyrus holstered his gun.

The screaming continued, attracting lookie-loos to their location. While Rohnert worked on cleansing the memories of the females, Cyrus jumped down to assess the damage. Aside from the ashes that littered the ground, the weapons of the deceased vampires were the only evidence left behind. It didn't take a second look to know that the weapons were Tack creations.

The distant wail of the sirens sounded. "Get the guns, and let's get out of here." He and Harrow gathered up the weapons while Rohnert tried to calm down the women.

With the witnesses' memories scrubbed clean, the men headed for the opposite end of the alley, away from the incoming squad cars. There was much to learn about how their guns had managed to end up in the hands of civilian vampires. The whole thing stank, and Cyrus was intent on finding out who the stinker was.

Back at the facility, Cyrus pounded the table with his fist. "What the fuck is going on?"

Harrow shook his head. "I have no clue."

"I have a feeling that some of the clients we've dealt with in the past are selling the guns to the public." Rohnert paced.

Not good. Not good at all. Cyrus turned toward the bar and grabbed the first bottle he could get his hands on, taking a quick swig. "What I need to know is who the bastard is."

"Welcome to the club," Harrow quipped.

"I'll put a trace on the unique number on each gun and see what comes up. I'll get to the bottom of this mess." He downed more of the bottle's contents and flopped down on the chair.

"I'll see what I can do to help." Harrow leaned in and took the booze from him. After a quick pull that left his eyes watery, he continued. "I'm going to have Rayce go over the transaction records and contact Leo to see if he can help."

The intercom buzzed, and Rayce's voice came on the speaker.

"Speak of the devil," Rohnert said.

"Boss, I think you need to get into the little girls' room quick." Rayce voice sounded too frantic to ignore.

The trio ran out of the I-room, and they found Jordan, Tor, and Allison racing in the direction of the bedroom Gail shared with Liv.

"What the hell?" Harrow ran faster to catch up.

Jordan and Tor were separating the girls by the time they reached the room. Jordan's voice was sharper than usual. "Hey, hey. No, girls. You can't do that."

"But, Mom, she's just going to check the vein in my neck," Gail said, her tone filled with innocence.

Liv blinked, seeming confused. "Gail said it's okay."

"No, no, Livvy. We don't check each other's veins here." Harrow managed to get the words out without making it sound like a big deal.

The little girl's lips began to tremble, and she blinked one too many times. "But she smells good."

Allison stepped in and placed an arm around the little one. "Liv, let's take a walk, and I will tell you a story."

"Can I come?" Gail pleaded to her adoptive mother.

Jordan's face blanched. "Why don't I take you swimming so we can talk also?"

Gail pouted and watched Tor and Allison hustle Liv out of the room. Then she turned back to Jordan and Harrow. "What is wrong with Liv and me playing? This is the first time I've have a playmate, and you're making a big deal about it."

This was too much for Cyrus. How had all the adults missed this one important detail? Liv was a child and a vampire who knew nothing about restraint or quelling her desire for blood.

If it hadn't been for Rayce's vigilance, Gail would've gone through the same thing he had. Cyrus left the room while Harrow and Jordan reasoned with their seven year old, and he found Rohnert leaning against the wall.

"This is messed up," Cyrus said, parking himself next to Rohnert.

"It's my fault. Why didn't I think of the repercussions of having little ones around Gail?"

That was Rohnert, ready to blame himself for every bad thing that happened. "It's not your fault, and you know it. We're all in this together."

Rohnert didn't look like he'd heard him. "I have to speak with Sawyer and warn him."

Cyrus jumped in. "Let me talk to him." The child was different and a bit on the sensitive side.

Rohnert didn't answer right away, which could mean he was still trying to grasp the recent development. It suited Cyrus just fine. Although Rohnert was a good guy, he had too much shit happening in his life. He felt responsible for every goddamn thing in the world.

"Give me an update, will ya?"

Cyrus nodded and turned to leave. He knew where he was headed next.

"Because if it won't work, I can take him to a childless couple."

Cyrus whipped his head fast and almost snarled. "No. The kid will be fine. Trust me."

Rohnert smiled unexpectedly. "I do." He left before Cyrus could say anything.

Cyrus jogged down to the stairwell until he reached the next floor. He could hear the television from the outside. It was on History Channel. Not his first choice, but hey, to each his own.

He rapped his knuckles on the door, and Sawyer answered right away. "Yes?"

"Boy, we need to have a little talk." That didn't come out right.

The young vampire's eyes widened. "Did I do something wrong?"

"No, it's another thing."

The door opened wider. "If you're talking about the birds and the bees, I know all about it already."

"Are you mocking me, child?" He chuckled and slapped the boy on the shoulder. "Sit down so we can talk."

After Sawyer closed the door, he sat on the couch next to Cyrus. Though still a bit cautious around him, the boy seemed more relaxed these days after spending more time with him in the training room.

"If I didn't do anything and we're not having a weird talk about sex, then what is it?"

Cyrus wasn't one to skirt around an important subject. "You know we value human lives here like we value our own, right?"

Sawyer nodded.

"We make sure every vampire has an ample supply of the blood of their choice. That being said, I want to make sure you are aware about the rules about taking humans." For a young kid, Sawyer seemed much, much older and very offended by his words.

"I know my place, sir. I wouldn't dare touch a human or vampire. I like the sterility of a blood bag over sucking direct from the source," Sawyer said with a straight face.

Cyrus couldn't help but laugh until his sides hurt. When his laughter ebbed, he found Sawyer watching him with a strained expression. "What's wrong?"

"I'm under the impression that we are not wanted here."

"That is not true. What gave you that absurd idea? Hell, I want you here."

Sawyer didn't look like he'd heard Cyrus' words. "I feel like we're being judged because of what our father did." The earnestness with which the boy declared his concern touched Cyrus' heart.

He took a deep breath, not certain he was the right person to talk about these things. If he wasn't, who would be? Rohnert, with all his infinite wisdom, was still fighting the demons of his wife's death and disappearance.

"I'm not going to lie to you. Your father did some horrible things that still give me nightmares. He condemned many to death, killed his kin, and stripped Rohnert of his rightful place . . ." He stopped when Sawyer began to look like he was going to throw up.

The boy heaved and cupped his mouth, taking quick breaths. Cyrus awkwardly started rubbing his back until the dry-heaving receded. Sawyer gazed up at him with glassy eyes. "Please continue."

Without even noticing it, Cyrus squeezed the boy's shoulder. "It's not easy to wave these things away as if they didn't happen. But I can assure you, Rohnert wouldn't have taken in you and your sister if it hadn't been for the best."

"Do you hate me?"

Cyrus was taken aback by the straight question. He shook his head. "The blood that runs in your veins isn't just your father's. I'm betting on your mother's good side."

That made Sawyer smile. "Thank you." He looked down at his hands. "What prompted this conversation?"

He stared at the boy and whistled. "Are you sure you're thirteen years old and not fifty?"

Another smile. "My mother told me that my human grandfather is a journalist. I guess it runs in the genes."

Cyrus smirked. This young vampire was too damn smart for his own good. "Liv tried to talk Gail into testing her veins."

Horror and anger were obvious in Sawyer's face, and he cupped his mouth once more. It didn't take long before he regained his composure. "What did you do?"

"Well, they were separated. Allison and Tor are explaining things to Livvy right now, while Harrow and Jordan are talking to Gail."

"Gail doesn't know about . . . us?"

Cyrus shook his head. "I have no idea if they will ever tell her. It's kind of difficult, with how she ended up with us."

"What happened?"

"It's not my business to talk about it. Let's just say we're not at liberty to tell her until her parents are ready to give her the whole story."

Sawyer turned silent, prompting Cyrus to study the boy. He was young for his age, whether vampire or human, yet he spoke and reasoned in a mature way—something Cyrus hadn't seen in the younger generations lately.

"Is it okay if I hang out with her?"

"As long as you can promise me that you'll keep her safe."

Palms on his heart, Sawyer made a vow. "I promise. I'll even watch my sister around her until she gets used to the idea."

"That's my boy." He tousled the boy's hair. "Now tell me about your mother."

As Sawyer launched into a series of stories about Hope, his mother, Cyrus leaned back against the cushion and closed his eyes, nodding and prompting the boy to talk more. Even with the little time he'd had with his mother, Sawyer had enough memories to last him a lifetime. Cyrus couldn't even trace his birth mother.

Cyrus continued to listen, but his mind had drifted to his hazy childhood before he'd landed in the caring home of the woman he regarded as his mother. Too bad it had been cut short.

A light rap sounded from outside the door. "Cyrus, can you take me to the winter formal?" Linda asked. With the carpeting inside his bedroom, it made it impossible for his foster sister to wheel herself in. Removing the darn carpet was the next on his list of projects for their foster mother, Elaine.

"Sure, booger-face. Didn't that cute boy ask you?" Cyrus pushed his chair away from his desk and walked to the door, where Linda always parked her wheelchair. He didn't bother asking if she wanted to come in, since Linda always wanted to spend time with him. Cyrus lifted her up, placed her on the edge of the bed, and sat next to her.

"I'm not a booger-face, and no, Simon didn't ask me. So if you don't mind going with me, I'll be your slave for the rest of my life."

He was on his last year in high school, while Linda was a junior. Cyrus knew why she was asking him. He'd overheard her telling her friend that no one would ask a crippled girl. Also, since he was graduating soon, this might be her one chance to go. He thought it was brave of her to risk being embarrassed by taking her foster brother rather than missing out.

"You can start by shining my shoes if you want me to go. And I will need breakfast in bed for two weeks. And—"

"That's a lot already!" Linda punched him on the arm.

"I'm not even close to done yet. You have to clean the bathroom, scoop up the dog poop, and wash my car."

Linda laughed, and her sad eyes were twinkling for a change. "You don't even own a car."

"That's right. Well, you can polish my skateboard." He nudged her playfully.

"Will it bother you that we can't even dance?" All of a sudden the smile was gone, replaced by the anxious expression he knew too well. Being born with useless legs had hindered her from doing the things most teenagers did. God knew that he and their foster mom had done their best to include Linda in every activity.

"Hey, who said I can dance? I think we'll have a good time, whether we dance or not. I will even take you shopping so you can pick out your dress."

"But you're saving your money for the trade tech."

"I want you to go in a new dress. We'll even take pictures. Just make sure you clean up well. No boogers allowed."

They were laughing hard when they heard a loud thud coming from the next room. Cyrus rushed out of his bedroom to find Elaine unconscious on the floor.

"Mom!" He tried to shake her.

"Cy, what's going on?" Linda screamed from the other room.

"Mom, Mom, Mom." He kept calling her. No response. This can't be happening.

"Sir, sir, wake up. You're having a nightmare."

Cyrus jumped up from the bed and found Sawyer staring down at him with a worried expression. He looked around and couldn't even remember how he'd gotten there.

"Are you okay? You were calling your mom, a lot." The boy asked, looking frightened.

"I fell asleep?" Cyrus ran his fingers through his short hair.

"We were talking, and then you were out. I left you to sleep because you looked exhausted. I heard you mumbling before you started screaming."

Cyrus shook his head, dispelling the remnants of the God-forsaken dream. "I'm sorry. I'd best be on my way," he said and stood up.

Sawyer followed him to the door. "I feel as lost as you do sometimes."

He looked over his shoulder at the boy. "Then I guess we're two peas in a pod."

Aemerria shifted her gaze from Gastarius toward the darkness that surrounded them. She inhaled the fresh air around her. The information the old diviner had provided didn't faze her at all. It wasn't a surprise that the people he'd trusted had betrayed him.

"I should've seen it coming." Gastarius ran his withered fingers along his beard in frustration. "I have lost my touch."

Sadness swept her entire being at his proclamation. It wasn't Gastarius' fault. He'd watched over their race for a long, long time. With the rapid increase in their population and vampires being created daily, his powers were stretched thin. Mistakes happened, and oversights were inevitable. In fact, Aemerria was surprised it had taken dear Gastarius this long before a slipup occurred.

"You're tired, my friend." She placed a calming hand on his shoulder.

When Gastarius closed his eyes, Aemerria did the same. Instead of calming, her senses plunged down to the deepest crevices of her long-forgotten soul. The soul she'd given up when her self-control failed her.

"You have to learn to let go of the past," Gastarius said. "Don't carry the burden of your ignorance."

Even though decades had passed, the memories still stuck with her. The guilt, though dulled by the passage of time, continued to haunt her.

"I have purged my soul for many years." She drew a sharp breath. "But why does it feel like it just happened yesterday?"

Gastarius leaned on her. "Because you haven't made peace with your mistakes. You've changed, and I think this is your chance to redeem yourself."

Every being, whether human or vampire, kept secrets—secrets that had the ability to create havoc and misery. Perhaps shame, fear, and cowardliness had prompted her desire to lock the truth away. When the need to face the truth became unbearable, this was the time when the true battle began.

"The truth shall set you free," she murmured to herself.

The irrelevance of fate had diminished any interest she had in committing righteous acts for a long time. She had been venerated for being one of the strongest figures in the thinning line of Shamans. Greed and personal aspirations had weakened their numbers. Another powerful priestess had committed blasphemy, and it was up to Aemerria to do the cleanup.

"Consider this your coming-out party. A debut."

Was it her, or did she notice a slight smile breaking through the corner of Gastarius' mouth?

Aemerria had been outcast once before. As a young apprentice with no memory of her past, she had killed without remorse. Ocean's quantities of blood and misery had been shed in her name. Back then, her thirst and the voices in her head were the only things that mattered. She hadn't listened to reason and had ignored the cries of her victims as her rampage continued. One wrong choice on her part had severed ties with the people who had trusted her. Aemerria had been changed by destiny, and her lapse of judgment had brought consequences that had dislocated her once rock-solid confidence. Through it all, Gastarius had remained her supporter. He'd continued to mentor her while she licked her wounds.

The torture of the memories surfaced anew and overwhelmed her. Her eyes, a dull myriad of colors, flickered like a slow, dying candle.

"Why do you torment yourself with the past you can't change?" Gastarius stood up from his battered chair and walked the length of the small room.

"Because these memories define me. If I let them go, I might lose sight of the path that I choose to lead now."

"Child, my one piece of advice to you is that you take on this project and prove that you have learned from your mistakes."

"What makes you think I won't commit another blunder?" She eyed the old vampire.

His gray brows furrowed. "Because I've seen it."

"Like you saw Ronestus' rise to power?" She knew the story too well—it had a sad ending.

"Just like I foretold the death of his beloved and the belated discovery of Lukan's betrayal. Yes, I feel the weight on my shoulders. Yet we don't dare change the course of their destiny or ours."

Aemerria saw it all—his death, her future, and everything else that gave her pause. "You're not going to change any of it?"

"Not a thing." The stubborn drawl sounded tired but resolute.

"What if I don't have what it takes to carry this out?"

"Then you will take comfort in knowing that you tried your best."

With a wave of his hand, Gastarius showed her the future in a ball of swirling events, stunning her. Aemerria gasped and covered her mouth to keep from crying out. How could she accept responsibility for several destinies that would later define hers?

Why me? What had made Gastarius choose her?

"You have the right amount of thoroughness to see it through, and the passion to prove yourself. Add a little compassion to your heart, and you shall be exalted. The darkness in you is still present. Use your best judgment to hand out mercy or justice as you see fit."

Aemerria wrapped her arms around herself to keep from falling apart. It was going to be a tough job, but it was a chance nonetheless. If she pulled it off, then maybe the crippling memories would go away. Her hands grew clammy at the visions she could sense. "Is there any other way?"

Gastarius shook his head. "I don't make these things up. My power is just as effective as the things that I see."

"If you believe in me, then I have no reason not to believe in myself." A burst of pure energy coursed through her veins. "If you find that I will stray from my path, do me one favor. Destroy me."

Gastarius shook his head. "I don't take lives. I just predict the outcome of them all." *Besides, I'm not going to be around much longer.*

Sadness gripped her heart. If Gastarius considered her fit to take over, then maybe she could change his destiny. "I can't lose you. You're my only family."

The old man laid a comforting hand on her head. "I will always look down on you with love, my child. Do not stray or act on impulse. Stay your course, despite your uncertainties and fear. Know that you are never alone."

Aemerria knew that Gastarius hated tears, so she swallowed the lump in her throat and took a deep breath. "You're still convinced that I can get things done for you?"

"Yes, you will ally yourself with Ronestus. He would be a tough sell, but I believe you will be able to find common ground. Just keep an ace up your sleeve."

"What might that be?" She narrowed her eyes. How convenient for Gastarius to have forgotten that little detail.

"You have seen it. It is all up to you now."

Aemerria found herself being transported to the future. Her hands fell limp.

"Don't fight what you can't change. Let your mistakes guide your present course."

The gravity of her past and what she had done steamrolled over her without compassion, clawing its way into her senses with mighty force. The guilt she had harbored now surfaced to remind her of what she had once been and the decisions that had affected her and the people around her.

It wasn't in Aemerria's nature to experience terror, and that fact alone fueled her resolve to rebel against her fears. "Fine. You're on."

Shaking her head in a gesture of helplessness, she tried to escape the need to open Pandora's Box. Once the truth was laid bare, she hoped to find some sort of release. Underneath it all, she had grown comfortable with the pain and regret. What would happen if she was devoid of such emotions?

At that precise moment, Gastarius gave her another glimpse of her next assignment. It was a heartbreaking reminder what death was capable of creating.

"Do right by them."

She pondered his words. "Hate and love. These two feelings oppose each other in every way except in what intensities they are able to reach. Love has the ability to heal scars, and hate has the power to destroy everything in its path."

Gastarius nodded. "I shall leave you to your thoughts."

Aemerria lingered within the walls of the diviner's chambers. It was a location disclosed to a chosen few. Deep in thought, a vision of the future snuck up on her. Staggering, she flopped into the chair and tried to understand the flashing images. Gastarius had seen this. No wonder he was prepping her to carry on in his stead. Death was imminent. Aemerria was powerless to change the course of destiny. She braced herself against the cry that bellowed from deep within her soul. It cut through the steel walls she had built around her heart.

Gathering the names of past clients had taken longer than Cyrus had anticipated. The damage to the computer systems from the last raid was not permanent, yet it had taken Rayce three days to put the data together.

Cyrus studied the corporation names and dates, most of which he vaguely remembered. He scanned the corresponding quantities with keen eyes, trying his best to track any patterns. One good thing came out of gathering the guns of the dead vampires during the recent clash. He could compare the identification numbers against their records.

"Did Pritchard mention anything about severed relationships with anyone?" Harrow asked.

Cyrus shook his head. "Not that I remember."

"Why don't we run the data through Leo? It might jog his memory."

"Sure. I'll have Rayce send him a copy."

"You didn't get to finish telling me about the shit with Drago."

Cyrus thought for a moment. "As I mentioned before, he is another bloodsucker. I sensed something shifty about him."

"What do you mean?" Harrow removed his sunglasses and rubbed his eyes.

"The guy is no ordinary vampire. There is more to him than meets the eye, and his backup singers are not your average vampires. Those guys were nasty."

Harrow raised an eyebrow. "Backup singers?"

"Well, they made some sounds that I haven't heard before. Creepy shit, if you ask me."

"What kind of sounds?"

"Hissing sounds." He stared at Harrow, knowing the guy was just playing him. "You're asking a lot of questions tonight."

"I'm killing time. I'm going to the warehouse in a little bit." Harrow flashed his fangs and laughed. As a new member of the Council, he had been given the role of keeping tabs on any humans turned vampire. This was a new position that had been created because of the great influx of new vampires. With Harrow's experience running the facility, he was most suitable for the role.

"Do you need help?" Cyrus asked.

Harrow studied him for a few seconds and then shook his head. "Nah. Keep that woman of yours happy. Stop finding more work to occupy your time. As it is, your plate is already heaped high."

Cyrus snorted. Issy was hardly his woman, but Harrow was right. She could use a bit of a downtime after the abrupt ending to their celebration a few nights ago. After shuffling a few responsibilities at the Council, Issy had been assigned to be the new keeper of the records, relieving Icarus, who had been named Council advisor.

It was a huge responsibility, but Issy had taken on the new role with grace. Cyrus had expected this from the young lady, though. She was strong, intelligent, and giving—and beautiful, and he was falling for her. It wasn't a revelation. Cyrus had known all along that if he stayed around her, there was no doubt he'd fall for her.

"You're spacing out." Harrow threw a piece of balled-up paper at him.

"If you don't need my help, then I'm going to see if Issy needs anything."

"Do that. I'm betting my money she needs you."

Smirking, Cyrus got up and grabbed the papers from the table. "Let me know what Leo says."

Cyrus left the I-room and went straight to Issy's suite, taking a deep breath before knocking. He pounded several times before the door opened. One look at Issy and he knew something was wrong. Her eyes were puffy, and her cheeks were mottled from crying.

"Hey, what's wrong?" He closed the door then gathered her into his arms.

Issy sobbed against his chest. While her body shuddered, Cyrus ran his palm up and down her back in an effort to soothe her. They stood in the middle of the room while she cried. He tried to figure out what could have caused her tears, but he drew a blank, so he waited until she'd calmed down.

"Issy? What's the matter?" he asked when her hiccupping stopped.

She looked up at him with miserable eyes. "I knew my parents had kept me in the dark to protect me. Their intention was noble, but as you can see. I'm screwed because of it."

"What are you talking about?" He tilted her chin just in time to see her lips quiver.

"They hid me because they knew Goran would be looking for me, so my entire childhood was spent within the walls of our home. They withheld information from me for my protection. I'm educated but also naïve. Even so, I never thought they'd keep something so important from me."

When her legs started to give out, he ushered her to the couch. "Tell me what it is."

Issy buried her face in her hands, muffling her response. "I have an older sister."

Okay, that was some news. In hindsight, he would have been shocked, too, if he'd been in her shoes. But why the tears? "Hey, care to tell me how you feel about this?"

It took a moment before she looked up at him. "I guess it came as a shock. I was brought up thinking I was an only child. I kept asking them why I had no sister or brother, and they always told me that was how it was supposed to be."

"Let's sit down." He led her to the couch. Once seated, Cyrus lifted up her chin. Looking into her eyes, he felt a wave of protective instinct. She was so beautiful and fragile. "Is that the only reason you're upset?"

She shook her head. "I read the black book. Just like me, she is in the dark as to who she really is."

"Who is she?"

"It didn't say."

"How will you know then?"

"The name was blotted out. It seems like no one wants us to know. It says there that this girl has powers beyond what is common in our race. She is destined to help our people, and under the circumstances, she is not supposed to know her background."

Cyrus rolled his eyes. "That is messed up."

Issy sobbed in response. "I know. I was hoping I would know who she was so we could be family. The thought that I wasn't alone would be a nice change."

This made his heart ache. "Oh, baby. You're never alone. I'm always here for you." And he meant it.

Drago wore a lazy smile. His ducks were in a row, and everything was proceeding as planned. Bretania was about to create havoc, and a glorious shaman was at his disposal. There was nothing else he could ask for until it was time to reap the fruits of his labor.

He pulled out a Cuban cigar from his suit pocket and popped it in his mouth, but a hand reached out and stopped him from lighting up.

"Let me do it for you." Lukan took the gold lighter from his hand. "Good evening, my lord." She flicked the thumbwheel and lit his cigar.

Drago took a few quick puffs then a long, clean drag. He savored the flavor before he released his breath. "Are you ready for this?"

Lukan sat on the floor by his feet and leaned her head against his thigh. She didn't respond right away. When she did, she glanced up and gave an angelic smile. "I've been waiting for this day since last year."

Drago smiled. "You were resistant at first, if I remember correctly." The memory of Lukan's wrath and punishment flashed before his eyes. She had imprisoned him for several weeks before she began to listen to his plan. Looking back, it had been a big gamble on his part, but it was worth the risk.

She closed her eyes and exhaled. "Mmm . . . that was before I'd heard your offer. You drive an irresistible bargain, my dear." He detected a slight quaver in her voice.

"I know what I want, and that is to have you by my side when all this is said and done." He took another drag from his cigar, feeling good about the prospect.

"I don't know if I can bear the thought of sharing you with Bretania," she said in a little voice.

"Patience, darling. We need her right now. She's doing great spreading the disease, and she has a big army at her disposal, something we can use on top of what we've built here."

Lukan stood up and walked over to the balcony, so Drago placed his cigar on an ashtray and followed her. He wrapped his arms around her waist and turned her to face him. "Don't be jealous. I have no intention of getting us infected." He skimmed his mouth along the nape of her neck.

His last encounter with Bretania had been well planned. After giving her a brief taste of what he could give her, he was able to hide the fact that he had protected himself from catching the disease. In her lust-induced high, Bretania had failed to notice he was wearing a condom. Drago smirked at the thought.

Everything had worked out just as he'd hoped. With Lukan's assistance, he was able to get rid of Goran, making it appear as though his demise was all about fulfillment of the prophecy. Even without possessing the black book and with having to depend on what little the priestess could gather from the thoughts of the brothers, Ronestus and Goran, Lukan had managed to manipulate the events that would make his ascent to power a reality.

Belonging to another coven had afforded him the chance to gather some valuable information on the comings and goings within the Vampire Council. Although he was relatively unknown in the vampire world, he had been moving in the background. His obscure existence had enabled him to study the others without fear of being exposed. Alongside building his business empire, he'd allied with the rare breed of vampires known as the Neroc.

The ugly sons of bitches were stronger and taller than the average vampire. Most would reach seven feet by the time they hit adulthood. Fast, lethal, and without the usual blood lust, the Nerocs were a fearsome enemy but a welcome ally.

Lord Marchec, the leader of the unsightly looking creatures, had agreed to work for Drago in exchange for protection. Unknown to many, most Council members shunned the hideous motherfuckers because of their lousy work ethic and untrustworthiness. After he got over his initial shock at the ugly face—the skull fitted with wafer-thin skin, eye sockets holding large-ass eyeballs the color of mud—he took a gamble. Drago had sat down with the head of the group and worked out a deal with him—their services for his blanket of security.

Thus, the alliance was born. With their help, his goals were within reach. He could almost touch success with his fingertips.

With Lukan pretending to have cast a spell on the Vampire Council and Tack Enterprises against detection by their enemies, the task was going to be simple. His army against that of the humans-turned-vampires and the soldiers of the Council.

Even if he couldn't stomach Bretania and her disease, he acted convincing enough. He'd even made her believe that she would sit alongside him when he began his rule as the head of the Council. Little did she know that he had already orchestrated her demise. Tonight might be her lucky night, depending on the outcome of her mission. Bretania's wicked efforts to spread the disease were a measure he thought would work to confuse the group who were endeavoring to administer the cure.

Bretania's group of vampires was spreading the disease through orgies and by brute force or at gunpoint.

This had divided Rohnert's attention between Council matters and those of the original group with which he'd been allied. Coupled with the death of his mate and the disappearance of her body, the great leader was guaranteed to crack soon. Their sole setback so far had been Gastarius' accidental discovery of Lukan's plans. Well, shit happened.

"Ugly creatures," Lukan commented, no doubt also pondering the alliance he'd forged.

"Shh . . . you don't want them to hear us." He ran his tongue along the exposed skin of her neck. When Lukan gave a delighted shiver, he led her to the sofa and patted his lap. "Sit down with me."

Lukan did his bidding. Her soft bottom, warm and inviting, rubbed against him, and he shuddered with desire. He'd known of her beauty and was delighted when she'd accepted his invitation to meet. It was a tricky maneuver since the shaman could read his thoughts. She could reduce him to ashes if he offended her. But now, with such a powerful entity in his arsenal, he couldn't imagine not achieving victory.

She wrapped her arms around his neck and nipped, kissed, and licked him all over. The woman was as lethal as the Neroc. The main difference between the two was that her face was pleasing to the eye.

"You have planned this to perfection," she murmured.

"I couldn't have done it without your help. Without your inside information, manipulation, and Academy-worthy performance, we wouldn't be here."

Lukan radiated with pride, her dimples deepening when she smiled. "It would've been better if the old bastard hadn't caught up with me."

Drago downplayed her misstep. "You're fine. I didn't even think we would get this far. Think of how Goran fell for your manipulation, believing you'd healed him. You got his brother to take him out then you stole his mate's corpse. What more could I ask for?" He kissed her mouth while his hands traced her soft curves.

Lukan watched him, her smile never wavering. She was reading his mind, he was sure of it. He knew she would see nothing that would prove that he wasn't telling the truth.

"If you keep showering me with praise, I swear my head will burst." She laughed and seized his mouth with hers.

En route to the warehouse, Harrow received a call from the facility.

"Harrow, I have a caller for you. I put a trace on it. The number is legit, registered to a Hill Monroe. I'm patching it through now."

He stopped at a loading zone and let the motorcycle idle. "Harrow here."

"Listen to what I say. Your warehouse is under attack right now. Get as many men as you can put together. Don't waste time." The caller, whose voice was familiar to him, hung up before he could ask questions.

Harrow thought for a second, deciding whether to heed the unsolicited warning. Erring on the side of caution, he punched in the facility's number. Rayce answered. "Get Cyrus, Tor, Rohnert, and Jordan for me. Hurry!"

It took a few seconds to get everyone on the same line. "Listen, I received a call to alert us that the warehouse is under attack. Get your men and meet me there. Jordan, stay and guard the facility. I have a bad feeling about this. I don't want a repeat of the last double ambush."

"We're on our way," Tor and Cyrus answered at the same time.

"Don't do anything stupid, Harrow. Wait for backup. We're leaving now," Rohnert said before hanging up.

"Listen to Rohnert, don't go yet," Jordan pleaded, sounding more scared than she would have admitted to being.

"I have to go, babe." He hung up before guilt got the best of him. Her request was one he couldn't go along with—not when the life of Jones, whose research made him one of the most important people in their organization was at stake.

Harrow revved the engine and gunned the gas. The tires let out a long squeal, leaving tracks on the pavement as he sped away. He went through the maze of late night traffic in haste. When he neared the warehouse, he turned off his headlight and parked the motorcycle behind a rundown building.

Unsheathing his Kalimetal, he made his way to the building amid the sound of deafening gunfire. In a few seconds, he found himself surrounded by Vampire Council soldiers headed by Rohnert. Incoming footfalls alerted them to Cyrus' and Tor's arrival. Once their group was assembled, Harrow called out instructions.

"Rohnert, take the back entrance." He pointed to the rear of the building. "We'll take the front." On his signal, they moved in. They made little noise until they ran into the group that had been firing at the vampires who had come seeking help for their disease. Screams bounced off the walls, and vampires were scrambling in all directions.

Jones was nowhere in sight. "Whatever you do, spare the lives of the diseased ones." Harrow gave the signal.

Cyrus jumped in and started firing at the attackers. This evened up the conflict and gave the civilians a chance to run for cover.

This also gave Harrow an opportunity to look for Jones. Along the hallway, the dead bodies of their human friends littered the floor, while mounds of ashes were scattered everywhere.

"Damn it," Rohnert muttered when they closed in on the lower level where the laboratory was situated. "Don't think of anything. Clear your headspace."

Harrow knew what Rohnert meant. Whoever was in the building was a mind reader, just like he was. Everyone nodded, and with slow, light footsteps, they made it to the door of the laboratory where a male vampire was questioning Jones.

The door of the side exit flapped, and Rohnert ran to it. "Bretania escaped. I'm going after her," he whispered and was gone in a flash.

"Who is the source of your cure?" the vampire asked.

Before Jones could answer, Harrow created enough noise to distract his interrogator. The man pivoted with one hand still locked on Jones' neck, the other gripping an automatic rifle. Harrow was certain he hadn't seen the vampire before.

"What is your purpose?" He inched forward.

The vampire pressed his fingers into Jones' neck until he shrieked in pain. "Who wants to know? Watch your step. Move any closer and I'll blow his brains out."

Arrogant bastard. "I'm Harrow Gates—a Council Elder."

The vampire sneered. "Ah, the infamous Harrow Gates. Your reputation precedes you."

"Let him go and I might spare your life." Harrow stayed where he was, eyeing the automatic rifle that was pointed at Jones' head.

"You sound too sure of yourself. I will have to make you eat your words."

The element of surprise was indeed a great ally. Out of nowhere, Tor moved in and tossed his axe straight at the vampire, smack in the center of his forehead. Harrow pulled out a throwing star and aimed it at the hand that gripped the gun, severing the wrist before he could do Jones any damage.

The vampire fell to the ground, writhing, and dragged Jones with him. Tor stared down at him. "Look who's eating his words now."

The disintegration process had started, but the vampire hadn't released his hold on Jones' neck and was still strangling him. Using the Kalimetal, Harrow moved fast to cut off the hand at the wrist. The man's cry was deafening, and Harrow pried Jones away.

Tor's laughter echoed across the room as the sizzle, crackle, and pop started. "Another one bites the dust," he said and turned away.

Harrow inspected Jones from head to toe. "Are you all right?"

"I need a drink. A stiff one," Jones said in spite of the shake in his voice.

"You'll get it." Harrow pushed Jones behind him when incoming footsteps sounded. They braced themselves for another showdown, but it was Gentry and Firman.

"What's going on here? Did you find . . ." Firman stopped when he saw Jones. "Damn it, you scared us."

"How does it look out there?" Tor asked.

"Cyrus is a fuckin' animal. The guy almost single-handedly annihilated the bastards." Firman holstered his dagger and gun.

Harrow was afraid to ask. "How many?"

"Only two humans survived—the ones who hid in the kitchen—but none of our vampire personnel." Firman let out a frustrated breath.

"Let's get this place cleaned up. Have the men take the humans and gather their bodies. Put the ashes of the vampires in the urn." Harrow turned around, sheathing his Kalimetal back in its holster.

Tor stood beside him. "We'll finish here. Take Jones home and secure the facility. I have a bad feeling about this."

Rohnert appeared from the side exit, a grim expression on his face. "I lost her."

"Who?" Tor asked.

"Bretania. That woman is fast, but I know she'll be back."

"Take some of my men. I will alert the Council. I won't be back until I get a hold of Lukan. Have Allison take my son to a safe place. She'll know where I'm talking about." He turned to Gentry. "Come with me."

After one look at Rohnert, Harrow all but carried Jones out of the room. "I'll see you guys in a few."

Harrow wasted no time. With the big group of vampires behind him, he powered the motorcycle to life, Jones clinging to his back. They shot through the city streets, zipping like a bullet while the rest of the men headed out on foot.

Rohnert ran at breakneck speed, with Gentry keeping pace. He needed to be in a place where he could summon help, preferably somewhere dark and without distractions. They were a few blocks away from the Council headquarters when he glanced up. Right in front of them was the famous landmark, St. Patrick's Cathedral—an ideal place.

"Let's go to the back," he said and moved toward the rear of the church. Construction was underway, and scaffolding surrounded the structure, making it easier to get into the church. They slipped through an unfinished window that was big enough to provide entry and found themselves face to face with the storied interior.

He looked around, trying to identify the best place to perform the summoning ritual. His last call for Lukan's help hadn't been pleasant, and he planned to mellow his attitude this time.

"Sire, this seems like a good place." Gentry pointed to a stairwell underneath the altar. "I'll stay here and keep watch."

Rohnert followed the stairs until he reached an area that seemed to be a tomb of some sort. Using his excellent night vision, he navigated the marbled corridor until he reached the middle of a long room. Several candles were already burning, providing a dull light.

Dropping to his knees, Rohnert closed his eyes and began chanting the words in their ancient language. He repeated the summons and then waited, his arms outstretched in veneration—also a sign of regret for not conforming to the ritual with the usual beads.

He waited a few more minutes and was about to call again when a strong gust of wind swirled around him—not the usual wisp of smoke unique to Lukan. Even the scent was different. Rohnert wanted to open his eyes but dared not risk offending the priestess.

"This is an odd choice of location to call upon me." A hand touched his head, but the voice wasn't Lukan's. "You may open your eyes."

Rohnert blinked but kept his eyes on the ground until the hand appeared in his line of sight. As was customary, he kissed the top of the hand. "Thank you for answering my summons."

"Aren't you in the least bit surprised?" the female asked.

Rohnert raised his gaze until he met her eyes. An unfamiliar entity stood before him, clothed in a hooded black robe. "I am."

"Tell me, what are you thinking?"

Rohnert wanted to be candid and say 'what the fuck is this,' but he knew that impropriety would cause unnecessary delay, and time was luxury he didn't have.

"You can be candid and say what you want. Just mean it." The rich voice was too enticing, and he felt fear for the first time.

"Where is Lukan, and who are you?"

The female smiled, showing perfect teeth. Beautiful and otherwordly, she looked almost delicate when she tossed back the hood to expose her shiny blonde hair, which reached past her shoulders. An inexplicable aura surrounded her when she spoke. "I am Aemerria, commissioned by Gastarius to respond to your call. As for Lukan, she has decided that she's done following orders."

When Rohnert stared at her in confusion, Aemerria laughed—a sweet and melodious sound like chiming bells. "Lukan has been evicted from her station. Gastarius caught her manipulating the course of our history."

Rohnert felt his muscles tightened while suspicions roiled within him. "How do I know if you're here to help?"

Aemerria brows furrowed before she responded with a blinding smile. "I understand your doubts, but you have no time for questions right now. Didn't you come here because you needed help?"

Rohnert lowered his gaze. "Indeed, I believe my people, the Council, and the Tack Enterprises facility's inhabitants might be in danger."

"You are not what I expected," Aemerria said as she moved away, walking toward the end of the long hallway.

He got to his feet while he waited for her to speak. It was several moments before she flitted back to him, her feet barely touching the ground.

"The Council has already been compromised. A few have perished, as was their destiny. The attackers are gone now, so it is safe for you to go back. I already cast a new unbreakable spell around the walls of the Council grounds. You can now ease your mind."

Rohnert closed his eyes and breathed deep, saying a silent prayer that the higher power would guide the souls of those who had died that night. He opened his eyes to find Aemerria watching him, and he stared back at her, returning her curiosity. Her eyes were a myriad of colors that seemed to change as her mood shifted, and she was small and fragile-looking.

"Appearances will deceive you."

"Is that a warning?"

She smirked and began pacing. "Your son is safe in the hands of the good people to whom you have entrusted him. Your facility will be under my protection, but I can only guarantee the lives of a few. Everyone's destiny has been written, and each individual's actions can alter the course of their existence."

"Why is this happening? Haven't my people suffered enough?"

Aemerria began walking around him, and Rohnert shifted his feet to follow her. "Suffering is as relative to happiness as death is to life."

"More deaths will come?"

"As more lives will be born out of those deaths." She stopped and took several steps closer to him. "You're facing powerful enemies, much worse than your brother. I cannot offer you the who and why. All I can tell you is to prepare yourself. You're surrounded by trustworthy people. Surprises will still happen, as was the case today. The anonymous caller has given some people a second chance at life. This is all I am allowed to say. Be well, Ronestus. Until we meet again."

"Wait." Rohnert took a step forward, but Aemerria waved her hand and disappeared. "Damn it."

Cyrus' heart was beating hard against his chest. He had left some fighters to finish the cleanup while he, Tor, and the rest of Rohnert's Council guards rushed back to the facility. Although they had some fierce fighters guarding the women and children, the worry was eating him alive.

Even Tor was quiet for a change, not slinging his usual wisecracks. They reached the lip of the tunnel and were granted access the moment Rayce had verified their identification. Each man had someplace to go. Tor took off for the elevator, no doubt in search of Allison.

Cyrus turned to Firman. "Get everyone situated. I'll meet you guys in the I-room in half an hour." Firman saluted and led the Council guards toward the stairwell. Cyrus needed to check on Isidora first before he could relax—and he wanted to check on the children, too.

He pounded on the door, too keyed up to give a damn. Isidora opened it and gasped. "You're here."

There was no way around it. He ached to hold her, to prove to himself that she was all right. Cyrus pulled her by the shoulders and wrapped his arms around her body. "Yes, I am. I just wanted to make sure you were okay after last night." It wasn't entirely a lie. Issy had been pretty shaken up when she discovered that she had a sibling.

"I'm fine. Jordan instructed us to stay inside. I have Sawyer and Liv here." She pointed to the bed, where the two children were fast asleep.

Just like one big, happy family. Moved beyond words, Cyrus cupped Issy's face and planted a soft kiss on her lips. He was new to this—the emotions flooding within him, and the tenderness that threatening to overflow.

Shit. He pulled away but kept his hands on her face. "Are you armed?" he asked, for lack of anything better to say.

Issy grinned and shifted, lifting her skirt up to her thighs to reveal a holster of daggers and throwing stars. "I learned from the best."

Pride welled inside him until he could no longer breathe. "You're special, Isidora, just in case I haven't told you." He kissed her mouth once more. *And I'm falling hard, fast.*

If Issy caught the last part, she didn't let on, but her smile told him she had. "You're one amazing man, Cyrus."

Compliments had never daunted him before. Coming from this woman, he wasn't sure how to take it. "I . . . uh . . ."

"Just take it for what it is."

Cyrus nodded, but then he remembered the meeting he was about to conduct. He pulled the cell phone from his pocket and instructed Firman to send up a fighter. "I'll have one of my men watch the children. I want you at the meeting with me."

Surprise spread across Issy's face, and she gave him a radiant smile. "It's about time you included me." They left the room together once the assigned sitter came, armed to the teeth.

The I-room was filled to capacity. Cyrus nodded to Harrow, who took the floor.

"First, let me commend you all for the rapid response and the display of courage and bravery." Everyone clapped, showing solidarity. "Moments ago, I received a phone call from Rohnert, and he would like me to inform you of our current situation. It seems that there is a new breed of vampires in our midst. They are strong and built for destruction. The Council headquarters were again compromised. I don't know about you, but I'm sick of always having to watch our backs."

Murmurs of agreement rippled through the room. Cyrus studied the faces of the fighters. Then he remembered the conflict back at the warehouse, noticing a pattern and the weapons used by the attackers.

When the room quieted down, Harrow continued. "Our warehouse, as you know, will be out of commission. Thus, the aid to those who require our help is temporarily halted. Jones is safe and out of harm's way. He is now deep in research, tucked away in his laboratory for the time being."

Cyrus raised his hand, unable to keep the information he wanted to share to himself any longer. Harrow stepped back. "Our new enemies are using automatic weapons, which gives us a small window in which to react. Therefore, I'm recommending that, starting today, we carry the same type of firepower."

"An eye for an eye?" Firman asked.

Cyrus nodded. "Sort of. I want each and every single one of you to be familiar with the gun. If you need help, Isidora is a fine markswoman, and I'm sure she'll be of assistance to you."

Issy blushed to a bright red but still managed a gracious bow.

He continued. "No one is allowed to leave the facility starting tonight except the Council soldiers. This is for your own safety and that of everyone else here. Until you hear otherwise from me, you will stay in and practice. Are there any questions?" Cyrus looked around. Everyone seemed content with the orders given. "Then have fun shooting."

The room emptied out, leaving him with Harrow, Issy, and Jordan.

Harrow slumped in his chair. "This is a fuckin' mess."

"You can say that again." Cyrus marched straight to the wall and pushed the button to reveal the bar. "Any drink requests?"

"Lag for me," said Harrow.

"Water here." Jordan took the seat next to her mate.

Cyrus glanced at Issy. "You?"

"I'll have what you're having."

He glanced over his shoulder and grinned. "Caol Ila it is." He poured their drinks and returned with them to the table. After taking a quick sip of his scotch, he sighed. "Man, I thought we were done when Goran checked out," he said.

Jordan snorted. "This is bigger than what that asshole started."

"That asshole is now rotting in hell." Harrow pulled Jordan into an embrace. "And we're going to relax tonight and regroup tomorrow."

Cyrus chugged his remaining drink. "Sounds good to me."

Issy downed the drink, straight up. Cyrus had never seen her drink, let alone chug a forty-five-year-old scotch.

"I guess it'll be an early night for us," she said.

Cyrus took her hand and kissed it. "You bet it will."

Zane knew he'd done the right thing by calling the facility to warn them of Bretania's plan. From his hiding spot not too far from the warehouse, he could smell the scent of death. There was no mistaking that lives had been taken tonight, but what pleased him was the knowledge that Bretania and her group had perished in the battle.

Call it a sixth sense, but he had the strange feeling he was being watched. He looked over his shoulder at Hill, who returned a blank stare.

"Boss, what's the matter?"

"Nothing," he said and waved off the feeling as paranoia. "Let's head back." Zane signaled his men.

Back safe in his own home, he slumped onto the couch and thought about his next course of action. With Bretania out of the picture, he was freed from her demands. The million dollar question remained. Did her death guarantee the group's freedom from further threat or danger? Or his? Somehow, he doubted it. The female hadn't struck him as dumb. Why would she risk her own life by attacking the warehouse? It didn't add up— unless someone had orchestrated her death. Deep in his gut, he sensed this conflict was far from over.

"Is there anything else you need for the night?" Hill stood in the doorway.

Zane shook his head. "You can go get some rest."

Hill nodded. "All right." His beady eyes studied Zane before he turned to leave.

Zane got up, propped his cane on the floor, and hobbled to the bedroom to strip his body of his weapons. Then he crossed the hallway to the treadmill. Although he didn't feel as weak as he had, his leg still gave him problems. The damage was permanent, and this was going to hinder him from doing many activities. This also meant that he would forever have to rely on someone else to do the legwork for him.

He was fine running on the equipment, but uneven pavement proved to be more difficult for him. There wasn't much he could do about his inability to get around, so he was reduced to delegating responsibilities to Hill and his men, which didn't sit well with Zane. His father always told him that great things were achieved by undertaking tasks personally.

With his defective leg, he was more of a liability out there.

"Fuck," he muttered and continued with his pace. Zane stayed a few minutes longer until exhaustion threatened to take over. It was nothing a long shower wouldn't fix. He grabbed the handlebar and stopped the machine.

He was limping to the bathroom when his cell phone buzzed.

The text message from Tack Enterprises' main line read: *You've saved many lives. We're grateful for your help. We would like to set up a meeting with you so we can thank you in person.*

Zane read the message several times before keying in his reply. *I wouldn't mind meeting with Rohnert tonight. Name the time and place.*

It took some time before the response came, and the tone had shifted. *Rohnert will meet with you alone. Don't try anything stupid if you want to continue breathing.*

Okay. At least they had gotten the threat out of the way. *Where and what time?*

Epitaph at the bar. Ten sharp.

Epitaph was a bar located downtown that was frequented by humans. The location would guarantee that neither of them did anything that might compromise their identities and the safety of humans.

Smart, very smart. *I'll be there.*

All righty—he had gotten himself a date with his great uncle. Whoopee!

Bretania reached her new hideout after an all-out sprint for her life. She had expected a total annihilation of the warehouse and its inhabitants, but that hadn't happened. Zane was supposed to meet her there, but it seemed like the little twerp had decided to sing instead.

Mason opened the door the moment she reached the steps. "I'm glad you're back," he said in a gruff voice, too territorial for her liking. He stepped out and glanced out at the front of lawn to see check if she had been followed.

"Are the children home? Nathan?" she asked, shedding her jacket and weapons.

"He's in the room. Where are the rest?" Mason took her weapons from the table and ushered her to her bedroom.

Bretania waited until they were in the safety of her room before she answered. "I was set up. Zane was a no-show, and I don't intend to contact Drago anymore. I'm sure the bastard orchestrated this fiasco. I've been an idiot, but we'll see who's going to have the last laugh. I didn't become a tactician and weapons expert for nothing. It seems like we have our work cut out for us." She flopped onto the mattress and kicked off her shoes.

Mason gave her a quizzical look. "Reid?" he asked.

It wasn't a surprise to Bretania how Mason felt about the other man. The two had an ongoing competition over whom she favored more. She wasn't picky. Whoever was available to satisfy her craving for sex or blood would be the It-man.

"He's gone. I left when the Council soldiers came. Damn Rohnert almost got me."

"Rohnert?" Mason walked over to the foot of the bed. He took her left foot and began massaging.

"He's the Council leader," she said, unable to think clearly. The foot rub was a welcome change since she had been running for quite some time. Bretania closed her eyes and thought about their current situation. With her army depleted, she would have to rebuild. It wouldn't be so difficult. She had done it already, and doing it again would be a piece of cake, especially when there was a pool of humans at their disposal.

Mason took her other foot and continued to provide her pleasure. "What are you planning to do now?"

Bretania opened her eyes and looked at him. She was glad he was still around. Between him and Reid, Mason was the tougher since he was a scum. Her scum. With his ruthless personality and no-nonsense attitude, he would make a good right-hand man. He followed orders, and most important, he adored her.

"I have a new position for you," she said, taking his hand and pulling him down.

His crimson eyes flickered with interest. Though she had infected him with the dreadful disease, the vampire didn't hold a grudge. He sat down and started running his hand along the base of her spine, moving upward. "Sure. What is it? Short-order cook?"

Bretania laughed and grabbed his strong chin so he was looking down at her. "Actually, I need a right-hand man. Are you up for the job?"

Mason seemed pleased. He smiled, showing his elongating fangs. "I'll be whoever you want me to be, as long as I get to share your bed."

"Deal," she said before pulling his face down for a kiss.

A lot of tongue action was happening, and she knew Mason was getting hard. There were issues she needed to settle first, so she pushed against his chest before they could get carried away. "Maz, go get Nathan for me."

His eyes were wild when he looked at her, yet he stood up and readjusted himself inside his pants. "Sure thing," he said then strode out of her bedroom.

A little over five minutes later, her door swung open again. "You asked for me?" Nathan walked in with his usual cocky swagger.

Bretania went to the adjoining room, which served as her office and weapons supply room. She gestured for him to follow. "Sit," she said.

She took the chair opposite him. Nathan had grown remarkably tall in just a few months, and the muscles in his arms were striking. Bretania ran her gaze over his proud face before she spoke.

"Drago set me up, and your nephew is likely in it with him. I'm not sure what the deal is, but I will find out soon."

Nathan leaned forward, his nostrils flaring. "I will hunt Zane down, just say the word."

"Down, boy. Let me get some intel first, and then we'll make our move."

"What happened to your crew?" he asked, sounding impatient.

"They're gone."

The young vampire snorted. "Want me to help find new recruits for you?"

Bretania hadn't really given this a lot of thought. Why not? They were quite a distance from the city, and it would be safe for Nathan to be out and about. "Go for it. Just give me your word that you'll stay in this part of the city."

His eyebrows rose. "Care to tell me why?"

"Drago's reach is quite extensive. I don't want him catching us before we're ready."

"What is up with this Drago character anyway?"

She smiled. If Drago thought he had made a complete fool of her, he was mistaken. Bretania had reached into his mind and had gotten some valuable information. The bastard son of Cantor wasn't as slick as he thought he was.

"Let's just say your father had a dysfunctional family."

Nathan nodded as though he knew what she meant. "Just save my uncle and Zane for me, and we'll be even."

Bretania reached out her hand. "Deal," she said. Nathan took her hand and gave it a firm shake. "Do what I say, and we'll get back in the ballgame, even it takes us months or years. We're not done yet."

His eyes gleamed, and he smiled, reminding her again of Goran.

Rohnert was just wrapping up the emergency meeting with the Council members when his phone vibrated with an incoming text. "Excuse me." He gestured for Wendell to take over.

He moved to the side. Instead of responding via text, he placed a call to Harrow. "Hey, what's up?"

"The man who alerted us of the attack would only meet with you. Are you willing to go?"

He thought for a moment. "Sure, when?"

"Tonight."

"Sign me up. Give me the details later." Rohnert hung up just as the meeting concluded.

Most of the Elders didn't leave right away. Some converged in small groups for conversation. Wendell approached him. "I don't think it's a good idea for you to go on your own."

Rohnert shrugged. "This has to be done."

He appreciated the concern, but their informer deserved his time. His invaluable tip had prevented the loss of more lives. If Rohnert hadn't gotten most of his men out to respond to Harrow's call, many if not all would have been caught unprepared. Meeting the informant was the least he could do. Besides, he could handle himself.

Wendell shook his head. "I know you're capable of taking care of business, but this Council won't survive without you, if anything should happen."

He gave the Elder a pat on the back. "You're too morbid. Don't worry about me."

They didn't notice that Issy had drifted closer until she spoke. "Why don't I come with you? And Cyrus is outside waiting."

Rohnert smiled at the sweet offer. "Thanks, but I don't think it's a good idea."

"Then you should at least feed before you leave."

He shifted his eyes to Wendell, who seemed uncomfortable all of a sudden. The Elder bowed and moved away, leaving them to continue with the more personal topic.

Issy was right. He hadn't fed for some time. However, with Cyrus in the picture, he doubted the propriety of their feeding situation. "I'll figure something out."

"Rubbish. Cyrus will understand. As we've already established, this is just a matter of survival."

There was no disputing her argument. The arrangement was convenient for them since they both needed each other's pure blood. He bowed. "Well then, I'll see you in my chamber in a few minutes."

If this was the right thing to do, why did it feel like he was betraying both Shelly and Cyrus? Rohnert shook his head in disgust. He left the meeting room and proceeded to his chamber, still plagued by guilt.

A knock on the door came after a few minutes. He answered it to find Issy waiting outside and Cyrus guarding the door, his expression unreadable. Out of respect for his friend, Rohnert didn't bother reading his mind. It was better to leave everything the way it should be—detached.

Rohnert stepped aside to let Issy in then closed the door. "Have a seat." He gestured to the chair in front of his desk.

She sat on the chair and waited, watching him while he hovered closer. "I know it makes you uncomfortable, but we've gone through the process before. Think of it as a matter of nourishment, nothing more. You're in love with your wife and I'm in love with Cyrus, but we need each other to survive."

He met her even gaze. Logic she said was right on the money, but the feeling of discomfort continued to gnaw at him. He eyed her neck and knew that prolonging the process would just make them both uncomfortable. "Please don't move. I'm going to make this quick."

Issy sat up straight and gripped both arms of the chair when he lowered his face to her neck. Rohnert spotted the biggest vein and latched on to it. He held her shoulders steady while drawing on her artery. When she relaxed, he began to tug harder. They both moaned when the flow of her blood began, coating his throat. He continued to pull until he had his gotten his fill.

Her pure blood had done its job yet again, and his strength multiplied. His senses were restored to their prime level, which was essential to his survival.

Rohnert released her, and she leaned against the back of the chair, looking depleted but resplendent. "Your generosity is appreciated. Thank you." He bowed before her then wiped his lips.

Isidora rose to her feet and walked to the door. "I will need to feed from you tomorrow," she said before she left his chamber.

Once alone, he held his head between his palms to keep the miserable thoughts away. It was an automatic response to purge himself after every feeding, after each overwhelming emotional betrayal. He went to the bathroom and took the dagger he kept for that sole purpose. With practiced ease, he created one deep slice. Rohnert took a sharp breath as the wound produced the pain and the reprieve he sought—a means to release his guilt. Blood trickled down his arm to the sink in a steady stream until he tied a cloth around it to stop the bleeding.

Rohnert looked in the mirror and gasped at Aemerria's reflection, watching him with disapproval written all over her face. He turned around to confront her. "What happened to privacy?"

She clucked her tongue and ignored his question. "There is no shame in taking another's vein out of necessity."

He shook his head and moved away, hurrying to the bedroom to gather his weapons. "You know nothing of my pain," he shot back.

She followed him, her footsteps muffled under her heavy robe. "You're not doing your mate any disservice by surviving, and I will continue watching you. It is a part of my job."

He glared at her. "I happen to like my privacy, and I don't appreciate being followed."

Aemerria smiled, not seeming in the least bit offended by his rebuff. "You're a tough one, Ronestus. I have a feeling I'll enjoy working with you."

"I can't say the feeling is mutual, but I'm willing to disregard my feelings if you will show me some consideration."

"Too bad. You'll have to endure my presence. I have the right to make an appearance whenever I want. Don't kid yourself into believing that Lukan and I operate the same way."

Rohnert gritted his teeth at her refusal to give in to his request. "Well then, you can do whatever you want. Just stay out of my way and don't speak unless it's necessary."

Her laughter echoed through the room. Rohnert was about to sling a retort at her when she disappeared before his eyes. He turned around, checking whether she was playing tricks on him, but the room was empty.

This made Rohnert seethe, making his bad mood worse. Too bad for the person he was getting ready to meet. The sucker had no idea what he would be capable of, given his foul mood.

Cyrus stood outside Rohnert's chamber like a statue, unmoving but raging inside. Sure, he understood Rohnert and Issy's superior makeup. He could accept that he couldn't satisfy Issy completely in that area, yet his emotions couldn't reconcile the idea of Issy feeding Rohnert, and vice versa.

He was jealous, but he wasn't going to act on his rage. They couldn't escape their bodies' need, nor could he disregard his reaction to this stupid arrangement. His plan was to take her back home once their feeding was over and then pick a fight somewhere.

Yeah, that sounded like a good plan.

The image of two bodies touching flashed through his head—a staggering reminder that he was out here while Rohnert and Issy were locked inside the room together. Cyrus felt his muscles tightening.

Just when he thought he couldn't take it any longer, the door opened and Issy stepped out. He raked his eyes from her head down to her toes. There was nothing out of place. Beside the dazed look in her eyes, she seemed fine.

"Are you okay?" she asked, her voice rising with concern.

Cyrus didn't answer. Instead, he grabbed her by the arm and hustled her to the far end of the hallway to her own private chamber. He closed the door behind them and pushed her against it. "I need to feel you now." He closed his mouth on hers, preventing any response.

Cyrus hadn't expected his instincts to take over. He thought he had a good grip on his sanity. Yeah right. He continued to kiss her with one thing in mind—the need to possess her. He traced his hands along the contours of her body.

Issy met his demands with total submission, arching her body and molding it against his. She understood his need for her. He needed to know she felt the same way for him.

She tilted her head and pushed him until he was at arm's length. "This needs to be said. I feel the same way about you. Maybe even more than you do for me."

Catching his breath, Cyrus stared at her, conflicted and aching between his legs. "That is impossible. You're the air I breathe."

"What are you going to do about it?" Issy's eyes were filled with challenge.

Cyrus licked his lips. Ready or not, he was going to take Issy. There was no mistake about that. With her back against the door, he studied her face, knowing that she was up for this. He kissed her. "I'm going to have you right now," he said between kisses.

"Take what is given freely."

Her words were like the ignition switch. "You have too many clothes on." Cyrus worked fast in removing every single piece of her clothing, revealing a figure he could worship for the rest of his life. "Beautiful." He cupped her ass and lifted her up until her breasts were level with his mouth. Cyrus captured one nipple with his lips and sucked hard. The pink tip was hard when he released it. "Like that?"

Issy whimpered.

His body tingled at the sound she made. "I guess you want more." Cyrus moved to the other nipple and took it with his teeth, nipping and biting until Issy writhed against his body while he fondled the other breast. She continued to moan with every flick of his tongue. Cyrus didn't stop—he couldn't. He set her down on her feet and continued to ravage the sensitive tip. Issy went wild when he ground his raging need against her thighs. He opened his mouth wider and seized her areola.

"Oh, Cyrus . . . that's it. Harder."

He sucked hard, tugged even more until she was screaming his name. He didn't let go until she was wriggling against him. Cyrus gave the other breast the same attention, pulling on the swollen tip. Issy screamed once more before she jerked, gasped, and froze.

"You're driving me insane with the sound that you make."

"Do something about it." She grasped his hair and arched her body closer, her mounds pressing against his face.

"Don't mind if I do." Cyrus pulled his boxers down to his knees and urged her legs apart with his hands. "I'm afraid this is going to be a quickie. I'm dying to be inside you."

"Take me." Issy took his swollen shaft in her hand and brought it toward her.

Cyrus almost unraveled at the feel of his tip against her skin. Unable to wait any longer, he gave one good push and was rewarded. She was as tight as a glove and so ready for him. "You're amazing," he rasped.

"Don't stop, Cyrus."

"It's been a long time, honey." He thrashed against her, his head spinning and his body screaming for release. "I—I might have some caveman tendencies."

Issy embraced him with warmth. Cyrus pulled back a bit and surged into her body again. The delicious friction was too much. He drilled into her with vicious impatience. He held her by the waist, pounded hard while their skin made slapping sounds with every strike. She undulated her hips, accommodating him.

He kept on thrusting until he couldn't hold off anymore. One hard pump was all it took, then he exploded violently inside her. Issy wrapped her arms around him, screaming his name while she rode her own climax. They held on to each other until the euphoria passed.

"Thank you," she said at last.

This brought his head up, and he cupped her face. "You're thanking me when I didn't even have the decency to take you to bed?"

Issy smoothed the frown from his forehead with her finger. "What have I told you before? I'll take you any way you want to give yourself to me."

He shook his head. "Unbelievable. This is what I get for being a jealous ass?"

"You betcha. But remember, I'm expecting another round soon." She winked at him then planted a soft kiss on his lips.

Drago raised a hand to stop one of Marchec's minions from talking. "What the fuck are you telling me?"

"We did as Lord Marchec instructed us. The headquarters had a skeleton crew, but a powerful and unseen force expelled us from the Council walls."

Om, the Neroc soldier, blinked, his dull eyes dilating in their sockets with aggression. Known for their impulsive nature, it would be prudent for Drago not to push it.

This was not happening. He had the plan mapped out like the goddamn New York City transit system. It was supposed to work. Besides, Lukan had guaranteed their success when she altered the spell that blanketed the Council walls.

"The plan was simple. Kill everyone in sight, you bastard."

In Lord Marchec's absence, discussing the matters with his lowly subject wasn't going to do anyone any good. The escalating tension between Drago and the ugly ass creature before him, plus the unsuccessful attempt to assassinate the key vampires in the Council, was driving his anger to the surface.

"Be careful. We might be allies, but I have no problem cutting you down." Om planted his grimy hands on Drago's desk and glowered down at him, showing off his jagged teeth.

Drago stood up, smoothed his suit jacket, and then pulled out a gun from underneath the desk. He aimed it at the fucker. "Threats make my balls tingle. That's all they do for me. You're better off leaving now before I blow your brains out."

Drago meant it, and from Om's expression, he believed it. Slow but steady, the repulsive looking vampire backtracked, hands raised, until he was out of the room. It wasn't until the door clicked shut that Drago replaced the gun in its holster.

Feeling tired, he sank down into the chair. That was unexpected. It was supposed to be easy. Damn it. He punched the intercom for his secretary's direct line.

"Sally, connect me to Tack Enterprises."

"Yes, Mr. Drago."

The line went silent until it began ringing. He waited and heard the voicemail kick on.

"Cyrus, call me. It's Jack Drago." He slammed the phone down. Mind racing and his anger meter bubbling over, he summoned Lukan while he paced around his office.

The Shaman arrived in a matter of minutes. "Darling, what ails you?" She snaked her arms around his waist, preventing him from walking.

He turned around. "Didn't you see these things would happen?"

From the expression on Lukan's face, he could tell she was already gathering the necessary information from him without asking. Drago pulled away and continued burning ruts in the gleaming hardwood floor.

Lukan paled. "I'm not Gastarius. I can't foretell what's about to happen. When I was banished from grace, every enhancement bestowed on me was taken away. I still have my innate powers, but that's all I have now."

Drago sucked in a furious breath. "Then we need to locate the black book."

She nodded. "I think I might be able to do that." A smile broke across her plump lips.

"Do that. I want to get around all this bullshit. I thought by now we'd be sitting pretty on the Council seat."

"I guess Bretania failed?"

"No word from her, and my scouts said the place is a ghost town right now." The botched attempt to gather information about the cure was a big obstacle. Then again, he wasn't going to miss Bretania. He was sick of worrying whether his condom would rupture while he was fucking the horny vampire.

"What about Cyrus?" Lukan flitted closer to him.

He stopped walking and faced her. "I have a feeling the man can be bought."

Lukan appeared unconvinced, prompting him to explain further.

"On the few occasions we've met, I've gathered some background from the man. He is loyal—hardcore to a fault. He has a foster sister who can be used as collateral, if you know what I mean."

She smiled, showing hint of understanding. "You're despicable."

Drago chuckled, feeling the tension in his muscles ease. All the cards hadn't been dealt yet, and he might be holding an ace up his sleeve. "We've played many hands, and most have gone our way. I won't stop the game now."

"When are you intending to carry this out?" Lukan took his hand and brought it up to the curve of her hips.

"I left Cyrus a message. As soon as he returns my call, things will be underway." He wagged his eyebrows conspiratorially and ran his palm along her back. "And you are going to get nailed tonight, my lovely Lukan."

"I love the way you think." Her voice grew huskier.

Drago didn't waste any time. He led her out of his study and into his bedroom, passing the Nerocs who lingered in the shadows, throwing furtive glances their way.

Inside, he rushed to disrobe her and then removed the ties that held up her honey-colored hair. He watched with open admiration as the honey-colored strands cascaded down her shoulders.

The priestess was the only living creature who could satiate his hunger. Maybe it was because she had a way of getting inside his head—and she knew how to satisfy him.

Lukan smiled and arched her body closer. "You can look or taste. Take your pick."

Drago bared his fangs. "I think I'll do both." He placed his hand at the nape of her neck and pulled her toward him. "This is just a prelude." He seized her mouth and nipped at her lower lip until she cried out.

That voice never ceased to turn him on. He continued his assault, his body humming in anticipation. Soon enough, Lukan was close to being insensible as the poison from his bites began to course through her body. This was his gift—a momentary disabling weapon he used to make his conquests. Maybe, if mass produced, the venom would help him in his quest for supremacy.

He inspected his handiwork once it had spread. Lukan was now at his mercy, and he could take her anyway he wanted.

"I love submissive women." Drago took her to his bed, the sound of her heartbeat the sole indication that she was still alive.

"Get away from me!" Cyrus tried to twist his head around to get a better look at Zane, but the bastard's foot was jammed against his neck, preventing him from seeing anything. Sweat trickled down his temples to the floor. Then his legs were spread wide apart until he could feel his skin tearing. He bit down on his lips to keep from crying out.

"Having fun yet?"

"Fuck you," he answered through gritted teeth.

Then with one mighty thrust, something was rammed into his ass—sick and terribly painful. His mouth opened, and he screamed on impact. There went his resolve.

"The sweet sensation of torture. Don't you just love it? Are you ready to tell me what I want to know?"

"Go . . . to . . . hell . . ." Cyrus managed to say in between cries of unthinkable pain.

"You first," Zane whispered in his ear. "Do you have any idea what I have jammed up your ass?"

He grunted at the torturous agony. "I'm sure . . . you'll tell me."

"This thing is what is referred to as a Pear of Anguish." Zane continued. "They also called it a Choke Pear."

Zane twisted something. A squeaky noise sounded and brought hell to his butthole. Cyrus screamed profanities, but that seemed to excite the half-vampire even more. He twisted the metal around for another demonstration, rattling Cyrus' wits to the core.

He writhed in pain, which doubled each time Zane twisted the device.

"This was used in the Middle Ages as punishment. It was a way to torture women who conducted abortions. It was also effective on liars and blasphemers. In your case, and considering the day and age, it's a way to make you sing like a soprano and give me the information I need."

Cyrus couldn't answer. His eyes were watering from the sheer torture as his anal muscles tore more with every little turn of the screw.

"Now, I think you are ready for more." Zane's voice was low, but Cyrus could hear every syllable with aching clarity.

Another squeak, and his long and agonized cry filled the room. Sweat poured down in torrents, mingling with the tears he hated to shed but had no way of stopping.

"This is what you're looking at. I gathered enough metal and screws and put this device together. Google really helps for DIY. I had to improvise, since it was either that or steal one from a museum. They don't make stuff like this anymore." Zane laughed.

Cyrus swore the bottom part of his body was going to separate from the rest of him soon.

Zane continued, enjoying the torment he was inflicting. "I scraped the metal with my bare hands. Mind you, I don't mind doing dirty work. I honed each piece into a spoon like shape, keeping it smooth for easy entry.

With Zane's slight movement, the metal lodged in his rectum elicited even more unbearable pain. Cyrus didn't dare move. He stayed still, hoping the madness would stop. Then Zane grabbed his hair and yanked his head back until he was bent in a terrible angle. His whole body ached like a mother.

"I attached the scraps of metal and screwed them together. It wasn't a daunting task at all. I enjoyed myself. This is my first venture in anything artistic. And it's been tested for accuracy."

There was no answer but a pathetic whimper.

"Don't you have anything to say?"

Cyrus, despite his predicament, still mustered enough energy to lash out. "Fuck you!" He tried to clamp his muscles together, to keep the throbbing pain from pushing him to madness.

"I think you're the fucked one here." Zane sounded so sure of himself.

He turned the screw once more, spreading the device farther apart. The sound of metal grated against Cyrus' skin, followed by the unbelievable feeling of his flesh tearing apart.

"Look at that! You're bleeding like a bitch."

There was no answer to give. Cyrus wasn't going to give the location of Tack Enterprises. Even the devil wouldn't find out where their underground hideout was. He closed his eyes, waiting until he could no longer sustain consciousness. He was going to let go. He was ready. Give him anything but this.

"Are you ready to talk?"

"Kill me now. I'm not going to say a word."

"You already have." Zane laughed with triumph.

"I didn't say anything . . ."

"I guess I forgot to tell you. I knew all along where you guys were hiding."

Another twist of the screw, one little inch was all it took, and Cyrus slipped into unconsciousness. The last thing he heard was the maniacal laugh of a man who got what he wanted and more. If this was death, he welcomed it with open arms.

"Cyrus. Cyrus, wake up." Issy's voice came through the haze of dark clouds as he surfaced from the mind-numbing nightmare.

His eyes popped open to the thundering sound of his heartbeat, and he pushed her away. "What are you doing here?"

"You invited me here last night," Issy said, looking scared. But instead of moving away from him, she inched closer. "Cyrus, I heard everything."

Shame washed over him like acid rain, burning his pride and ripping at his threadbare ego. He turned his back on her, an effective blockade to hide his embarrassment. "You didn't have to see that."

"But I did, and it's okay." Her voice changed into a low growling sound. "Hell, it's not okay. I understand now why you've been clinging to your hatred. What Zane did to you is unthinkable. I would want to kill him, too . . . With my bare hands. I would twist his neck so hard his eyes would bulge out of their sockets."

Cyrus looked at her in disbelief.

After a few moments, she took a deep breath. "What I want to say is that you have nothing to be ashamed of."

Issy placed a comforting hand on his shoulder. His muscles coiled, but Cyrus remained glued to the spot. When he didn't shake her hand off, she moved until they were facing each other.

"I'm filthy. That's the reason why I couldn't make love to you." His voice shook, making him loathe himself even more.

Issy shook her head. "No, no. That is a lie. I've always known you were keeping something from me, from Sawyer, and everyone else. We all deserve your love and affection, if you would let us in. You don't deserve what has been done to you, and I love you now more than ever."

The revelation startled him, and he wasn't sure just how to respond. Cyrus went for the safer subject. "What about Sawyer?"

"The child needs someone to look up to, someone to anchor him. I can tell he is drawn to you, but you've been keeping him at arm's length."

"I'm not big brother material." Cyrus shook his head at the thought of taking another soul under his wing.

"Give both of you a chance," Issy whispered.

Despite the turmoil in his head, he heard her loud and clear. The idea of people wanting to be around him was too absurd to be believable. "I'm not sure why you would want me to be with me. I can't even touch you without thinking of what has been done to me. You deserve someone better, a purebred vampire, someone like Rohnert."

Her face turned red with indignation. "Let's get this straight. I'm a grown woman, and I know who I want. If you don't feel the same way, that's all right. I can handle it. But don't ever push me toward another man. I don't have to be told who I should be with."

"Issy, I've felt something for you since the day we met." Cyrus recognized defeat and heard it in his voice. He wasn't going to hide anymore and risk losing the woman he loved. "I have the overwhelming urge to protect you—"

Issy covered her ears. "Stop it! Don't try to protect me. I want your love more than your protection."

Cyrus held her hands and lowered them. With a brittle smile, which was the best he could offer, he spoke the words he'd been longing to say but was too afraid to even think. "You cut me off. I wanted to love you ever since I laid eyes on you, but I've been afraid because I feel you could do better. You have no idea how difficult it was to deny you, to turn you away."

Issy's eyes misted over, and she offered a tentative smile. "You've loved me that long?"

Cyrus nodded. "It could've been longer. It seems like I've been waiting for you all my life." Taking her chin, he planted a soft kiss on her mouth. For the first time, he felt as though he was no longer drifting. He was finally anchored to a safe place he could call home. All along, he'd only needed someone to accept him for who he was and what he had to offer. In Issy's embrace, life held a new meaning.

With Isidora in his arms, Cyrus found comfort from the torture of his nightmares and his past. The warmth of her touch and the sweetness of her kisses made him think of nothing but the present and the desire he had long denied.

Cyrus had no idea how to take things between them. He had given her rough sex because he had been a jealous ass. If he'd been thinking clearly, he wouldn't have done it. Yet he had given in to the intense need to possess her. Maybe, if he took things slow and started from the beginning, he could make do with the little kisses and touching. However, the tenting inside his pants was a cause for concern. It didn't take long for her to notice.

Issy broke their kiss and smiled up at him. She had that gleam in her eyes, the kind that told him she knew what he was thinking. He rotated his hips, trying to create room between their bodies, but she refused to let him go.

"This is a good time to see if we can work things out."

"Damn it," Cyrus muttered. Was he ready? The answer was out of his hands. With the massive wood he was sporting, even a long dip in an icebox wouldn't chill him out. His body needed Issy, and there was no doubt she wanted him, too.

"Cy, you can take charge of everything. We'll go at your pace and on your terms. I'm here to enjoy the ride."

This made him smile. "Even if the ride is bumpy?"

"As long as I'm with you." She tightened her arms around his waist. "I don't care how rough, how easy—just take me with you."

Cyrus' heart skipped under her intense gaze. He kept staring at Issy, reacting to her words. He was a goner when she seized his mouth. This time, her kisses were hungry, teasing him to take what was being offered. How could he even consider letting this moment pass?

He pulled away and held her face, making sure she understood. "My fears are real. I would hate to hurt you."

Issy pressed a finger to his lips. "I know, and I share your fears. The only way you'd hurt me is to push me away. Remember, we're taking this nice and slow. You're in the driver's seat."

Cyrus took her mouth once more and shut everything else out. He gave her gentle kisses, enjoying her soft lips before sliding his tongue deeper into her mouth. Issy tangled her fingers through his hair and rubbed her body against his.

He broke the kiss but kept holding her. "Woman, you're going to give me a heart attack here."

She just smiled and sat up, tugging on his shirt. "May I?"

Cyrus nodded. Rational thinking wasn't possible with her looking at him with those pleading eyes. He watched her hands tremble as she released the first button. He took her hand. "Are you okay with this?"

"Yes." She kept at it until the last button was undone. Then her hands glided along his chest, touching, feeling, and probing the ridges of his muscles.

Watching Issy elicited delicious ripples of want in him. Everything about her made him want to scream, to tell her, to make her see, and to make her believe how much he worshipped her. How much he loved her.

"You have to say it. I've been longing to hear it."

"I . . ." Cyrus hesitated, feeling a bit out of his element.

"It's okay if you're not ready."

"But I am. It's just that . . . I'm not used to . . . Oh, God. Isidora, I'm in love with you. I've never met someone like you." It came out in a rush, but it didn't matter. He loved her, and she loved him back.

Happiness shone in her face when she smiled. "Thank you."

"Why are you thanking me? It should be the other way around."

She moaned. "Hush now. I'm dying to feel you inside me."

Cyrus replied with a sheepish grin then took her mouth again while his fingers worked on relieving her of the dainty dress. It was difficult to kiss her and still maintain restraint, and he was dying to just rip her clothes off.

With the garment off her body and tossed on the floor, he allowed their mouths to separate so he could take in Issy's lovely form with his eyes. Unlike their first time together, he intended to go slow and enjoy the moment. Cyrus wasn't going to go ape man on her again. She needed tender loving, and he was going to give it to her.

"I want to do right by you." *Even with my fucked-up headspace, I can do this.*

Issy grimaced, and he could tell she'd caught his unspoken thoughts. She took his hand and rubbed his sweaty palm. "Baby, we don't have to do anything if the memory is still fresh. I understand what you went through. Maybe it's too soon. We . . . I can wait. We can just hold each other tonight."

Cyrus glanced down at their entwined hands and shook his head. They fit perfectly. He wasn't going to let this woman go. His bad experiences had taken so much from him already, and he'd be damned if he would allow them to ruin the rest of his life. Not when he had this beautiful and caring woman who wanted to share her life with him.

He smiled and lifted her hand to his mouth for a kiss. Then he looked into her eyes. "I'm going to make sweet love with you. We'll do rough and tumble another time."

Isidora blinked. "Are you sure?"

"More than anything." Cyrus eyed the black lace bra, imagining his mouth grazing the pink tip of her breast while his hand worked its way into her panties to touch her.

"You're teasing me." Issy closed her eyes but not before he saw the raw desire burning there. Her chest heaved up and down with the cadence of her steady breathing.

"Issy . . . you're beautiful." Cyrus uttered the words in adoration as his gaze continued to sweep across her body. "You have no idea how long I've wanted you."

"How long has it been?" She licked her lips, a simple act that was still enough to unhinge him.

"Since I first laid eyes on you." His voice was haggard while he strained to keep himself together.

She purred. "Touch me now."

Issy unclasped her bra and took Cyrus' hands to lay them over her breasts. He glanced down to where his hands cupped her softness, and fever raged through his body. Cyrus had been on fire without even touching her. Now he was blazing with need.

She shivered with pleasure when his finger played with one nipple. He circled and teased until her throaty moans echoed across the room, feeding the flames within him. Unable to keep himself from tasting her any longer, his mouth descended. On first contact, Issy's body jerked, and her nipples hardened when he pulled the perky tip with his teeth.

She squirmed. "I know you said you wanted to take this slow, but I'm dying here. Can I get a rain check on mellow and have you take me fast and hard?"

Cyrus barely comprehended what she'd said, but one look at her face and he knew that his woman was unwilling to wait. "You're an impatient little thing, aren't you?"

Issy trembled and moaned. "I want to feel you inside me now. I can't . . . I don't want to wait."

Her invitation sounded like church bells, drawing Cyrus to his knees. "You don't need this." He ripped the bikini off her body.

Lit with the same longing, Issy followed suit and took charge of removing his clothes. Once every garment was gone, Issy cupped his butt, freezing him for a moment.

She jerked her hand back. "Oh dear, I'm so sorry. I didn't mean to startle you."

Cyrus held her gaze. He wasn't going to freak out. This was Issy. He got this. "Honey, don't worry. I'm okay."

Still hesitant, Issy waited for him to make his move.

"How do you really want your kisses? Soft and gentle, or hard and deep?"

"I can't believe you're making me choose. All I can want is your mouth on—"

Issy didn't get a chance to finish before Cyrus closed his mouth on hers, thrusting his tongue deep and letting her know he meant business. It was time he manned up and pushed the vicious memories away. He needed to undo Zane's damage and move on.

Whether he took her rough or slow, he would be free of the shackles of his past. "I'm in the driver's seat?" he murmured.

She responded by dropping her hands to his hips to pull him closer.

Screw it. He could do the worshipping later. Cyrus shoved inside her and joined their bodies as one. Stars exploded in his eyes at the sweet invasion. "God, I love you."

"Oh, keep saying it." Issy embraced him with her warmth and clenched. Cyrus moaned at the heady feeling while chanting his love for her until his throat constricted and he could no longer breathe.

Damn, she was much too lethal for him. Even if he tried to pace himself, he was too far gone. Cyrus ran on autopilot, letting his instincts take over. Circling his hips and finding that sweet spot, he was rewarded with a series of delirious moans. Issy arched her back and spread her legs wider to accommodate him. He thrust into her until the bed was shaking under the force of his pounding.

Each push and pull brought him closer to the peak. He pumped harder and claimed her mouth when the climax closed in on him. Cyrus held back a little when he felt Issy was reaching her own peak. Her head arched back when she claimed her bliss, shuddering and crying out his name. His release followed right after, sending him into a convulsive state when he shattered inside her.

They collapsed next together, both grinning from ear to ear. "That wasn't so bad, was it?"

Issy's eyes held a mischievous gleam. "I have no complaints. Do you?"

"I'm sure we can do better." Cyrus grinned then wrapped his arm around her. Issy nuzzled in the crook of his arm, and he sighed and stared at the ceiling, feeling a pang of regret. "I wanted our moment to be special and gentle. I didn't plan on turning into a madman with you."

She turned to face him, looking bewildered. "It was special. We needed this, whether you like to admit it." Then her eyes twinkled. "Besides, that means we have to do it again."

That brought a smile to his face. "You know what I want to do with you?"

She shook her head.

"I'm going to make love with you again. This time, I'm going to explore every inch of your body. I will worship you with my hands and praise you with my lips. Then after you can think of nothing else, I'll take you and show you how precious you are to me."

"Should we start now?" Issy's tone was filled with hope and longing. It would be a shame to make her wait.

Cyrus sat up and pulled her toward him until they were face to face. "We start now." He trailed a finger along her collarbone and watched her shudder with want. He was setting the tone—slow, nice, and easy while listening to the erratic beating of their hearts. True to his word, Cyrus made love to Issy with his hands and mouth. He made her feel as if she were the most precious thing on earth. He touched her, kissed her, and teased her.

Cyrus didn't stop until Issy was begging for mercy. He took her to heaven, and they both soared and gloried in the ecstasy of love.

Spent but radiating with bliss, Issy turned to face him. "Now, what are we going to do about the sleeping arrangements?" Her mouth twitched into a playful smile.

Chuckling, he tousled her hair. "You're already planning on moving in?" The idea was unnerving, but also exciting at the same time. He'd been living on his own for such a long time. What if it didn't work?

"Stop overthinking this. We're going to make it work." She turned and tangled her legs with his. "Besides, I'm not letting you off the hook. I want rough and tumble."

The concept of being in a relationship was staggering, but he wasn't going to fuck this up. Grinning at the prospect of endless time together, he wrapped an arm around her and cuddled her close. "I would love having you in my bed." With a smile on his face, Cyrus fell into a contented slumber.

He awoke a few hours later with Issy still in his arms. "Are you awake?" he asked, running his hand across her back.

"No, I'm asleep." She giggled. "I've been thinking about sharing a bed with you."

Picturing the life he'd not dared dream of in the past, he saw them together for a long, long time. An overwhelming happiness rose inside him. "I like the idea, but I want to keep this quiet for now."

He felt Issy stiffen before she glanced up, frowning. "Are you embarrassed to let people know?"

Cyrus shook his head. On the contrary, he felt he was going to burst into song. Yep, he had it bad. "I just hate the teasing. You know how the guys are, especially Tor."

Sighing, she nodded in understanding. "Okay. I'll play along until you're ready."

"I can't promise you I know the first thing about being in a relationship. It's been a long time, and I'm pretty rusty. I hope you won't hold that against me."

Issy rolled her eyes. "You're overthinking again. Will you—"

Her words were cut off by the shrill ringing of the phone. Cyrus reached toward his nightstand and picked up the call. "Rayce, this better be important."

"Drago left a message for you. He wants you to call him back."

"Did he say why?" He glanced at Issy.

"Nope. He sounded pissed."

"Call me back when you have him on the line." Cyrus got out of bed and picked up his pants from the floor while Rayce patched through the call. He was pulling his jeans up when the phone rang and Drago's voice went live.

"Cyrus, listen well. I'm in possession of precious cargo. If you want to see her alive, come and see me, alone."

"What the hell are you talking about?"

"You underestimated me. I know exactly who you are—everything about you. Your past, your job, and when you were turned. Your sister is not going to like it if you don't come for her. Don't let her down, Cyrus."

His grip tightened on the phone. Not Linda. "Fuck you, asshole! Touch her and I promise you, I won't stop until your ashes are blown away."

Drago laughed, making Cyrus want to scream. "I'm *really* scared here. You will meet me at this location tomorrow at midnight." While the vampire on the other line recited the address, Cyrus pounded his palm on his head. Issy stood next to him with questioning eyes.

"One wrong move and your sister is dead. This is not a joke, so don't even think of fucking this up. Come alone. I have eyes everywhere. If you want to see her alive, do what I say."

"Lay a finger on her—" The phone line went dead before he could finish. Cyrus glared at the phone then threw it across the room. It hit the wall and fell on the floor with a resounding thud.

He walked to the door, not knowing what to do or say. Issy moved toward him, wrapping her arms around his waist. "Stop. What's going on?"

Cyrus turned around, his eyes burning with rage. "You heard the man. He will kill Linda if I don't come."

"Your sister?"

"Yeah." He rammed his fingers through his hair, hating that he had to explain why he'd kept his sister a secret from everyone. "I didn't tell anyone about her because of the nature of my job. I don't want her involved in any way."

"What are you going to do?"

"That is a stupid question." He glared at her then realized how he was acting. "Issy, I'm sorry. I just never thought anyone would do something this low."

"Don't apologize. I understand how you feel. I've lost everyone I loved already, but like hell I'm going to let you go alone."

Stunned at her words, Cyrus stared at her.

Rohnert reached the meeting place minutes after Aemerria's rather distracting surprise visit. How dare she barge in on him unannounced? She might be an important figure, but she had no right to invade his privacy. Seething, he stalked to the front of the long line. He zipped up his ever-present trench coat and breezed through the entrance by flashing a hundred dollar bill so the door man would let him in without a thorough pat down.

Sure, he was going to meet with the Good Samaritan, but he wasn't fool enough to go in there unarmed. Once inside, he unzipped fast and looked around. He was not familiar with this place, but a quick call to Rayce had given him a quick description of the setup. The club was comprised of three levels, which boasted different types of music—jazz on the ground level, pop music on the second, and hip-hop on the third.

Rohnert walked up a series of steps that to a dark room offering the more subdued jazz music and ambient lighting, just as Rayce had described.

Once his eyesight adjusted to the darkened surroundings, he began to scan the patrons. He spotted a lone figure in a corner of the bar. This must be his guy. Rohnert strode over and took a good look at him. Rage replaced curiosity, and he hissed under his breath. Zane glanced up at him for a brief moment then diverted his gaze right away.

"You'd better have a good reason for asking to see me." Rohnert took the empty barstool next to the vampire, but Zane refused to make eye contact. He had no time for bullshit, so he got down to the point of their meeting. "Why did you do it?"

"Anything to drink?" Zane signaled for the bartender, who came over right away.

Rohnert ordered a double scotch and focused again on Zane, watching him turn the ice inside his glass with his finger. He'd had several tussles with the vampire in past, but tonight was different. Zane's emotional grid was calm for a change. No static, no rapid heartbeat, and not an ounce of aggression. Still, he couldn't get past Zane's merciless treatment of Cyrus or his spearheading the attack on their facility that led to Shelly's disappearance. His heart clenched at the memory.

"I should kill you now and end your miserable life." He eyed the cane that hung on the counter between them.

Zane didn't even blink. "You're welcome to do as you please."

Rohnert seized Zane's thoughts, every unspoken sentiment inside his head, and staggered at the weight of the man's regrets and misgivings. "I think it's best to leave you alive for Cyrus." He downed his drink and gestured to the bartender for another.

"That's probably the best thing to do." Zane chugged the remaining contents of his glass.

"I have to say that was ballsy of you to go against Bretania. What's with the change of heart?" This could be a trap, and Rohnert began combing every single thought in the room. He refused to be a sitting duck in case there was a plot going on around him.

Everything and everyone checked out all right. Still, he kept one hand on his weapon.

Zane sighed then turned to face Rohnert. "I'm done being manipulated."

"You left a lot of damage in your wake."

There was remorse in the eyes that met Rohnert's. "I can't take back the past. My father's dead. Melissa was sent to her death. I've done things I can't begin to explain. There's no excuse, and an apology isn't going to cut it."

"You're damn right." Rohnert grunted, feeling his muscles tighten at the tension of having to sit next to this bastard. He clenched and unclenched his fists, trying his best to stay calm.

In the thick silence that followed, Rohnert absorbed dark thoughts from Zane he couldn't comprehend. His order came, and this gave him more time to gather more information from the vampire. It wasn't every day he stumbled on insider information. But then Zane's mind wandered off to Shelly and the circumstances leading around her death.

Rohnert gripped the glass until it shattered in his palm, slicing it open. "Tell me what you know. I want it all." His voice had dipped so low that it was almost inaudible.

Zane spoke in a calm manner. "Goran called on me for surveillance. I watched her . . . Shelly, from afar. There were so many things I've witnessed back then that I later reported back to Goran. I saw when you rescued the injured human out of the hospital. I also knew of Goran's plan to seek Shelly out.

"That was the reason why I came to the warehouse, to warn you that he was coming. But Cyrus blew his top, and I had to leave."

Rohnert's mind began to race. He couldn't believe what he was hearing. If Cyrus hadn't driven Zane away . . . Shelly would still be alive.

"Shit . . . shit . . ."

His eyes grew dim, and he couldn't process anything after that. Then his breath caught in his throat, and he felt like he was going to suffocate.

"What's going on?" Zane placed a hand on his shoulder.

"Don't fuckin' touch me," Rohnert said through gritted teeth. He stood up and banged his palm on the counter. "If you are lying, you better pray I don't find you." He turned to leave.

Zane stood up, propped his cane on the floor, and followed him. "Rohnert, I know what you're thinking. If it's—"

Rohnert pivoted on his heel. He grabbed Zane by his jacket collar and then dragged him against the wall. "You have no idea what I'm thinking."

People began to gather. "Hey, take your shit outside," one man said.

"Mind your own business." Rohnert glared at the human. "Stay back."

Zane shook his head, trying to pry off Rohnert's fingers, but he was beyond pissed. "You . . . you . . . want revenge. You think Cyrus . . . could've prevented Shelly . . . from dying . . . he is as much a victim as you and Shelly."

His head was spinning. All he could think of was his loss and what could've been.

Rohnert hissed. "Shut up, mother fucker."

He released his hold, and Zane staggered backward as his cane clattered to the floor. Gasping for air, he looked up at Rohnert and shook his head. "Don't make the mistake I made. Vengeance blinded me. I went to battle based on faulty information. Look where it got me."

"I'm not going to listen to your lies." Fury raged within him, making it impossible to see the truth behind Zane's words. He walked toward the door then swiveled, pointing a finger. "You better not skip town, because I will hunt you down."

Zane trailed behind him. "I'm done running."

Rohnert's phone chimed. With anger coursing through his veins, he yanked it out of his pocket. "What, Rayce?"

"Rohnert, Harrow's on the line for you."

He heard a click, and then Harrow was on the line. "Rohn, Rayce caught a conversation between Drago and Cyrus. He's blackmailing Cy into seeing him or else his sister will die."

Speak of the one person Rohnert wanted to see. He drew in a sharp, angry breath. "Cyrus has a sister?"

"It's obvious he didn't tell anyone in order to protect her. Cyrus has no idea we know. Drago specifically instructed him to come alone."

"Why are you telling me this?" Rohnert asked.

Harrow was silent for a moment. "Where the hell did that come from? Our friend is in a jam. This is not a joke."

"The fuck, Gates. Shelly was killed, and it could have been prevented if Cyrus hadn't driven Zane away."

For once, Harrow had nothing to say. The line went quiet for a long stretch before he spoke again. "We will not let this happen. We've seen too many deaths. You're doing Shelly a disservice by turning on the people who have been there for you."

"I will not let you go alone." Issy followed Cyrus to the closet, where he began loading up his weapons.

The eyes that met hers were cold. "You have no say in this. That is my sister we're talking about."

Issy was so done being told what she could or couldn't do, say, or think. She grabbed Cyrus' arm and didn't let go. "I won't lose you. It won't happen." Tears threatened to fall, but she refused to succumb to the terror or weakness.

Cyrus took one good look at her, and his expression softened. He cupped her face. "Issy, you won't lose me. Not today or ever. I need to do this. Linda is fragile. She's been through a lot."

"But this might be an ambush. Let me go with you. I can wait from a distance. My aim is good."

He shook his head. "No . . . you will stay here, where it is safe."

Another person intent on protecting her was the last thing she needed. "I'm not a piece of delicate china. I can take care of myself." When Cyrus refused to yield, she went for another tactic. "Wear a vest. Protect yourself."

Cyrus considered her plea before he conceded. "Fine. I will swing by to see if that project Jones has been working on is done. Promise me you'll stay here and you won't do anything stupid."

"I'll be right here waiting for you."

He gave her a hurried kiss and then continued holstering his weapons. The amount of daggers and guns inside his jacket should put her mind at ease, but somehow her fear continued to strangle her.

"Take care of yourself." It wasn't until she heard the door shut behind him that she allowed the tears to fall.

It took a decent amount of time before Isidora collected herself enough to call on the one person she thought might be able to help. Rushing to her suite, she took the black book from her nightstand drawer and searched for guidance. She went to the center of the room and kneeled down.

Issy had heard her father chant the sacred words while she was growing up but had never expected the day would come when she would be in grace to summon the shaman. Her knowledge of the ancient language had been taught by a private tutor, and the mere thought of invoking the ritual scared her. She closed her eyes and took deep breaths, willing herself to relax. Slow in the beginning, she began reciting, gathering more confidence with every passing second.

Not knowing what to expect, she kept her eyes closed and waited. Minutes passed, yet there was still no sign of the shaman. Her patience was wearing thin, and her hope quickly dissipated. Isidora repeated the call with urgency, her voice shaking with emotion.

Just when she thought of giving up, a gust of wind rattled the furniture around her. Issy kept her eyes closed, afraid to offend the entity in her midst. She bowed her head low in veneration. The scent of wildflowers swirled around her, tickling her nose, yet Issy remained in her position.

"Open your eyes," the melodious voice said. Issy obeyed but kept her head bent low. "You can look up at me."

She did as she was told, raising her eyes until she saw a woman whose face reminded her of her mother's—kind, exquisite, and familiar. A strong current of emotions shot through her veins when their eyes met. The priestess smiled down at her and offered her hand. Issy stared, her mind a blank, not sure what to do.

The female smiled. "I can tell that this is your first time." Issy nodded. "You will kiss the top of my hand before you can ask me for favors."

Issy took hand in front of her. It was soft, yet she could feel the strength in it. She pressed her lips to the skin and closed her eyes at the warmth it offered. It felt strangely comforting and intimidating at the same time.

"I am Aemerria. Cast the weight of your heart on me so I can help you." The shaman did not let go of her hand. Instead, she pulled Issy to her feet.

"I requested an audience to ask for a favor." Isidora stopped to see if she had spoken out of line. When Aemerria gestured for her to continue, she began to pour out her deepest fear. "I have lost so many people in my life. I implore you to guide and keep safe a man dear to me, if it wouldn't offend."

Aemerria smiled and opened her arms. "Come and let me ease your troubles."

Walking into her embrace, Issy felt as though she was home. It was the same sensation she had gotten in the presence of her parents. She relaxed in an instant. "Why do you feel so familiar?" she asked before she could stop herself.

Silence was Aemerria's answer.

"Have I offended you?"

The shaman ignored her question. Instead of answering, she pulled away and took Issy's hands. "This former human you speak of, tell me about him."

"I met him not too long ago. He has taken me as his . . ." *What should I say, lover or friend?*

Aemerria's laughter filled the room. "You're a breath of fresh air, my dear Isidora. But I'm afraid I cannot alter the course of one's destiny."

"He is a kind being, strong and loyal to our race. We need people like him."

"Your faith in him is enough. I'll be watching from the sidelines, as I am powerless to alter the path each of you must take."

Issy cried from the fear that gripped her heart. "I beg you to return him to me."

"He is strong—a quality most of us possess but do not always use to our advantage. If his heart and mind are the same, he will come back to you. I'm afraid you will have to leave it to faith."

With those words, Aemerria vanished from sight, leaving Issy dazed and more confused than ever.

Cyrus slipped out of the facility, hoping to stay undetected. Fat chance. He might as well try shooting the moon. Without a doubt, Rayce would have alerted Harrow and the others by now, so he pushed his boots on the pavement and sprinted to get a head start. He checked over his shoulder to see if he was being followed. Nothing but darkness greeted him. Just like the way he wanted it to be.

He thought about Linda. Sweet Linda, caught in the middle of it all. Cyrus had stayed away all these years to protect the one special person from his past, but it seemed like his present had a way of catching up with him. For Drago to use his sister as a pawn was beyond despicable.

There hadn't been a time when he hadn't thought of his foster sister. Many times, he had to stop himself from checking on her, and he had made arrangements for her care at the group home. God, it pained him to be away from her, yet the nature of his associations demanded it.

"Fuck!" he screamed at the top of his lungs as he ran past the field that bordered their facility. With his temper flaring, he doubted he would be thinking straight once he found Drago. The bastard better make good on his promise to release Linda. God knew Cyrus would be ready to throw down if Drago decided to try bluffing.

Slated to meet on the rooftop of his penthouse, Cyrus glanced at the tall building. He rejected the idea of taking the elevator and went to scale the walls in the back. It would give him a little time to think things through before the showdown. Then he remembered a very important detail. Drago could read minds, so he was better off shutting his down if he didn't want to give his position away.

He reached the top of the building in no time, and he wasn't the least bit surprised to find Drago sitting on a lounge chair, looking too relaxed and far too cocky for his own good. Then he saw Linda sitting right next to him, with her wheelchair not too far from reach.

The sight of his sister looking helpless next to the vampire infuriated Cyrus. He broke into a run, but he stopped in his tracks when Drago aimed an automatic at him.

"Damn you, Drago. You should've left her out of this," Cyrus said, feeling the burn of fury in his veins. It didn't come as a shock to find that the gun aimed at him was the same weapon their company had supplied to the asshole.

"You wouldn't have come if I didn't use her as bait. Remember this. I'm always one step ahead of you, Mr. Crackenbush." Drago's laughter echoed in the dead of the night.

Cyrus ignored the reference to his last name and made eye contact with Linda.

"Cy, don't do whatever it is he wants you to do."

Confused by her words, Cyrus shifted his gaze to Drago. "What the hell did you tell her?"

The vampire smirked and raised a hand. "Take her away." Out of nowhere, a creature came out of the darkness and plucked Linda from the lounger, leaving her wheelchair behind.

"Linda." He rushed to stop them, but Drago kept the gun pointed at him.

"Sit down, and we'll talk. If you do as I ask, you two can have a happy reunion." Drago gestured at the lounger.

"You're digging a deep grave for yourself, Jack." Cyrus crossed his arms.

"Not if you beat me there."

"What the fuck do you want from me?"

"I need an insider. Someone who would be willing to give me information in exchange for the life of a crippled little sister. You must have put her away because you were ashamed of her."

Cyrus' anger spiked to an unbelievable level. "You shouldn't go there."

"I'm there already. Despite her useless legs, she's quite a looker. I'm sure the Nerocs wouldn't mind playing with her." Drago sneered.

Blood rushed to Cyrus' face. "Don't you dare lay a finger on her."

"That can be arranged. My demand is simple. Get me inside the Council grounds." Drago smiled, exposing his fangs.

He knew what he'd heard, but Cyrus couldn't think how the idiot knew of his connection to the Council.

Drago snickered. "I know everything. How about that girl of yours? She's rather pleasing to the eyes."

Before Cyrus could respond, gun shots rang out not far away. Drago looked at him in surprise and pulled the trigger, but Cyrus managed to launch a dagger just as the first bullet exploded out of the muzzle. Then the force of the successive shots threw him several feet away.

"Fuck," was all he could say. Expecting to disintegrate any time, Cyrus closed his eyes. *This is it. I'm done.* Stunned, it took several seconds before he realized that none of the pop, sizzle, and fizzing was happening. He opened his eyes to find Drago gone, but he was still breathing and in one piece. Damn. The bulletproof vest Jones had given him had worked its magic.

Cyrus staggered to his feet but slumped back down from the pain radiating from his chest. He struggled to get up.

"If I didn't know any better, I'd think you were goddamn cat with nine lives," Tor said, reaching down to help him up.

Cyrus took Tor's hand and hoisted up his aching body. "What the hell are you doing here?"

"Oh, we're just out for a midnight stroll." Tor laughed and nodded to the rest of the gang. "We figured you're not one to ask for help, so we just made sure Drago wouldn't have anything on you."

Clutching his chest, Cyrus glanced at the far side of the roof and found just about everyone he knew from the facility. In the center of it all, Harrow was cradling Linda in his arms. Fuck crying, fuck happiness, he was giving in to the tears. He took a step forward and stumbled. Tor caught him. He watched with tears in his eyes while Harrow deposited his sister in her wheelchair.

"You're setting a world record for getting shot and living to tell about it." Tor absorbed his weight as they walked toward Linda.

Cyrus felt a flush radiate throughout his body as if he'd been submerged in hot water. Sweat broke out on his face, and his legs shook underneath him. Overwhelmed, he kept nodding his head at the sea of faces surrounding him. "I'm so happy to see you, sis."

Visibly shaken, Linda's face broke into a hopeful smile. "Does this mean we can be together now?"

"Nothing and no one could keep us apart from now on," he answered and then took her in a tight embrace. "I'm so glad to see you, booger face."

Linda laughed, despite her tears. "Oh no, not that again."

"You'll get used to it." Cyrus kissed her on the forehead and then ruffled her hair. Out of the corner of his eye, he saw Rohnert lurking in the shadows, watching the reunion with lifeless eyes.

Back in the facility, Harrow's order trumped his, leaving Cyrus without a say. Instead of being at the meeting in the I-room, he was hustled to the clinic to be examined by Rick. Assisting the doctor as his interpreter, Issy appeared both calm and relieved. Rick helped Cyrus out of the heavy, bullet-riddled vest.

Issy fidgeted before she voiced Rick's thoughts. "You're a lucky bastard for getting out of this one alive."

Cyrus' eyes flickered to Issy before he answered. "That's what I gather. Any damage?"

Rick did a quick visual examination then shook his head. "Lie down for me." Once he did, the doctor ran his hand over Cyrus' abdomen and up to his ribs, where he started to flinch. "Bruised ribs for sure. Let's get you x-rayed. If there's anything broken, there's nothing I can do. It'll have to heal on its own. It'll be a pain to move for a few weeks and painful to breathe. I recommend several days of rest, and no strenuous activities for now."

"Damn it," he muttered. "How about my sister? Have you seen her?"

The doctor helped him get into a sitting position. "She's next." Then he looked at Issy as if there were a silent conversation going on. "The vest saved your life. I suggest wearing it from now on. That goes for anyone else going out there."

Cyrus jumped off the table, but the pain shot through his entire body, making him stagger backward. Issy was quick to brace his body against hers. "You don't take suggestions well, do you? You heard Rick. Rest is what you need."

Feeling like a child being scolded for bad behavior, he offered an apologetic smile. "I know, I know." He gave her a quick kiss on the mouth. "Can you help Linda out while I attend the meeting?"

Issy nodded. "You know I'd do anything for you," she whispered.

"Thanks."

Rick cleared his throat and had a quick silent conversation with Issy before leaving the room.

Cyrus smiled. "I'll be back for the X-ray after the meeting. I'll see you right after." Another kiss from Issy made him forget the ache for a moment. "You're getting good at this kissing thing."

"I think practice makes it perfect." She blushed. "I'm so glad you're back here in one piece. I don't know—"

He silenced her with a finger to her lips. "Shh, I'm here. We're together. Linda's safe."

Her eyes misted over, but her smile was brave. "I need you to be with me for a long, long time."

Touched by the sentiment, he traced a finger along her soft lips. "I think we can arrange that."

Issy grinned. "Go on before I hold you hostage in here."

Cyrus laughed. "Harrow might send out a search party."

Once he managed to pry himself away from Issy, Cyrus made his way to the I-room. The bruises he'd sustained from the impact of the bullets made each step difficult. His chest felt like it had been run over by a bulldozer then wrung out several times for good measure.

The meeting was already underway when he got there. Everyone looked up with curiosity when he flopped rather clumsily into a chair. Harrow watched him with a pinched expression.

Cyrus knew this was as a good time as any to ask his question. "What in the hell were you thinking, going in there without telling me?"

Harrow narrowed his eyes then laughed. "You told me before that Drago is no ordinary vampire. He can read minds. If you went there knowing my plan, then you'd be jeopardizing Linda's life and yours."

Cyrus thought about it for a moment. Harrow was right. "That's sneaky. You could've been killed. Next time, don't pull a stunt like that without telling me."

Tor snorted from where he sat at the end of the table. "This is the time to say 'thank you, suckers'."

"You're beginning to bore me," Rohnert said.

Under normal circumstances, Cyrus wouldn't mind the jab, but he'd sensed an unspoken hostility coming from the vampire earlier. "You have a problem with me, Rohn?"

The room grew quiet. Some fighters shifted in their seats while he met Rohnert's gaze. Cyrus saw Rohnert's nostrils flare, and a murderous glare was directed at him. "In fact, I do."

Cyrus flashed toward the vampire's grill, ignoring the screaming pain from his ribs. "Mind enlightening me?" His growl echoed in the silent room. All eyes were focused on them.

Harrow jumped in, wedging his body between two men. "Hey, hey. We have a meeting to finish." He looked at Cyrus, then Rohnert.

"You have something to say, say it now." Cyrus edged closer, prompting Tor to muscle him away.

"Jones has something important to say," Harrow said, still acting as if they were just having an ordinary argument.

"Let's step outside and get this over with," Rohnert pinned him with another killer glare.

"Jones, care to tell us about your new invention?" Harrow continued.

"Uh, sure," Jones said, seeming uncertain.

Harrow gestured for him to stand up. "As you can see, it worked on Cyrus."

Jones stood up, which halted the escalating confrontation for the time being. He grinned, looking pleased with himself.

The scientist drew a breath then addressed the group. "I've been working on a the prototype on and off, but I pushed forward these past couple of weeks when Harrow brought up the issue of high-powered guns being used by subversive vampires." He pulled out a vest from underneath the table, one similar to the vest he'd let Cyrus use. "Instead of using steel or titanium plates, I used a sheet of metal similar to graphene."

A collective murmuring circulated around the room while Jones waited to continue. "Cyrus' body absorbed much of the impact of the bullets, thus the bruised ribs and aches in the contact areas. However, I can tell the thin sheet did its job well. It is known to be one hundred percent stronger than steel and can absorb force better. Now that I have the test vest back in my hands, I will do further studies to see if there are any thermodynamic reactions resulting from the impact."

Cyrus kept his eyes straight. Still fuming, he heard few of the details. He was a lucky bastard, yada, yada, yada.

Question after question came up, and the room was buzzing. Harrow raised his hands to quiet the group. "Jones will give us more information as his research progresses. It is good to know that we have in our possession a countermeasure against our enemies. We will try to produce this ballistic armor as fast as we can."

"Are we going to manufacture them like we do guns?" Gentry asked, voicing the growing concern among the fighters.

Harrow's answer was quick. "No. This is going to be used by our fighters and no one else. With the rapid spread of illegal automatic weapons out there, and may I add that most were bought from us, I feel this new invention will better serve our primary purpose, which is survival."

This pleased everyone. Harrow continued. "Each one of you will be fitted with your own personal vest as soon as we can obtain the metal. I'm afraid you'll have to be patient. The development of this metal is still in its early stages, and production doesn't come as easy as we thought."

The discussion went on for several more minutes while Cyrus fought hard to sit up straight. The pain had been too intense to ignore, but he kept up the brave face. Indeed, Rick had been spot on when he suggested rest, because the goddamn pain was disabling to the point of immobility.

He glanced up to find Rohnert glaring at him from across the room, where the vampire was leaning against the wall. Cyrus returned Rohnert's stare without batting an eyelash. This went on until Harrow dismissed everyone, leaving the core members of the team.

As soon as it was just him, Harrow, Tor, Rohnert, Firman, and Gentry, Harrow pounded his fist on the table. "What the fuck was that about, Rohnert?"

Rohnert wasted no time pulling Cyrus out of his chair by the collar. "You shouldn't have driven Zane away. Shelly would still be alive if you'd allowed him to give us a fair warning about Goran's plan."

This was so not happening. Cyrus refused to allow anyone, even the revered head of the Vampire Council, manhandle him.

Pain or no pain, he pushed against Rohnert as a growl tore from his lips. "Get your fuckin' hands off me." Cyrus' eyes flashed.

Everyone jumped out of their seats to pull them apart. Cyrus managed to close his hands around Rohnert's neck. They strained against each other's death grip.

"What the fuck are you talking about?"

Tor and Firman held Cyrus back while Harrow and Gentry eased Rohnert away. The tension was high, but Cyrus wasn't about to back off.

Rohnert drew a sharp breath, his eyes blazing. "Zane came to warn us that Goran was after Shelly. If you hadn't stepped in, she might still be alive."

Cyrus heard the despair in Rohnert's voice, but he wasn't going to own up to the accusation. "Try to be in my shoes. You might've done a lot worse in my position."

Rohnert shook off Harrow and Gentry's hands. "You have no idea what has been taken from me. Shelly's death could've been prevented." His face hardened, and he let out a primal cry.

Cyrus shrunk back. Did his act really cost Shelly her life? Was he so caught up in his own problems that he forgot to think of others? He fucking had no idea what to think anymore.

"Let me go." Cyrus struggled from Tor and Firman's grasp, and they released him. He contemplated trying to comfort Rohnert, but he thought better of it. The vampire wouldn't appreciate it. Besides, what could be said at that point?

Instead, Cyrus strode to the bar and poured a drink for himself. After chugging it down, he looked up and asked. "Anyone want to get drunk with me?"

"Leave us, please," Rohnert said, depositing himself in one of the chairs.

Harrow appeared dubious. "If you guys are going to go at it after we leave, you—"

Cyrus cut him off. "This goddamn room is rigged with cameras."

Once the place emptied out, Cyrus brought the bottle along with two glasses to the table. "Look, I couldn't have known what the motherfucker was going to say back then." That was the best explanation he could offer.

Rohnert buried his face in his massive hands. He stayed that way for a long time—long enough for Cyrus to finish half the bottle's contents. When Rohnert looked up, his pained expression did a number on him.

"Look, I'm not good at this talking shit." Cyrus slid a glass along the table to Rohnert.

Rohnert caught the glass with his hand. "Then don't," he warned, downed the scotch, and slid the glass back to him. "The damage has been done."

With those words, Rohnert left the room, leaving Cyrus guilt-ridden and confused. He buried his face in his hands and groaned. If he wanted to salvage his friendship with Rohnert, he had to find a way to do right by him. He'd loved Shelly, too, and missed her more than anything. "We'll find you, Shelly, if it's the last thing I ever do," he swore under his breath.

Drago cradled his hand inside his suit jacket and rained curses down on no one in particular. For the second damn time, things hadn't gone his way. It was enough to ruin his mood. He had everything figured out and executed to perfection. The sister had been cooperative out of fear of hurting Cyrus. Such loyalty made Drago want to throw up.

How had Cyrus managed to keep his thoughts from him? How in the hell had Linda gotten away? That was the question of the century. Unless . . .

He called for Lukan, who appeared within minutes. Lord Marchec eyed him with amusement but remained quiet on the sofa opposite his desk. The priestess bowed before approaching the desk, her lithe body moving faster than eyes could follow.

"My lord, what happened?"

"Tell me, is there anyone more powerful than you?" He pulled her by the neck until her face was close to his.

He heard a scratching noise as Lord Marchec rose to his feet. "If there's nothing else you need from me, I'd better be on my way."

Nodding without sparing a glance at the leader, Drago continued to wait for Lukan's response.

He noticed her paling but wasn't going to ease up on her. "Answer me."

"There was one, but she was wild and uncontrollable. She was out of commission after she succumbed to bloodlust just after we found her."

"Who is she?"

Defiance crossed Lukan's lovely face before she responded. Truth was, Drago didn't care if he offended her. "Her name is Aemerria. She was taken from her parents at a young age. She has no memory of who she is or where she came from."

"Is it customary for you people not to remember your past?"

Lukan shook her head. "It was her, just her, because Gastarius projected great things about her."

He prodded her for more information. "Great things?"

"I don't have any idea what he knew, but he predicted that Aemerria would have incredible power. So imagine his disappointment when she went on a rampage."

"Tell me more." Drago could see Lukan's discomfort, but he had to know. If his questions were doing a number on her fragile ego, there was nothing he could do about it.

"She was too young. Confused and lost. She went out one day, not knowing what the outside world was like. She stumbled upon a village and sucked everyone dry. It was a tough cleanup for us. Gastarius had no choice but to keep her locked up as punishment. I only saw her the day before he hid her."

"Where was she before you left?" He flinched from the pain radiating from the stump of his missing forefinger. Damn Cyrus for having a good aim. The vampire had clipped Drago's finger before he went down. At least he got the bastard good and hard. He should've stayed for the grand finale, but with his finger blasted, he wasn't going to be any good at firing the weapon.

Lukan bristled and ignored his question. "There's another thing, my lord. Cyrus is alive. Bruised, but alive."

His mood turned black in an instant. Here he had a severed finger, and the vampire was alive? If he remembered correctly, he had gotten Cyrus in the chest, many times. How could he have survived a round of Dangeran bullets?

Drago shot out of his chair and pushed Lukan back. "Explain to me how that happened," he said through gritted teeth.

"I don't know. It has to be the bulletproof vest he had on." Lukan began to backtrack, but he stalked her until she had her back against the wall.

Drago hissed. "You used to be sharp and accurate."

Lukan appeared offended by his words. He could see it in her eyes when she blinked, as though she didn't understand. "I have served you well, to the point of sacrificing my very nature. If my best isn't good enough, then I think it's best for us to part ways."

He searched her inner ruminations, as he was well aware she had been doing to him. They were similar creatures—scheming and full of greed. They deserved to be together. Besides, he wanted the highest seat as much as she wanted to sit next to him when the time came. It all made perfect sense. They needed each other if they wanted to see their year's worth of work come to fruition.

Drago closed his eyes and breathed deep. When he opened them, he changed the tone of his voice to appease the former shaman. "Please accept my apologies. I was out of line." He touched her cheek with his good hand.

Lukan moistened her lips with her tongue and pressed her body against his. "You're forgiven." She kissed him on the mouth then pulled away when his excitement shot up. "Let me look at your hand."

He eyed her warily but offered his injured hand. "I cut it before more damage occurred."

She removed the bandage and stared at the stump. He had cut his right forefinger at the knuckle before the poison of the Dangeran could ride up and affect the rest of his hand.

"You treated it yourself?" she asked, her voice dipping lower as her lashes concealed her eyes from him.

"Yes. I applied menthe, which helped with the stinging, but it's throbbing like it has a life of its own."

Without a word, Lukan covered his injured finger with her mouth. The warmth of her mouth felt twenty times better than the cooling sensation from the plant extract. With her tongue, she swirled around the affected area, leaving Drago gasping. Lukan's face held that eroticism he'd come to appreciate in her. Drago grew hard with desire.

"You're going to make me forget the pain?"

She nodded. Then she guided his finger deeper into her mouth and pulled back. Lukan repeated the push and pull with his stump until he groaned. With his pain forgotten, he removed his finger from her mouth and lifted her onto the nearby couch.

"Did it help?" Lukan rearranged her body in the small space, removing her robe to display her glorious body.

"You know how to ease me, milady."

Drago worked on freeing himself from his pants and settled his body on top of hers. At his first grind, Lukan arched her body upward to meet him. This was turning out to be a good night after all. With his anger dissipating, he fell under her spell. He penetrated her deep and thrust hard.

Lukan's cries reverberated around the room. He loved that sound, the cry of passion. She dug her nails into his skin, creating the pain that drove him to the brink of orgasm. He pounded into her harder as her cries intensified. This was quick and easy, just what they both needed. Without stopping, he drilled into her until she broke into a passionate scream.

His own high came seconds after as he bit into her exposed neck. He pulled at her veins while he pumped himself empty. She jerked at the force of his bite, then her body gyrated at a slow and languid pace.

Once satisfied, he licked the entry area, lapping several times to seal the puncture site. "You're as exquisite as ever." He pulled his body up into a sitting position next to her naked body.

She smiled, her face radiating the calm he knew so well. "I have an idea that will make your balls tingle," she murmured.

"I'm all ears," he said and leaned closer.

Weary, Issy collapsed in the chair after Cyrus had collected Linda. Rick glanced over his shoulder at her from the sink.

His sister is a smart girl. I can tell she has a lot of questions about us and the operation. I'm sure you know that already, being a mind reader and all.

"Yeah." She was afraid of the questions, so she'd ended up being a spectator while Rick examined Linda. Issy wasn't in a position to divulge anything until Cyrus opened up to his sister. "She has a lot of questions. I can't even begin to think how Cyrus will answer them. The one question she kept asking herself was why Cyrus left her in the home."

I guess that's got to be addressed soon. Rick pulled a paper towel from the dispenser then sat down next to her while he wiped his hands dry. He tossed the paper at the garbage can, and their loud sighs came out at the same time. *It wasn't easy talking to her by paper. I've gotten too used to having you speak for me.*

She looked at Rick, who had grown a beard. He looked tired but contented. "You did great. It doesn't matter whether you talk or not, you're getting the job done. All the people here adore you."

Rick sighed again, and the rest of his inner ramblings were left for Issy to digest. He thought about his friend, Shelly. He missed her. Then Rohnert was working himself into the ground, running the Vampire Council and going out on patrol rotation while being a father to his son. And then there was her.

Sometimes, she couldn't understand it herself. Did Rick feel something for her? She didn't want to know, because it would complicate things, most of all their working relationship. She liked Rick, but it wasn't romantic. She could talk to him more easily than to others. Rick knew how she felt about Cyrus, although God knew she'd tried to hide it.

I bet you're wondering how I feel about you. Rick took her hand and squeezed it. Issy nodded. *I thought I was attracted to you in the beginning. It must be the fact that I'm alone and you were, too. It just made sense to gravitate to someone who understood you the most. The truth is, I've been in love with one person all my life. One . . . and I don't think I'll ever get over her.*

She watched him struggle with his reality. It couldn't be easy to love someone who didn't return your affections and then watch her die.

"I love you like the brother I never had. I wish you'd find someone who would love you the same way you have loved in the past. Don't give up on the idea of finding that special woman."

The sound of the shutters lifting signaled the start of a new day and time for bed. Issy rose to her feet, feeling weary and elated at the same time. The former sensation was the consequence of worrying about Cyrus and whether she'd see him again. The latter was from seeing him alive and well, though banged up. Also, getting Linda out alive and unscathed was news worth celebrating.

Rick stood up and placed a hand on her shoulder. *Look at me.* When she did, he took her hand and lifted it to his mouth for a kiss. *You're a wonderful woman, Isidora. Cyrus is lucky to have you. You are doing your race a great service by helping Rohnert. I know it's a tough position to be in, but you're doing the right thing. I'm lucky to have you as a friend. Don't ever feel that you can't come to me for anything.*

His words made her smile. Although she had lost her parents and the people she had known, she'd found another set of family. She was indeed lucky. Now, if she could find her long-lost sister, she'd be an even happier woman.

"Thank you. I'm also here for you." She stood on her toes and kissed him on the cheek.

The doctor beamed. *Shoo, go get some rest. Who knows what the new day has in store for us.*

Grinning, Issy left the clinic and went straight to her room. She thought about checking on Cyrus, but she decided against it. He needed some time alone with his sister. Maybe he would answer all the burning questions running through Linda's mind.

Cyrus was settling on the couch after a long argument with Linda over who should take his bed. As usual, he'd won, and she was comfortably situated, with her wheelchair waiting close by.

"Cy, are you still awake?"

"No, I'm not, booger face." He heard her laugh in the darkened room, followed by the rustling of the bed sheets. He reached her before she could grab her wheelchair. "What are you doing?"

"I can't sleep, and I want to talk to you."

Great. This was the part he'd dreaded the most—the questions. He reached for the lamp, turned it on, and slid into the vacant space on the bed. He paused when pain radiated down his chest.

Linda pulled herself up into a sitting position. She looked so tiny and adorable wearing his shirt and pajama bottoms.

"What's up?" He leaned against the headboard.

"Are you still in pain?"

What was the point in lying when anyone could see that the simple task of breathing was an excruciating struggle for him? "I ache everywhere imaginable."

Linda snuggled closer, prompting Cyrus to put his arm around her shoulder.

"I missed you and the time we spent talking."

"You have no idea how much I wanted you here with me." He inhaled her scent. It hadn't changed. She still smelled like the strawberry shampoo she'd been using since childhood.

"Tell me how you got here. This job . . . everything."

Cyrus took a deep breath, despite the pain that came with it. He started with the troubles he'd gotten into after their foster mother died and his inability to locate her. Then he went on to talk about meeting Pritchard and landing the job that had given him a direction and purpose in life. How he had paid an investigator to track her down and make arrangements for her housing and caregivers. He watched Linda's face turned somber while he gave his reasons why they couldn't have been together back then.

"I thought you were ashamed of me." Her voice was too low to be heard, yet he heard the hurt in her voice.

"Just because you can't walk? I thought we'd gone over this already. It doesn't matter if you can't walk. You do everything else sitting down. That's not too bad, right?"

"No, but when you arranged for me to stay in the home, you didn't even come to see me."

Cyrus' heart shattered into million pieces. What he'd thought was good for her had made her think he was abandoning her. This was as a good time as any to rectify that misapprehension. "You see, what happened tonight is what I was trying to avoid. We have enemies who would use anyone or anything to get to us. I hated the idea of any of them using you."

Linda pulled back to look at him. Her big brown eyes were wide with worry. "I hope I didn't make matters worse."

He shook his head. "What could be better than us being together now?"

"I got so scared when I heard the gunfire. I thought I'd never see you again."

Cyrus pulled her in for a hug. "I'm here. You're here. No worries. We won't ever be separated again. I'm going to take care of you."

"I don't want you stressing over me. I can do things on my own. I'm a grown woman, you know."

That part would take a lot of getting used to. "I know, but you'll have to let me be the big brother."

"You're not back to making me clean your room and making you breakfast, right?"

Okay. Cleaning the room might still stand, but the latter wasn't applicable to him anymore. "We'll see."

Linda laughed. It was the glee-filled tone he'd been missing all these years. Then she nudged him. "I have something to ask you, but promise you won't get upset."

Here we go. Cyrus gestured with his hand for her to go on.

"Your friends, and the creature who took me, they're not normal."

Cyrus couldn't suppress a smile. "Are you calling us weird?" He feigned an insulted tone.

"What are they? You? And that thing was some scary creature."

There was no getting around the topic anymore. If Linda was to live in the facility, she was better off knowing the type of beings that surrounded her.

Cyrus scooted on the mattress until they were face to face. Then he took her hands. "Okay, this is not going to be easy for me to say, but since you'll be staying here with us, this is something you have to know. When Pritchard took me in to work for him, he needed people who would work on finding a cure that was running rampant in the vampire world."

Linda's eyes grew wide, her breath hitched, and she gasped. "They're all vampires? Even Rick, the doctor?"

"Not Rick, he's human. So are Cheryl, the nurse; Jones, our mad scientist; and Rayce, the tech guy. We have several human fighters and Gail, Harrow and Jordan's daughter." Cyrus watched the expression that crossed Linda's face and stifled a laugh.

"Are you?" She sounded almost afraid to ask.

"Well, duh. I wasn't at first. Then a bastard . . ." His voice trailed off. "It's not important. I was changed not too long ago."

"Are you going to eat me?" Linda's hand gripped his hard enough to solicit a hearty laugh from him.

"I don't eat humans, Linda. I drink their blood, yes—but donated blood."

"No more pancakes and steaks for you?"

"I don't enjoy them as much as I did before. Any more questions?" It hadn't been too bad except for the 'eating her' part.

She thought for a moment. "Am I safe here?"

"This is a safe place as long as our enemies don't get to us. As far as the in-house vampires, they won't bother you. We have a great group here. We're like a family."

"The vampires, I mean. Won't my being human pose a temptation for them?"

"They don't like booger-face women."

Linda wrinkled her nose in mock disgust, but his words seemed to have put her mind at ease. "Will you give me something to do? I have been trained to help out at a local clinic. I was helping with reception duties and assisting the nurse with supplies before that horrible thing snatched me from my bedroom." She shuddered, no doubt from the bad memories.

The thought of Linda being abducted from her safe environment was enough to get his blood boiling. Drago was going to pay for this. Cyrus took another painful breath and then tried to push the thoughts away.

"Clinic?"

She nodded. "I know I'm good at it."

"Let me ask Rick if he has something for you to do."

Linda's face lit up. "Thanks. You won't be sorry."

"Okay, now that that's settled, can we go to sleep?"

"But it's daytime."

Cyrus had forgotten about that little detail. Linda would need a room of her own, considering the difference in their sleeping schedules. "Our time is the opposite of yours."

"Any aversion to garlic and crosses?"

"No." He rolled his eyes.

Linda grinned. "What can kill vampires?"

"Any weapons or bullets made of Dangeran."

"Danger-what?"

He blew out an exasperated breath. "Can we continue this after I get some sleep?"

"Okay, but you have to tell me more."

"I'll get you your own room before you drive me insane."

"Wow. My own room?"

Cyrus nodded and slid off the bed. "Yes."

"Now we're talking."

"We're done talking. Good night, booger face." He leaned over and gave her a kiss on the forehead.

Linda lifted her thin, lifeless legs and adjusted them before she lay down. "Good night, Cy."

He turned off the lights and walked with slow steps to the couch, still reeling from the pain of being shot and the shock of seeing his sister. His chest puffed with happiness at having her in his life again. This was a good day—even with the goddamn aches he had to endure for the time being.

Before he'd had no one, and now he had two special women in his life. *Is this really happening?* he asked himself before he fell into a dreamless sleep.

Harrow and Rohnert stood outside the abandoned warehouse surveying the damage. The place hadn't been trashed like their main facility had been during the raid. Still, with the current state of affairs, it was wise to err on the safe side instead of continuing their mission and compromising lives.

"I'm getting sick of these types of surprises." Harrow removed his sunglasses to rub his eyes.

Rohnert kicked a pebble under his boots. "I wonder where Bretania got her leads."

"Who knows if there's a connection between her and Drago. Or maybe even Zane. It's déjà vu all over again."

He could still remember the slaughter at their upstate home as though it had happened yesterday. Too many lives were lost that night. "I suspect a connection between Bretania and Drago. Too bad she's not around anymore. I don't know about Zane. I don't know how to say this, but I think the man had a change of heart."

Harrow threw him a skeptical glance. "He's an asshole, and it's best if we don't trust him."

Rohnert felt the same way. He still couldn't reconcile Zane's motivation in his head. "I understand."

"What about Drago? Do you know if he survived? Cy said he clipped the guy."

Rohnert shrugged. "Who knows? I don't know much about him. Maybe we can ask Aemerria."

Harrow gave him a blank stare. "Amer-who?"

Perhaps this was a good time to break in Harrow and give him some inside information. As a new inductee into the Council, he should be able to summon the Shaman any time he needed her. "She guides our race. She's sort of a priestess, doctor, and part-time protector."

"I thought you had Lukan?"

"She disappeared without a word. I didn't bother asking. These things are better left alone. I'd hate to offend Aemerria by asking."

"Sounds like a tough woman." Harrow chuckled.

Rohnert arched an eyebrow. "We're surrounded by tough females."

"You got that right."

"Let's head inside and call on her." He moved toward the side entrance and keyed the combination on the keypad.

Harrow followed. "You mean now?"

Rohnert nodded. "This is as a good a time as any. Besides, you have to learn how to reach her." The door swung open, and they stepped inside.

"Why?" Harrow absentmindedly glanced at the strewn furniture in the foyer.

Rohnert sighed with exasperation. "You're an Elder. We do this if we need her assistance."

"How?"

He glanced sideways at his friend. "You're starting to sound like Gail." They reached the little conference room, Harrow trailing him like a lost puppy. "We can do it here."

He went on to describe the ritual at length, and Harrow listened. Rohnert kneeled in the middle of the room and gestured for Harrow to follow.

"Under normal circumstances, we would need beads and candles as a part of the summoning rite, but because we are not prepared, we have to be patient. Repeat the chant if you have to."

As he started chanting the words, Rohnert felt a prickling sensation at the back of his neck as if someone were watching them. He repeated the hymn until the gust of wind hit his face, listening to Harrow's mind ramble while he braced himself for the meeting, Aemerria's voice flitted inside the room.

"I'm beginning to enjoy these rendezvous of ours. You're taking me places." The happy lilt to her voice prompted Rohnert to open his eyes. "Who do we have here?" Aemerria eyed Harrow with interest. She lowered her hand for Rohnert to kiss before gliding over to Harrow.

Rohnert nudged Harrow. "Do the same thing."

As Harrow kissed the hand being offered to him rather awkwardly, Rohnert made the necessary introduction. "Aemerria, I would like to introduce Harrow Gates, one of the newest members of the Council."

Aemerria narrowed her eyes, and Rohnert could see the fast thoughts about Harrow running through her head. Then she smiled. "Ah, the infamous Gates Syndrome, the originator of the disease that ravaged our race. This is unprecedented."

Harrow twitched but remained impassive. Rohnert had no idea how to take the shaman's declaration. When they continued their silence, Aemerria laughed, her melodious voice echoing around them.

"I'm not judging. I find it amusing that after being away for so long, I have come back to find that our Council has made remarkable changes to its way of thinking." She nodded as if approving information in her head. "I like the direction you're steering this race, Rohnert."

"If it doesn't offend, we would like to find out some information on our new enemies." Rohnert's head remained low, as did Harrow's.

"Why don't you cut the formality and talk to me?"

They raised their heads at the same time and looked at each other before Rohnert spoke. Aemerria's multihued eyes were focused on him. "We have been attacked on two fronts at almost the same time. This had happened before. We're wondering if there is a connection between Bretania and Drago."

If Rohnert had been privy to Aemerria's inner thoughts before this, she closed him off this time. She paced the room, circling them while her robe rustled with her every movement.

"Drago is cunning and dangerous. There is no limit to the disgusting machinations he could let loose. He wants your seat. Greed and vengeance are reigning in his heart. Lukan has fallen from grace. From what Gastarius shared with me, she and Drago have been manipulating events and people. My knowledge is limited due to the nature of my past indiscretion."

Past indiscretion? This piece of information had trouble written all over it. "Bretania, where does she fit in?"

Aemerria stared at him, challenging him to say something. Rohnert returned her gaze without saying a word.

"Drago used Bretania to penetrate the warehouse and halt the treatments. That's as far as she could get." Aemerria stopped in front of Rohnert and offered her hand.

He took it and was pulled to his feet, but he pulled his hand back as though he had been hit by a jolt of lightning. Her strength didn't surprise him. These shamans, despite their beguiling appearance, could crush anyone with their innate power. It was the flashes of images their touch sparked that created the wave of anxiety within him.

"What's wrong?" she asked, placing a hand on his arm.

He backpedaled, not relishing the idea of losing control of his head. "When you touched me, I saw something. I don't know what it is. A figure . . . flashes of light."

Aemerria frowned. "I don't know what you're talking about. I didn't see a thing."

She wasn't lying. Rohnert sensed her emotional grid. All he got was a whole lot of "what the hell."

Shaking his head, he moved away from the priestess so he could keep his head straight. Harrow watched them with interest but maintained his silence.

"Forget it." Rohnert changed the subject. "So Lukan and Drago are in this together?"

Aemerria moved to the end of the room. She picked up a chair and sat down. A frown remained on her face. "They are."

"Can we thwart any attacks they might be planning? Can you see anything?"

She closed her eyes, and any movement ceased for a moment. When her eyes opened, the usual kaleidoscope of colors had turned into a dark pool, depthless and rather disturbing. "I see bloodshed and deaths but not faces, time, or place." She shook her head as if she was dispelling the bad images. "I'm sorry."

Rohnert cursed. "Haven't we suffered enough?" he asked no one in particular.

Sadness swept across the shaman's lovely face. "One thing I can assure you is that no one can infiltrate the charm I have used to surround both the Council headquarters and the underground facility."

At least their families and comrades were safe. That was a big measure of consolation. "That is all I ask of you." Rohnert bowed his head with reverence, and Harrow followed suit. Then he remembered her reference to Drago's plan to unseat him. "Will Drago be successful in taking my place?"

Aemerria took a deep breath, looking rather uncomfortable and shutting him out so he couldn't gather unspoken information from her.

"I'm sorry. I can't share future details, but don't ever doubt that I will never forsake you."

Rohnert still wasn't sure if he could trust her fully, but his options were limited at the moment. He'd have to be extra vigilant if necessary.

Then Aemerria switched gears, turning to Harrow. "You made a fine addition to the Council."

"Thank you." He dipped his head graciously.

"You can call on me anytime, just used the proper protocol." Aemerria laughed, and in the blink of an eye, she vanished into thin air.

Harrow scratched his head. "Damn, that woman is intense."

Rohnert nodded. He had so many things competing for his headspace. The shaman was intriguing and unnerving at the same time. If what she had said was right, then they'd better get their troops ready. Death had taken too many of his people. This train of thought led him back to the one person he missed most—Shelly.

Drago smiled at Lukan's brilliant idea. If her well of information from her former position had dried up, she was still one step ahead. Just the way he liked it.

He pulled her up for a quick kiss and hopped out of bed. "Let's do this now."

Lukan raised an eyebrow. "You have no concept of patience." It was a fact, and they both knew it.

"If it can be done today, what's the point of waiting for tomorrow?" He picked up his discarded pants off the floor and slipped into them, while Lukan donned her velvet robe. "I want to personally see this is executed properly."

She offered a gracious smile. "As you wish."

He worked on the buttons of his shirt, but his missing finger made the task difficult. "Damn it."

"Need my help?" she asked, gliding over to where he stood.

Drago dropped his hands and let her button the rest. After she was done, Lukan picked up his right hand and blew on the injured digit. The relief was instantaneous. With his forefinger cut short, pulling the trigger would be impossible. That would be a problem.

Lukan read his mind. "You'll have to learn how to fire with your left. It's quite easy. All you need is a little practice."

He grunted at the thought of spending time retraining himself. It wasn't appealing, but did he have any other option? He dismissed the disgusting prospect and focused on the task at hand.

"How many backups do we need?" He walked to the door and held it open for her.

"None. All we need tonight is the exact location. Which one do you want to visit first?"

It was a no-brainer. "I want that asshole dead."

"I'll meet you there in a few minutes?" Lukan gave him a sideways glance when they reached the lobby door.

"Yeah."

Since he was unable to travel the way Lukan did, he had to go by foot or drive. The latter option was a no-go. The traffic would drive him mad. Drago sniffed the air around him, taking in the general mood of his surroundings before digging in his heels and taking off at a sprint.

Lukan was already surveying the area by the time he cleared the bridge that connected the main artery to the area that bordered the Tack Enterprises facility. He knew the area all too well. With Pritchard's social standing, the famous circular building had been featured in every architectural magazine there was, and it had been photographed countless times. Since the building had been demolished and leveled, the exact location of the facility was now a big question mark.

With an active group of fighters, risking open warfare against the Tack team was best avoided for the time being. Lukan's idea would serve just as well. He stood next to her and continued eyeing the perimeter.

"You'd better stay back," she said.

He took several steps backward as Lukan began a rapid incantation, too fast for him to catch. The words *fire* and *surround* were the only ones he was able to decipher. Her hands moved fast in a circular motion, gathering momentum. Smoke appeared within the confines of the ball she was creating until fire sparked.

She threw the first ball of fire in an open space and the area started burning. With quick movements, she continued to throw the burning fury in the wide area until pockets of fire and smoke billowed everywhere the eye could see.

As the orange hues lit up the night sky, a shimmering glow in the shape of a dome appeared, translucent and definitely invisible to the naked eye. He could see the size that encompassed the facility.

"Bingo. Mark the perimeter."

Lukan's smile was sinister. It revealed the malevolence he'd always known she had in her. Drago watched her rubbed her palms together. Then she extended her arms toward the burning embers of grasses and vegetation until glistening stakes appeared, marking the area.

The sound of sirens blared from a distance. It was their cue to get lost. "Let's go. We're done here. At nightfall, have the Nerocs guard the perimeter until the rats come out of their hiding place."

Pleased at the progression of his plans, he grabbed Lukan's arm, and they broke into a fast run, blurring past the speeding fire trucks that had been summoned to put out the blazing inferno she had created.

"Remind me again how lucky I am to have you by my side." Drago laughed.

Cyrus walked into the training room and was surprised to see Rohnert in the middle of the mat. The leader of their great race had his face down and was silent and motionless. Once he'd had a chance to think things over, Cyrus had wanted to talk to his friend. This would be as a good a time as any.

Rohnert looked up and heaved a deep breath. "What do you want?"

In the tone of the vampire's voice, Cyrus detected the pain that had been eating at him, too. He walked onto the mat and sat in front of him.

"Rohn, I know it's difficult to wrap your mind around everything that's happened. And I won't try to downplay the severity of your circumstances. I apologize if what I did caused you pain, but I can't take it upon myself to accept the blame for what went down. I wish I could turn back time and change it, though."

Rohnert's jaw tightened, and he gave Cyrus a hard stare. "I don't know what to think. Everywhere I look, memories of Shelly surface, reminding me that I failed her."

"I feel your pain. I know it's tough, and but please give me a chance to prove to you that I would never do anything to hurt you or your family."

His friend released a deep sigh. "I know it wasn't fair of me to put the blame on you. I just don't know what to do."

That makes the two of us. "I loved Shelly, too. I wish it had been me instead of her. Malin needs a mother."

Rohnert stood up and started pacing. "I've killed and brought justice to those who murdered Shelly. Why does it feel like it's not enough?"

Cyrus understood Rohnert's predicament. The wound was still fresh, and the pain would never go away. He couldn't imagine losing the one he loved that way. What could he say to ease his friend? No words could console a broken heart. Nothing.

"You don't have to say anything."

"Maybe sparring would help?"

Rohnert nodded. Cyrus knew he was at a disadvantage. With Rohnert's expertise and rage, he was looking at nursing bruises and possibly some broken bones. Oh well, this had to be done. If he could ease his friend's pain, then it would be worth the trouble.

"I'm ready." Cyrus extended his fists, tucked his arm, and spread his legs.

What happened in the next few minutes wasn't a surprise. Rohnert moved with unbelievable speed, kicking, punching, and landing strikes anywhere he could inflict pain and embarrassment. Cyrus tried to keep up, dishing out some damage, but it was nothing compared to what he was taking. With anger serving as Rohnert's fuel, it was no surprise when Cyrus landed in a heap of limbs on the mat.

"Care for some more?" Rohnert stood above him.

He glanced up and saw the fury still burning in Rohnert's eyes. "I knew I had a purpose here. A live punching bag is better than anything out there, right?"

Rohnert shook his head. "Nothing numbs the pain."

"For what it's worth, I feel wretched. I promise you this, I won't give up until we find Shelly."

A hand reached out, and Cyrus clasped it and was pulled to his feet. "That is good enough for me."

"Thank you," he said in a solemn voice. "I've been meaning to say this. I appreciate that you guys got to Linda on time."

"To be honest, I wasn't sure I wanted to be there at first. But then, I was their best bet for avoiding detection. You know, reading minds and all."

"Well, for whatever its worth, I'm glad you came." Okay, they were headed into oversharing territory.

Rohnert smirked. "That thing that almost got Linda is some sick creature. I wonder how that asshat Drago dragged them out of their cave."

Cyrus exhaled with a curse. "What is that ugly mother fucker anyway? I think I saw several of them before when I met with Drago, but somehow I forgot about them until tonight."

"That's Drago, erasing your memories. Those creatures are called Nerocs—a rare breed of vampires. They can't be trusted. I've heard about them, but for hundreds of years they've managed to hide underground. No one knows how to find them."

That wasn't comforting to hear. Their new enemy had forged an alliance with that nasty band of hideous fuckers. "How did you get her?"

"I did a little mind trick. It wasn't my most shining moment, but I had to do it."

"What do you mean?"

"I manipulated the vampire while Harrow moved in."

He remembered an incident with Rohnert and a human female in an alley more than a year ago. Rohnert had called it thought insertion. To Cyrus, it was just freaky. Still, he wasn't complaining. It had worked, and Linda was safe with him. Then he remembered he needed to check on his sister.

"You have no idea how thankful I am for what you guys did for us."

Rohnert accepted his gratitude with a nod. "There is something I want to say."

"Spit it out, Rohn."

"This feeding with Issy. I know it's tough on—"

"We do what we have to do." Cyrus turned toward the door. It wasn't a lie, but he didn't want to think about the arrangement. He saluted Rohnert before walking out the door.

The ear-piercing wail of the facility's alarm pulled Cyrus from his sleep. He scrambled out of bed and grabbed his discarded jeans from the floor. Issy did the same and quickly ran her fingers through her hair. Then she hurried to the closet and came out with their weapons. The protocol for this type of situation was to arm yourself and listen for an announcement.

"Is this just a drill?" Her voice sounded sleepy, and she handed Cyrus his Glock and daggers.

"I have no clue." They rushed outside like the rest of the inhabitants who were scrambling out of their respective rooms to wait for further directions.

Rayce's voice came through the speaker system. "All personnel must report to the I-room now." Cyrus glanced around and saw Tor ushering Allison and the children next door. Sawyer and Liv were tucked under Tor's protective arms while Allison held the weapons.

Everyone moved in the direction of either the elevator or stairwell, but Cyrus scanned the entire area, hoping to get a glimpse of his sister.

"Get to the I-room now!" he shouted while they made his way toward Linda's room a few doors down the hall from his. The door opened, and his sister awkwardly propelled her wheelchair out of the doorway.

"Here, let me help you." Without waiting for her answer, he lifted Linda out of her chair.

"You don't have to carry me like a small child," she protested.

"Linda, not now." This was not time for them to get into an argument about how he babied her. In moments like these, all his effort and energy were focused on getting everyone to safety. Linda's body turned rigid, her way of showing her displeasure.

"Let's take the stairs." Cyrus led their group up the stairwell until they reached the second to the top floor. They made it to the I-room and found it filled to capacity. Harrow was standing in the front conferring with Tor and Firman, while Jordan and Allison were comforting the children.

"Sir, take my chair." Sawyer got up the moment he saw them.

Cyrus nodded at the young boy and deposited Linda in the chair. The big screen was turned on and was showing views of a fire raging. Fire fighters were busy battling the blaze.

The location seemed familiar. "What the hell is this?" Cyrus looked around.

Harrow grabbed at his hair and pulled at the roots in frustration. "The fire is outside. It is surrounding our property."

A collective gasp spread across the room.

"Say that again?" Tor shouted, clearly as surprised as everyone else.

"Someone must've set that up." Firman was shaking his head.

"I already called General Krever, and I'm hoping to hear from him soon." Harrow turned back to the screen just as a military vehicle was seen arriving in the background.

Issy took Cyrus' hand while they watched events unfold. It wasn't the general who emerged from the car, but it had to be one of his men.

"When did this start?" Cyrus asked.

"Rayce said just a few minutes after five this morning." Harrow pinched the bridge of his nose.

This got Cyrus thinking. How could a fire break out by itself? The facility had maintained a modern sprinkler system around the areas with vegetation and ran it on a regular basis. With what he could see from the media coverage, the burning patches all surrounded the general area of the underground facility. Plus, the timing made it hard to believe the fire was accidental.

"It's suspicious," Tor commented as if he'd read his mind.

"Who called the fire department?" Jordan asked.

"Rayce did," Harrow answered. "There's nothing we can do since daylight is coming."

"Too damn suspicious." Cyrus pounded his fist on the table. From the corner of his eye, he saw Rick leave the conference area.

The news coverage continued to flash images of the affected areas in the waxing light of dawn. Then the camera focused on a newscaster who was interviewing the fire chief.

"What can you tell us about this particular fire?"

The fire chief rubbed his forehead before answering. "We're still investigating the cause. As you can see, there were several patches, all of which have now been contained."

The picture cut away to show the burned vegetation, black and still billowing thick smoke.

"Isn't this the area where the Tack Enterprises building used to be?" the newsman asked.

The fire chief nodded. "That is what our blueprint shows."

"Is there a reason you would suspect arson?"

"I wouldn't be able to answer that until we have concluded our investigation." The fire chief shook his head.

Harrow turned the television off and wheeled around. "Okay, folks. We're not going to assume anything at this point. Let's head back to our rooms and wait for announcements. Thank you for responding in a quick and orderly manner. Does anyone have a question or concern?"

A few people raised their hands, but Cyrus tuned them out. Operating on little sleep, he found it difficult to think straight.

"I think you need a massage to help you relax," Issy murmured.

He glanced at her and offered a grim smile. "Why don't you get Linda's —?"

His request was cut short when the door opened and Rick came back with Linda's wheelchair. This halted the ongoing discussion for a moment. Cyrus glanced over at his sister, who was sitting ramrod straight and looking very sulky.

"If there are no more questions, let's head back to our rooms." Harrow concluded the emergency assembly.

As everyone else left, Cyrus watched Rick approach Linda with her chair. It was difficult for him not to interfere, but Issy held him back.

"Let her be," she whispered.

After Linda transferred herself to her wheelchair with practiced ease, she wheeled herself out of the room without even glancing his way. Rick followed close behind.

"That didn't go well," he muttered to himself.

Issy squeezed his hand. "Let's get you back to bed."

"Cy, we'll get together later." Harrow waved them out.

Cyrus nodded. He knew Harrow would be burning the phone lines talking to Leo about the situation. There wasn't much they could do until the fire department's investigation was over.

He and Issy walked out of the I-room and returned to his suite, which they now shared. The bedroom trade-off between Linda and Issy had worked out well. His sister got her privacy and could go with her usual sleeping schedule, while he and Issy could keep theirs. It was a win-win situation, except the day's events continued to niggle at him.

"What if there's an emergency like this again and I can't get to her fast enough?" He flopped on the bed.

Issy worked fast to shed her clothes and then sat next to him. "Hey, don't stress yourself out about this. You got her in time." She began to rub his temples with her thumbs.

"She hates me . . ."

"She'll get over it."

He looked at Issy. "What did I do wrong?"

A few seconds slipped by before she answered. "To be honest, I kind of understand how she feels. Regardless of Linda's condition, she still wants to have a say in things. She may not have the capability to walk, but she can decide for herself."

He drew in a sharp breath. Why was there always a big stink when he took the initiative with his sister?

Issy answered his unspoken question. "Imagine being handled without your consent. This has nothing to do with good intentions. We're talking about giving her the respect, the choice. These are the things most people forget when they deal with people with a disability."

"I care for her. I don't want her hurt. She needs to be protected."

"Turn over."

When he did, she straddled him from behind. "I get what you mean about wanting the best for her, but don't forget she has feelings. No matter your intention, give her the chance to decide for herself."

He closed his eyes and rested his cheek on the pillow. Maybe Issy was right, but old habits were hard to break. "You think she hates me?"

She laughed while skimming her palms along the expanse of his back. He felt some of the tension leaving his muscles at her touch.

"Linda has already forgiven you. It's just her pride that needs a little restoring."

Cyrus snorted. "Rick made me look like an ass."

"Oh, stop it. The man is a doctor. They have special sensitivities that we don't." Her fingers dug into one coiled muscle, making Cyrus jerk.

He opened his eyes and turned his head to catch a glimpse of her face. "Are you in cahoots with the doctor?"

"Rick is a good friend, and I'm sure he meant well."

Resting his face back on the pillow, he thought about his sister. "Do you think she'll talk to me after this?"

"There's one way to find out." Issy continued kneading his shoulders, easing a tight muscle on his shoulder.

He began to relax. "I guess I'll check on her later."

"Just remember, always put yourself in the other person's shoes before you act."

"Sure . . ." he mumbled.

There was no way of knowing how fast he fell asleep after that little talk with Issy. Cyrus surfaced from a restful sleep to the sound of his phone ringing. He groped in the darkness to pick up the call.

"Cyrus here."

"Cy, I'm afraid we have a problem on our hands." Harrow's voice sounded strained.

He glanced at the luminous digits of the clock and was surprised to see that he'd slept for almost ten hours. It was close to six in the evening, and Issy wasn't next to him. "Oh, fuck. I overslept. What's going on?" He rubbed his eyes and tried to focus.

"Six men haven't reported back from their patrolling duties."

"Did Rayce call them?" he asked, bolting to a sitting position.

"Several times. No one is answering."

"Who's on tonight?"

"Vince, Matthew . . . five humans, and Barth."

"Ah . . ." All the humans were rather new to the operation. Although they were disciplined, they were young, and who knew what kind of trouble they could get themselves into. "Let's give them time. This is not the first time this group has failed to report when scheduled."

He heard Harrow sigh. "Okay, fine. I'm not going to stress about it right now. When you're up and about, start calling them."

"Sure thing. Let me just check on Linda, and I'll get on it."

"Your sister didn't look pleased with you last night."

It seemed like everyone had caught on. "Yeah, I know. I can be an ass sometimes." He got up and walked to the bathroom.

"Your words, not mine." Harrow chuckled.

"Shut your hole, man." Cyrus ended the call and threw the cordless phone on the bathroom counter. "I can't help it if I want to keep her safe," he said to himself while looking straight at his reflection in the mirror.

Minutes later, he was groomed and standing outside Linda's bedroom. He pounded on the door a couple of times and waited. There were sounds of laughter inside before he heard tires squeaking against the hardwood floor.

"Who is it?" Linda asked from the other side.

"It's me."

There were more scraping sounds before the door opened a fraction and Linda navigated her chair to open it wider. "Hey."

"Mind if we talk?" He allowed her to move her chair and then closed the door after him.

Linda didn't answer right away, but it wasn't necessary when he caught the scent of the man sitting on her couch. Cyrus advanced into the room and glared. "Are you making house calls now?"

Rick stood up, looking offended. He scribbled fast and hard on the tablet he was holding, then he flashed it for Cyrus to read. *None of your business*, it said.

"The hell it isn't." He bristled. "She's my sister."

Before Rick could write anything else, Linda propelled her chair close enough to bump Cyrus' leg with her footrest. "And Linda can decide who she wants to entertain in her own room."

Cyrus wheeled around and stared at her. "Damn, Linda. This is not coming out right."

"Then make it right," she said then crossed her arms.

He raked his hands through his still-damp hair. Lord, this was going to be another long day. "Where should I start?" He glanced over to Rick, who was scribbling furiously on the paper.

The doctor turned it around. *I'll leave you two alone, but you and I aren't done talking*. Rick glared at Cyrus then marched toward the door after giving Linda a quick peck on the cheek.

When there was just the two of them left, Linda transferred herself to the sofa. "Now talk."

Gastarius heard the gust of wind and knew it was time. Even if his vision had come too late, he had seen the ending in his mind. His ending.

Trepidation seized his heart for a brief moment, but he refuse to succumb to his doubts. His fate had been decided. He was ready. His guidance had been given, and his time had come.

With grace, he straightened up from his chair. He had been staring at the blank parchment on his desk for the last few hours before deciding against putting his final thoughts on paper for fear of it landing in the wrong hands. Instead, he had delivered an urgent message to a chosen few with his last words of advice.

He looked up to find Lukan standing in front of the desk with a dagger in her hand. Her lovely face was devoid of any emotion but the determination to finish the deed.

"I have seen this." He leaned back in his chair and met her empty gaze.

"Your time is up, old man." Even her voice was a dull monotone.

"Before you carry out your mission, answer this. What made you turn your back on your sworn oath?"

Lukan laughed. "The day you took Aemerria as your successor decided your fate."

Gastarius wasn't surprised. Jealousy was an insidious passion. "When you strike me, remember cause and effect. It's a vicious cycle that will persist until you breathe your last."

"You're a fool. You could've lived forever." She advanced and stood next to his chair.

"Everything has to come to an end. I welcome death, but I pity those people who continue a fruitless existence. You shall feel my wrath when I'm long gone."

She lifted the dagger, and Gastarius closed his eyes, his life flashing before them. He had done everything he could in this endeavor, and he was ready to face the afterlife.

Peace embraced him like a protective cocoon. His mind and soul were ready. When the blade struck his heart, he gripped the arm of the chair until he felt his body exploding in million pieces. His dying thought was for the pupil he left behind.

May the grace of the universe watch over you, Aemerria, my child.

One of the benefits of playing sleuth for his father while growing up was developing a gut-feel for what might happen—or just being able to be in the right place at the right time. Driven by the desire to make it right with one person, Zane drove to the area where the Tack Enterprises office building used to be. After learning about a fire on the news, he decided to check it out for leads. After all, stakeouts were the only thing he could do these days.

Two miles away from the general vicinity, he sensed a nasty vibe—something he hadn't encountered before. This prompted him to park his motorcycle about a mile away to see what was going on. Driven by the same instinct that had brought him to this place, he took off by foot with his trusty cane. Navigating the muddy ground made it difficult for him to move faster.

When he got closer, the feeling of malevolence wrapped around him like a stifling blanket, and he stopped in his tracks. Patches of land were burned down, and traces of water from the firefighting effort still remained. He was certain he'd gotten the location right, since he had made several trips here in the past.

Then he heard movement not far away from where he stood. Several fast-moving creatures were hiding behind some bushes and vegetation that had escaped the fire's wrath. Even in the darkness, Zane could see the creatures well. Tall, lithe, and ugly, they had the type of face only their mothers could stand. Each one held high-powered guns. Suspicious by nature, Zane hid behind another bush to wait.

He pulled out his weapon and stayed calm. If there was a fight breaking out, he wasn't planning to engage. If it had anything to do with the Tack fighters, he was going to help them whatever way he could. It was a few minutes later when the action began. Four fighters emerged out of nowhere. There were no doors opening, no mist that appeared or a hazy cloud. Nothing. The foursome just came out of nothing. Zane suspected that the area was protected by a charm similar to of the one at the Vampire Council headquarters. Many times in the past, he'd tried to locate his father, but he could never find the entrance or any hint the place even existed.

They walked with the swagger he'd come to expect from Harrow's fighters. All of them wore almost the same attire—dark jeans, shirts, and jackets. Underneath those jackets, judging by the bulges, they were packing hard-core weapons.

From each fighter's movement, it was easy to tell that two were vampires and the others were human. The four-man team reached the edge of the property that led to the bridge before another group, this time a five-man team, came out.

A lick of fear shot through his system. It was same feeling he got when something wasn't right. Zane pulled out his phone to make the call and dialed, even if it wasn't the smartest thing to do. At that moment, the creatures began emerging from their hiding places.

Cyrus was inside the training room, finishing one of the classes he was teaching, when the alarm blared.

Rayce's voice came through the speaker. "Harrow, Cyrus, and Tor. You are needed in the control room. Now!"

"What the fuck." Cyrus wasted no time before grabbing his daggers and throwing stars from the cabinet and securing them in his holster. The new recruits jumped to their feet, looking ready to rumble. "Stay here until you hear from me. Joe, you're in charge. No one is to leave this room."

He ran up the stairs, taking them two at a time, and found Harrow and Tor running when he emerged from the stairwell. "What the hell is going on?" he asked.

"I have no fuckin' idea," Harrow said as the three of them blazed through the hallways. Firman and a few other vampires were rushing in, as well.

"What's going on?" Harrow scanned the monitors, which were flashing different images of the facility's exterior.

"Josh and his group left for patrol several minutes before Dirk's group. This is happening right now."

Rayce punched the keyboard fast and several monitors showed Josh and his party of four about to clear the bridge. Then gunshots fired. The sound reverberated through the speakers while they followed the gruesome event unfolding right before their eyes.

"The hell, another ambush!" Tor raged. "Let's get moving."

The main phone line rang and when Rayce flipped another key, the caller went live.

"This is Zane. You have to stop more people from coming out. There is an ambush outside your hideout."

Cyrus' blood boiled upon hearing his voice, and he felt the itch to run outside. He gripped his gun, raring to go.

"You heard the warning," Harrow said and moved fast to hold him back.

"That bastard might be in on it." He twisted his arm and shook Harrow off.

Tor drew in a sharp breath. "I don't have a good feeling about this."

"You're not letting those people die!" Cyrus shouted then turned to Rayce, who was bringing several more screens to life. "How many are there?"

Cyrus glanced at the monitor and saw Zane shoot a nasty-looking creature, similar to the one that had almost gotten Linda not too long ago.

"There are ten of them," Rayce said above the din of voices. Everyone was talking at the same time.

"I'm taking that fucker down." Cyrus lunged for the exit.

"What the hell are you thinking?" Harrow screamed after him.

"He's mine." He took off before anyone could stop him. "Rayce, side exit."

Gunfire erupted, nonstop and deafening. Bullets upon bullets blasted out of gun muzzles until the first group of men fell like flies. Zane dove to the ground, tracking the second group, who were startled but had gotten into position fast. With much of the vegetation surrounding the area burned to the ground, the group had a tough time securing a safe hiding spot.

The facility's voicemail kicked in. "This is Zane. You have to stop more people from coming out. There is an ambush outside your hideout," he screamed the words amid the gunfire that was slinging around him. He sat back up and fired at the creature closest to him. The thing went down and fizzled before his eyes.

When he crawled out of his hiding spot, he could tell that the second team had been fully engaged in the battle. He aimed at another advancing creature and clipped the sucker on the leg. Before he could fire the next shot, the thing snarled and cut off its leg.

Zane scrambled to his feet and was running back for cover when a shot was fired. He dove to the ground, and the bullet zipped through, narrowly missing his shoulder. Pivoting around, he aimed and pulled the trigger, catching the bastard in the abdomen.

"That should keep you down." Glancing at the area near him, he found several disintegrating creatures. The battle continued to rage, but from his vantage point, he could see several men had joined the party.

At least this time the odds were tipped in favor in the facility's fighters. As the newcomers engaged the remaining creatures, Zane began his retreat. He crawled for about ten feet until he could stand, but then he realized he had lost his cane.

"The fuck," he said and tried to pull himself up.

Just then, one shot was fired, then another, knocking him to the ground. The familiar blast of pain rippled across his abdomen and down to his legs while he scrambled to get up. He expected the fizzling to follow within seconds, but nothing happened.

"You're not thinking I'd let you off that easy." It was Cyrus' familiar voice.

Zane glanced up despite the crippling pain and saw pure hatred in those eyes. This was going to be over fast. "I didn't expect anything less." He struggled to get to his feet.

Cyrus stalked forward, aiming the gun at his head. "I told you. Even hell could not keep me from killing you."

Zane rose to his feet and straightened up, raising his hands. "Do it," he said, looking Cyrus straight in the eye.

Several footsteps approached, and before he could even blink, Rohnert was standing between them. "Cyrus, this is insane."

"Rohn, move over. I won't hesitate to shoot." Cyrus kept his aim even.

Rohnert shook his head. "I respect you, Cy, but I'm afraid I can't let you make this mistake."

Silence surrounded them. Zane tried to keep his body upright, but the pain became unbearable. His legs gave way, and he crumbled to the ground. It felt like time stood still while Rohnert chanted some words he hadn't heard before. Then Cyrus' body went slack, dropping the gun to the ground. Another soldier grabbed him before he went down and slung him over his shoulder.

"Gentry, take him inside." Rohnert turned and stared down at Zane. "You're coming with me, but I'm warning you—one wrong move, and I will kill you myself."

Those were the last words he heard before everything went black.

Issy and Cheryl were showing Linda around the clinic, going over the inventory of medications, and quizzing her on the different instruments when the speaker blasted with an announcement.

"We have three gunshot victims, two possible amputations. All medical personnel, report to the clinic now."

Issy looked at Cheryl and nodded. They both ran to the sink and began the washing procedure. They'd done this too many times before, and the steps were automatic. Linda wheeled herself toward a corner of the room.

"Linda, come here and wash up. There are too many victims. We might need an extra pair of hands." Issy waved her forward. "Remember everything we're doing. You need to have presence of mind, and whatever happens, do not crack under pressure."

Cyrus' sister nodded and did what she was told. Issy was finishing with the lathering process when the door opened and Rick came bursting in. Cheryl made room for him at the sink while she wiped her hands clean. Next came the music, a relaxing piano tune to that Issy had grown accustomed whenever Rick was around.

I'm going to be working fast and will attend to the gravest case. You will assist me and have Cheryl work on the less severe one.

She looked at Rick and nodded. "Cheryl, Rick wants you to take the second case. If you have a question, just say it."

Cheryl snapped on her gloves. "I'm ready," she said. "Linda, stay beside me."

Rick had just donned a surgical mask when they heard the sound of incoming footsteps—too many to number. Issy stood aside the minute Firman and several other vampires brought two fighters in. Rick did a quick assessment and turned to Issy, and she translated without delay.

"Rick will take George. Cheryl, Dirk is yours."

Cheryl began barking orders, efficient and sure of herself. Issy admired the woman. Despite her personal troubles, she kept her head straight and focused on getting the job done.

"Linda, bring me some towels, and I need—"

Rohnert burst into the room carrying a man Issy hadn't seen before. His blood soaked his clothes, as well as Rohnert's. It took a few seconds for her to realize that Cheryl had stopped talking, and her face had turned pale.

"Zane will need some help, too." Rohnert deposited the man on the farthest examination table in the room.

It dawned on her who the man was, and Issy stumbled back. Tor was quick to steady her. She balled her fists and felt the overwhelming urge to kill. Rage boiled inside her, remembering the countless nights she had listened to Cyrus and his tormented nightmares.

Issy, you need to focus. I need you to clamp George's leg while I work on him. Rick gave her a steady eye, and his orders were rigid. *Is everything okay?*

Issy took a deep breath. "Yes . . . yes . . ." she said and forced herself to concentrate. Her protective instincts were shooting high, and all she wanted to do was to kill the sorry excuse for a man.

"Issy, Rick needs you to focus. Revenge will have to take a back seat at this moment," Rohnert whispered.

She glanced over at him, aching to defy his order and avenge the man he loved.

Rick's loud thoughts got Issy's attention. *Tell Cheryl to focus. She has work to do.*

Issy drew a sharp breath. "Cheryl, Rick wants you to focus. Can you get this done?"

Rohnert walked up to Cheryl and took her hand. "Look into my eyes," he murmured.

Whatever Rohnert did, it must've worked. Cheryl jerked back and started working with fevered intensity for the next hour. Rick worked faster than Issy had ever seen him do before. He had Tor take over the bandaging when they moved over to Zane, and she interpreted the remaining procedures to be done.

Rick picked up Zane's wrist and looked up at Issy, his expression grim. *I need the defibrillator.*

Issy debated for a moment. "I don't want this bastard alive," she hissed under her breath. The only two people who caught her words were Rohnert and Tor. They both stared at her, their faces grim.

Rick shouted his thoughts again. *Issy, now!*

This got her moving. She wheeled the instrument closer and handed the paddles to him. He glanced at her and nodded.

"Clear," Issy said. She wanted to vampire dead with all her heart.

Isidora closed her eyes when she heard Cheryl gasp, which was followed by a heartbreaking cry that echoed across the room.

Cyrus came around, feeling lightheaded and dazed. He opened his eyes but did not recognize the room at first. It was to be expected, since he wasn't in his own room. He bolted up, but Allison jumped in front of him.

"Harrow's orders are to keep you here for another hour."

He glared at Allison and stepped to the side. "What the hell for?" he asked. The top of her head just came up to his nose, and she weighed almost nothing. It wouldn't be a problem getting away from her, although he wouldn't enjoy manhandling a woman he admired.

"Because we won't let you kill Zane." Allison stepped right in his path, blocking his way to the door.

"Better think twice about that. You might be able to get around Ally, but not me." Tor got up from the couch and stood next to the exit.

"The fucker isn't dead?" Cyrus sidestepped again, but Allison grabbed his waist, holding him so tight he couldn't breathe.

"Cy, hold your fuckin' horses, will you? Get your head out of your ass. Your anger is turning you into someone you're not."

Cyrus stiffened at the sick memories, feeling his muscles lock down on him. "I have to finish him off." He gritted his teeth to keep from saying more.

Allison went all out on the hug. "You might not have to. Rick is still trying to revive him, and it's killing Cheryl . . ." Her voice broke off.

"Cheryl?" Cyrus asked, staring at Tor while Allison sobbed against his chest. Was she for real, crying for the spawn of the man who had killed her father?

Tor nodded. "I left right after Doc started using the paddles on him. Cheryl's reaction is messing with my head. It's damn heartbreaking, too."

He'd be dammed. How had he not seen this before? No wonder Cheryl had protected the bastard so many times. She had fallen for Zane.

"Fuck . . . fuck . . ." Cyrus held Allison, not knowing what else to say.

"I know what you're thinking. His father killed Daddy. I should be angry, but honestly, I'm so sick of getting angry. We're much better than the things going on around us. I've seen enough killing to last a lifetime. I want to live in peace, to help people, and to achieve Daddy's dream."

Cyrus shared the same goal, except it was difficult to let go of the rage and thirst for vengeance. He'd held on to this for a long time, and his plans for revenge were all that had kept him going until Issy came into his life. Shit. This was all wrong. Maybe it was a good thing that Rohnert had hypnotized him, ending his momentary madness. Even so . . .

"I can't believe we're keeping that asshole here with us."

Tor patted him in the back. "You know, I can think of a lot of other ways to get even with the guy."

Cyrus glanced up to see Tor grinning. Judging from the glint on his eyes, there were a lot of torments the man would inflict if given the chance.

Allison pulled away to look at Cyrus. "I don't know how to ease your pain because I don't know what he did to you. But now is not the time."

"I can't promise anything." He heaved a long sigh.

Tor chuckled. "With two boy scouts urging you to stand down, I don't know what else you can do at the moment," he said, referring to Harrow and Rohnert.

How had he lost sight of what was most important to him? Cyrus had everything he needed, together with the people who mattered most to him. Whether Zane lived or died wouldn't matter much to him, but his death would kill Cheryl. She was like family to him. Was he losing sight of the more important things?

Cyrus pulled away from Allison's embrace, but he tilted her chin up until they were looking into each other's eyes. "I still can't see past the things this guy did to me, but I'm done with the killing." *For now.*

She nodded. "I love you, Cy. I'm . . . glad you're coming around."

Oh, he was far from getting over it, but there was no use pushing the issue right now. He cleared his throat. "You know you're one of the few people who can get through to me. Did Harrow put you up to this?"

Allison punched his stomach playfully. "Harrow is up to his neck in everything that's been going on. This was that beautiful man's idea." She glanced at Tor and winked.

"Cheryl, it's out of our hands. Time will tell if he's going to make it," Issy said.

"Then I will be here, holding his hand, when that time comes." *No one deserves to die alone.* She didn't care to say the latter out loud. Even if it killed her, she would stay right there with Zane.

If Issy heard what she'd thought, she gave no indication. The vampire squeezed her hand. "I'm going to turn in. Call me if you need anything. Rick is also a phone call away. He wants you to know that he did everything he could for Zane."

"Thank you," Cheryl said, unable to tear her eyes away from Zane's ashen face.

Issy reached down and lifted her until she looked up. "If I was a betting woman, I'd say he's going to make it," she said, then she left to join Rick and Linda in the hallway.

Zane had been moved to a room next to the clinic. It was closest one to the OR, just in case he coded again. Cheryl glanced at the multiple machines he was hooked up to and prayed that the one monitoring his heart function would stay silent. She couldn't stand the piercing sound of flat lining anymore.

It had been a long night—too darn long. After Rick had stopped the bleeding for George and had revived Zane enough to be able to operate on removing the bullets, he'd coded twice. It hadn't been a surprise when she couldn't finish her task and Rick had to take over with Dirk, too. She used to be much better under pressure.

"You still are, Cheryl. Don't beat yourself up for things you have no control over," Rohnert said from behind her. She glanced over her shoulder. How had he managed to slip inside the room without her noticing?

"It was too much for Rick. One of the men could've died because I failed to do my job." She looked down at her hands.

Rohnert pulled up a chair and sat across Zane's bed from her. "Rick is an experienced surgeon. He lives for moments like these. Just think of Shelly . . ."

Cheryl looked up to see Rohnert's pained expression. "Yes, they're both one of a kind. Sometimes, I still imagine she's here working."

The vampire nodded, looking too distraught for words.

So she continued. "There are days when I forget that Rick prefers classical music, and I'll end up playing Led Zep or Clapton. It was always the louder, the better for her." She smiled at the memories. "I miss her so much."

Rohnert nodded. "There is not a second that I don't think of her."

"I feel the same way about him," she said, unable to shake the fear that continued to claw at her. "I know he'd done unthinkable things to us, but I can feel deep down that he is capable of redemption."

Kind, dark eyes met hers. "I'll reserve my opinion for later, but I've seen glimpses. He saved us from several incidents that could've taken more lives. Like tonight, he called when he discovered the ambush. I have a feeling that he was looking for you."

This shouldn't make her feel good, but it did. God knew how many times she'd wanted to call him, except her loyalty to her adopted family had won out. The one time she had gotten Zane on the line, she couldn't get herself to say a word.

"Life is strange. Just when we think we have a grip on everything, something happens that can either shake our belief or strengthen our faith. It's bizarre." Rohnert leaned back in his chair and closed his eyes.

Cheryl leaned forward and rearranged the sheet covering Zane's legs. His skin felt cold, and he looked so helpless hooked up to all those machines. He seemed almost vulnerable, like he would be incapable of the deeds he had committed in the past. Then she glanced up to find Rohnert watching her, his expression unreadable.

She asked the question that had been nagging her for some time. "Am I betraying everyone by feeling this way?" There was no point in keeping it to herself when she knew Rohnert could read her mind.

"I'm not going to tell you what is right or wrong. You can't help who you love. But I'm going to warn you, be careful. We're not sure what Zane's motivations are."

Cheryl nodded. "I'm not sure how I feel." She covered her face with her hands, too embarrassed by the admission.

Rohnert laughed, but it sounded brittle. "I know how you feel. I tried pushing Shelly away because I couldn't figure it out, and I almost lost her."

Cheryl glanced up. "Shelly was smitten with you from the beginning. I could tell because her voice would change when you were around. She lit up like a string of Christmas lanterns." The fond memories of her former boss made her smile.

"I caught her several times, but I pretended not to care. I was too damn afraid to show her how I felt. I mean, look at us. She was a doctor, I'm a vampire—not a good combination."

This made Cheryl turn to look at Zane. "Kinda like me and him?"

Rohnert cleared his throat. "I guess." He stood up. "I'm going to check on the baby. I'll be around if you need to talk."

He left before she could thank him for his understanding. Christ, this was a mess. Life had taken them all on a wild ride.

She reached over the side rail of the bed and dimmed the lights. In the darkened room, Cheryl studied the contours of Zane's face as she had done the first time she'd been watched over him. His once-short hair was longer, reaching to his chin, and it was duller than the fiery red she remembered.

Stubble was peeking out from his smooth skin, and his cheeks were unnaturally hollow, as if he hadn't been eating.

For crying out loud, the man didn't eat. The man drank blood, just like almost everyone she knew in the facility. Had he been neglecting himself? Cheryl continued to watch him. His stomach was wrapped with bandages, and his breathing sounded shallow. She glanced at the machine to check the readouts once more.

"You're going to make it. You're going to make it." She took Zane's limp hand in hers, lifting it to her mouth to kiss it. "I'm rooting for you."

After an hour, exhaustion won, and she fell into a fitful sleep. She kept waking up every thirty minutes or so to check the readings on the machines before falling back to a restless slumber. At some point, she felt a hand touching her hair and a warm blanket being placed on her, but she was too damn tired to open her eyes. The whole time, she was clutching Zane's hand.

It was in the late afternoon before she felt human enough to stand and let go of Zane's hand. Although his condition remained serious, the fact that he'd made it through the morning without another episode made her hopeful.

Cheryl rushed to the bathroom and came out as fast as she could, since she was afraid to leave Zane alone. He remained unmoving, but the steady rise and fall of his chest reassured her. Cheryl returned to the chair and sat down, despite her aching back. She reached for his hand and continued to watch him.

She must've dosed off again, because the next thing she knew, she woke to find Zane flailing in his bed. An alarm sounded, and she panicked before realizing that the wailing sound wasn't coming from one of the machines. It was an alert that the patient had moved. She jumped to her feet to neutralize the alarm, but Rick beat her to it. Harrow, Tor, and Issy also came running in.

Rick went to check on Zane's vitals while they looked on, wondering why Zane kept moving. His breathing was raw, but Rick didn't seem worried after checking the readouts on the machines.

When Cheryl gripped Zane's hand, he settled down right away. Harrow and Tor exchanged a knowing look then grinned.

"Rick is going to give Zane another dose of sleeping pills to keep him from moving."

"Is he all right?" Harrow stood behind Issy.

She turned silent while she listened to Rick. "He wants everyone out for a few minutes while he checks on Zane's wound, and then he'll let us all back in."

"Can I stay?" Cheryl asked.

Rick nodded, and Issy translated. "It's the only way this guy will stay put, so yeah, you have to stay."

Once the trio piled outside, Cheryl went into nurse mode. She moved to the other side of the bed so she could assist Rick. The moment she let go of Zane's hand, he began thrashing again until she picked it up and gave it a light squeeze.

"How is this even possible?" she muttered, handing Rick two gloves.

The doctor smiled and scribbled on his note pad. He turned it around for her to see. *That's the power of love.*

Cheryl couldn't say a word.

The sun was on its gradual ascent, and yet Drago continued to pace inside his penthouse office. Lord Marchec was in a corner of the room, no doubt avoiding any possible confrontation.

"I can't believe this. We sent ten mother fucking vampires," Drago said, and he held up his fingers to prove his point. "None returned. What the hell is wrong with this picture?"

The head of the rare breed looked on, refusing to meet Drago's eyes. Dressed in a loose black tunic and dark pants, Marchec's appearance made it clear that he was one nasty package of terror, just like his reputation. Tall, slim, and agile, he moved like a nightmare and was a force to be reckoned with. The vampire raked his fingers along his short, dark hair and remained silent.

This, of course, further provoked Drago's anger. He stalked to where Marchec stood and glared at him. "You got something to say?"

Marchec took a step back. "Nothing that will help the situation. It would be better if you backed off a bit, Drago."

Feeling his rage spiking, Drago inched closer until their faces almost touched. "How's this?" he taunted.

The temperature inside the room dipped lower while Marchec glared at him with his beady eyes. "Don't tempt me to cross the line. I'm not having this conversation with you."

"Threatening me won't get you anywhere but in a fuckin' heap of trouble."

Lord Marchec smirked. "Let's get one thing straight here. You gave us lodging in exchange for the work that we do for you. Does that fucking sound like an even trade to you? And now you're bitching about how many of us fucking died?"

Drago sneered. "You're too smart for your own good. But don't underestimate me." He moved away, creating distance between them. "I know you're motivated by more than just the chance to return to the land of the living. Don't underestimate me, Marchec."

"My motives are not your concern. As long as I hold up my end of the bargain, I consider our agreement satisfied. Do not at any time think that you can order me or my men around."

The burning rage inside Drago multiplied. "I think you and I should have a better understanding here. Will this do?" He drew out his gun and aimed it at the vampire. In a blink of an eye, he was surrounded by Nerocs, tons of them.

The leader stepped back, allowing his minions to circle Drago. With a sneer, Marchec pulled out his own weapon, a sword with jagged blade. "Don't think for one minute that I would hesitate to rid this earth of your presence. I lost men out there. Not just soldiers, but friends. So forgive me if I don't tremble at your warning."

Drago was certain the motherfuckers were going to take him down, but fear had no place in his heart. "Honor our deal. You said you'd get the job done."

Out of nowhere, Lukan appeared in a blinding light. The Nerocs covered their lidless eyes, staggering back. "It seems like we have a little problem here." She moved closer to Drago, shielding him with her body.

Her proximity, as well as her courage in the face of the ugly motherfuckers, made him harden. When the light diminished, the Nerocs drew their guns and aimed at Lukan.

This is it. Showdown! Drago pulled her to his side. "Let me handle this," he whispered, his eyes trained on Marchec.

Lukan squeezed his hand, and he looked down at her. "I already did."

Wondering what on earth she was talking about, he glanced at Marchec's men. All were holstering their guns as if their mission had been accomplished. Their eyes were glazed over, and their expressions were blank.

He turned to her. "What did you do?"

She gave him a shrewd smile. "It's a simple spell for the weak-minded."

Marchec turned toward the door. "For the simpleminded. I guess that doesn't include me and Om. I'm calling a truce, not because you scare me, but because your woman's tactics are beyond what I can squash at the moment." He exited the room.

They could hear Marchec barking orders, and the creatures began to disperse. One Neroc, Om, lingered a moment longer, sizing them up. His eyes were glacial, and his teeth gnashed together. "I don't like you, Drago, or your cheap tricks. This is not over yet."

Surprised, Drago leveled his revolver at the Neroc. It would seem he'd made himself a new enemy. "Get out of here, you bastard, before I blow your head off."

Om smirked. "Not over yet, *sir.*" He stressed the last word before leaving the room.

He lowered his weapon once the door closed and turned to Lukan. "Spell . . . what kind of a goddamn selective spell was that?"

She blew out a nervous breath, a habit of hers he had noticed lately. "I said it works for the weak-minded. It seems like Marchec is not the only smart one in the bunch." She laughed, but Drago recognized the worried tone of her voice. Lukan was acting concerned about the Nerocs in particular. It seemed like the spell had worked but was only temporary. Soon, the Nerocs would be a group to reckon with. Their breed was far more resistant to influence than your garden variety vampires—even tougher than their pure blooded counterparts.

Drago walked over to his desk and deposited the gun inside the drawer, pretending he hadn't noticed her lingering doubt. He shook off the unwanted gloom that had descended on him like a nimbus cloud and dropped in the chair, weary but relieved they'd avoided a tussle with Marchec and his band of ugly ass shitheads. Lukan stayed glued to her spot. "Come here." He beckoned her to sit on his lap.

Lukan shook her head, but she projected her thoughts until Drago had a clear picture of what she had done. She had not discussed what she'd done with another living being. When he learned of the deed she had committed, he was shocked that she was just telling him now.

"What in the world were you thinking?" Drago felt a knot in his stomach. "You killed Gastarius?" Even in his vilest moments, he didn't think he'd be capable of committing such a crime.

"I did everything I could to please the old man, but he set me aside because he didn't think I was worthy. I didn't know what else to do. We needed the black book so I . . ." She buried her face in her hands.

He stood up and rushed to Lukan, encircling her in his arms. "Shh . . . give me some time to think this over." As they stood in the middle of the room, Drago's mind raced. This was a definite glitch in the overall plan, but if she had located the bearer of the black book, seemed like they were back in business. He was working on getting other covens to back up their conspiracy to take over the Council. This should be a cakewalk.

"The black book is with this minx Cyrus is screwing?"

Lukan nodded but continued to remain silent, pressed to his chest. His head swam with the new ideas this gave him. He ran his fingers through her hair and chanted calming words in her ear. When he sensed her anxiety abating, he cupped her face and kissed her on the lips.

"I have a plan. We're going to test your powers and see what happens."

She shook her head. "I don't know if I can do it."

Drago wasn't one to be fazed easily. "You will. You're not going to fuck this up."

Lukan looked up at him through veiled lashes. "I'll try." The uncertainty was still strong in her voice, but her thoughts were more confident.

That was all he needed to hear. This was the Lukan he knew, undeterred and always up for the task. He smiled, revealing his fangs in delight.

Zane fought through the haze of pain and misery. Death was imminent. All his energy had left him, and he was helpless to fight it. The face of death was knocking, taunting him with an empty, dark eternity. Its claws dug into his body, dragging him away. This was the end he had hoped for.

An abrupt wave pulled him back, taking him for another spin.

Through the agonizing experience, he felt a presence. There was an anchor that refused to let go—a warm and comforting touch, urging him not to give in. So he hung on in the midst of the black abyss that surrounded him. He persisted through the pain and the flashes of light that shocked him to the very core of his being. It wouldn't be a surprise if he found he'd been delivered to hell. And he didn't even believe in the idea of heaven or hell. Yet here he was, forcing himself to latch on to the dim light he could see through the lonely tunnel where he was suspended for endless time.

He heard voices—many, at one point. Then they disappeared, and he lost himself, unable to fight the darkness. After a time, he came around again amid flashes of light and too many voices. Another drawn out silence engulfed him.

Zane had no idea where he was when his heavy lids opened. The room was stark, bounded by white walls wherever his eyes could reach. The stench of blood wafted around him like an invitation to sink his fangs into a healthy vein. He drew back, and it earned him a shot of pain to his midsection. Death had a scent, too, except it wasn't he who had bitten the dust. He was alive, although God knew in what condition.

Was he glad? Not an ounce of relief washed over him at the discovery that he was still a part of the living, until he felt the light grip on his hand. He tried to move his head, but even that fraction of a movement made him want to scream. A pitiful moan escaped his lips, and he panicked. What had happened to him? Where was he? As influx of information came barreling down at him, and he remembered being shot. Twice.

Christ . . . and he'd thought the Dangeran particles were bad. Being shot felt as if he'd been bulldozed many times over. He hadn't disintegrated, so Cyrus must have used regular bullets, intending for him to suffer through the pain.

This was pain, all right. As he lay wondering whether the bottom portion of his body was still attached, the pressure on his hand tightened, then was followed by a gasp.

"You're awake . . . you're alive. Thank God." *That voice.*

"Che . . . ryl?" His throat felt like sandpaper, rough and dry.

Her eyes glistened when she came into view. "Stay there. Don't go anywhere." She sounded frantic, like she had been put through the wringer.

He might have run away if he could manage to move an inch. As it was, he was plastered on the bed, his body weighing him down. He managed to nod his head since he couldn't speak. *What am I doing here?* Then he remembered Rohnert's warning all too clearly. He was in the Tack facility, and the venerated leader himself would kill him if he tried to flee.

Cheryl let go of his hands, and he wanted to scream. It was pathetic, but not having personal contact for a long time could do that to a person. He heard the door open, and the sound of her footsteps grew faint. If she was calling in the big guns, he'd better get ready to face the firing squad.

The moment he tried to sit up, an ear piercing alarm sounded. Zane had no idea if this was their way of keeping tabs on him. Maybe it was, considering the things he had done to their group in the past. The wailing continued, leaving him unable to achieve the simple task of getting himself upright.

He heard incoming footsteps, too many to track. Cheryl was the first to come into view. Then there was the male doctor he had seen in the news. Dr. Rick Whitaker had been maimed by Goran at the same time Shelly was killed. The third person who came into his line of vision was someone he hadn't seen before. The female looked at him with as anger in her eyes while the doctor made incoherent noises.

"Rick wants to know how you feel," the female asked.

Zane closed his eyes and willed himself to speak. "I . . ." *I can't feel my legs. Other than that, I'm here, I guess.*

The female nodded then turned to the doctor. "He can't feel his legs." Her voice was flat.

Now wasn't this just dandy? Another mind reader in his midst. Zane wasn't sure if it was a good thing or not. Beneficial since his voice box had gone MIA on him. Tough because she'd know everything he was thinking. It was time to shut the lid on his thoughts.

A silent conversation ensued while he fought the pain of turning his head to get a glimpse of Cheryl. The mind-reading female, with her dark orbs, watched him and nodded.

"Do you feel any pressure around your abdominal area?" she asked.

Before he could answer, Cheryl spoke, sounding almost hysterical. "Issy, can you ask Rick if this is temporary?"

What is temporary? "Some . . ." he couldn't get the words out. *Someone tell me what's going on.*

Zane turned his head to see the doctor shaking his head and rubbing his chin. Rick glanced at him before turning to the female Cheryl had addressed as Issy.

"Cheryl, Rick has no way of knowing until he runs further tests. For now, get a shot of painkiller for the patient. We'll check him once he gets some rest."

Zane drew in a harsh breath. These people were talking about him as if he weren't there.

"I have to know."

"Cheryl, focus. Zane needs some sleep, and you've been here for forty-eight hours. It's time for you to get some rest." Issy's tone no doubt expressed the doctor's personal sentiments. A choked sob came from Cheryl, and Zane tried to make heads or tails of what the hell was going on.

What is temporary? What made Cheryl cry? Damn it. He wanted to know, but when he struggled to say the words, he felt a cold flush running through his veins. Everything started to dim until he could no longer keep his eyes open.

The phone rang just as Cyrus was getting ready to head to the training room for a class. He picked up to hear Harrow's agitated voice. "I-room, stat." The line disconnected before he had the chance to ask what the hell was prompting the emergency meeting.

Cyrus reached the I-room with the rest of the key personnel. He found Harrow in a deep conversation with Rohnert while he, Tor, and Firman took their seats.

Harrow glanced up and nodded at Cyrus before calling the room to order. "I just received a call from Leo. This is happening as we speak." He took the television remote and turned on the news. Everyone fell into a hushed silence, trying to the digest the events unfolding before their eyes. From what Cyrus could see, a group of unknown individuals was firing at crowds in an undisclosed subway station. Chaos ensued while humans scattered in every direction.

"Vampires?" Firman asked.

The question was unnecessary. The attackers' movements were far faster than those of average humans, and remorseless expressions were another dead giveaway.

Tor grunted. "No doubt."

"Course of action?" Cyrus asked.

Harrow walked over to the television screen, looked at the ongoing telecast, and then turned around to face everyone. "Leo advised us to stand down, but Rohnert and I feel we must intervene. Humans are not to be touched, and this crosses the line."

Tor pounded his prosthetic fist on the table. "Damn right. Slaughtering humans is not a sport. I think it's about time we started flexing our muscles."

That was Tor, all right. The guy would rather let his axe and gun do the talking.

This much was true, though. Humans were not a part of their war. Harming them would prompt the authorities to get involved, which was a complication they had managed to avoid in the past.

Rohnert bristled. "This has gone too far. We will take action."

Cyrus was down with that decision. He'd been itching to get things done. They'd been taking too many hits, and it was time they retaliated. His body began to hum with anticipation.

Harrow bared his fangs, a good sign that their leader was ready to get down to business. "With those horrid sons of bitches stalking the perimeter, I think it's a good time to use the chutes."

"Aemerria assured me that everyone is safe inside this facility. Taking the chute is the only way we can stay undetected," Rohnert added.

There was a murmur of approval at his decision.

"What do you have in mind?" Firman asked.

Cyrus had knowledge of the chute spanning its inception and construction. Pritchard had discussed his intention to build a secret passage in case their location was compromised. He had to hand it to their fallen leader. The man's long-term plan had been a lifesaver. If it hadn't been for the chute, Tor, Allison, Jordan, Shelly, and Jones would have been killed along with most of the underground inhabitants during Zane's surprise attack.

Wasn't that a buzz kill? The thought of Zane made his blood boil. Cyrus shifted in his seat, trying to block out the thoughts of the man whose presence provoked him to murder. He glanced up and found Rohnert staring at him.

The vampire was reading his mind, no doubt. Cyrus didn't care. He had gotten a small amount of satisfaction from shooting the motherfucker. Zane could still be fighting for his life, but he was beyond caring. If the fucker lived, then he would be smart to stay out of Cyrus' way. If he died, then this was his destiny.

Rohnert shook his head, but Cyrus wasn't the least affected by his unspoken disapproval. He turned his attention to the television screen still showing the same news as earlier.

"This is when we try to get them from behind," Harrow said.

Now we're talking, Cyrus thought.

"Rohnert is calling for an emergency meeting of all the Elders tonight to discuss this. Issy and I have to attend, so this means Cyrus will be with us. We'll discuss this with the rest and try to get the Council approval. Once we get the go-ahead, we'll coordinate with you and hit these suckers from behind, where they least expect us to attack."

"What time do we leave tonight?" Cyrus stood up, unable to contain his excitement.

"We're leaving right after this meeting. I suggest wearing the vests Jones has given most of us. Those who don't have one will be providing support from afar." Harrow tossed vests to several them, and they fitted the armor underneath their clothes.

"Tor, I'm going to be in contact with you and Firman once we get the Elders' support. In the meantime, familiarize the rest with the chutes and establish a meet-up location," Harrow said. Then he turned to Cyrus. "Meet you at the chute in five."

When Cyrus hurried out of the I-room, he found Issy waiting outside, did a double take, and stopped in his tracks a few feet away. Issy, in all the time he had known her, had been quite simple in her wardrobe choices. Instead of her usual skirts and simple tops, tonight she wore jeans that clung to her body like second skin. Her leather jacket was snug over her bulletproof vest, but it still accentuated her curves. Two guns were slung low on her hips in a holster. A low whistle sounded from behind, and Cyrus glanced over his shoulder to find Tor grinning like an idiot.

"Guess your girl had taken a few pointers from Allison and Jordan," he said when he walked by, stopping to give Issy a knowing look.

Tor continued to chuckle while he walked down the hallway. Cyrus returned to gape back at Issy, running his eyes up and down her body. When he settled on her face, she smiled, seeming pleased with the attention.

"Your mouth, dear." She grinned.

Cyrus snapped his mouth closed. He had been enamored with Issy from the moment he first laid eyes on her. She was always a vision to behold in her usual attire, but he had to admit, this new outfit was a total knockout.

Then he realized he had been staring, hard. He cleared his throat. "Sweetheart, you're going to give me a heart attack."

Issy smiled, and he just about melted on the spot. "Not sure if I should be pleased or offended."

He closed the small gap between them and pulled her into his arms. "I'm incapable of offending you. You, my girl, take my breath away." He skimmed his mouth along her exposed neck.

"Hey, hey . . . what have I been saying about public displays of affection?" Harrow said. "We're ready to go."

Cyrus clucked his tongue. "Your timing is as impeccable as ever, Gates." He shook his head and ushered Issy through the long hallway, followed by Harrow and Rohnert.

None of them had used the passageway before, and the blueprint Rayce had rustled up showed that each chute led to a different ending point. "We're going to meet over where the ice rink used to be. Take the middle, Cy. I'll take the right one, and Rohn will use the other." Harrow saluted then took the plunge.

"I'm off. See you at the meeting place." Rohnert disappeared into the dark hole, followed by a swooshing sound.

"Are you ready?

"As ready as I'll ever be," Issy said then planted a kiss on his lips.

"I'll be right behind you." He tapped her on the butt. "Go."

Issy jumped into the mouth of the tube. Cyrus allowed a few seconds to tick by before taking the plunge himself. The damn chute was dark as hell, but Issy's giggles continued throughout the entire drop, making the experience more fun than he would have expected.

The downward slide lasted for a few meters until they had to crawl on their hands and knees. This took longer. The tube was big enough to fit two people abreast, enabling them to crawl next to each other. They continued forward until they reached the end of the dank passageway. Cyrus grabbed the lever and pulled it down. The vacuum seal sucked air from the outside with a hiss, and he wiggled out. Once upright, he took Issy's hand and guided her. The little room they'd dropped into was nothing but a tight space that could fit three people at most. One wall held a door made of rusted steel.

"Ready?" Cyrus pulled another lever and opened the door. With his hand resting on the butt of the gun inside his jacket, he stepped out and looked left to right. Their particular chute had led them to a deserted alley. He turned to Issy. "It's safe."

They trod toward the end of the alley and discovered they were somewhere in the vicinity of Wall Street. "I'll follow your lead." Issy pointed her nose upward, taking the customary precaution of checking their immediate environment.

"Stay close. Keep your eyes open." Cyrus broke into a sprint, and Issy kept pace with him. Their speed was more for the benefit of the humans around them, since they were packing ammo like mercenary soldiers. They covered several blocks in a heartbeat and heard gunfire when they closed in on the agreed meeting place.

Cyrus' first instinct was to grab Issy and shield her with his body. "Stay behind me," he instructed. Issy did as told, releasing one of her guns from its strap. They zigzagged in and around cars toward the sound of gunfire. Once they got close enough to see, a bullet zipped by, missing his shoulder by mere inches.

Protecting Issy with his body, they dived to the ground next to a car. "I have to get you in the Council walls." He started firing back in the direction the first bullet had come from. The exchange was rather lopsided, and bullets were in their direction from all sides. Not too far from them, Cyrus could see a full-on battle happening close to the Council headquarters entrance. Humans were screaming and fleeing the scene. Shots thundered around them, and he spotted fallen humans and comrades alike.

"This is not good," Issy said.

"We need backup." He glanced sideways to check on her. It was surprising to see her firing at will, in her element. Once she finished the round, she reloaded.

"Help me." The faint voice of a woman cried from inside the vehicle they hid behind. Cyrus inched toward the window then ducked as a bullet swished by him again.

"Issy, check the woman inside. I'll provide cover." Cyrus crawled toward the rear of the car and began firing while Issy worked her way to the driver door.

He could hear her assuring the human female while she assessed her medical condition. The bullets continued to rain on them even as he reloaded. "Damn it. Where are Harrow and Rohnert?" he muttered. He pushed in the casing then resumed firing.

Taking his phone from his pocket, he speed-dialed the facility. "Rayce, we're outside the VC headquarters. Send some backup. Whoever you can find."

"Lemme find out who's closest to you," Rayce yelled over the noise. Bullets continued to swish by them while he waited for Rayce's response. "Boss, I'm sending Luke and his team. ETA seven minutes."

"Okay," he said then dropped the phone in his pocket. He checked on his last two rounds. *Fuck, we won't last long if we keep exchanging fire with them.*

"I have to get her out of here and take her to the nearest hospital. She's bleeding bad." Issy was right next to him and wasted no time reengaging in the shoot-out.

"We'll have to get these fuckers off our backs before we can do that." Cyrus continued to exchange fire while thinking of a way out for Issy and the woman. "Okay, I'm going to take the heat off you. Once they're focused on me, drag her out, get somewhere safe, and call 911. Stay with her and wait for my call." That was the best he could do at the moment.

"Okay." Issy leveled a shot that took one enemy down.

Cyrus spotted an abandoned car about ten feet away. He nodded to Issy and crisscrossed to avoid the incoming bullets headed his way. He was a few feet away from his intended cover when he got zinged in the chest. He went down hard on the pavement, his gun clattering on the asphalt, as another bullet pounded on his safety vest.

"Cyrus, Cyrus, are you okay?" Issy screamed amid the deafening sound of the nonstop gunfire around them.

While he crawled to the vehicle for cover, his leg got clipped by an errant bullet. He howled as pain exploded in his left leg. He knew an instant decision had to be made. He pulled out the dull dagger each one of them carried for times like this. Without thinking beyond his desire to survive, he thrust the weapon into his leg and severed the Dangeran-affected site below the knee.

The pain, though unbearable, was better than exploding into pieces. He glanced at Issy and found her waiting for his answer. "I'm fine." He turned to search for his gun and discovered it was several feet away from him. "Fuck."

There was no way he could get to it fast enough with the lower part of his leg missing. Crawling was out of the question. He'd get shot before he could retrieve the gun. The sound of gun fire continued raging, but the shots concentrated on them had ceased. It didn't take long to realize the reason for this.

He looked up to find three of the same unsightly vampires he'd seen before staring down at him. The one in front sneered.

"Om, can I take the woman?" one of the other two asked the leader.

"She's mine. I've never tasted a pureblood before," the one called Om said. Then he jammed his foot in Cyrus' bleeding stump.

Cyrus howled on contact.

"You're time's up, asshole," the vampire said and pointed the gun at his head.

"Wrong thing to say," Issy said from behind them. "You go first."

How Issy had ended up behind the vampires undetected was beyond Cyrus. Through the tears blurring his vision, he watched the three vampires whirl around in surprise. Issy, calm and resolute, began firing her high caliber automatic at them. The element of surprise worked for the ones in front. They didn't have a chance to even pull their triggers, but the one called Om managed to fire several shots at her. A shot to the chest threw her across the lot, and she landed head first.

A wave of cold dread hit him. "Oh, God," Cyrus cried and unleashed all the throwing stars in his arsenal, nailing the vampire on the head, chest, and lower torso. "You're not messing with my woman."

A series of fizzle and pops followed as the vampire disintegrated into ashes on the ground. Cyrus pushed his body up by his elbows, despite the pain, and began the excruciating task of crawling to Issy. She was attempting to get up, but she was having trouble. Her face was contorted in pain. Blood pooled on the ground around her head.

"Issy, I'm coming," he yelled. His sight was short circuiting on him, but he plowed on.

From out of nowhere, something resembling a dart zipped by him, hitting Issy on the neck. Her movement ceased right away. Before he could take action, he felt a sting in the back of his own neck. As he lost grip on consciousness, he caught a glimpse of men clad in dark clothes closing in on them.

Zane was pulled out of a nightmare by the sound of voices around him. A low conversation was going on, so he kept his lids shut and his body still. Not that he *could* move.

Two females were talking in a corner of the room. He was certain the sweet but melancholic voice belonged to Cheryl, but he wasn't sure about the other.

"Don't lose hope. Rick said it might be temporary." This came from the female whose voice he didn't recognize.

Cheryl answered with a sigh. There was no way of knowing her present condition without the benefit of seeing her. Zane felt his anxiety soar sky high. He wanted her to be okay. What had caused her tears?

"He's gone through enough, Linda. He could barely walk with the cane. I don't know if I can bear him not being able to walk at all."

Are they talking about me? Zane kept up the pretense of sleeping despite the havoc this information was causing in his system. He turned his head away from the voices and flinched when panic began to claw at him. If he wasn't ever going to walk again . . . he was fucked.

The sound of a tire squeaking on the tiled floor startled him, but he kept his eyes closed. "You know, Cyrus told me a long time ago that I do things differently. It doesn't matter if I can't walk. I do things sitting down. It's not too bad."

The door opened. This was his cue to open his eyes in time to see the doctor walk in.

Zane glanced at Cheryl and found her distraught. The woman sitting in a wheelchair next to her looked at him with curiosity written all over her young face. Human. How was she related to Cyrus?

Fuckin' shit. Focus, damn it, focus.

Rick took one look at him then scribbled fast on the paper and turned it around for him to read. *How are you feeling?*

Zane opened his mouth to speak, but nothing came out. He swallowed several times and attempted again. "How long . . . was I out?"

The doctor flashed two fingers on one hand and four on the other while his mouth moved, producing nothing but air.

Cheryl jumped up, moving closer to his bedside. "You were asleep for almost twenty-four hours."

He tried to find any sign of anger or displeasure in her eyes. Sadly, all he could find was pity. Compassion wasn't something he'd grown accustomed to when growing up. His father, Demetrius, had zero tolerance for weakness. Zane wasn't accepting pity from anybody, especially from Cheryl. Her body was rigid in her stark white coat, and her hair, though tied in a bun, had several strands sticking out. The dark circles under her eyes indicated that of the two of them, he had gotten more sleep.

Zane stared straight ahead, refusing to succumb to the urge to touch her. He could do without her sympathy, even if he craved the warmth of her hand touching his.

"When do I get out of here?" he asked.

All three of them looked at each other. It made him wonder where the mind reading translator was. Rick wrote on the tablet and showed it to him. *You're not going anywhere. Not in your condition.*

That was a newsflash. No doubt they wouldn't hold him against his will, but what would make them want to help someone like him? Anger and confusion welled inside him, giving him the extra oomph to push his body up into a sitting position. Cheryl and Rick rushed over to restrain him.

"I'm leaving at sundown." What the hell? He didn't even have an idea what time it was.

Rick shook his head, mouthing words he couldn't understand while Cheryl held his arms down against the mattress. "You're not going anywhere until we say you're ready to go."

Her words set off a primal response in him. He reached forward and grabbed her by the nape of her neck, pulling her down for a kiss. Time stood still for the briefest moment when her lips touched his, but then he abruptly ended the sweet torture.

When he let her go, she stumbled backward. Good thing Rick was able to catch her by the arm. The doctor tilted her chin until she met his eye, as if he were searching her face for an answer. A tear trickled down her face. Cheryl ran off, with the woman in the wheelchair trailing behind.

Once it was just him and the doctor inside the room, Zane pinned a steady gaze at him. "Am I going to walk again?"

Rick's brows furrowed. He sighed and took to writing on the notepad. It was more than a short scribble, so it took him longer to hand it to Zane.

CT scan showed no organ damage. However, your sciatic nerve is swelling, which is causing the lack of sensation in your legs. This may be temporary. I don't know. Only time will tell, and your being a vampire with quicker healing might just do the trick. It's a wait and see situation for us right now.

Zane threw the writing pad across the room for lack of a better way to channel his frustration. *Time. Who has the luxury of time?* "How can I get out of here if I can't walk? I'm not welcome here."

Rick walked over to where the tablet landed and picked it up. He returned to Zane's bedside, scribbled some more, and handed the sheet of paper to him. *On the contrary. Harrow and Rohnert want me to make sure you get the best possible treatment.*

Somehow Zane doubted that. Who would want to be around him with all the death and misery he'd caused these people? No, sir. This wasn't happening. He pulled the flimsy sheet off his body to swing his legs off the bed. That was what he'd intended to do, but nothing happened. His damn legs didn't budge, which caused him to topple over, sending the motion sensor blaring to high heaven. The wail agitated his sensitive ears, and he thrashed at Rick's attempt to steady him.

The door went flying off its hinges when Tor burst in, looking like a battering ram ready to slam into him. "Stay in your fucking bed. Your legs aren't going to take you anywhere. Stop giving Rick problems and be a good fuckin' vampire."

Before he could voice his protest, Tor's fist connected with his face, sending him back against the mattress. The punch was hard enough that his lights flickered and began to dim, but not before he heard Tor say, "That's for Cyrus."

Things had gotten out of hand this time, and Rohnert couldn't believe his eyes. He managed to get a few of the Elders to the safety and out of sight before the cops arrived in hordes. Helicopters circled the night sky like overgrown vultures seeking their next meal, their megawatt lights pointing to the ground, looking for anything or anyone they could pin this massacre on. Desider, Tiber, and Clotilde, along with most of their armies, had perished in the surprise attack from the collected vampires and Nerocs.

With cops combing the perimeter of the Rockefeller Center and the adjacent streets, it would be impossible to walk in and out as they pleased.

"Let's head back to the facility," Harrow said. Their group made their way to a chute location and crawled their way back to the underground facility.

"What the hell is happening?" Harrow lashed out once their small group had assembled in the I-room. "Did you see what those bastards did to the humans? They were gunned down like it was a goddamn video game."

Rohnert sat down, feeling like he was about to explode. He looked each Elder in the eyes and soaked in their own battered emotions. Wendell, Icarus, and Bardos wore glazed expressions of disbelief. Death had taken more of their friends, and since humans were now involved, their existence would no doubt be brought to light unless General Krever could pull a trick out of his sleeve again. Rohnert glanced around at the soldiers of their departed brethren.

"You are free to leave now that your masters are gone."

There was a ripple of murmurs from the group, and one answered, "I'm Cisneros, sire. I'm the head of Clotilde's personal army. My men and I will stay and serve you."

"So will we," two soldiers from Desider's and Tiber's groups said in unison.

"Thank you." There was nothing else to be said under the circumstances.

Harrow continued to call the rest of the MIA members. Each time he couldn't reach one, he rained curses that echoed against the walls of the silent room. When he finished his calls, Harrow stood up, pinching the bridge of his nose.

"Regrita is back home. There are no answers from Serena, Virgil, or Isidora."

Rohnert closed his eyes and breathed deep. Though he had a strong bond with each Elder in the Council, Isidora had been a constant source of pride for him, just like a sister, if he had one. To think she and Cyrus had left the facility at the same time. There was no reason for them not to come to their aid, unless . . .

Damn. He wasn't going to think morbid thoughts. Besides, she had Cyrus with her. The man would skin himself alive before he would allow anything to happen to Issy.

The phone rang, halting his musings. Harrow pressed the speaker button, and Rayce's voice came on. "Turn on the news."

Harrow pressed the remote, then hung up. He muttered an oath the second two familiar faces were seen being carried unconscious into a dark SUV. The camera zeroed in on Cyrus' blood soaked pant leg, where a shoe was noticeably missing.

"Jesus, we have to get them right away," Rohnert said.

Then the camera zoomed in on Issy, her head covered in blood. If Rohnert wasn't mistaken, the people taking their friends were human.

"I'm calling Leo now." Harrow was on the phone right away.

Rohnert continued to half listen to the news reporter while he delved deeper into speculations about Cyrus and Issy's role in the shooting.

However, the newscaster wasn't giving any leads about the particular organization involved in handling the case.

He heard Harrow's voice rising while he continued a somewhat heated conversation with the general.

"I'm all for getting them out by any means possible," Wendell said in a resolute voice.

Icarus released an exasperated sigh. "I have no problem with that plan. Besides, we can scrape everyone's memories before we leave. The biggest problem we have is finding where Isidora and Cyrus are being held."

"It's time we stepped out of our comfort zone. Now that the Nerocs are mobilized, I think we need to show the vampire world what we can do." Bardos added, his voice oozing with confidence.

Rohnert glanced at August's brother. Although he was much younger than his deceased sibling, Bardos had a wealth of knowledge about their race. His outlook was more in tune with the changing times. Rohnert acknowledged his sentiments with a nod of his head.

Harrow finished his call, punching the button on his cell phone with disgust. He paced the room as though deliberating what to say, but the Elders already had gotten the gist of it. When he looked up, his eyes were wild, and his face red with anger.

"Leo can't do anything right now because Issy and Cyrus were taken by a paranormal agency. According to Leo, he's been under pressure from a guy named Pete, the head of the agency, to give them more information about us. Leo hasn't given them any details, but he promised to talk to Pete in the morning regarding Cy and Issy. In the meantime, he wants us to sit tight and make sure no more blood is shed until he's able to field questions and get a damage control plan in motion."

"Sit tight? These are people we consider our brother and sister." Rohnert ground his teeth to keep from saying more.

"Bro, I share your sentiments. Believe me. I want Cyrus and Issy out of there right this minute."

"Cy is bleeding. He cut off his leg." Rohnert hated himself for pointing out the obvious. He couldn't even begin to imagine the torture Cyrus was going through at that very moment.

"Damn it." Harrow paced.

"If I may say something, that's bullshit." Bardos was bristling with frustration. "I vote to get them out now."

Harrow nodded slowly. "If we're all in agreement, then let's do it. Screw laying low. I'd hate for the man to bleed to death if those people won't help him."

"I'm calling Tor for backup now." Rohnert took out his cell phone.

"I'll get Rayce to track their location." Harrow said and started dialing as well.

"We have three hours until sunrise," Wendell reminded everyone.

Cyrus heard the several voices around him even before he opened his eyes. Hazy vision and a foggy mind greeted him the moment he tried to get up, but something held him back. Then he realized that his wrists were bound.

"Where the hell am I?" Even his voice sounded like he'd gone through hell and back—hoarse and shaky. The ongoing conversation ceased, and several men surrounded his bed. With his blurry sight, he tried to focus on the one closest to him.

"I recognized your face. You're with Leo—"

Cyrus didn't give the guy a chance to finish. "Where is the female?" If his hands weren't bound, he'd choke the bastard. When his eyes adjusted, a growl rumbled in his chest. He remembered this man. He'd seen him during the commotion in the hospital when Shelly was killed. If he recalled correctly, the man's name was Pete, and he was an official from an agency dealing with paranormal shit.

Anxiety closed in on him the moment reality sank in. How would he get Issy out of there if he was missing a leg? Never mind the pain. He should be used to it by now, having been stabbed and shot already. Losing a leg was just icing on the cake.

"Where is the female?" he asked once more.

"I do the questioning here." The man pulled out a chair and sat down while the rest of his men remained at full attention. "I'm Pete, and—"

"I know who you are." Cyrus struggled against his restraints and turned his head to glance around. With the black-clad men surrounding his bed, it was impossible to see anything beyond their big bodies. "Where is she?" he asked again.

Pete rose to his feet and glared down at him. "Shut up. You're at my mercy here, bloodsucker. I've been watching your kind for some time now. I was just waiting for you guys to screw up so Leo couldn't protect you anymore."

"What the hell are you talking about?"

The human smirked. "Did you think Leo could keep you guys all to himself forever? He's been using government resources to keep Tack's operation on the down-low."

"You're making a big mistake by taking us." Cyrus hissed, baring his fangs.

Pete laughed. "You made the wrong call by involving humans. You guys were untouchable until you made this mistake."

"Where is she?" Cyrus sniffed the air. He caught her scent and knew she wasn't far away. "Where are you keeping us?"

"You're in Unit 1260. And you will stay here until I say you can go."

Straining against his cuffs, Cyrus pinned the human with a death glare. "Let the female go. Keep me. Just let her go." As much as he hated to beg, he couldn't bear the thought of Issy having to endure captivity under the hands of these humans. Damn it. She shouldn't be going through this shit at all.

"You're not convincing me. Besides, I'm sure there is much to learn from *two* vampires. So if I were you, I'd cooperate and not be a pain in the ass."

Wrong thing to say. "You're going to regret this."

Pete seemed amused by his threat. "You're tied, and I'm not. I think you're getting things mixed up here." Then he nodded at one of his men, who came forward with a needle. "You need to sleep. You're going to have a long day tomorrow."

Cyrus thrashed, shaking the bed, but strong hands clamped around his arm. The needle went into his skin, delivering another unwelcomed slumber. He continued to struggle until his lids shut against his will and he lost consciousness.

He had no idea how long he was out, but the moment he resurfaced, his first thoughts were of Issy. Still restrained in bed, Cyrus let his eyes roam the room. She was at the far end, unconscious. He studied their surroundings and realized that it wouldn't be easy to stage an escape with the cameras trained on them. There was a big glass window that must also be a means to monitor them.

Issy started mumbling, as if she were having a dream. He could smell her blood and hoped to god those bastards had attended to her head wound. Cyrus glanced at the wall clock. They had two hours until daybreak. He had to try to rouse her while they still had darkness on their side. If she remained here, there was no telling what these people would do to them.

Being a guinea pig was not appealing at all.

"Issy . . . Issy. You gotta wake up, babe."

Two little girls were walking in the meadow, which was lit by the glow of the moon. Their paths were parallel to each other, yet there was no connection, no conversation between them. The taller one moved with obvious purpose. Half her face was covered by the long, blonde hair that fell to the small of her back. Her white dress touched her ankle, and while her feet moved fast, they barely touched the ground.

The smaller girl's pace was slow by comparison, and her steps were hesitant. She would look around, seeming unsure if she was headed in the right direction. Her red hair was pulled into pigtails, and her confused expression was punctuated by the pout on her plump, red lips. Dressed in a dark velvet dress that reached her knees, her tiny legs were hard at work to keep up.

They were headed in the same direction, but the disparity of their movements made it easy to guess which girl would make it to their destination faster.

"Issy, follow my lead," the older girl said, her hand beckoning her to take the same trail.

"Who are you?" the smaller of the two asked, quickening her steps to catch up.

When she managed to get closer, the blonde girl looked over her shoulder and took her hand. "I'm your sister, silly."

Issy gasped at the strong current created when their hands twined together. "Aemerria?"

"Issy. Issy, can you hear me?" Another voice called her name. It was a man's voice, which didn't make sense. Yet the sound was familiar and comforting.

"Issy . . . girl. C'mon, wake up." The voice sounded desperate. "I need you to wake up."

The plea jump-started her like a jolt of lightning, pulling her from the weirdest dream ever. *Aemerria is my sister?* The thought left her reeling, but the dream had felt real. Deep in her heart, she believed it was true. Aemerria, their shaman, was her sister. How? Why were they separated? She has a sister! Too much questions vied for answers, but the realization was a welcome one. She still had a family.

"Issy baby, please, wake up," the voice pleaded again.

Her eyes snapped open to the glaring overhead light. She sprang up, but the cuffs on both her wrists made it difficult. Issy sank back onto the mattress. Where was she? She looked down to find two wires attached to her chest and felt a slight vibration on her skin.

"Where am I?" She looked around but only registered beeping apparatuses. The place was not familiar. White walls, bright lights, and it stank of human and . . . blood. She had a splitting headache.

"You have . . . to escape . . . here."

She turned to follow the voice, which sounded broken and pained. "Cyrus?" Her eyes widened when she found him restrained by handcuffs on another bed at the other end of the room, his head tilted in her direction. A quick read of his mind brought back the events of the last hour or so. The fight, the ghastly looking creatures, being shot . . .

Her gaze traveled to his leg, and she cried. "Cyrus, we have to get you out of here."

He shook his head. "You have to get out of . . . here if you can. Don't waste . . . time."

Issy continued to comb his thoughts. It was no shocker that he'd rather rot there than slow her down, but she wasn't on board with his plan. "No . . . I'm not going to leave you."

Cyrus' smile was sad. "You have two hours left before sunrise. You can make a break for it."

Pain radiated from her chest, no doubt from the impact of the bullet. But it was her head that was giving her the most trouble, and the bright light overhead wasn't helping. "I'm not leaving you here—"

"I'd slow you down."

She frowned. "We'll get out of here together."

Concentrating, she compartmentalized the sounds swirling around her— the ones coming from the beeping machines hooked up to Cyrus, and his haggard breathing. She could hear too many voices in her head. A few sounded like doctors, but the rest were some sort of military personnel. They were being monitored, especially Cyrus. The general mood was a mix of fear and disbelief regarding their existence.

Issy looked up to see a camera pointed at her. She turned her head and found another one focused on Cyrus. The pristine white walls and the sterile scent in the air identified the place as a laboratory of some sort— with a steel door, to boot. It was hard to tell what lay beyond the big glass window at the far end of the room.

Feeling a choking sense of panic, she stifled a sob. She wasn't going to disgrace herself by crying. There would be no tears. Cyrus needed her, and she was going to figure a way out for them.

Wracking her brain for the quickest way out of her cuffs, one thought came to mind. She closed her eyes, took deep calming breaths, and began a series of chants. Uttering the summons in the old language, she beseeched the higher being that might be their sole salvation.

"Issy . . . please . . ."

She blocked out everything around her—Cyrus' plea, the noises, and the unseen threat outside. A few minutes passed, but her supplication remained unanswered. Issy begged for mercy and continued imploring for help. Her call would be answered. She was sure of it. The great shaman wouldn't leave them high and dry. They were going to make it out alive.

A loud clang sounded came from the steel door when it opened. Issy heard Cyrus hiss, and she strained against her cuffs. The damn things were too snug to allow movement. Tied and desperate, she bared her fangs, hoping she could get to her gun.

A burst of air blew in from the doorway.

"Let's get you guys out of here," Rohnert said in a low voice.

Before she could register what was happening, Harrow, Tor, and Firman were moving in to work on Cyrus' metal cuffs.

"Get Issy out of here first." Cyrus was more than adamant.

"We're getting you both out of here," Harrow said. "Tor, take Cy."

"Tor, take it easy. He's hurt," Issy said.

"He's in good hands, girl. Don't worry." Tor slung Cyrus onto his shoulder as if he weighed nothing, despite that Cyrus was big even by vampire standards.

The blare of the alarm startled them. Bardos peeked through the doorway. "We have to go. They're sending the big guns."

Whatever that meant, Issy knew they weren't going to get off as easy as she'd hoped.

Thundering footfalls sounded from a distance. Rage and terror warred inside her. This shouldn't be happening. They weren't animals to be tied down. A snarl escaped her lips as the sound drew closer.

"Let's get moving. Sunrise is coming. Spare lives if possible," Rohnert said as he worked on her metal cuffs. Harrow hovered, glancing back and forth the between her and the door.

The lock popped, releasing her. Issy worked fast on removing the wires that were taped to her chest, then she pushed her body off the bed and stood up. Once upright, her vision began to spin, and her head throbbed.

"Harrow, take Issy. I'll take the lead." Rohnert signaled to Bardos as soon as their group was ready to go.

She raised her hand to stop him. "I'm fine. I can walk."

Harrow grunted then pulled a gun from his holster. "Take this. You have perfect aim. If things get sticky, shoot at will."

Issy had only a moment to think of Harrow's words, which contradicted Rohnert's call to spare lives. She palmed the weapon and followed the rest out the door.

The alarm continued its piercing noise while their group made it out the first series of doors without interference. Issy could see Cyrus glance back at her, wishing he was holding her instead of being handled like a goddamn piece of meat. She couldn't even begin to think about the pain he was going through at the moment. Keeping her head straight, she gripped the gun and focus on the incoming footsteps. Rohnert was running ahead with Bardos and Wendell, along with Council soldiers. Firman and Gentry were providing cover from behind while she and Harrow ran side by side, following Tor with his cargo.

Before they reached the stairwell, gunfire erupted, and they had no choice but to dive for cover. She heard Cyrus howl in pain when he and Tor hit the ground.

An announcement blared from the overhead paging system, calling for reinforcements. The sound of helicopters approaching meant this was not going to end peacefully. The situation was changing from a clean getaway to all-out war. So much for quiet and bloodless.

While bullets zipped back and forth around him, Cyrus tried to stay upright. He was sitting against the post behind Tor, who was slinging gunfire at the humans. Cyrus looked down at what was left of his leg and winced. Though some sort of doctor had attended to it, the work wasn't what he'd come to expect—not even close to what Shelly or Rick could do. If he had to guess, he'd say the haphazard job was deliberate and planned for observation's sake. Although the massive bleeding had stopped, the wound continued to hurt like hell, and blood continued to seep through the wrappings. At this rate, he would bleed to death before the night was over.

He could hear Rohnert's efforts to convince the humans to stop firing, insisting they talk and clear the air. No one was listening, and they kept the assault going. Pete's voice was in the thick of it all, barking orders and pointing his men to areas that would best surround their group.

"Give me a gun," Cyrus shouted over the din of gun fire.

Tor tossed one of his reserves while assessing his condition. "We have to get you out of here."

"Yeah, yeah." Cyrus wasn't even going to get his hopes up. Things would be all right so long as Issy came out of this alive. A movement at the corner of his eye caught his attention. Issy was on her elbows, crawling in his direction. That was the last thing he needed. His instinct to protect rose up. A human aimed at her, and Cyrus fired a shot, catching the man in the head. No, sir. No one messed with his woman.

Issy made it to him, and he put his arm around her protectively. "That was so stupid of you."

"No, it wasn't. I want to see what I can do for your leg. You're going to bleed to death." She touched his lips, her face filled with worry. When she glanced down, he saw her frown, and her eyes filled with tears. "I won't let you wait any longer for help."

From the sounds of incoming shots and the fizzling fireworks around him, Cyrus could tell the battle was an even match. It could go on indefinitely, and yeah, he didn't have the luxury of time. Regardless, all he cared about was getting Issy to safety.

Before he could put his thoughts into words, Issy stood, her automatic poised, and began firing. She took down two men right away. Since she'd become an open target, the nearby humans shifted their focus to her and began firing in her direction.

"No!" Cyrus' warning was drowned out by the rapid succession of shots headed her way. This couldn't be happening. Issy was stupid to risk her life for him. His chest tightened, and his sight grew blurry with tears, but he continued to fire.

"What the fuck?" Harrow curse and jumped in with his Kalimetal to deflect incoming bullets away from her. Rohnert did the same, while Tor started flinging a series of throwing stars. Their team was suffering casualties, fallen soldiers disintegrating to ashes faster than human eyes could follow.

Then the shots trickled off. Rohnert recognized the small window of opportunity. "Let's get out of here." He gestured at the stairwell and communicated with hand signals that he would provide cover while the others made a run for it.

Issy turned to Cyrus. "Let's go." She pulled him to his feet. "Lean on me. Tor, cover us."

Cyrus dared not disagree when he glanced at Issy's wild eyes. The usual kindness there had been replaced by a pool of fury and determination. He wrapped an arm around her shoulder, and together they made the first awkward step.

"I'm heavy," he said.

"You're fine." She absorbed his weight. Together they made it toward the stairwell, Harrow leading the way while Tor brought up the rear. Harrow signaled for everyone to follow just as Rohnert and the rest of the Elders engaged in another barrage of gunfire. The stairs were difficult to navigate, and each time he hopped, excruciating pain radiated from his bleeding stump.

"Oh, no!" Issy cried, but it was too late. Men in full combat gear were waiting for them below. They'd walked into an ambush. Shots were fired, and the sounds were deafening in the enclosed area. Bullets zinged past them, hitting metal and concrete, creating a thundering noise. Tor got hit, and the big vampire staggered back under the weight of the shot.

"Score one for Jones' bulletproof vest." Tor winced but righted himself.

Harrow continued to deflect shots left and right with his Kalimetal, but Cyrus knew that he could only hold them off for so long. He continued to fire, but a new problem was fast becoming obvious as the ammo began to run out.

Much to their surprise, a blast of air swirled around them, and a woman appeared.

"Aemerria." Issy gasped.

Cyrus had a second to see the shaman who had replaced Lukan.

Calm as still water, Aemerria nodded to them and waved her hand. She created a blinding light that was bright enough to incapacitate the humans. "Take this exit." She pointed to the small window. "Go by way of the chute back to the facility."

"What about Rohnert?" Harrow asked.

Aemerria smiled. "Never worry, Harrow."

While the humans cowered and covered their eyes, the group of vampires made it out of the opening in one piece. Issy was talking to Cyrus, rousing him, but the sound of her voice grew fainter, duller, as she called his name. Blackness followed, and he slipped into oblivion.

Issy thought their getaway would be guaranteed once they cleared the exit. Yet another wrinkle stood in their way the moment they emerged from the side of the building. Squad cars were scattered everywhere, surrounding the structure. Uniformed men were hiding behind their vehicles, guns drawn and ready. She could hear their thoughts, and most weren't pretty. The orders were to take down their group in any way possible, dead or alive. Harrow gestured to a wall they could use for cover.

"We'll have your back," he said.

Dragging Cyrus' dead weight made it difficult for her, but adrenaline got her moving faster while they made a mad dash for it. Their not-too-covert movements caused a huge commotion among the waiting humans.

"You're surrounded. If you want to get out of here alive, you will lay down your weapons and surrender." The warning, delivered via bullhorn, was loud and clear.

She leaned against the wall, still holding Cyrus upright. Despite the fear she felt in her gut, she had to push on. They had to get out of there and get Cyrus to the safety of their facility. Passed out, he was much too heavy for her to handle. With dawn within striking distance, their options were limited. She eyeballed Harrow. Her mind was made up.

"Tor, take Cyrus."

He hesitated, no doubt sensing her plan. "Issy, Cy is not going to like this one bit."

She wasn't listening anymore. "We have no other choice. You're the one who has the best chance of getting him back to the facility in one piece." Tor shook his head, thinking he was better off doing the damage himself, but she was done with these guys' macho crap. "Take him!"

"Issy's right." Harrow looked at the group surrounding them. "There are too many of them." There was no fear in his voice, just straight-up assessment.

With a heavy heart, she kissed Cyrus on the temple and relinquished her hold on him. Tor slung Cyrus over one shoulder and nodded. "Tell me when," he said.

Mustering her strength, she nodded with grim determination. "Tor, I need your gun and ammo."

Tor produced a weapon and a round for her. "That's all I've got."

"Don't worry. This will be enough to get you out of here."

Issy caught a number of scents and felt a sudden burst of energy. More backup was in the area, waiting for a signal. "Time's running out. Please get him to safety."

Tor seemed skeptical. "You better get your ass back to him, Issy. I swear to God this man will skin me alive for letting you out of my sight."

Harrow bristled when his phone rang. He picked up, head bobbing at the latest news. "Firman's here. Let's roll." He looked Issy in the eyes then turned to Tor. "Be safe."

Issy took a deep breath and said a quick, silent plea to the higher power. On Harrow's signal, they moved, guns blasting. Their sudden emergence surprised the humans, enabling Tor to streak through the parking lot undetected.

Their backup, led by Firman and Gentry, attacked from behind. Instead of killing the unsuspecting humans, their group fired on the vehicles, creating diversions and eliminating hideouts. Cars began to explode one after the other while the humans scampered for cover. Fires broke out, giving the vampires a chance to run for it. As the orange glow rose to disperse the waning night, shouts came from the immediate surroundings.

Helicopters zeroed in on them with their megawatts of light, following them while they darted across the parking lot.

"Let's try to lose them." Harrow looked over his shoulder at her. "Meet you at the chute entrance."

"Got it," Issy said through gritted teeth. She veered toward the empty patch of land that bordered the building they were held in. Harrow darted in the opposite direction, creating raucous noises to attract attention to himself. The choppers separated to follow each of them.

Issy's heart raced as she ran as fast as she could, dashing toward the street where she hopefully could lose her pursuer. She looked up to see the chopper's light singling her out like a fugitive. She zigzagged between people and cars, any way to shake off it off.

Most of the humans stopped in their tracks to check out what the fuss was all about, making it easy for Issy to move faster. The helicopter continued its pursuit while she wracked her brain for a way out of its line of vision.

Sunrise was closing in. She didn't need a watch to know that it was coming. Her skin prickled, and her eyes begun to sting.

"Damn it," she cried while she continued to run, heading for a cluster of high rise buildings that would make it difficult for the chopper to stay low to the ground. Cars beeped when she dashed across the street to get to the next alley. The whir of the blades grew fainter, but she dared not look back. Her skin continued to tingle, yet she refused to slow down.

"A few more blocks to go," she said to herself. "A little more." She kept going, despite the blistering pain that had begun to slow her down. Fear started to creep in when the first of the sun's orange beams came into view.

Her ears started ringing, mixing with the confusing chatter and thoughts of humans around her. "One block to go." Heart pounding in her chest, she continued her efforts to move forward. Her steps slowed down as the sting of the sun began to spike. Issy leaned against a store window, hoping to get a second wind. Curious people began to crowd around her.

"Are you okay?" one woman asked.

"She's on the news. I saw her," another said, gawking at her as if she was a part of the circus.

Death this way wasn't welcome. She wasn't going to be burnt to a crisp. Issy had to make one final stand, but her feet wouldn't cooperate and her energy was flagging. While more people cornered her, Issy thought of dying. She had never been afraid of it, but she hadn't thought her grand exit would be like this.

Sweat continued to bloom when she made one last ditch effort to get to the chute. Her eyesight was failing because of the glare of rising sun. *I'm not going to make it,* she thought as tears blurred her vision. She covered her eyes with her arm and thrust forward, feeling her way. Swimming in a sea of panic, Issy thought of Cyrus. If he made it, then her existence wouldn't be for nothing. She had loved and offered her life for another. She had been a part of something important. It wouldn't be a waste after all.

Random thoughts fired through Issy's brain as her knees buckled underneath her. When she crumpled to the ground, she whispered, "I want to be your wife, Cy," hoping she could see him one last time.

"You're going to tell him that in person," Harrow said, his arms encircling her waist and pulling her up on her feet. "Now, let's get you home."

In a fit of rage, Drago launched himself at the desk, throwing things across the room as if they weighed nothing. The resounding crash did nothing to relieve his burning desire to kill, and it left him feeling more agitated than ever. Lukan and Lord Marchec looked on.

"This is unacceptable." His fury continued to multiply as the television continued to show the same footage over and over.

Lukan rushed over, close but not within striking distance in case she became an outlet for his rage. "My lord, some things are beyond our control," she said in a frightened voice.

Lord Marchec was quiet, but Drago knew what was on his mind. The leader of the Nerocs was not to be underestimated, especially with the death of his brother, Om. Drago could sense the brewing wrath within, and God knew what the vampire was capable of doing.

"We were so close to victory. We've taken down Elders and guards. We should be celebrating right now."

Lord Marchec's head snapped in his direction. "A fierce soldier died today. Om and I have been through many battles together. He was not just my brother but also a trusted comrade. Your so-called celebration won't happen until I get my hands around his killer's neck." He glared at Drago, and his daunting eyes glowed, spewing a wave of disturbing wickedness.

Drago pried into Lord Marchec's mind, wanting to be a step ahead in case the leader went berserk. "I share your grief, Marchec. We shall find a way to avenge your brother."

With a wretched expression, Lord Marchec stood up and cursed. "I want revenge," he said and hissed. "This just became personal."

Good deal. Drago smiled to himself. This could just be what they needed—an incident to ensure the leader's full commitment. Drago knew that Marchec could be lethal and ruthless. If it weren't for their abhorrence of being seen by others, the Nerocs would be leading the vampire order based on their innate, unique powers. Instead, the leader and his group preferred to stay hidden and forgotten.

This was going to be a lot of work, but Drago was no stranger to playing a long game. Besides, he hadn't gotten this far without being persistent. If he set his mind to a task, he was going to get it done, one way or another.

He nodded at Marchec and smiled. "You will have it, my friend. Are your men still camped outside the facility?"

"No one will be able to go in or out undetected." Marchec's eyes flickered with ire. "Unless they're taking a different route, which I suspect is the case."

Drago walked over to the floor-to-ceiling window and gazed out. "You may be right. If that's the case, you know what needs to be done."

Marchec stood next to him, and Lukan drifted to the other side. "Grant me the autonomy to do what I think is necessary, and you'll get your seat."

Good thing he can't read minds, Drago thought, *or else he'd know that I don't trust him one bit.*

Lukan, of course, heard him as if he'd spoken aloud. She glanced at him, a wicked smile playing on her lips.

Drago shrugged. "You do what you want as long as we get the results *I* want."

A grim smile tugged at Marchec's mouth, reeking of the evilness that wrapped itself around him like a fiery blanket. "Oh, you'll get that and more."

Drago had an idea of what Marchec had in mind and celebrated in silence. He made a mental note never to piss off a Neroc vampire unless he had a death wish. "How long will it take you to get the job done?"

Marchec turned and pinned him with his spine-chilling gaze. "Don't demand a deadline. I don't think well with time restrictions. I will study each of them and strike when the moment is right."

Drago seethed inside but schooled his expression. "So be it."

"Good. If that is all, I have things to do." Marchec turned for the door. Before he cleared the room, he looked over his shoulder at Drago. "Stop reading my mind. I don't appreciate the invasion of my privacy." He pulled the door shut.

Drago growled. Another hiccup. He turned to gaze out the window again at the waning darkness. The sun's tentacles were already reaching upward, ushering in another day of waiting. "I want you to keep a close eye on that one. If he's up to no good, I want to be informed."

Lukan sighed. "As you wish. What do we do about Goran's children?"

Screw the girls. He was more interested in the oldest son, Nathaniel. The trouble was that he and the rest of Goran's brood had disappeared without a trace when Bretania vanished. No one could give him a straight answer about what had happened to the whore. Did she perish in the warehouse attack, or had she broken away from their agreement?

Lukan looked at Drago. She understood his need to obtain Goran's oldest son. He wanted to show the world he had arrived. The illegitimate son of Cantor would not linger in the background any longer.

"That kid has so much potential. I want him found, along with Goran's whore."

Lukan stepped between him and the glare of the rising sun. She snapped her fingers and the shutters began their steady descent. "Is there anything else you need?" Her smile held an invitation he couldn't refuse.

"Bed me and ease my worries," he said, knowing it was what the shaman needed to hear.

"I thought you'd never ask." Lukan flashed a dazzling smile. Then she snaked her arms around his waist, resting her head against his chest. "Have I told you that every beat of your heart is music to my ears?"

The words were meant to fluff his ego, and it worked. He stroked her hair and let his thoughts run free about the things he wanted to do to her. "I meant to thank you for ridding this world of Gastarius."

Drago felt her shiver with need.

Zane was alone in one of the clinic rooms when the speaker blared with an urgent call for Rick, Cheryl, and Linda to report to the clinic. He tuned out the rest as he tried to push himself up into a sitting position. His arms were strong enough to support his torso while he leaned against the steel headboard. The effort zapped his energy, and he found himself having to catch his breath. What a fucking joke. A paraplegic half-vampire. Wasn't that a hoot?

He glared at the wheelchair next to his bed, loathing his present predicament. His legs continued to remain nonresponsive, and this had aggravated him more than anything in his puny life. Being in a wheelchair was a no-go. He would rather rot in hell than be limited that way.

Cheryl still visited, but she her lack of eye contact and her stiff medical inquiries left him cold. He could tell she had been worried on his behalf. There was an undeniable attraction between them. Yet sometimes, it felt like he had just imagined those things. Left to his own devices most of the time, he wished he could get up and leave.

Hurried footsteps sounded outside—a heavy and determined gait, together with light and efficient little steps. Funny, he could tell which one was hers. He strained his ears to catch the muffled conversation between Cheryl and Linda. Tor's voice boomed in the hallway, and his heavy steps echoed against the tile floor, followed by a muffled description of the current situation.

Zane couldn't tell who was injured, but he had the sudden urge to know what was going on. Little by little, he inched his body closer to the edge of the bed until his legs dangled on the floor. He gripped the side of the bed and could see that his feet were touching the tiles. Without the benefit of feeling the floor underneath him, he decided to test his lower limbs and heaved his body upright.

It was no surprise that his legs balked at the weight and he crumpled down to the floor. His bed alarm sounded. With his limp legs unable to support his movement, he relied on his upper body strength to scoot up until he could reach the alarm button. Once the blaring stopped, he slumped against the side of the bed. Good thing everyone was too busy to check on him. This was embarrassing. The last thing he needed was to be seen in such a humiliating state. Exhausted and hating himself for acting irrationally, he waited until his heart stopped racing and contemplated his next move.

The bed was too high to reach, leaving the wheelchair as the more accessible alternative. Zane eyed the thing with disdain, hating that he would need to use it, but he would rather give in than to ask for assistance. Pride was a terrible sensitivity to contend with, and his lack of options made him do the unthinkable.

He reached over to the footrest and folded it out of the way. Using the lower frame to get closer, he gripped both sides and pulled himself up. A prickling sensation in the soles of his feet felt like there were thousand needles poking him. Zane looked down at his legs and found them shaking violently. His palms closed in on the arm rests to steady his body while he rode the tide. It took several minutes before the spasms ebbed.

Beads of sweat peppered his temples when he righted his body on the damned wheelchair. Tired and pissed off, he remained unmoving. He hated being an emo jackass, when he'd brought this on himself. He covered his face with his hands and tried to contain the emotions that seemed to hit him from every direction.

It took a great deal of time before he could muster the strength to look up. Once his emotions were in check, he tested the wheels, propelling himself with difficulty. He released the right wheel and pivoted with the left, and his foot hit the leg of the bed.

Zane yelped in pain, but then stopped himself. His eyes widened with surprise. He'd felt pain. That could mean just one thing—he was feeling. Feeling was good. A sliver of hope coursed through his veins at the thought of being able to walk again.

Feeling elated, he pushed the rims forward until he reached the door. With some maneuvering on his part, he was able to clear the doorway. In the hallway, Zane could hear the commotion inside the clinic. Classical music was drifting through the quiet corridor while he decided where to go.

Zane looked down the long hallway, not certain what to do next. He had been in the facility for days, but this was the first time he'd set foot outside his room. He looked up and found one of the cameras trained on him. That didn't come as a surprise. He knew they would be watching his every move, and he couldn't blame them.

He was turning back to his room when the clinic door opened and Cheryl stepped out. She didn't notice him right away, and this gave him the chance to see the depths of suffering on her face.

She bumped into his chair and stumbled forward. Zane reached out just in time to catch her, and she ended on his lap.

"Oh God, I'm so sorry." Cheryl turned, and her sad eyes widened in disbelief once she saw who it was. She scrambled to her feet, but he held her, not wanting to lose the warmth she provided.

"Are you okay?"

"I didn't see you." She ignored his question and pulled away. Once on her feet, she smoothed the fabric of her pants, refusing to look him in the eye.

This stung more than any weapon could. "Cheryl, please look at me." He hated the quiver in his voice as he reached for her hand.

She stepped back, and her gaze traveled down to the wheelchair. "How did you manage to get up?"

"Desperation." Zane pulled back his hand back. "I asked if you're all right."

Her hands went to her hair, and her fingers ran through the strands. "I'm fine." She still avoided looking him in the eye.

"Is there something I can do?" He wheeled closer to her but did not attempt to touch her.

Cheryl shook her head, her lips trembling.

"What's going on? Who's in there?"

"Cyrus . . . Rick managed to revive him, but his leg is gone." Cheryl managed to get around his chair and ran down the hallway, leaving him tongue tied and unable to believe what he'd heard.

Cyrus had some vague thoughts about what was going on the moment he lifted his heavy lids. He recognized the ceiling, the massive lamp staring down on him, and the familiar dread in his gut. So he was back in the facility, inside the clinic where he'd been flat on his back three times already, not counting this current episode.

"You're awake," Tor said, standing by the door.

He realized he couldn't speak with a tube running down his throat. When he began tugging on it, the machine next to his bed started beeping.

Tor rushed over to restrain him. Rick clamped down on his hand to stop him, and his eyes spoke volumes. This just agitated Cyrus more.

He fought back, wrestling out of Tor's grasp and muscling Rick away. With a mighty yank, he pulled the tube out of his mouth and sputtered.

"Dude, you've flat lined. Stop pulling this macho shit on us." Tor bristled.

Rick pushed a button, and the annoying sound stopped.

Cyrus swallowed the lump in his throat and tried to speak. "Where's . . . Issy?" He tried to push himself up, but something heavy underneath the sheet made it excruciatingly difficult to move. He sank back against the mattress and blew out a frustrated breath.

Tor looked at Rick and didn't answer right away. Cyrus didn't miss the nervous glance between the two men, and he looked at the clock on the wall. Six-thirty in the morning. His heart began racing, and he thought his chest would explode. "Where is she?" he rasped.

His vision blurred, and tears started pouring out of his eyes like a sprinkler gone bad. "Please tell me she got back in time."

Tor sat down next to the bed with a grunt. "We haven't heard from her . . . or Harrow."

"Christ." This wasn't happening. Not to Issy. Harrow had shown resistance to dusk before, but they hadn't tested him against the early morning sun. They should've left Cyrus there.

Rick's hand rested on his arm, providing comfort. Cyrus closed his eyes and let the pain settle in the pit of his stomach. Knowing that his life would be worthless without Issy, this was going to be one huge hell he had to wade through.

Unable to utter another word, he blinked several times, but the tears continued to flow. Screaming inside and distraught beyond belief, he cried in silence. The room had grown quiet while he wrestled with the ache in his chest.

All three of them remained in daze until they heard Rayce's frantic voice over the speaker system. "All available hands, please proceed to the chute location now!"

Tor and Rick raced out of the room, leaving Cyrus wondering if he should hold up hope. He scooted to the edge of the bed and reached for the phone. Rayce came on the line right away.

"Who is it?" he asked, not even bother with pleasantries.

"It's Harrow and Issy," Rayce said. He could detect the worry in Rayce's tone.

"Are they okay?"

Rayce didn't answer right away. Cyrus had a sneaking suspicion that he was weighing his answer.

"Tell me!"

"Harrow seemed sluggish but upright. Issy, on the other hand, isn't moving at all."

Cyrus hurled the phone and hollered at the image that came to mind. His blood pressure plummeted. "Oh God . . . oh God . . ." Even though he was seeing double, he disconnected the wires attached to his body and pushed himself up with his elbows.

Once seated, he realized the dead weight slowing him down was his stump. Cyrus pushed the sheet away to reveal a whole lot of bandages covering his abbreviated leg. He cursed under his breath and glanced around. There were no crutches around. Not a fucking thing to help him move.

There was a knock on the door before it opened. He was hoping to see Tor, or at the very least his sister, to give him the deets, but he didn't expect to see Zane. The bastard was propelling himself on a wheelchair.

"What are you doing here?" He felt anger shooting out of his pores.

"I heard a scream." Zane advanced into the room but left the door open. "Is there anything I can do for you?"

Cyrus snorted. "I don't want your help," he said, wiping the tears away with the back of his hand. Then he thought better of it. "Give me your chair."

There was no hesitation from Zane. He wheeled close to the chair next to the bed. Cyrus watched him lock the brakes, and in awkward movements, transfer himself over to the vacant seat. Then he turned the wheelchair around for Cyrus.

"I would help if I could," Zane said in a quiet voice.

"No need," he shot back. Using the side rail to steady himself, he guided his injured leg then his good one until they dangled off the bed. Blood flowed down to his lower limbs, and an unwelcomed pressure caused him to pause.

"Wait a moment before you make a move." Zane held the chair in position.

Cyrus was going to sling an angry remark but thought better of it. He lowered his right foot to the floor. The cold surface greeted the bare sole, and he shifted to swing his body over to the wheelchair. A dizzying sensation made him halt every movement while he muttered curse after curse, but he'd made it.

The spinning stopped soon enough, and he wheeled himself out of the room. The hallway held an eerie silence, but he heard distant noises coming from the elevator. He pivoted the chair and focused in the direction of the shaft opening. Harrow emerged first, supported by Rick. Cyrus felt his insides roil in sick anticipation. Then Tor followed, cradling Issy in his arms.

"What happened to her?"

"Exposure to the sun, but don't worry, she just passed out," Harrow said when their eyes met.

Cyrus sighed in relief and moved out of the way. Cheryl had already prepped the examination table by the time they reached the clinic. Tor lowered Issy onto it while Rick assisted Harrow into a chair. The doctor picked up the pad and wrote in haste.

A quick visual check told Cyrus that Issy had blisters on her face, arms, and wherever else skin was visible. She might even be suffering from shock.

Rick turned the pad around for Cheryl to read. She then moved in quick successive motions, lining up gauzes and small bottles on the tray. Then she hustled over to Harrow.

Cyrus wheeled to the foot of the bed to catch a glimpse of Issy, who was beginning to moan and stir. His heart leapt in joy. "Hey baby, are you okay?"

"Where are you?" Issy reached out her hand.

Rick gestured for him to come closer, and Cyrus propelled the chair to the side of the bed. He took her hand. "I'm here, baby. I'm so glad you're all right." He began to weep as relief swelled within him.

Issy struggled to sit up, but Rick made a frantic noise that prompted Cyrus to hold her back.

"Stay there and let Rick examine you first."

She gripped his hand. "I'm glad you're okay, too," she said while tears streamed down her cheeks. Then her head whipped in Rick's direction. "Okay, he wants everyone to clear the room. Cyrus, you can stay and watch, but after this, you will be flat on your back for the next week or so. It's too soon to be applying pressure to your stump."

Cyrus nodded, overwhelmed with happiness.

Tor snorted on his way out, and Cheryl assisted Harrow out of the room. Once it was just the three of them left, he watched Rick begin a silent conversation with Issy, who kept still. Then she turned her head to Cyrus. "He's going to cut my clothes off to check on the blisters. Then he will check my eyes."

"Check your eyes?" The statement confused him. "What's wrong with them?"

"I can't see much except blurred shapes. I'm only able to pinpoint your location by following your thoughts and voice."

Rick began working on cutting off her clothes, starting with her leather jacket.

What the fuck was that about? Cyrus felt as if he had been doused with cold water. His precious Issy couldn't be blind. That was not how it was supposed to be.

She squeezed his hand. "There goes my first attempt at making a fashion statement," she said, trying to make light of the situation.

Cyrus smiled, but sadness gripped his heart. "You don't need nice clothes. You'll always be beautiful to me."

Rick nodded at him, and Issy smiled. "Rick wants you to know that he shares your sentiment. He also wants to remind you that this procedure is clinical, so don't go jumping on him when he inspects the rest of my body."

"I know." He watched Rick removed everything, down to her bra. Once Issy's chest was bared, Cyrus flinched at the sight of the dime-size blisters covering her exposed skin. The ones that had been under her clothes were much smaller in size. "Does it hurt?"

Rick took one bottle of mentha extract and began the process of applying the balm onto each and every blister. Cyrus could see the instant change the moment it touched her skin.

"It's pretty bad, but I'm not complaining. You've been through worse than me." She smiled.

Cyrus shook his head before he realized she probably couldn't see him. "You're such a brave woman." He kissed her hand.

"Not as brave as you." Issy turned to Rick, who seemed to be saying something. "Rick said he'll leave the rest for me to treat. At least he can see that they're just second degree burns. And he wants us to cut the emo crap." She laughed.

Cyrus had to laugh when he realized that he'd been crying. He brushed the tears away, and then flipped the doctor a middle finger. "Thanks, Doc. I owe you one."

Rick smiled then urged Issy to close her eyes. He pulled out a penlight from his coat and checked the area surrounding her lids. Then Issy opened her eyes and gazed up the ceiling, blinking several times while the doctor continued to move the light around her pupils.

Cyrus waited with bated breath while Issy's gripped on his hand tightened. "What's going on?" He searched Rick's face for an answer.

From where he sat, he couldn't do much but stroke Issy's arm to comfort her. He felt impotent for the first time, unable to hold her as a man should.

She took a deep breath and faced him. "My retinas are showing signs of burns, and blood flow is not like it should be. But with my ability to see blurred shapes, there is a chance I'll regain some of my vision in time. It depends on how the healing process goes."

Issy turned her head back, and Rick began applying a clear solution. Cyrus wrestled with the weight of her situation, trying to make heads or tails of what it meant. Damn it. How in the world could he allow her to suffer like this?

"You've got nothing to feel guilty about." Issy squeezed his hand.

"Damn it, Issy. You should've left me there."

She whipped her head in his direction, her eyes blazing with unconcealed annoyance. "I will never do that. So stop with it already. We're going to be okay, no matter what happens from this day forward. What's important to me is you're alive. That is all I care about, not you missing a leg or me having fucked-up vision."

Taken aback by her sudden bout of temper, not to mention her first time cursing, Cyrus began to laugh. Rick joined in, and before he knew it, they were all laughing together like fools. Once their outburst of mirth ended, Rick finished checking Issy's eyes.

"You will be a good vampire and return to your room. Rick isn't afraid to humiliate you by dragging you back to bed if you resist."

"Is that a fact?" Cyrus said and gave the doctor a challenging stare.

"He said you can bet your life on it."

Rick smirked then walked over to the sink and started rinsing his hands. After that, he left the room, and they were alone.

"I'm so happy to see you. You're right, nothing matters. Not my leg or your vision, so long as we are together." Cyrus struggled to get up.

Issy sat on the examination table and pushed him back down. "Stop it. You've just been to hell and back." She let go of his hand and climbed down, using her sense of touch to orient herself.

"Wait. You're in no position to move around. Just lie down for now. I'll be here to watch you."

"Oh rubbish. I only have little blisters, and I can feel them healing already."

Cyrus inspected the sores that were indeed healing right before his eyes. "But you shouldn't be moving around yet."

"You didn't hear Rick say anything to that effect. Did you?"

He shook his head then added, "No."

"Good boy. Now, tell me which way to go so we can tuck you back into bed." Before he could protest, she was pushing his chair toward the door.

"Make a left." Cyrus knew in his heart that everything would be all right in their world.

Drago roused Lukan as soon as sundown arrived. He had a brilliant idea that could cripple the damn Tack Enterprises vampires. So much for their righteous acts and compassion for silly humans. This time, he would hit them where it would hurt the most. Just because Marchec was bidding his time, Drago didn't have to sit around and wait.

He knew how the group operated and their silly notions about keeping puny humans away from the conflict. It was noble, but nobility wasn't going to keep their bellies full. Nobility wouldn't give them what they needed the most. This scheme would put an end to their hiding. Once their supplies dwindled, they would have to come out and search for food. That was when he would be waiting for them.

Lukan reached for his arm, trying to pull him back down. "What's going on?" she said in a sleepy voice.

"Get up. There is something I want you to find out for me." Drago kissed her on the forehead and slipped out of bed.

Her eyes opened and focused on him. "What is it, my lord?"

"I want you to find all the blood banks in the area."

It took Lukan a few moments to figure out what he had in mind. When she did, she raised her hand as if scanning an imaginary book, and then she smiled at him, her eyes twinkling. "There are three here in the immediate area, and many across the state."

"Great. I shall put my men to work," he said with a smile.

Rohnert breathed a thankful sigh after they escaped the clutches of the humans who had been closing in on them. They had been outnumbered three to one. There was no way in heaven or hell to flee the escalating bloodbath until Aemerria showed up.

Aemerria's presence had eased his worries. In all his years in battle, he'd never imagined going up against humans. It would have been easy to take them all out, if it hadn't been ingrained in his mind that they didn't warrant enough of a threat. Their inferior makeup couldn't be considered a challenge.

Aemerria had spread her blinding spell and blasted bright light everywhere, stunning the countless men surrounding their position. She had created a path for them to escape their pursuers and reach the safe haven of the nearby lot until all his men had been accounted for.

Then she'd led them back to the old apartment building where he used to spend all his time after his abrupt departure from the underground facility.

Bardos collapsed next to him while Wendell and Icarus spent some time debriefing their soldiers. It wasn't lost on him that these men had narrowly escaped death, and for that he was grateful to Aemerria intervention.

He followed her with his eyes while she paced in the tight space. The floorboards squeaked under her nonstop movement.

"Why here?"

Aemerria stopped to face him. "The headquarters is surrounded by Nerocs. Everyone is safe as long as they stay inside the walls, but it's the coming and going I can't guarantee." She resumed her pacing.

"What happens next?" he asked, echoing Bardos' exact inquiry.

"You will gather for a meeting and regroup. This is a different breed you're fighting. I have no power against them. All I can do is help with the other aspects."

"Why don't you have—"

She regarded him with weary eyes. "They can negate my power. Somehow, their leader knew this."

"Would Gastarius be able to offer some wisdom?" Wendell's brows were creased together into a solid frown, still unable to believe the events that had led them to this place.

Aemerria inhaled deep, her petite form heaving when she released a lungful of air. Her eyes were like a black abyss when she faced them. "I'm afraid Gastarius is no longer with us."

Rohnert's heart banged his chest at the news. Sure, he hated the diviner for withholding vital information from him, but he could never have imagined their world without the old man.

"How did it happen?" Wendell stood up, his expression pained.

The shaman continued to pace, leaving them all watching and waiting. "Gastarius had seen it. He asked me not to intervene because he believed he had served his purpose in this world. What I can't fathom is how Lukan got to him."

Icarus drew in a sharp breath. He was known as one of the wisest Elders, despite his fairly young age. "He didn't hide from her. As you said, he asked for you to look the other way."

Aemerria considered this then shook her head. "It doesn't mean I can't have my revenge on Lukan. She made this personal. Gastarius was a good man, and we needed him."

"You're talking about vengeance. Does your status allow you to kill?" Rohnert asked.

Her eyes flickered with dark undertones. "As I said, this is personal. I will answer for the rest, but I will only find satisfaction when she is no longer breathing."

"Christ, what's next?" Wendell asked.

The shaman answered with a bitter laugh. "We'll dip into a cesspool of uncertainty?" she said.

Rohnert ignored her reply because he detected that it was her fear talking. If his read was accurate, then they were headed into some serious fuckery.

Then Aemerria asked herself a silent question. *Where is the black book?*

He had no idea what to make of that. Shouldn't she know, since she was the woman running the show now? Aemerria shot him a questioning glance, but Rohnert merely shrugged in response. He now recognized that without Gastarius' wisdom, Aemerria being a newbie would encounter numerous challenges along the way.

"Who should we turn to for guidance now?" Bardos asked.

"You're looking at her." Aemerria's voice dipped lower, as if she couldn't believe it herself.

Rohnert stared at her. Sure, she was great, talented, and knowledgeable, but she was also terribly young . . . and they had no idea of her past. How did he know that she could be trusted? What would become of their powerful and once-proud race?

She offered a brittle smile. "Thank you for your kind thoughts. Yes, I'm young. In fact, I'm one of the youngest in our little group, but all the others seem to support Gastarius' decision to leave me with this huge responsibility. I should inherit the position since Gastarius spent the most time with me. I have no recollection of my past except the dark secret I've come to embrace. But I can feel it in my bones that one of you holds the key to unraveling one of my life's mysteries." Then she locked eyes with Rohnert. "As far as trust, I guess there is nothing I can do to put your mind at ease until I prove myself."

Rohnert continued to stare at Aemerria, unable to believe the weight she was carrying on her shoulders. "Are you up for this?"

She shrugged and resumed her pacing. He and Bardos watched her lithe form move back and forth. "It would be accurate to say that he has imparted his vast knowledge to me, but I've yet to test my full powers. I've been cooped up for too long."

This piece of information was intriguing, and Rohnert was careful to store it in his memory. He would have asked what she was referring to if it weren't too personal, but he left it alone. Both Aemerria and Bardos glanced at him. It was Aemerria who responded. "Thank you. It'll make a good bedtime story, kinda like the Wicked Witch of the West."

"So this will be our headquarters for the day?" Rohnert changed the subject, not willing to corner the great shaman into sharing her secret until she was ready. Something about her made him want to distance himself. She might as well be playing them just like Lukan had. Who would know?

"I'm afraid we'll have to stay here until sundown." Aemerria ended her pacing and settled on the battered cot that used to be his bed. He watched her cross and uncross her legs. If he was guessing by her actions, she was nervous and unsure of herself.

It seemed as though Rohnert would have to make the call. He beckoned over Wendell and Icarus. "I think we're safer if we all stay in the facility instead of being divided in two places. We can hold the meeting there among the remaining Elders. Track Virgil, Serena, and Regrita. Have them settle their families in a secured location. After that, cut all contact with them until we can guarantee their safety. I'll meet you here tomorrow at sundown. That should give you enough time to get your kin in a safe shelter until the situation calms down."

Wendell gave Rohnert's suggestion thorough consideration. "I agree."

"What about me? I have no family." Bardos said.

Rohnert had forgotten that Bardos was still unmated. Apart from August, he was the last remaining representative of their bloodline. "Come with me. I can use another strong hand."

Bardos nodded.

"We still have a little time before the sun hits. It's best for us to go now. We shall meet you back here tomorrow. I'll let the rest know." Wendell,

Icarus, and their personal armies departed, leaving the three of them to their thoughts.

The building quieted down. Rohnert continued to run scenarios in his head, and he belatedly noticed Aemerria was sharing her unspoken ideas with him. Together, they welcomed the sun beating down onto the boards that made up as their only defense against its harmful rays.

Cyrus had no idea how long he'd been asleep, but as he tried to shift his position on the small clinic table, he noticed an arm was draped over his waist. He turned to see Issy's serene face. Her even breathing told him she was dead to the world.

He gazed upward and recalled the moment they'd come back to this room, Issy pushing the wheelchair, and she had started talking about her ordeal.

"When I was feeling the heat on my face, I thought that was it for me. I had no way of making it back to you. I said something and hoped you would somehow feel it coming from me."

Cyrus had turned his body and caught her smiling. He had taken her hand and led her to sit on the bed, facing him. He would've had her sitting in his lap, but he doubted his legs could handle the weight.

"What did you say, babe?" he had asked, staring at her beautiful face.

She had deftly traced her fingers along his cheek, running along the contours of his mouth until she had reached his eyes. "I said I want to be your wife, Cy, or whatever you call your mates. I whispered it to myself, but Harrow heard it when he came for me. He urged me not to give up so I could tell you in person."

He had taken both her hands and kissed each one before gazing into her eyes. It didn't matter if her focus wasn't right on, he'd known she was seeing him just the same.

"Jesus, I will marry you as many times as your heart desires. Anywhere, any time. We could do it now if we could manage to get a minister in here, or maybe your sister could do the honors." His chest had felt like it would burst from happiness. "Issy, I've loved you since the moment I set eyes on you, and I will love you until my last breath. Marry me, because I want to make you mine forever."

Issy's eyes had filled with tears, but her smile was radiant, lighting her face. "I think forever sounds like a good idea."

Then it had dawned on him that he wasn't prime husband material, but her mouth had already closed in on his, preventing any other doubts to creep in. When she had stopped for air, she whispered the tender words. "I'm not looking for perfect. I want what you can give me."

"What would that be?"

"Your love and affection."

"You'll get that every second of the day," he had said and kissed her again.

The kiss had taken them further than they had intended. It was followed by the heated passion of a lover showing his partner that he needed her like he required air to breathe. They'd ended on the clinic bed. Somehow they'd figured out the positioning and worked around his injured leg.

Cyrus smiled at the memory of their lovemaking, feeling the heat rising in the pit of his stomach. Hell, they needed to get out of there now, if he could find a way to arrange it. His recuperation could continue in the comfort of his own bed, holding the woman who meant everything to him.

Issy stirred in his arms, and her eyes opened. He could tell she was searching his face. "I'm on board with that idea. This bed is not comfortable."

He laughed, marveling at her forthrightness. "If you help me into that chair, I think we're on our way to freedom."

Her laughter filled the room, and she snuggled against the crook of his neck. "Give me five more minutes. Besides, Rick and Linda are on their way here."

Cyrus almost fell off the narrow bed in his haste to cover her naked body with the hospital sheet. Issy grabbed his arm just in time. "I love it when you get worked up."

"You're going to get a lot of that from me."

Within a few minutes, his sister and Rick entered the room without knocking. The newcomers gave Cyrus and Issy an odd look but said nothing.

Issy broke the awkward silence. "Cyrus wants to know if he can continue his recuperation in his own room. This bed is too small for us."

Cyrus almost fell over again at Issy's candidness. This time, Linda was there to brace his body. Rick cleared his throat while she giggled.

"I think that's a good idea, unless we put a mattress on the floor to catch his fall." Linda winked, adding to his discomfort.

"Rick says that's a good idea. He would like to check on your leg right now." Issy eased off the examination table, taking the flimsy sheet with her. Cyrus grabbed the pillow to hide his hard evidence.

Rick chuckled, knowing full well what was going on, then went right to work.

"Where is Cheryl, anyway?" Cyrus asked while Rick unwrapped the thick wad of bandages that covered his attenuated limb.

Issy answered for Rick. "She's packing. She asked for a leave without pay to visit a sick relative." The doctor shrugged.

This made Cyrus think. When Pritchard hired Cheryl for the job, she had made it clear that she had no living relatives, so he suspected this had more to do with Zane's presence in the facility than anything. Her "visiting-a-relative" crap was just an excuse to get away.

"Harrow let her go by herself, with all the Nerocs guarding the perimeter?"

"Cheryl was insistent, so Harrow let her go with Luke as her escort. They're taking the chute, and Harrow feels she won't be in danger because she's human.

Cyrus had his doubts but wouldn't question Harrow's call. He wasn't the leader of their group for nothing. Besides, Luke was a great soldier, one of the few humans they had left on the roster.

He saw Rick wince and look down at what used to be his leg. The area surrounding the amputation site was swelling and emitting a rather nasty odor.

"He wants to make sure we monitor the site until he can remove all the Dangeran bits that might have splintered. He can't do anything right now while there is swelling because it would hurt like . . ." Issy paused, then continued, "hell."

"That's fine." He turned his full attention to Rick. "I need a prosthetic leg after this thing is healed. Is there anything you can do for me?"

Rick continued to cleanse the site and nodded. He wrapped the leg with a fresh bandage before he looked up.

"He said since the stump is not in good condition, it might take a bit longer to get you fitted with a prosthesis, but he'll make sure you get the best C-leg he can find for you."

Cyrus reached out his hand to the doctor, who clasped it back. "Thank you for everything you've done for us."

Rick grinned when Issy interpreted. "He said you're a . . . geez, you want me to say that?" He nodded. "He said you're a sturdy motherfucker, and you're welcome."

Issy punched the doctor on the arm. "I'm done doing this shit for you. You're on your own now," she said, teasing.

Hours later, they were in the comfort of his room when a soft knock sounded. Issy felt her way to the door and opened it. Outside, Sawyer stood, his face mottled and his eyes puffy.

Cyrus pushed his body up into a sitting position. "Hey boy. What's wrong?"

"I wanted to see you, but Allison wouldn't let me." Sawyer glanced at Issy before walking inside.

"I'm going to check on Cheryl before she leaves. Call if you need anything." She smiled in Cyrus' direction then addressed the boy. "I'm glad you came to visit, Sawyer." Cyrus could tell that Issy had gotten a read on the boy's thoughts, and that had prompted her to excuse herself. The door closed behind her.

He patted the spot next to him. "Come here and tell me what's troubling you."

Sawyer sat on the bed and took a deep breath. "I know I have to be man and all, but I was worried sick when I heard you were injured." He looked down on Cyrus' leg, then tears started trickling down his cheeks.

Cyrus felt a pinch in his heart at the boy's anguish. "Allison was right. I wasn't in good condition when I was brought in. It wasn't a pretty picture. But I'm good now. I appreciate your visit."

It didn't seem like the boy had heard him at all. He turned and wrapped his scrawny arms around Cyrus' neck. "I wanted to ask you if you could somehow be my father since I have no one else. Rohnert is a relative, but he already has a son. Allison and Tor love Liv, and I'm—"

"Your idea is perfect." He stroked the boy's back and felt a wave of pride wash over him. For as long as he could remember, he had nurtured younger kids in every foster home he'd stayed in, and this was as a good time as any to foster another. Someone who *wanted* to be in his care for a change. Just like that, he had gotten himself both a mate and a young son to complete his family. "You know, I've grown so fond of you. Issy and I would love to call you our own."

Sawyer looked up at him and smiled through his tears. "I hope you're not just saying that," he said between sobs, burying his head against his chest.

Cyrus shook his head. His son—Christ, he still couldn't believe it— hung on to him for a long time, but he continued to stroke Sawyer's hair until he got his control back.

Once his boy looked up, clear happiness was welling in Sawyer's eyes. "Thank you. I'm glad you came back"—he gazed down at Cyrus' leg then continued—"alive."

"Me, too. Believe me, I feel the same way." He pulled Sawyer against his chest.

Harrow's phone rang just as Jordan finished dabbing more mentha extract on the blisters he'd sustained. He reached for his cell and pressed the talk button. "Rohn, I'm glad to hear from you."

"Gates, I have a favor to ask."

"Anything."

"The Council headquarters is surrounded by Nerocs. Everyone is safe inside, but there's no guarantee bloodshed can be avoided if they find anyone entering or leaving the place. Can we house the Elders and soldiers there?"

Rohnert wasn't one to ask for favors until he'd exhausted every other possible option. Harrow wasn't about to turn down his comrade.

"Come anytime. All I ask is that they be careful taking the chutes. Once we get everyone in here, I'm issuing a lockdown for the time being. We're all over the news, and Leo won't even return my calls after that incident at Unit 1260."

"I'll make sure I'm the last one to get in the chute. No need to worry."

After they hung up, Harrow flicked on the television. He glanced at Jordan, who was staring at him, her face grief stricken. "What's wrong?"

When she didn't answer right away, he got up and pulled her toward him. "Is something the matter?"

She shook her head, but he knew her damn well. Jordan wasn't one to fuss. He urged her to sit down, and he took the space next to her. "C'mon, tell me what's bothering you."

Jordan sighed then closed her eyes. "You've been pushing yourself too hard. What if the sun affected you the way it did Issy?"

"Ah . . . you know I have been tested before. I'm durable." He tried to make light of the matter, but Jordan didn't seem amused at all.

"That was during sunset. You shouldn't have done it." She cupped his face with her hands and rested her forehead on his. "I know how much everyone here means to you, but you can't always sacrifice yourself. You have Gail and me to think of, too."

Harrow kissed her on the lips before pulling away. "Anyone here would've done the same thing for us."

Jordan nodded in understanding, yet he could still sense an internal battle raging within her. "I know . . . but I don't think I would survive a day without you."

He twined their fingers together and kissed the back of her hand. "I love you, Jordan. Never forget that, but I made a vow to protect everyone in here. I will have to go where I'm needed."

"I love you, too. Just promise me you'll try to stay safe."

Harrow didn't fancy feeling guilty about his decisions. Although he knew he'd inevitably hurt the people he loved in the end, this was the life he'd chosen, and there was nothing he would do to change it.

A newsflash halted further discussion as their attention was glued to the television. The head of the paranormal unit, Pete Mitchell, who he'd seen at the clash the night before, was speaking to a group of reporters.

Harrow adjusted the volume and got the tail end of the statement. "The local city officials are cooperating with our agency to hunt down all vampires in the city. Upon capture, they will be placed in a holding cell until we find out who was responsible for the shootout near the Rockefeller Center." While the head of the unit was speaking, there were flashes of panic from different locations throughout the city. This was what they had been trying to avoid all along. "Sightings should be reported to the hotline number we're providing. I advise all residents of the city to stay indoors from sundown to sunrise to avoid being victimized by these vicious creatures."

Pictures of Nerocs were plastered on the screen, followed by Cyrus, Issy, Rohnert, Tor and himself. Even Bardos, Wendell, and Icarus were included in the lineup of creatures the unit had proclaimed dangerous fugitives.

Just perfect. Curing the disease would not be their main focus anymore. They'd be more worried about staying alive and hidden, pushed even deeper into the underworld. Their troubles would never end. Harrow released a long-drawn-out breath.

"Let me check on Gail," Jordan said, slipping out the door. "Just relax and allow the blisters to heal."

Relaxing was the last thing on his mind. Harrow turned off the television and dialed Leo's number once more. Just when he thought his call would be left unanswered, the general picked up on the fifth ring.

"Harrow, what the hell happened?" Leo's normally schooled voice was replaced by a tone of reprimand.

"We were going to the headquarters for an assembly when we got jumped by this group of vampires. They're a part of Jack Drago's team. You know we never attack humans unless provoked."

"I have the president breathing down my neck, pressuring me to turn you guys in," Leo said with exasperation.

"Why us? We didn't start it."

"You may not have, but your escape has been highly publicized. You have to admit that your group has killed humans, too."

Harrow ran his hand over his hair in frustration. "Yes, but just to save Cyrus and Issy. They were going to let Cyrus bleed to death. There was no way I was going to let that happen."

"Pete claimed their surgeon checked out Cyrus' wound."

"There were pieces of Dangeran left . . . look, you know how Pritchard ran this place, and I'm following his example. He would've taken the same steps if he was still alive."

There was silence on the other line, a long one, before Leo responded. "Yes, he would have. Listen, I'm in hot water because Pete knows about my association with you guys. The moment humans were killed, he considered our agreement to leave your team alone null and void."

Harrow pinched the bridge of his nose, hating the path their lives had taken. "So be it. I understand your position."

"Remember, I'm on your side. I believe in the cause my good friend championed. Make sure you don't veer off course. I can't promise anything right now, but I'll keep on trying to get them off your back. Keep everyone off the radar. Don't patrol, and stay low until you hear from me."

"That's all I can ask of you. Thanks, Leo."

They talked for another minute, and then hung up, leaving Harrow feeling bereft. Why did it feel like the weight on his shoulders had just gotten heavier?

Five days and counting, but Zane felt like he'd spent an eternity cooped up inside the facility. It had been one day since he last saw Cheryl. Although he wasn't looking forward to her seeing him in his pitiful state, he had to admit that the highlight of his day was when she visited him.

The minutes crept by at a snail's pace while he counted the seconds until his next dose of antibiotic. So far, it had been Linda coming in and out to check on him and deliver his medication. He heard the squeaks of her wheelchair tire even before she knocked on the door.

"Ready for your medicine?" Her voice was chirpy. She wheeled close to the bed and handed him the tiny paper cup that contained his pill.

"Thanks." He popped the tablet in his mouth and took the glass of water from her.

"What are you planning to do today?"

Linda was one of those kind souls, naïve almost. He had been observing her during her routine visits, with or without Cheryl or Rick. She could be just the one to answer the burning questions in his mind.

"I know you visit everyone here." Linda nodded. "Can you tell me how Cyrus is doing?"

He watched her hesitate before she applied the brakes on her chair. When she looked up, her usual cheerful demeanor had been replaced with a somber expression. "I know what you did to my brother . . ."

Wait, did her hear her right? "Cyrus is your brother?"

"We're not blood relatives, but we came from the same foster home. He has been watching over me ever since our foster mom died. To me, he is much more than a brother. He is my protector and friend."

This left Zane speechless. How could Linda bear talking to him after what he had done to Cyrus?

"We're taught to be professionals here, so I'm giving you the benefit of the doubt. I'm doing it for Cheryl, because she believes there is some goodness in you." Zane stared at her. "Cyrus is going to be okay. He has a good woman who loves him and people who adore him."

Bam! That stung. He drew back at her words. It was crystal clear that his past had caught up with him. He'd been so caught up in the material things that he'd forgotten what was important in one's life—to have someone to love and be loved in return. He'd cared about a few people in his life. Two to be exact—and they were both gone.

Zane also cared for Cheryl more than he was willing to admit. At first, he'd thought this was out of a sense of obligation after the care she'd given him. But no, his desire to see Cheryl had nothing to do with his feelings of gratitude. As days passed, he found himself dreaming of her and wanting to see her in any way possible.

Of course, this was difficult considering his past history with Cheryl's associates. He had been instrumental in his father's discovery of this underground facility and the eventual death of Mr. Tack himself at his father's hands. Zane had bitten a huge chunk out of the Council leader's shoulder. He had abducted Cyrus, tortured him, and turned him. The list of offenses went on and on.

"For the record, I don't like you. If Rick hadn't made me promise to protect his patients' best interests, I would've poisoned you."

Zane wasn't surprised by her animosity. "Fair enough. Just for the record, too, I'm not proud of what I did in the past. I believe that whatever is coming my way now is much deserved."

Linda studied him for a second, her eyes narrowing beneath her glasses. "You know, I'm a big believer in second chances. I'd like to think that Cyrus is the same. He might just take a little longer to realize it."

Zane attempted a smile. "I don't expect him, or anyone else, to forgive me. I vowed to make it right for these people I've hurt in the past. The last thing I expected was to be a recipient of their generosity."

"Let me guess. You're thinking that your condition is some sort of penance for all the bad deeds you've done in the past."

How astute of her. He nodded. "I will add well deserved, too."

"Do you think I'm confined to this wheelchair because of some heinous sin I've committed?" she challenged.

Not sweet Linda. "No, I don't think so."

She smiled. "Then do yourself a favor and think of your situation as a blessing or a lesson learned. Besides, there's nothing else you can do. It's not like you'll be walking out of here anytime soon."

He smiled at her observation. "Are you saying I can't go whenever I'm ready?"

"No sir, we're on a lockdown until boss Harrow says it's over."

That was news to Zane. "Lockdown?" he repeated.

"Yeah. It's a good thing Cheryl was able to leave before Harrow made the announcement this afternoon."

His chest tightened. "Cheryl left? Where did she go?" This was turning into a nightmare. It was okay if she was just avoiding him, but leaving? He didn't realize his presence had affected her enough to make her leave her home.

"Oh, she didn't say. She just mentioned a sick relative she had to visit."

"For how long?" He sagged against the mattress.

"I don't know. She didn't even say goodbye."

There was a hint of sadness in Linda's voice that echoed his feelings, except his was ten times stronger. He buried his face in his hands, not too keen on showing Linda how badly the information had affected him.

"Zane, are you okay?" she asked in a worried tone.

He nodded, afraid that his voice might give his emotion away.

"Well, I have to go. I still have another delivery to make."

After Linda left the room, he spent the next hour berating himself for Cheryl's departure. He didn't believe her excuse at all. It was he who had driven her away. If he could get up and walk, he'd go out and find her and make sure she returned to her home.

He squeezed his eyes shut. *Oh man, what have I done?*

A determined knock on her door roused Bretania from sleep. She glanced at the clock and shook her head. It was only ten in the morning. The pounding continued. "Come in," she said, sitting up. Mason was dead to the world next to her.

Nathan peeked his head in before he entered. He eyed the sleeping figure next to her with disdain. It wasn't a secret that Nathan didn't share her enthusiasm for Mason as her second-in-command. "You have to watch this," he said then grabbed the remote control next to the television.

The early news was showing footage of devastation battle in front of her old hideout. Humans were screaming and running for cover. The ugly creatures she had seen in Drago's penthouse were firing at them, as well as other vampires. She saw ashes on the ground, which could only mean one thing. An all-out war had erupted. She smiled. "Increase the volume." When Nathan did, Mason jumped up.

"What the hell is going on?" He grabbed his dagger from the bedside table.

Nathan rolled his eyes while Bretania laid a comforting hand on his arm. "It's all right, sweetie. We're just watching a very important event."

Mason replaced the weapon and leaned against the headboard. There was footage of several vampires, most of whom Bretania knew—Rohnert, Harrow, Wendell, and Icarus—and a few others she didn't recognize.

She burst out laughing, which made Nathan and Mason look at her with an odd expression on their faces.

"Care to share the joke with us?" Nathan asked.

"Can't you see? The tables have been turned. The Council members are now being hunted, and Drago's precious Nerocs are out in the open." She clapped her hands in glee. "I think we have to step up our recruitment so we can share a piece of the pie."

Nathan's fang punched his lips as he realized the opportunity this gave them to get even. "You have no worries about that."

True. Goran's son had been hard at work recruiting. She couldn't hide her pleasure with his choices, either. Like choosing a side of beef, he made his selections with care. Just the premium cut, the cream of the crop. Criminals and murderers had been piling up on their doorstep. This enabled Bretania to concentrate on training. It didn't hurt that Mason had instilled fear in the hearts of their men. Greta was running the household with Jackson's assistance, so the girls were well fed. Her army was left with enough spare time to spread the disease. Just like a goddamn well-oiled machine.

"You're doing great, my boy. Step it up a notch, and we'll be having our breakout party soon." She smiled, loving every minute of this. The second time was a charm, wasn't it?

Rohnert, together with the rest of the surviving Elders, made it to the facility by way of the chutes. As they were designed more as exit alternatives, using them as a gateway back into the facility was much more challenging. The uphill incline was tougher since they were crawling on their hands and knees, but it was safer. They proceeded in single file, led by Bardos and with Rohnert watching everyone's back.

It was too bad the rest of the Council soldiers had been trapped inside the walls of their headquarters. With the Nerocs standing guard outside their hideout, Rohnert wasn't about to gamble with his people's lives and risk getting them killed. The remaining Elders and their armies totaled about fifty, and they were all taking refuge in the underground facility until they could figure out what to do next.

It didn't help that humans were hunting them down, too. The nonstop television coverage of the bloodbath outside Rockefeller Center had instilled fear. Therefore, the only thing they could do was to stay hidden for the time being.

"Welcome to our facility," Harrow greeted the moment Rohnert emerged from the dark passageway. He gestured for his men to stand down.

Rohnert wasn't surprised that Harrow, Tor, and the rest of the fighters had their weapons trained on the newcomers. Their unit had suffered too many breaches in the past, and this was their last line of defense.

Rohnert took Harrow's outstretched hand and allowed him to pull him up on his feet. "Thanks. Are you sure we have room for everyone?" he asked.

Harrow laughed. "Of course. Welcome to the Tack Hotel." He patted Rohnert's back before turning to Wendell, Icarus, Serena, Bardos, and Virgil. "Firman will show you to your rooms so you can settle in."

They moved toward the main hallway. "Can we get everyone in a meeting in, say, an hour?" Rohnert said.

"Sure. I'll make an announcement."

Then Rohnert turned to Tor. "How is Ally doing with Malin?"

Tor's eyes lit up. "I'm afraid you'll have to pry Malin from her. She's going gaga over your little boy."

Conflicting emotions coursed through him—happiness at having someone who cared for his baby while he was away and guilt for not being able to spend enough time with his son.

Tor seemed to have sensed his inner torment and placed a hand on his shoulder. "You're doing fine. You have so much on your plate, and we're more than happy to help. It gives Allison something to focus on, so she hasn't been asking us to put her on rotation," Tor said knowingly.

"Thanks. I appreciate your help. I'll see you guys in an hour." They reached the wing where most of the bedrooms were situated. Firman took charge of room assignments while Rohnert made a beeline for his own suite. He knocked softly before walking inside. There he found Allison placing Malin in his crib.

"You're okay?" she asked once she'd gotten a good look at him.

"As good as I'm going to get." Rohnert headed straight to his walk-in closet to remove his weapons. "How is he doing?"

Allison smiled. "He's wonderful. He can hold his bottle for a short time and is responding to my voice when I talk to him. He's quite a talker, you know."

Rohnert walked over to the crib and glanced at the baby. The sight of his boy sleeping peacefully warmed his heart, but it also brought back painful memories. He clenched his teeth and took a deep breath. Shelly was always on his mind. Moments like these made it even more difficult to overcome his grief. His son should have his mother around, not dead and missing.

A hand touched his shoulder, bringing him back to the present. "Rohn, I'm happy to help. You don't have to feel guilty for not being around all the time. You're doing us a great favor by serving the race."

He turned around and nodded. "I know, but why does it seem like I'm not doing a good job?"

Allison took his hand and led him to the couch. Once they were seated, she answered. "On the contrary, you have brought the Elders together. You have freed us from that monster, Goran. There's nothing you can do to control the evil elements out there. Ride the tide and know that everyone believes in you for a reason. We have faith in you."

Somehow, he wasn't convinced. The bloodshed was continuing, and with the recent involvement of the humans, the vampires' once-peaceful existence was in jeopardy. "What if I run this race into the ground?" Uncertainty began to creep into his voice.

"Stay your course. You have our support," Allison said, her expression earnest.

Rohnert attempted a smile. He still had his doubts, but with friends like her, he sure would keep trying. "Thanks," he finally said.

Allison patted his hand then rose to her feet. "I'm going to check on Liv now. I'll be back before the meeting."

Once alone, Rohnert closed his eyes to stop the tears that were threatening to spill. He was overwhelmed, and the situation was more than he'd bargained for. He missed Shelly too damn much, which made it impossible to breathe. God, how long could he manage without her by his side?

While Cyrus was catching up with lost sleep, Issy sat against the headboard and hugged her knees against her chest, thinking. She hadn't forgotten about her dream. Though distressing, it made so much sense now. From what she had read in the black book, she had an older sister. Nothing much had been said except that her sister was destined to have great accomplishments.

From the looks of things, Aemerria had been getting a lot done. She had saved Isidora and the rest from certain doom. How could Issy go through life with this little secret? Wasn't Aemerria entitled to the truth, just like her? Their lives had been disrupted, and a secret of this magnitude was left to her to keep. Could she carry on and pretend she had no idea of their relationship? The thought was too painful after they had been deprived of each other. Of the two sisters, Issy was better off. Aemerria had to go through her existence not knowing her past.

The black book carried more secrets than Issy had ever imagined. It explicitly instructed the bearer to keep her ancestry hidden from the next diviner, so Issy had to keep the information to herself. Aside from Cyrus, she hadn't told a soul, but since Rohnert was a friend, there wouldn't be any harm in sharing this bit of information with him.

Life had indeed taken a sharp turn for her. First, she had lost her parents, her best friend, and lover Finn. In exchange, she had stumbled upon this great group of people who meant the world to her. She had been welcomed into their big family. Then there was Cyrus, who had become her sole reason for living. Funny how fate them had thrown in a bit extra in the form of a living, breathing, and totally unreachable sister.

Heaving a sigh, she glanced at Cyrus through her blurred vision. She could see signs of improvement, but Rick couldn't give her an exact timeframe since such a case was unprecedented. Issy had downplayed her fear, and Cyrus', but deep down, she was scared of being visually impaired for the rest of her life. But then it was a small price to pay to have Cyrus back in her arms.

Scooting over to the edge of the bed, she peered at the numbers on the clock, but no matter how much she tried to focus, her vision didn't improve.

"If you want the time, all you have to do is ask." Cyrus snaked an arm around her waist before glancing at the clock. "We have plenty of time before the meeting starts."

She smiled and slid down to snuggle with him. "That's enough time to get things done."

Cyrus' smile grew wider, and he rearranged his bandaged leg, propping it on a pillow and then opening his arms. "One trip to heaven, coming up."

Issy straddled his waist and leaned closer until she was nuzzling his neck. "I hope you don't mind me doing this." She licked the bare skin and then plunged her throbbing fangs into his inviting vein.

On contact, Cyrus arched his back, scoring her shoulders with his nails as his moan filled the room. She tugged harder while his body strained against hers. This was something he'd always wanted her to do. Tonight, it seemed perfect. She didn't ease up until she felt his blood in her veins. It didn't matter if it wouldn't nourish her the same way Rohnert's could. His responses and hearing his rush of satisfaction were enough for her.

Issy gave one last pull, eliciting another groan of contentment from him when his body shuddered. She sealed the puncture site with her tongue and looked up to see the pleasure in his eyes.

"That's what I'm talking about," Cyrus said, his voice sounding raw.

"That's all I have time for."

"What do you mean? I don't mind a minute-man session right now," he said. His arms tightened around her waist.

"I need to see Rohnert for a bit. I have to discuss something with him."

Cyrus' eyes flickered. "Fine, I'll be here waiting for you."

Issy kissed him on the mouth. "I love you, you know that?"

"Yeah, yeah. Get your ass back here so we don't miss the meeting."

Issy walked to the closet and dressed in her other pair of jeans, dark shirt, and leather jacket, which was fast becoming her favorite attire.

She blew a kiss to Cyrus, who watched her leave the room. She made her way to Rohnert's room and knocked on the door. He answered with Malin in his arms.

"Issy, what brings you here?" He opened the door wider for her.

"There is something I want to bring to your attention." She walked in, using the wall to guide her.

"Here, hold my hand and let me help you to the sofa."

She sat and smiled. "How's Malin?"

"Heavy," Rohnert said and then chuckled. She watched his blurry form walk across the room and lay the sleeping baby back in his crib. When Rohnert returned, he sat next to her." What's up?"

Issy dove into to the subject she'd been dying to discuss with the leader. "As the caretaker of the black book, I read its contents, and I have something I thought you should know."

She sensed the sudden shift in Rohnert's mood. The black book's pages had been where Gastarius had divulged his vision of Shelly's demise. The air in the room dipped lower while Rohnert's silence persisted.

"This has something to do with me . . . and Aemerria."

"Oh?" Rohnert leaned forward, and he let out a long sigh.

"I discovered that I have an older sister."

Jesus, any more surprises and I'm going to crack. She heard his unspoken thoughts. "You and her?"

"The book didn't mention her name, but I had a dream of us together."

"Are you sure about this?"

She nodded. "It makes sense. When she held my hands, I had visions I couldn't explain. Her face is just like my mother's and . . ." She hesitated. "Call it gut-feel."

Rohnert shook his head. He remembered the night Aemerria had offered her hand to him. He'd also seen flashes he couldn't explain.

"If you're right, what do you want me to do?"

"Nothing. You just need to know. This is just between you, me, and Cyrus."

"How do we keep something like this from her?"

"We never speak or think of it beyond this day. The book specifically demanded that her memory be wiped clean for a reason."

It took Rohnert a long time to respond. "She mentioned something about needing to see the black book since she had nothing to go on. After being voted in as the leader of the priestesses after Gastarius was killed by Lukan, she wanted to see if the black book could offer her something."

"As the caretaker of the black book, I will make sure no one sees it until it's ready to be transferred to the possession of the next caretaker."

Rohnert nodded. "That damned thing sure carries more burdens than good news."

Issy couldn't agree more. "Now that I've gotten that off my chest, I'm going to get ready for the meeting." She stood and turned for the door. "Oh, your next feeding should be done soon. If you don't mind, let's do it at the same time, and with Cyrus around."

"I think that's a good idea. The clinic sounds like good neutral ground." Rohnert walked her to the door.

"Tomorrow night is fine?"

"I'll be there."

Issy returned to the room after her conversation with Rohnert and found Cyrus waiting for her. "Are you sure you want to attend the meeting?" She walked over to the bed and glanced at his leg, uncertain whether he was up to the task.

"I wouldn't miss it for the world." He squeezed her hand. "I'm going to be fine. I won't do much except sit there anyway."

"The leg must be elevated at all times," she said, still unconvinced.

"Damn, the wheelchair isn't mine. I got it from . . ."

She didn't have to hear the name to know who he was referring to. She pursed her lips to keep from saying something unpleasant. To say that she hated Zane was an understatement, but she wasn't going to compound Cyrus' rage.

"You have anything to say, dear?" Cyrus asked.

"I will kill the asshole, just say the word," she blurted, unable to keep her own fury from surfacing.

"Baby, I'm done with the killing for now, but I promise you this. I will make his life a living hell."

"You don't have to do anything, darling." Issy grazed her lips against his then straightened up. "Let's get you up and dressed."

A few minutes later, they were on their way to the I-room with her walking alongside Cyrus' wheelchair, which he insisted on propelling himself. The place was already filled with the facility's inhabitants as well the remaining Elders and their armies. Good-natured greetings and handshakes were offered to Cyrus while they made their way to the front of the meeting room next to Harrow and Rohnert.

Issy soaked in the general emotions of those present and recognized their grim outlook. When she glanced around with her blurry eyesight, it became obvious that their hunted status weighed heavily on all involved. She herself wasn't intending to set foot outside anytime soon. At least, not until her vision was restored.

Harrow cleared his throat and stepped forward to address the congregation. Issy sensed his emotional grid and could tell he was operating on autopilot. She could imagine this wasn't easy for him.

"I'm sure by now you're all aware of our predicament. The entire vampire race is under close scrutiny by humans and their government. This does not come as a surprise, considering the countless lives taken during the massacre outside Rockefeller Center. We're going to lay low for some time. I'm afraid another group has decided to wage war against the Council and our organization. We don't know their motives at the moment, but believe me we'll get to the bottom of this."

A murmur of speculations began spreading across the room as everyone started stating their opinions. Issy closed her eyes, compartmentalizing each distinct voice and letting Harrow's words sink in.

A warm hand covered hers, giving her a promise of security. She opened her eyes to find Cyrus looking up at her. He didn't have to speak for her to know what he wanted to tell her. He loved her, and everything would be okay. Despite the fear in her heart, she knew he was right.

She bent down to plant a kiss on his mouth, not caring if anyone was watching them. Her heart was overflowing with gratitude and love for this man.

Harrow called on Rohnert to step up and address the situation. Rohnert's face was grim, and his emotions were in turmoil. He glanced around before speaking. "I've given this a lot of thought, and after conferring with the few remaining elders, I've come to the conclusion that we need to go into stealth mode. I will ground all activities outside our two main residences. No soldiers will patrol for the time being until I lift the ban. A rare breed of vampires most of us haven't heard from for a long, long time has resurfaced to create chaos under Drago's leadership. They have struck us where it hurts the most. Three of our Council Elders have perished in the recent attacks. Some of our fighters have been taken by the group called Unit 1260, a governmental department dedicated to tracking our activities. It has been brought to my attention that they are now on the prowl to capture all vampires in the city, dead or alive."

This announcement brought a ripple of discontent to those present. Harrow silenced them right away.

"Harrow is also implementing the same protocol here. Every activity must be reported to us, and we will continue to monitor the situation outside. I'm afraid the attacks committed by our brethren have forever tarnished our reputation. The widespread media coverage of the incident has placed the government on high alert. I have been warned that they're not going to go easy on us.

"Harrow has been gracious enough to let all surviving members of the Council take residence here for an indefinite period until the smoke clears." Rohnert bowed his head amid the clamor of questions coming his way.

Issy watched the ongoing talks when a strong current of an unfamiliar emotion coursed through her veins. Her knees weakened, and she braced herself by leaning on Cyrus' chair.

"What's the matter?" he whispered, looking up with concern written all over his face.

"I don't know." She shook her head. Her heart began racing as the sensation of being summoned grew stronger. "I have to go."

Before Cyrus could speak, she flew out of the room and raced to the stairwell, her feet hardly touching the floor. She heard the elevator door open, and Cyrus maneuvered his chair out of it.

"Issy, what's going on?" he yelled across the long hallway.

She covered the length of the corridor to meet him. She kneeled down until they were at eye level. "I think she's here."

Cyrus gave her a blank stare.

"My sister."

Cyrus narrowed his eyes. "Are you going to be okay?"

Once she'd convinced him she was all right, Issy walked back to the bedroom she shared with Cyrus. She needed to do this alone, without an audience. It was a family matter, so to speak.

The air swirled around her when she closed the door. Inhaling deep, she recognized her sister's scent. She closed her thoughts to keep the secret safe with her. There was no need to rock the boat. If Gastarius had demanded secrecy, then she was going to follow his instructions.

Issy walked to the middle of the room and kneeled, awaiting Aemerria's appearance. The gust continued to swell while the scent grew stronger. When the current dulled, she sensed the being before her, but she kept her eyes on the ground.

The toes of Aemerria's bare feet came into view while Issy waited for her command. A soft hand touched her head, calm and comforting. "Rise, Isidora, daughter of our beloved Iden and Chandra."

She got to her feet, and Aemerria stepped back, studying her. "To what do I owe this surprise visit?" she asked, meeting her sister's eyes. Though still blanketed with haze, Issy saw her smile.

"I sensed an inexplicable pull to see you. I have no explanation for it. I'm wondering if you felt the same." Aemerria took her hand and led Issy to sit on the edge of the bed.

The truth was hard to deny, but Gastarius' wish prevailed. Issy mustered a forced smile and shook her head. "All I feel is the usual gust of wind to announce your arrival and the calming presence when you're around."

Aemerria turned to watch her. Just like Issy had done, she closed off her thoughts, making it impossible to guess what she was thinking. Under the shaman's close scrutiny, Issy began to sweat, yet she kept up the pretense. A flicker of emotion passed over Aemmeria's face, but Issy couldn't see well enough to read it.

Finally, Aemerria spoke. "You have been brave and stupid out there."

Surprised, Issy stared at her. "I wanted to get him to safety. I didn't—"

"The power of love." Aemerria shook her head. "It makes us do impossible things."

Issy had no idea how to respond to that, so she stayed silent.

Aemerria lifted her hand and just before it touched Issy's eyes, she caught the glow emanating from her palm. "You shall see the great things around you again as you sensed them. Your heart is pure, and your wisdom is advanced for your age. Your presence is a calming reprieve for me."

In an instant, the blurry veil blanketing her eyesight disappeared, and her vision was restored to normal. Issy gasped in disbelief. She took Aemerria's hand and kissed it. "Your kindness knows no bounds. I'm indebted to you."

Aemerria smiled and shook her head. "You owe me nothing. Your existence brings me joy I can't explain, and for that, I'm thankful."

Happiness overwhelmed Issy as tears began streaming down her face. "Thank you. Thank you." She wanted to throw her arms around the shaman, but such an act might not be welcomed, considering their difference in status. "I want to give you a hug, if it would not offend," she said before she lost her nerve.

The shaman already had her in a tight embrace before Issy had a chance. "I thought you'd never ask."

Issy clung to Aemerria and felt her strengths, weaknesses, fears, and triumphs all in the same breath. They hung on to each other for a long moment before Aemerria broke contact. "I knew that man of yours was a good catch. There is no way I will allow you to feel the pain of losing a beloved again, even if I had to contravene destiny. Be well, my sister in fate."

With those words, Aemerria disappeared in a cloud of smoke.

Issy stared at the vacant spot where the shaman had been. Digesting her parting words, Issy's chest expanded with joy. If Aemerria's claim were true, then she owed Cyrus' life to her sister. This was a gift she would celebrate for the rest of her life.

Cyrus went straight to the clinic after heeding Issy's request to be left alone with her sister. He still couldn't wrap his mind around the revelation. Damn, weren't they an interesting bunch of mismatched beings? It was funny how everything had come to a head for him and Issy.

He rolled into the clinic in his borrowed wheelchair to find Rick and Zane *talking* in earnest. They both glanced in his direction.

"I didn't mean to interrupt. I was just going to return the chair and ask for crutches." Cyrus propelled one wheel and pivoted around to leave.

"No . . . I was just finishing up in here," Zane said.

Cyrus kept his back to them, not enthused with the idea of being in the same room with the vampire. He had been hanging on to the anger for a long time, but deep within, he recognized the sacrifice Zane had made on their behalf. Penance could be hard to gain, and even if Cyrus couldn't bear to look him in the eye, he wasn't going to carry the grudge in his heart. He had too many good things going on his life to dwell on the past.

Cyrus shrugged and turned around. "Thanks for letting me use the chair."

Zane nodded. "I'm glad it served its purpose, because I don't want it."

The denial in Zane's voice was hard to miss. Cyrus felt a twinge of pity for him, but tamped down the urge to say anything remotely sympathetic. Rick looked on, not attempting to jump into the conversation.

"I'm going to start working out this stump in a few weeks. I don't mind having company if it'll give me a chance to shove your face into the mat."

Zane's fangs elongated, and he gave a rueful smile. "Don't rule out the chance for payback. You shot me, twice!"

Apologies were overrated, and forgiveness at this point was unnecessary. Sometimes, some things were better left unsaid. Cyrus pumped his fist in the air in response before turning to Rick, who had assumed a fly-on-the-wall position. "I need crutches. I want to get around faster."

Rick studied him for a moment before picking up a pad of paper and writing. He turned it around for Cyrus to read. *You're supposed to be on bed rest except for bathroom runs. Stay off your feet if you don't want me to tie you to your bed.*

"Don't even think about it," Cyrus shot back. Even so, he could tell the doctor wasn't bluffing. "Fine, off my feet, but please give me crutches. I don't like sitting on my ass."

Minutes later, he was swinging awkwardly on forearm crutches along the hallway. At least he was vertical, just the way he liked it. Cyrus turned the bedroom doorknob and walked in with a bit more confidence than he had when he left the clinic.

He found Issy on the edge of the bed, crying. Cyrus' breath left him, and he hurried over to her. Leaning his crutches against the mattress, he sat down and rubbed her back.

"Issy, look at me. What happened?"

She looked up. Fearing the worst, he was surprised to see her smiling amid the tears that stained her face. "Nothing . . . I'm just happy . . . thankful you're alive and . . . somewhat healthy," she said in between hiccups.

Relief rocked his body, and he gathered her into his arms. "Oh baby. I thought something bad had happened. And yes, I'm happy to be alive, too, because I want to spend the rest of my life with you." Cyrus rained kisses onto her face until he found her mouth. He poured his happiness and gratitude into their kiss, but when her response intensified, other parts of him wanted a piece of the action.

"I see the color in your face. And I can smell the lust—"

"You can see? Like clear . . . right now?"

Issy laughed. "Yes . . . very clear."

"How did it happen? Did she give you—?"

"Among the other gifts she bestowed on me." She quelled his questions with a kiss.

"I want to be inside you right now," he said, feeling the heat rising up his body until he thought he'd explode.

"I love you, Cyrus."

God, he loved her so much he felt like crying. Damn it. He fought it, yet his tear ducts were not listening, and he broke down like a big idiot. He was beyond caring. It didn't matter if his weakness showed, because she was strong enough for the two of them. Issy held him as he wept, rocking and whispering soothing words in his ears. It took a long time before his pathetic sobbing dried up.

He reached for her face and stroked her cheek. "I love you so much, Isidora. Thank you for bringing light into my lonely world."

"Always?" She smiled and opened her arms

"I have eternity in mind," he said and then launched himself into her embrace.

Zane slid onto the wheelchair after Cyrus left. With some sensation returning to his lower limbs, he should be celebrating, but his spirits hadn't lifted since he heard the news of Cheryl's departure.

Rick tapped him on the shoulder and mouthed something. Zane tried reading his lips but couldn't make out what the doctor was saying. He waited while Rick scribbled on his tablet and turned it around for him to read. *We miss her, too. It's not the same without her here.*

He stared at the doctor, wishing Rick couldn't see right through him. Zane shrugged. "Are you a mind reader now?" he asked, irritated at being so transparent.

The doctor shook his head and placed his palm over his chest, then mouthed something. If Zane read it right, Rick said something along the lines of *from one heart to another*. Weird, but he could sense the doctor understood.

Zane wheeled out of the clinic, still feeling the burden of Cheryl's absence. He wished he could change his past and undo all of his mistakes, but there was no turning back. All he could do was move on and hope he had enough time to make it right.

Instead of heading to his newly assigned room, Zane proceeded to the I-room to avail himself of the countless bottles of alcohol he'd seen when he was captured by Harrow. Tonight, he needed a stiff one, or maybe more—something that packed enough punch to get his mind off Cheryl.

Opening the door, he found Rohnert and Harrow deep in conversation. Both looked up when he tried to back away. Harrow stood and walked over to him. "Come in, we were about to call on you." He held the door open for Zane.

This is it. They're kicking me out. That was fine. He didn't expect them to put him up for a long time. With a shrug, he wheeled inside to find Rohnert watching him with those intense dark eyes. There was nothing to hide from his great-uncle. The great one knew everything. Besides, he was done hiding. Zane had given up on the tough guy routine.

He applied the brakes once he reached the long table and parked opposite Rohnert.

Harrow took a seat at the head of the table and cleared his throat. "As I was saying, we wanted to talk to you—"

"I know it's time for me to go." Zane wanted to spare him the trouble of coming up with excuses. "I will leave now."

Rohnert clucked his tongue in a rare display of annoyance. He glared at Zane and then shook his head. "Boy, if you're going to stay here indefinitely, you'll have to learn to hold your tongue."

Stay . . . indefinitely? What the fuck was that about? "What do you mean?" He ignored the mild scolding.

"Well, since you seem to be an expert in stalking . . ." Harrow laughed. "I mean, trailing people, we're going to need your help tracking down some people for us. It doesn't hurt that you're friends with the sun. That alone will be a big help." He pushed his glasses to the top of his head.

Zane leaned on the table, his curiosity piqued, but he had to get one thing straight. "Are you sure you want to trust me after everything I've done to you guys?"

Harrow rubbed his eyes then leaned back. "To tell you the truth, I still don't trust you, but we're going to remedy that. Before we give you the details of what we want you to do, Rohnert and I have conditions for you."

He glanced at Rohnert, who in return gestured with his hand, giving Harrow first dibs.

Harrow did not speak right away. Instead, he went reached underneath the table and produced a familiar-looking accessory. It was the same thing he had seen when he and his father, Demetrius, had attacked some soldiers several years ago.

"You want me to wear that?" he asked.

"Trust is something to be earned. I have to tell you, everyone in this facility would fight over the chance to kill you. This is necessary to appease them." Harrow continued to dangle the anklet in the air.

"Sure thing. I don't mind a new accessory." Zane kept a stoic face, even if the idea of being tracked like a pigeon was unappealing.

"Now that's settled. You're not at any time to go out of this facility without giving notice. Any of your associates must be declared to us or we will eliminate them without notice."

Zane had no problem with that. He looked up at Rohnert, who was staring at him with dead eyes.

Rohnert stood up and started for the bar. "With your record, the murders you have orchestrated, and your inhumane treatment of Cyrus, you will be brought in front of the Council so we can hand down the punishment you deserve."

"That's fine." He looked Rohnert right in the eyes. This had been a cakewalk so far. He'd expected far worst treatment after what he had done.

"Consider this a luxurious prison. Be careful with the inmates, because they will strike you even from behind." Harrow laughed.

Zane kept a straight face.

Rohnert came back with a drink in hand and gulped it down.

Harrow continued. "When you started your Good Samaritan shit, I thought you were onto something diabolical again, but you've managed to convince us otherwise. Besides, your great uncle here seems to have taken a liking to you."

No emotions showed in Rohnert's face except his eyes, which darted in Harrow's direction.

Zane kept looking straight ahead. He was fine with whatever punishment they deemed necessary. Living in the facility would only mean that Cheryl would have to endure his presence the moment she came back. He had already driven her away. "How about Cheryl?"

"What about her?" Rohnert answered this time. His eyes were trained on Zane, his gaze unwavering.

"I've driven her away. I don't know if this is a good idea."

"She's coming back. She promised." Harrow's statement sounded too damn certain.

Zane couldn't refute it, but he had his doubts. "When should I start with this project you were speaking of?"

"Whenever you're ready."

"I don't know if I'll be able to walk like before." There, he'd said it.

"I'll have Jones create a super wheelchair for you." Harrow chuckled.

The prospect made him flinch. If he had to spend night and day in the training room to get himself back in walking form again, he'd do it. The limp he'd been sporting before was far better than this temporary paralysis shit.

"Let's get this straight. You're getting a once-in-a-lifetime chance to get your act together. Do this right, or I will kill you with my bare hands." Rohnert shot him a level stare.

"I'm doing it," he said, unblinking. "Tell me what you have in mind."

Rohnert nodded to Harrow, and for the next few minutes, he gave Zane the details of what they wanted him to do. The task sounded simple enough. This was his forte.

"As I mentioned, since you have no aversion to the sun, we'll get you a partner as soon as he is up on his feet, too."

Zane groaned. Yep. Partnering up with the vampire who hated him with a passion was his penance. "Bring it."

Cyrus woke up before Issy did, still thinking about her impending feeding with Rohnert. Sure, he wasn't jealous anymore, but the damn prospect still made him uncomfortable. He loved the woman, and that alone made the upcoming ordeal bearable.

"You're thinking again." Issy placed an arm across his chest and drew him close.

"I love you." He kissed her on the mouth.

"I know, but I need you to understand this. No more pouting."

He forced a smile. "I understand. It's just hard to share you with anyone, even if it's clinical."

"Believe me, I wouldn't do it if there's any other way."

Taking a deep breath, he ran his palm along the small of her back in a caress. "I've been thinking. What if you have Rick draw your blood and store it for Rohnert's use? He can do the same."

Issy digested the information and nodded. "It's a great idea. I think it might work. Let's discuss it with him after the feeding."

Cyrus smiled, relieved that Issy didn't take his suggestion the wrong way. "I know I'm being a territorial idiot. I feel for Rohnert. This arrangement is hard for him, too. The man is cutting himself after every feeding."

The news made Issy sit up. "God, it must be so awful for him." Disbelief was written across her face.

"Tor found him passed out and shit. I know it sounds like a gossip, but he swore with his life it was true."

"Is there something we can do for him?" Issy stood up and paced.

"Not much right now. He doesn't need to take another hit by finding out that we've been talking behind his back."

She nodded in understanding. "I've been good with keeping things to myself."

Cyrus knew Issy was referring to her sister, Aemerria. Apart from Rohnert and him, she had kept this secret nice and tight. They both recognized the peril should Aemerria find out. The powerful entity might go on a rampage, considering her earlier record, if she found out that she had been taken as a child from her parents and wasn't given a chance for a normal childhood.

"But promise me, no secrets from me."

"You have my word." She looked at the door. "Sawyer is outside."

Sure enough, there was a soft knock on the door, and Issy went to answer it. Outside, she found the young boy in his PJs, looking miserable.

"What's going on, son?" Cyrus beckoned him to come closer. Sawyer walked in, holding a piece of paper in one hand. Issy led him to the bed. Together, the sight of Issy and the boy made his chest puffed with pride. "Sit here." He patted the mattress next to him.

Sawyer climbed onto the bed, facing him. Without further probing, he mumbled. "I had a dream."

Cyrus squeezed his shoulder for assurance. "It's just a dream. You know they're not real, right?"

He nodded. "I know, but it stayed with me long after I'd fallen back to sleep and woke back up."

"Care to tell me about it?"

"It's this creature." Sawyer unfolded the piece of paper and turned it for Cyrus to see.

It was a drawing of a Neroc vampire wearing the same getup he'd seen them wearing in the last battle. The one Sawyer had drawn looked like he had some power of some sort, judging from the crest on his breast. Cyrus coughed, unable to believe his eyes. He glanced at Issy, who was cupping her mouth in disbelief.

"Is there anything you remember from your dream, like something they said?"

Sawyer nodded and dove down to cry on Cyrus' chest. He patted his son's back, providing comfort while he tried to recall the clash outside headquarters.

Once Sawyer calmed down, he sat up and looked at Cyrus, his mouth still quivering. "This creature kept saying—I'm going to kill you. You're going to pay for killing my brother. He said it over and over."

Cyrus had no idea why Sawyer was seeing that, but if his gut was right, it might have something to do with the creatures he and Issy had killed. But why was their son seeing this? That was something to ponder.

"Now . . . now . . . . it's just a dream. Come stay here with us tonight so we can watch over you."

Sawyer nodded, and Cyrus could see the unspoken fear in his face. While Issy helped their boy to settle down, he grabbed the phone and summoned Barth, one of their vampire fighters. "Come to my room right away."

It didn't take many minutes for Sawyer to fall asleep. Even in his slumber, Cyrus could see the strain on his young face. The poor boy had been through a lot already.

"Here are your crutches," Issy said once Sawyer had gone deeper in his sleep. He and Issy got ready while Barth waited on the sofa.

The fighter got up when Cyrus walked closer. "What do you need me to do?"

"Issy and I will be at the clinic. Watch over him and call me if he starts dreaming, okay?"

"No problem, Cy." Barth glanced at the sleeping child on the bed.

They hurried to the clinic, as fast as Cyrus could manage on crutches. He glanced at Issy and found her frowning. "What's on your mind?" He wanted to hold her, but the damn crutches made it impossible.

They reached the clinic, and Issy turned to him. "I'm scared for Sawyer."

He leaned one crutch against the door and balanced himself on one foot. Then he held her chin and tilted her face up. "Don't be. I won't let anything happen to him or you."

"This isn't over yet," she murmured.

Cyrus couldn't answer. He wanted to deny her words, but he felt it in his bones, too. "We're safe in here," he said instead. He lowered his mouth to hers and planted a soft kiss on her lips. "Are you ready?"

Issy nodded and offered a weak smile. Cyrus turned the knob and pushed the door open with one crutch. To his surprise, they found Linda and Rick instead of Rohnert.

"What's going on here?"

Linda looked at Rick, then to Issy, before she spoke. "I was just having him check my legs."

Cyrus felt a nagging suspicion that there was more to it than what his sister was telling him. "What about your legs?" He threw a glare in Rick's direction. The doctor returned his stare, standing his ground. Cyrus moved closer until he was right next to the examination table. He saw some instruments he hadn't seen before.

Linda pleaded with Rick. "Can you put me back in my chair, please?"

Rick did so with obvious ease. Then he looked at Issy. "Rick says it's none of your business, Cyrus. You can talk to your sister if you want, but he is not violating patient–doctor confidentiality."

After Issy was done translating, Rick walked out the door, followed by Linda. Cyrus flopped onto the exam table. "Aren't you going to tell me what's going on?" he asked.

Issy sighed. "I'm bound to the same oath as his translator. I'm sorry, love." She kissed him. "Don't worry about it. Linda is of age. Her big brother shouldn't fret about her."

Cyrus blew out an exasperated breath. "You people are going to drive me crazy." Maybe Issy was right. It was time for him to trust Linda and her decisions.

"Of course I'm right. I'm sure she'll tell you when she's good and ready." The smile Issy gave him held a secret he wished he could share.

"Where is Rohnert?"

The door burst open. "I'm here. Sorry I'm late. Little boy burped out his dinner, and clean up took a while." Rohnert eyed them then flopped next to Cyrus on the table. "How do you guys want this?"

Cyrus patted Rohnert on the back. "I'm going to watch from the chair so I can elevate this damn leg." He eased off the table took the chair next to it.

"Issy?" Rohnert tapped the vein on his neck. "Ready?"

Cyrus watched his mate approach Rohnert, and without as much fanfare, latch onto his vein. This was the first time Cyrus had seen the process. While it was disturbing from a mate's point of view, the act was clean and involved nothing that would make him want to kill anyone. Rohnert groaned one time, and Cyrus could see that it came with the tug and pull.

Things happened fast, and before he knew it, Issy was sealing the puncture site.

Yet when Rohnert's turn came, Cyrus found his fists balled up at his side and his breathing came rapid and hard. Rohnert kept his hands on Issy's shoulders to steady her. Aside from the moan that came out of her mouth, it was over before Cyrus could react.

After Rohnert placed the sealing touch on her neck, he looked at Cyrus and dipped his head. "Thanks to you both for doing this," he said.

Issy looked at Cyrus before she spoke. "Rohnert, I've been wondering if we could have Rick draw our blood instead of doing it this way."

Rohnert nodded, looking relieved. "I have been thinking of the same thing. I'll talk to him and arrange something before we need to feed again. If you both will excuse me," he said and left the room in a hurry.

Issy jumped off the table and ran into Cyrus' arms. "I love you. Thanks for understanding."

Cyrus released the breath he had been holding. "Anything for you," he said and meant it.

In the dead of the night, several beings streaked across a deserted parking lot. The slapping of their boots on the damp pavement was the only sound for miles. With weapons drawn and carrying a big, plastic container, they reached the lonely building with its decaying sign dangling from a lone hook.

"Are you sure this is the right place?" one of the masked beings asked.

"Can't you fuckin' read? It says blood bank. What else are we looking for?"

"Oh, I was just making sure," came the dumb reply.

One hand tested the glass door, pushing to feel its strength, then gave it one hard pound. The glass splintered, and the shattered particles landed on the ground, creating a symphonic melody of ting, ting, ting.

The lock was disengaged, and as the alarm began to wail, the three people rushed in. One of them took care of the blaring nuisance. As the last of the beeps sounded, the other two began to work in perfect sync, combing through the first floor, knocking down chairs and scattering papers from the desks.

"Nothing here," one said.

"The second floor, I can smell it."

The trio bounded the stairs in no time until they reached the next level. The temperature dipped lower, and chills ran down their spines. This was definitely it. The aroma of the sweetest gift to those of their nature assaulted them when they opened the massive double stainless doors that took up almost the entire second floor.

Bags after bags of sweet human blood awaited them. Marked as positive or negative, the rows of bags tempted each one of them to have a taste, but orders were orders. With difficulty and hesitation, they were able to carry out their deed.

Each one secured their weapons before emptying the gasoline container into the refrigerated area. They stood back, inhaling the faint smell of blood that was now overpowered by the explosive fuel. The flick of a lighter was followed by a plinking sounded when it touched the ground. Fire blazed on contact, prompting the trio to leave in a hurry.

The crackling sound grew louder while they watched from outside until it developed into a full-blown inferno.

One of the masked beings pulled out a cell phone from his pocket while they darted back into the darkness. "Yes, it's done. We're headed to the next one."

"Good job. Your bonus awaits you. Tell the others to make this fast and simultaneous. I want it done and over in an hour."

As soon as the line went dead, Drago turned to Lukan. "Turn on the news in fifteen minutes. In the meantime, come here and let us pass the time." He drew her by the neck and plunged his fangs onto her vein, smiling against her soft skin.

The game wasn't over by any means.

"Pops, are you sure this is a good idea?" Sawyer stepped onto the mat.

"Do as I say, son. I'm giving you an edge here." Cyrus tried to balance himself on one leg.

"It's not you I'm worried about. Don't think Is . . . I mean Mom, would be happy if she saw us sparring again."

"It's been eight weeks, and I don't feel any pain. We're good. Just keep your voice down so she won't hear us."

Given that it had been a couple of months since he amputated his own leg after being shot during the confrontation with the Nerocs, Cyrus was feeling much better. Especially after he and Issy had been officially mated. His residual limb had healed, despite a few setbacks stemming from the remaining Dangeran bits that Rick managed to remove after the swelling had gone down.

Cyrus had grown accustomed to hopping on one leg over shorter distances, and his arms were much stronger from crutch usage. At least he was up on his feet rather than sitting on his ass for long periods of time. Although Issy still gave him static whenever he pushed himself too hard, she had begun easing up on him. It didn't take a mind reader to know that he was about to go insane with such limited activities.

Sawyer rolled his eyes then bared his fangs. "If you say so. I'd just hate it if I kicked your butt again."

With his right foot planted firmly on the mat, Cyrus followed Sawyer while he danced in front of him, teasing him to make the first move. True, the boy had kicked his ass during the first few sparring matches they'd had, but that was just because he had still been favoring his injured leg. Now that he was close to one hundred percent, Cyrus was going to show his son a little humility.

The lockdown had everyone taking turns using the training room, and this was their only chance before the other fighters clamored for their turn.

Sawyer held his arm up as Cyrus taught him, jabbing to see his reaction. With limited movement on his part, Cyrus paid attention to where Sawyer's fist would land. He needed to conserve energy if he wanted to sustain his upright position.

The door opened with a creak, and he glanced up to see Tor walking in. The momentary distraction afforded Sawyer the window to swipe his leg, and down Cyrus went. He fell on the mat with a loud thud to the beat of Tor's roaring laughter.

Cyrus pushed himself up into a sitting position. "Shut it, Burns," he said, but kept his eyes on the little boy, who seemed grief stricken at taking advantage of him.

"Sawyer, show your old man how to fight." Tor was having a blast at Cyrus' expense.

Sawyer ignored the good-natured teasing. "Are you okay, Pops?"

"Of course I am. Don't worry about it, but please help me up." Cyrus tousled the boy's hair before he was pulled to his feet.

Unknown to Sawyer, Cyrus was killing time in order to avoid dwelling on his upcoming appointment with Rick that evening to try on his prosthesis. As much as he tried to tell himself that everything was going to be fine, he was still nervous as hell.

He blocked out Tor's continued banter and concentrated on his son alone. When the boy tried to punch, he countered with a block, and then twisted his arm until they ended up on the ground. Trying not to use all his strength, he pinned him lightly until Sawyer pounded on the mat, signaling that he was beaten.

Another round produced a draw. They continued to go at it until they were both sweating and Cyrus felt his right leg was about to give up on him. He was getting up when the door burst open and Issy walked in, hands on her hips.

"Cy, what the hell? You're going to be late." She glared at Sawyer but smiled when the boy looked like he was about to cry. "Off to the shower young man, then time to feed."

Sawyer scrambled to his feet then offered a hand to Cyrus. "I told you she was going to go off again," he whispered.

"C'mon, Issy. Lighten up. I'm going, I'm going." Cyrus hopped on one foot to the desk and grabbed his forearm crutches. "I'm ready." He grinned.

Issy walked alongside him, huffing. He stopped and seized her by the waist. "You're pretty when you're upset." He kissed her on the temple then released her.

"You're insufferable, Mr. Crackenbush." She blew an errant hair out of her face.

Cyrus winced at her use of his last name. He reminded himself to strangle his little sister for disclosing that tiny detail to his mate.

They reached the laboratory, where Jones and Rick were huddled together by Jones' desk, inspecting the C-leg he was about to try on. Both men looked up when Cyrus and Issy walked in.

"Ready to feel like Superman?" Jones stepped back and crossed his arms.

"Oh, yeah. I have a need . . . a need for speed," Cyrus quoted a line from one of his favorite movies.

Rick grinned and gestured for him to sit. Cyrus sat in the chair and released the crutches. Then he lifted his shorts to reveal his left stump, which had healed well. Issy sat next to him, and he could hear her rapid breathing. He glanced at her and knew she was as nervous as he was. "It's going to be okay," he said, then squeezed her hand.

Jones became Rick's voice box while the doctor fitted the prosthesis to his leg. Then they had Cyrus remove it so he could practice attaching it on his own. They did this several times before he was confident that he wouldn't fuck it up.

"How does it feel?" Jones asked. "Is it snug?

Cyrus nodded. Looking down at his state-of-art C-leg, he felt apprehension seeing something attached to his stump. He had grown used to his abbreviated leg, and the prosthetic limb felt foreign.

Rick tapped him on the shoulder, and then Issy began translating. "You'll get used to it. Just think of the things you can do again with it."

Still nervous, Cyrus checked out the prosthesis again. "Okay, let's see what this baby can do." Rick held out his hand and helped him up. Once standing, Cyrus let go and concentrated on staying upright. "Whoa, it can support my weight," he said, looking at Issy.

She smiled and translated again. "Once you're comfortable using it, we're going to get you every make and model that your heart desires. Anything to fit your activity and mood."

Cyrus laughed as he jabbed Rick on the ribs. "You're all right, doc. Thanks."

"Now, let's go for a walk, and you can see if the fit is good. Hold on to your wife . . . oh, I mean me," Issy said, and they all laughed.

Holding her hand, Cyrus felt his anxiety diminish. Everything would be all right. He could feel it from his heart all the way to his missing limb. Everything would be just fine.

A week later . . .

Upright and holding the treadmill handlebars, the view was better like this. But why did he feel like he was going to be sick?

"C'mon, Cy, press the button. We've gone through this before," Rick said through Issy. They stood next to the machine that tested his endurance and the strength of his new and improved C-leg.

He had been fitted with several prosthetics over the last week, and by far, this model was the best fit. His stump had healed well enough to endure several exercises a day, but this was the first time he would attempt to run.

The prospect was exhilarating and scary as hell. Cyrus had been looking forward to this day, but as he pushed the on button, he wasn't sure anymore.

The machine whirred to life, and the wide conveyor belt underneath him began to move slowly. He started to walk along the platform, still gripping the handlebar for fear of stumbling. It had been different doing this on solid ground. Rick increased the speed, and Cyrus was forced to adjust his pace.

"Concentrate on your stride for now. Don't worry about falling. You're doing well." Issy was still translating on behalf of the doctor.

Cyrus glanced at his new wife for a brief moment and grinned. "I look like an idiot."

Issy shook her head. "You're wonderful. Doesn't it feel great?" He knew those were Issy's words.

He kept going, mindful of every step, until Rick upped the speed again, forcing him to adjust to the quickening pace.

"How do you feel? How's the pressure on your stump?"

"No pain. It's holding up. How about I take over the speed adjustment?"

Rick waved his hand with a flourish. Both he and Issy stepped back, giving Cyrus free rein. Feeling confident with the prosthetic leg, he pressed the speed button and was able to match the increased speed of the belt.

He got more confident with every stride, and he released his death grip on the bar and began to enjoy the run. He watched his form in the mirror in front of him and was astounded at the sight of himself running at full speed.

Cyrus continued to push himself and the C-leg, reaching a considerable speed. He wasn't letting up. He'd waited for this for months. Now that he was up and running again, there would be no stopping him. Thanks to Issy's insistence on massaging his limb regularly, there was lingering discomfort in his knee but nothing he couldn't handle. Pushing harder, he kept increasing the speed until the machine was powered to the max.

He lost track of time and didn't even notice that Rick had slipped out of the room until Issy stood in front of the machine. Her face was radiating with the happiness.

"Hey, Mercury, is there any chance we can do this tomorrow? I'm ready for bed."

Damn, the mere mention of bed had Cyrus punching the off button. He jumped off the platform and landed on the floor with a loud thud. In two big strides, he was next to Issy and seizing her by the waist. He held her up against him. "Bed? Hey, I'm there."

Issy looked up with a wry smile, her eyes twinkling. "It doesn't look like you're ready yet."

Nope, Issy did not just go there. Without a word, Cyrus lifted her off her feet and slung her over his shoulder. She laughed and pounded on his back.

"Put me down."

"Not until we reach our bedroom." He stared straight ahead, focusing on his steps as they headed out of the training room. "I'll show you how serious I am about heading to bed." Halfway back, he shifted her into his arms, and her hands twined behind his neck.

This was what he'd always wanted—a life filled with laughter, and a promise of more happiness ahead with the one he loved. Could a vampire's life get any better than this?

"No, because it's already perfect." Issy rested her head against his chest.

His grin got bigger. "Ready for bed, Mrs. Crackenbush?" Cyrus crossed the threshold of their bedroom and laid her down on the bed.

Sneak Peek from
Redemption,
the fifth book in
The Gates Legacy series
by Lorenz Font

When they emerged from the secret passage to the underground facility, Zane waited while Cyrus pointed up his nose to check for the scent of trespassers.

"It's clear," he said with a glare back at Zane.

It had been one year and counting since he took up residence in the facility, and the treatment he'd been receiving from most of the inhabitants ranged from indifference to contempt. This was expected. At least the attempts on his life had stopped. His great-uncle, Rohnert, had enough problems to juggle without playing cop to the vampires who wanted Zane dead. After he had issued an edict to this effect, the constant challenges stopped.

Since the Nerocs had stepped up their efforts to block the entrances and exits on both the Vampire Council site and Tack Enterprises' underground location, the residents of these strongholds had to hunker down and remain hidden.

The Nerocs were creatures of the night, just like the rest of their vampire brethren. Harrow, the current head of Tack Enterprises, could withstand some sunlight, but he was still susceptible to burns and blisters if exposed during the middle of the day. That meant that as daywalkers, Zane and Cyrus were their group's one hope of locating their biggest enemies to date, as well as the vampires who had no aversion to the sun. So Zane was stuck with the man who hated him with a passion.

He stepped out after Cyrus to join the city's daytime population. "Where to now?" Zane asked. He took mental inventory of weapons hidden underneath his jacket. Like Cyrus, he was armed to the teeth, and together they could wage war on battalions if necessary.

"To your penthouse. We'll stay there until sundown."

Cyrus began a steady jog, and Zane followed. His legs were strong enough to support him, but the pain was ever-present. Too bad Rick couldn't extract the particles of Dangeran that were still imbedded in the muscles of his leg. Too much time had passed before an effort was made to extract the granules.

They ran through several busy thoroughfares that couldn't be avoided. The city's alleys would be filled with delivery trucks dropping off merchandise to businesses, and the commotion would slow them down. Their best bet was to run through the middle of the snarling traffic, even if it meant crisscrossing the busy avenues.

Words between them were few. Cyrus may have forgiven him enough to work with him, but that was the extent of their relationship. Zane knew the road ahead was still a big question mark for him, but with Cheryl's condition, he was willing to endure anything.

His anklet weighed heavy with every step, a sad reminder that, although he was accepted as part of the underground operation, he still wasn't trusted. Could he blame them?

They reached his penthouse. As usual, the doorman acknowledged Zane with respect and threw a doubtful glance at Cyrus. "Good morning, Mr. Drew."

He acknowledged this with a nod before ducking into the elevator with Cyrus. When they reached his penthouse door, Cyrus grunted, "Key."

Zane pressed the button to deactivate the motion sensors that had been installed in his suite. Handing the key to Cyrus, he turned around, hand poised on his gun as a precautionary measure. It was better to be ready for the unexpected. As soon they were safely inside, Zane moved first, gun ready to go. He darted from room to room, checking for unwanted visitors.

"Coast is clear," he said, and then inserted his weapon back into its holster.

Cyrus nodded. "I'm going to park on the balcony."

Zane knew the drill. Cyrus would be scouring the city with his long-ass telescope. They had made strides in ridding the city of some of the Neroc mother fuckers, but they still had a lot of work ahead of them. This war was far from over. The seat of the Neroc leader still had not been located. This Lord Marchec was as elusive as Drago, their vampire ally.

Sitting at the desk, Zane began to activate the secret cameras that had been installed inside the building and around its perimeter. With Drago being a resident of the building, he or his henchmen were bound to make frequent appearances. Zane was reviewing the first camera, which had been dedicated to Drago's penthouse, when his phone vibrated, announcing a call.

He glanced at the caller ID and pressed the button to answer. "Hey, babe. What's going on? You're missing me already?"

"Yes…" Cheryl sounded breathless. "Zane, I think you should come home."

"Cheryl, what's wrong?" He shot out of the chair, startling Cyrus in the process.

The vampire was right next to him in a heartbeat. "Zane, what is it?"

He didn't answer, focusing instead on Cheryl's reply.

"My water broke, and the contractions are coming hard."

What the fuck! She'd been fine when he left the facility. "I'm coming. Hold on."

Cyrus chuckled from behind him. "Welcome to fatherhood, asshole."

Acknowledgements

Writing a series takes a lot of work, patience, diligence, and time—not only for the author, but also for her support team. I'm so lucky to be surrounded by a group of wonderful people who have taken the journey with me since Book One. Thanks to Wendy Depperschmidt, Claudia Trapp, Judith Somera, Eric Banaag, Lucia Morales and Trenda Lundin. Your help with the different aspects of this series, and my writing journey, has been invaluable. Thank you for your gift of friendship.

To my street team, "It's All in the Font," Wyndy Dee, Paula Kangasniemi, Cynthia Ogg, RE Hargrave, Melissa Hardy, and Lori Divine—I wouldn't be able to get the word out without your help and dedication. Thanks for taking the chance on an unknown author. You girls rock!

Also, thanks to my editing team, my Sensei, Mavvy Vasquez and Wendy Depperschmidt for helping make this baby shine.

Claudia of Phantasy Graphic Design- Your book cover rocks!

And to the following for making my life easier—Sam Pitterman, Edwin and Joy Del Carmen and JC Clarke.

About the Author

A professional daydreamer, Lorenz Font discovered her love of writing after reading a celebrated novel that inspired one idea after another. Since being published in 2013, she has been conspiring, butting heads, and enjoying her spare time with vampires, angels, samurais, and other creatures she has created in her head.

Her perfect day consists of writing and lounging on her garage couch (a.k.a. the office) with a glass of her favorite cabernet while listening to her ever-growing music collection. She finds writing urban fantasy exhilarating and places an intense focus on angst and the redemption of flawed characters. Her fascination with romantic twists is a mainstay in all her stories.

Lorenz lives in Southern California with her supportive family and three demanding dogs.

www.ingramcontent.com/pod-product-compliance
Lightning Source LLC
Chambersburg PA
CBHW071221250626
47163CB00001B/64